ARTISTIC VISIONS

In Company:
Robert Creeley's Collaborations

IN COMPANY

Robert Creeley's Collaborations

AMY CAPPELLAZZO AND
ELIZABETH LICATA, EDITORS

Essays, interviews, and archival images of this prize-winning poet's artistic collaborations, with accompanying CD.

"[Creeley's] influence on contemporary American poetry has probably been more deeply felt than that of any other writer of his generation." —*New York Times Book Review*

108 pp., 9 1/8 x 11 1/2, 45 color / 45 b&w illus., $24.95 paper with CD

Distributed for the Castellani Art Museum of Niagara University and the Weatherspoon Art Gallery, University of North Carolina at Greensboro

LIGHT WRITING AND LIFE WRITING

Photography in Autobiography
TIMOTHY DOW ADAMS

"Fascinating. . . . [Illuminates] the quasi-fictional nature of both photography and autobiography . . . with detailed discussions of Kingston, Auster, Momaday, Ondaatje, Price, Welty, Morris, and Weston. [This] will be an indispensable addition to the growing work on literature and photography." —Miles Orvell, Temple University

Approx. 368 pp., 54 illus.
$49.95 cloth / $22.50 paper

MIRROR TALK

Genres of Crisis in Contemporary Autobiography
SUSANNA EGAN

Explores new directions in autobiography, including drama, film, and comics.

"Timely and important . . . maps the extensive territories—genres, cultures, hybrid forms—that are going to be the country of autobiography in the time to come." —Paul John Eakin, Indiana University

296 pp. $49.95 cloth / $19.95 paper

SOUND STATES

Innovative Poetics and Acoustical Technologies
ADALAIDE MORRIS, EDITOR

Both editions include accompanying CD

"Tuned in to the twangs and calibrations of poetic listening and fine-tuned to cultural studies of modernism, contemporaneity, and poetics. An original and innovative anthology by people thinking with an 'ear-mind.'" —Rachel Blau DuPlessis, poet and critic

"Impressive." —*Virginia Quarterly Review*

368 pp., CD $55 cloth / $24.95 paper

THE UNIVERSITY OF NORTH CAROLINA PRESS

AT BOOKSTORES OR CALL [800] 848-6224 | www.uncpress.unc.edu

COMING UP IN SPRING AND FALL 2000

An Important Two-Volume Anthology
AMERICAN FICTION & AMERICAN POETRY
States of the Art

For the year 2000, *Conjunctions* undertakes an ambitious two-volume project that will help to map the literary landscape of innovative contemporary American fiction and poetry.

Our spring issue, *American Fiction: States of the Art*, gathers unpublished and commissioned works by a pantheon of writers, from new voices to recognized masters, and with particular emphasis on those who are currently midstride in their writing lives.

Among the three dozen novelists and short story writers included in *Conjunctions:34* are Jamaica Kincaid, Padgett Powell, William T. Vollmann, Rikki Ducornet, Rosario Ferré, Rick Moody, Mary Caponegro, Paul West, Dale Peck, Alexander Theroux, David Foster Wallace, William H. Gass, Robert Antoni, Lydia Davis, Jessica Hagedorn, Ben Marcus, Joyce Carol Oates, A. M. Homes, Lynne Tillman, Walter Abish, Sarah Gaddis, Steve Erickson and John Barth, as well as many other distinguished contributors.

Emerging writers such as Pamela Ryder, Christopher Sorrentino and Jonathan Safran Foer will also be featured, along with in-depth conversations between Bradford Morrow, Richard Powers and Joanna Scott.

Conjunctions:34, American Fiction: States of the Art will be complemented by a companion volume to be published in the fall of 2000, *American Poetry: States of the Art* with work by some forty poets.

These groundbreaking volumes will be essential reading for everyone interested in where contemporary American fiction and poetry is headed in the new millennium.

Novelist and *Conjunctions* founding editor Bradford Morrow will edit both volumes. For updates on contributors and previews of work, please visit our website at www.conjunctions.com.

CONJUNCTIONS:34

Richard Powers
Rikki Ducornet
Padgett Powell
A. M. Homes
Alexander Theroux
David Foster Wallace
American
Fiction Rosario Ferré
Rick Moody
Mary Caponegro
States of The Art Lydia Davis
Joyce Carol Oates
William H. Gass
Joanna Scott
William T. Vollmann

CONJUNCTIONS

Bi-Annual Volumes of New Writing

Edited by
Bradford Morrow

Contributing Editors
Walter Abish
Chinua Achebe
John Ashbery
Mei-mei Berssenbrugge
Guy Davenport
Elizabeth Frank
William H. Gass
Jorie Graham
Robert Kelly
Ann Lauterbach
Norman Manea
Patrick McGrath
Joanna Scott
Mona Simpson
Nathaniel Tarn
Quincy Troupe
William Weaver
John Edgar Wideman

published by Bard College

EDITOR: Bradford Morrow
MANAGING EDITOR: Michael Bergstein
SENIOR EDITORS: Robert Antoni, Martine Bellen, Peter Constantine,
    Elaine Equi, Brian Evenson, Thalia Field
ASSOCIATE EDITOR: Jonathan Safran Foer
ART EDITORS: Anthony McCall, Norton Batkin
PUBLICITY: Mark R. Primoff
WEBMASTERS: Brian Evenson, Michael Neff
EDITORIAL ASSISTANTS: Courtney Scott, Alan Tinkler

CONJUNCTIONS is published in the Spring and Fall of each year by Bard
College, Annandale-on-Hudson, NY 12504. This issue is made possible in part
with the generous funding of the National Endowment for the Arts, and with
public funds from the New York State Council on the Arts, a State Agency. We
are also very grateful for a gift from an anonymous donor.

SUBSCRIPTIONS: Send subscription orders to CONJUNCTIONS, Bard College, Annandale-on-Hudson, NY 12504. Single year (two volumes): $18.00 for
individuals; $25.00 for institutions and overseas. Two years (four volumes):
$32.00 for individuals; $45.00 for institutions and overseas. Patron subscription (lifetime): $500.00. Overseas subscribers please make payment by
International Money Order. For information about subscriptions, back issues
and advertising, call Michael Bergstein at 914-758-1539 or fax 914-758-2660.

All editorial communications should be sent to Bradford Morrow,
Conjunctions, 21 East 10th Street, New York, NY 10003. Unsolicited
manuscripts cannot be returned unless accompanied by a stamped, self-
addressed envelope.

Conjunctions is listed and indexed in the American Humanities Index.

Visit the *Conjunctions* website at www.conjunctions.com.

Printers: Edwards Brothers.

Typesetter: Bill White, Typeworks.

ISSN 0278-2324

ISBN 0-941964-49-3

Manufactured in the United States of America.

TABLE OF CONTENTS

CROSSING OVER

From Plowing the Dark
Richard Powers

AND WHEN YOU FELL BACK on mutual bitterness, when rage reprised itself, when you took to throwing darts again at the world map, at last it hit you. Simple choice: replay the old routine, the self-triggering cycle of accusations, the verbal razor cuts daubed in love's alcohol. Traipse down the path of tender sadomasochism yet one more soul-shredding time. Or turn around and walk. Escape down the path that must still lie somewhere to the south, the way you walked in.

One more tearful reconciliation would only further demean you both. The place you pushed for—the tumble-down house in the country, your dream of intimacy that always made her bite in fear—now vanishes in fantasy, gives way to that darker late-night venue, where hisses of desire shade off into abuse, abuse feeding back into desire.

You've been each other's shared addiction, slinking back repeatedly to the nightmare rush that you'd both fought to be rid of. You've come back from the dead a dozen times only to spin out worse, whole weeks at a time. You've suffered the delirium of total withdrawal: one month, two, without so much as a word. Then, clean, virginal, at peace, calling again, just to see if you can. Just to see who's in charge. Just a quick little needle, dipped into the waiting vein.

All that changes forever, this Friday. You're off to a place where you can't ask her to hurt you again, where neither of you can backslide into care. Where you can no longer reach one another, however much mutual tenderness revives. It rocks you, just to imagine.

Among your friends, the plan produces only stunned hilarity. "You're going *where*? Don't they shoot people in the street there, without even asking whose side they're on?"

"No," you shit them back. "You're thinking of D.C."

At last they realize, these friends who've witnessed your worst whiplash for years now. You mean it, and it rocks them.

You rush to assure everyone. The school you'll teach for is a virtual armed compound. Tensions are nowhere near what they were this time last year. The civil war is ending; all sides are talking compromise. The foreign armies have left. Their president has finally taken the reins. All that insanity is a thing of the past.

And it's only for two terms, anyway. Eight months. Safer than a daily commute on the Edens Expressway.

You sleep well on the long flight, crushed up against the window with one of those squares of cotton gauze the stewardesses pass off as pillows. In your sleep, you already speak fluent Arabic. Even your dream marionette is struck by the strangeness: these guttural rapid bursts issuing from you, part nonsense, part gift of tongues.

Over the cabin speakers, the pilot warns that he must take the standard evasive maneuvers upon approach. Passengers are not to panic. The plane will simply lose a few thousand feet in a matter of seconds. Many on board seem used to the procedure.

You Stuka to a landing, safe, even exhilarated. The guard at the baggage claim totes a machine gun resembling an haute couture coat hanger. The school bursar is waiting in the terminal to meet you.

The metropolis lies dark and quiet. You cock your ears toward the south suburbs, but can hear nothing except traffic. The chauffer from the school laughs: what did you expect? Grenade-toting crazies lurking behind every street vendor?

In the morning, you tour the compound. The school buildings are mostly intact. They sit up on a bluff, with a view down to the Corniche and the sea beyond. Your office balcony looks out on precarious pyramids of rubble being bulldozed into the water. You search for the Green Line, the vegetation growing up through the cracked concrete that divides the city. You see only a stand of high rises, their pock-marks blending into this day's dappled shadows.

It's better than you imagined. All white and marine and accepting. A recovering place. A good place to recover. The resinous air, the olive mountains. Arid, azure, clear. Your sinuses haven't been this open since childhood. This city is returning. You can live here.

*   *   *

The staff at school exudes a nervous optimism that no one will jinx by speaking. They give you the guided tour prepared for all new hires. They leave the school driver to orient you, although all parties tastefully avoid that verb.

"I take you anywhere, Mr. Taimur. You tell me, I drive."

He brings you down a newly broadened thoroughfare. On all sides of your closed car, life returns to trade. You pass the financial district and the open-air *suqs,* once again breathing with people. The anti-Ottoman statues in Martyrs' Square seem almost crater-free, from a distance. You hook around the Corniche along the Riviera, avoiding the checkpoints.

Here and there, steel girders tear loose from building sides, dragging along sprays of concrete veil. Balconies crumble off the high rises like so many dried wasp nests. Fresh-scrubbed laundry hangs from the ones that remain, blinding white in the Levant sun.

Here is the Paris of the East, the once-chic orchid of the Eastern Med. You speed along the shredded Rue des Banques to a palm-lined plaza, down by the turquoise bay. Fifteen minutes after setting out, the chauffer spreads his hands in the air, palms up, disarmed. You see? Things are calming down. Returning to livable.

"Where does that street lead? No, this one here."

"Ha. Don't worry, Mr. Martin. Very boring. Very nothing."

"Can we head down this way? I'd just like a quick peek."

"Later, maybe. *Inshallah.*" *God willing.* As if healing required hiding the wounds.

9

No matter; you see it already. The thing your friends back home saw, even before you left. The thing you've half wished away, half sought out. Just behind the ivory facing, just beneath the glinting amethyst, this world is shelling itself deeper into rubble.

You can't help but hear it, rumbling off in the direction of the Metn foothills. It growls like linen scraped over a plywood drum. One shell barrels overhead, close enough to break your guide's composure. This war is not over. This war will never end. Yet this rumble is cartoon thunder. The bursts come no closer to hurting you than scoreboard fireworks. They detonate impotently, more inert than the explosions of your recent American bug-out.

In fact, living on a powder keg has much to recommend it, providing one's driver knows a safe way back to the impregnable compound. A city's self-inflicted scars offer unlimited further diversions.

The following week treats you to your first teeth-rattling blast. The panic passes, leaving you more alive than you've felt in months. An artillery plume rises on the horizon like an old movie's Indian smoke signals. Your life is not yet over, whatever the last two years insisted. Thirty-three is still young. The future remains your dominant tense. You're alive, unhit. Anything can still happen.

Simply being here proves that. You couldn't have scripted such a trip. Six years in Chicago, explaining your inexplicable country to Japanese businessmen, riding the emotional tilt-a-whirl with a miserable woman on a largely ceremonial salary. Now living like a sultan, on hazard pay, in a place even more desperate than that woman.

A kind of harsh humor: acing the job interview because of your Muslim mother. Because you don't currently drink, no matter the reason. Because they mistake you for one who understands the Faithful. Because tenacious Lebanese have need of the same English as Japanese businessmen.

You like them, these violence-inured twenty-year-olds raised alongside the Green Line's furrow. They have an intensity you've never seen in any classroom. Pitching one's tent under the mortar's arc does wonders for a student's motivation.

"Why do you want to improve your English?" you ask them, on the first day of your new tenure. The diagnostic ice-breaker, cheap but to the point.

It helps with trade, Phoenicia's descendents inform you. It's the world's second tongue, say the refugees of Sidon and Tyre.

A smiling, bearded Nawaf in the front of the room summarizes. "America bosses the world around in English. We need English, just to tell America to go to hell."

The whole class laughs. When learning another language, comprehension always outstrips production. Its true, the class agrees. Americans speak nothing and own everything. The world needs to learn English, just to talk back to its owner.

Your very existence astonishes them. "How can an American have your name?"

"How can you let yourself be coming from such a place?"

The ones you like best explain the delusions you've been living under. "Black people, in your country, are killed like sheep here for the end of Ramadan."

"Americans pay forty million dollars to one man for putting a ball in a ring. Instead they could buy hamburgers for forty million starving people."

They offer these earnest proofs of Sodom for your own good. But greater needs pull them toward this evil. Their interest dribbles out over your first two weeks. "This Rocky, Sir? You think he fights so good? He doesn't last five minutes against my cousin with Mujahideen."

"This Terminator? He's not so great. Take away the big gun. . . ."

"The Terminator is Austrian," you tell them. "He's not our fault."

"Mr. Martin? What means this? 'I am leaving the material world, and I am immaterial girl?'"

11

"We'll work on that one next term," you promise.

Ardent children of civil war, they seem still bathed in first innocence, strangely unhardened, even by the odds against survival. They
might sit basking, afternoons, out by the marina under the St.
George, if that neighborhood still existed. But they stay on, by choice
or compulsion, after a million of their countrymen have thought
better and bailed. Each of them, too long trained by collapse to continue hoping, yet too angry to give it up. All of them hungry to learn
the true size of the world beyond this city: a world of glossy fictions,
stable, rich, progressing, theirs to glimpse only through the shadow-
boxes of bootlegged videotape.

You are their model, their messenger from the outside world. Your
job: to chat them up for hours at a shot, training them to survive the
force of their imaginations. You work to hold them to the rules of
polite conversation, in a city trying to believe again in rules, in
words. It is by any measure the perfect job description—the ticket
you've been trying to write yourself for years. A golden existence. All
that's missing is someone a little brave, someone just a little kind to
share it with.

"Tell me how you got here," you assign them, early on. The topic
provides a high personal interest. Good practice with the tricky past
tenses. And it's easy to answer without straying too far outside core
vocabulary.

"How did *you* got here, Mr. Martin?" Nawaf baits you.

The whole class becomes a sea of colluding head-bobs. "Yes. Yes. We
all want to know."

"Nothing to tell," you tell them. "I came here to make sure that
your subjects and verbs all agree with each other."

"What job have you done before being our teacher?" Nawaf asks.

"What did I do before coming here to teach?"

"Yeah. You said it."

"A lot of things. Most recently, I trained Asian businessmen to survive Chicago."

The sly bastard persists. "Why did you change your jobs?"

"Now why in the world would that interest you?"

"It's very interesting, Mr. Martin," the very interesting Zarai chips in.

"Well, for a lot of reasons. But we're not going to get into that."

"It's a secret?" Nawaf taunts.

"That's right. Yes. It's a secret."

"Top secret?" Zarai smiles at you from beneath her head wrapping.

You smile back at her. "Tip top secret."

* * *

They say that you know more about this place on the day you first touch your foot to it than you will ever know about it again. And they're right. Each day that passes leaves you more confused about this stew, let alone the recipe that produced it. You understand Shiite versus Sunni, Maronite versus Orthodox, Druze, Palestinian, Phalangist, Amal, the radical Party of God and their fanatical cell the Holy Warriors. . . . But the fourteen other religions and splinter factions plunge you into the same despair that your students feel when confronting irregular verbs.

This al-Jumhuriyah al-Lubnaniyah: even the name is a maze. The country's politics, like some unmappable Grand Bazaar out of Ali Baba, cannot be survived alive except by chance. Here the ground rules of civilization disperse into fantasy's mists. Standing agreements, tenuous at best, collapse back into the law of armed camps, each local militia staking out a few shelled blocks. No one is allowed to cross from zone to zone, not even the Red Crescent. Your students scrape by in a decaying landscape, one of those post-apocalypse teen movies they find so intriguing.

13

But for all that, the streets still seem safer than Chicago's Near North. Tomorrow feels more affirmed here, this city's pulse more surrendered to pleasure and devotion.

You learn a few words: *Na'am, la, shukran, merhadh, khubuz.* Yes, no, thank you, bathroom, bread. You begin to fantasize about meeting a woman, perhaps even a woman in head covering. Taking a crash course in the rules of her grammar.

Then the real woman calls you. Dead on schedule. Just as one of you recovers some semblance of health, some solidifying core of self-esteem, the other one calls to crash it. At least now, the two-dollar-a-minute taxi meter and the audible satellite lag protect you from extended conversation.

Or they would, if she weren't wild. Cost means nothing to her. Her words come through the phone like a violent cough. "Taimur. Tai. Thank God you're alive. You have to come back. Tonight. Now."

Too pathetic, even for retaliation. You can't even rouse yourself to decent brutality.

"I don't *think* so," you sing-song into the receiver.

"I skipped my period."

You recover before the satellite link can click. "You skip every other month, Gwen. You're a high-strung, finger-pointing, street-brawling drama queen who never menstruates in the middle of a fight. Which is pretty much all the time."

Too many adjectives, and you've lost another round. Lost her. Lost yourself. Lost the person you were trying to become by coming here, who refuses to return knee-jerk hurt for hurt.

She starts to sob, but softly, horribly. You hear her give up on the hope of consolation. And that, where nothing else could, makes you want to console her. Succor, once more, becomes your secret sickness. Your awful, tip top secret.

"Gwen. Don't start. We can't do this again. We both promised."

"I need you, Tai. I can't do this by myself."

"Cut the theater, Gwen. You're fine. Give it another couple weeks."

"I've given it *eight*."

It blossoms in you again, in the space of a second. Full-blown, the old, loving parasite you carry around inside, awaiting its chance to graze. A pillar of purity expands in your chest, so righteous it can't even be called anger. "Don't you think you ought to call the father, then?"

"You, Taimur. *You*. Don't you remember? Our long goodbye?" The weekend window when she seemed almost happy, knowing you were already gone. "Nobody before. Nobody since. . . ."

The words are whiplash. And yet: they must be bluff. Florid, desperate, sadistic, even by the standards that the two of you perfected.

"Gwen. As far as I remember from high school biology, sperm must actually meet egg in order to. . . ."

"Oh fuck. Oh fuck. I knew we shouldn't have. . . . I told you that we shouldn't. . . ."

"What you said was, 'Sex with your ex is asking for trouble.' In a soft, slinky voice, if I remember correctly."

She starts shrieking, the performance over the top, incredible.

"Come home, Tai. I can be better. You can."

The accusation maddens you. You: *better.* You, who she always punished, just for being you.

"I need you. I can't do this. Come home. Now."

The *now* is hideous; it gives the game away. You don't bother to tell her: you are home. Or as close as you're going to get, for the foreseeable future. You place the still-pleading stream of hysteria

15

back into the cradle. And you don't pick up on the ringing phone again, for several days.

* * *

You leave the compound sometimes, for fried fava beans or a breath of air. A non-cigarette break. Escape from Butt Central. Staff doesn't like it, but no one can stay cooped up forever. You keep close, always doubling back after a few minutes.

Today, a knot of men a little younger than you mill around on the pavement outside school, examining a flat tire. Someone approaches for help. You walk toward him and he shows you something. And the something is metal, and a gun. And then, he is not. Not asking for help.

"Please enter the car. Fast, fast."

Three of them persuade you of the idea. They're all shouting quietly, like a Chinese fire drill. An improvised skit of confusion. One ties your hands behind you. Another shoves your head down to clear the car's roof, just like in the cop shows. Too fast even for fear. A crazy mistake that'll have to wait to be straightened out. Wait until they remove the greasy rag they tie around your face. Wait until they settle down.

The engine starts. The car lurches forward. *There is no flat*, you realize, your thoughts even stupider than this crisis. The one sitting next to you pushes your head to the floor. On your way down, he presses close to your ear. "Don't worry. Don't worry. This is just political." The comic diction comforts you. These men are amateurs.

On the floor of a dark car. Someone's foot rests on your temple, just for the thrill of disgracing you. They drive at least an hour. Maybe two. Time enough to catch up with your own pulse rate, with what's happening to you. Your fatal stupidity. You give in to the heat of the floorboard, to the nail of the shoe on your skull, the sponge bath of terror.

The car traces an enormous circle. They are playing some insane charade of distance, doubling back, trying to throw you off. You want to call out to them to get where they're going. You're long since lost. But every sound produces a hiss and a heel crush.

They stop. They bang you out of the car. You cock back your head, to see beneath your oily blindfold. Someone chops you hard in the neck. They drag you, doubled over, inside.

They take your keys and your pockets' trinkets. Your Swiss Army knife causes a buzz out of proportion to its two pinkie blades and nail clippers.

They confiscate your wallet, pull it apart piece by piece. They demand an account for every scrap and wrapper. Your expired organ donor declarations. Your eyeglass prescription. Your student ID, ten years obsolete. Bank cards that you couldn't use anywhere within a thousand kilometers.

"What is this?" a venomous tenor shouts at you, sticking each enigma under your blindfold for inspection. "What these numbers mean?"

"Those . . . are phone numbers. Phone numbers of friends in America."

"Don't lie!" Another pair of hands slams you from the rear, more for the drama than the pain.

"Codes," a neutral voice declares.

"Not codes. Phone numbers. Go ahead. Call them. Tell them I say hello."

The voice laughs without humor.

Another bodiless voice draws close to your face. "You American? Why you look like a Arab?"

You curse your failure to memorize the fourteen splinter groups. Who are these people? What do they need to hear? They'll kill you for your political ignorance.

"Why?" your interrogator shouts. "What kind of name is Taimur Martin?"

The question that you grew up with. Your gut snaps tight. You roll the die and answer. "I am . . . half Iranian."

Rapid bursts of translation pass among several people. They argue, climbing up the pitches of virulent Arabic. You've never realized how much you need your eyes to converse.

"Where your passport?"

"I . . . hadn't planned on sightseeing when I stepped out of the compound."

For a moment, they soften, pat you on the shoulder. They shuffle around in the invisible room, collecting your things. They'll put you back in the car, return you to the school, drop you off, and fade back into whatever lunatic cabal of posturing boys put them up to this stunt.

They strip and search you. The hunt grows violent.

"Please, not the necklace," you beg. "That's a present. A gift from a . . ."

"Don't call us thieves." Spit sprays your cheek. And the necklace, Gwen's good luck charm, disappears into the political.

They want names. Names of who? It's absurd. They can spot an American from ten kilometers, if they care to look. What would they do with names? Saunter up and down the street, calling them out? Still they ask, but listlessly, a dry read-through, the script's barest minimum.

"Tell us what we ask. We know how to use . . . electricity. You understand?"

You understand. You tell them you'll do whatever they ask.

"What are you doing here?"

"You kidnapped me."

Something cracks you just above the left ear. Lights explode against the curtain of your blindfold. You bite into your tongue. You vomit, stinging and dry, in your mouth.

"What are you doing here?"

"I am a teacher. I give conversational English lessons at . . ."

"You are stupid. Big shit. You are American spy. You are CIA."

The first objecting syllable out of your throat whips your interrogator into fury. "You lie. You *lie!* We know why you come here. We know about your big secret."

Connection lights you up at last. It comes back to you, the vanished lesson from your teacher-training days in Des Moines. The first rule of any classroom: never resort to irony.

* * *

Now that you've explained the mistake, they'll let you go. It may take a few hours for permission to filter down whatever chain of crazed command these hoodlums follow. But you explain to them: a schoolteacher. A teacher who used to have a decent job in industry before his private life fell apart.

Teacher. No spy. Joke. Bad joke. Very sorry.

You cost more to kidnap than they can hope to get for you. Not worth ten shekels a pound on the international terrorist spot market. Even these amateurs have to see how ludicrous the whole mix-up is. What a story this will make, when it's all over. The greatest, most unbelievable letter back home ever.

They take your watch, along with everything else. They wedge you into some kind of root cellar, where you can't tell day from night. Two dozen hours have passed since they grabbed you. Surely not more than thirty. It might take a couple days, perhaps even a week, to straighten everything out. You fake a state of patience and settle

19

in for however long a wait it takes.

The crib where they've dumped you is too dark to see. Inch by inch, your fingertips cover every surface. Good for passing a couple hours, if nothing else. You're on a dirt floor, in a more or less rectangular room, maybe ten feet by six. The floor is little more than the flight of five steps they shoved you down. It stinks of soot and vegetables. Three of the walls are wooden; one is stone. The crumbling plaster ceiling is too low to stand up under.

Above the flight of steps lies a wooden trap door. You nudge at it. It does not move. After some time, the trap opens. Through the flood of light comes a crisis of arms and legs. Someone barks three Arabic syllables. The trap closes, and the room fills with a putrid odor. You grope your way to the steps. On the top one sits a tin plate covered with a steaming mass they can't possibly expect you to eat.

It's some kind of evil game. See what the prisoner will put in his mouth, down there in the dark. The scent gags you. You remove your nose as far from the plate as the cramped quarters allow.

After the rush of danger passes, fatigue slams you. Fear has run you through a marathon. Only now do hormones give up pointlessly dousing your muscles. You need to sleep as you've never needed to sleep in your life. But you can't. The room is too small and hard to stretch out in. The pain of your first handling still pounds you. The stink of the refuse they've tried to pass off as food keeps you from losing consciousness. Above all—sheer stupidity—you want to be awake when they come release you.

The need to urinate grows unbearable. Banging on the trap and peeing in the corner seem equally humiliating, and you refuse to be humili-ated. You try to ignore the swelling pressure on your bladder, to focus on making them open the trap. They will break before you do.

Enough time must now have passed for the school to mark your absence. Your docile flock will have told administration that their teacher has failed to show up. You try to figure how many classes you've missed. Surely, in such a city, in such a climate, someone will know to expect the worst. Someone will pull the alarm, raise a search party. . . .

Others have been taken before you. Others, with more powerful institutions lobbying for their release. Another thought to shove out of your mind. Still, your case is different. By now, your kidnappers know they have made a mistake. You aren't what they thought you are. You're a schoolteacher. You have no secrets. None that would interest them, in any case. You'll be out in a matter of days, at the most.

You pee in the corner. You try to break up the ground beforehand, with your fingernails. So the liquid can soak down.

You fill the time by going over the details of your abduction. You replay the car, the thugs, the questioning. You work up the details, making them more threatening or more comical in the recap. It's the most fantastic story that has ever happened, even without embroidering. But you'll wait a while, after your release, before sending your mother even a sanitized account.

Soon you'll have to defecate. If your bowels revolt before anyone comes, you'll be in deep shit. Another thing not to think about. Thoughts to avoid begin to crowd the already cramped quarters.

Your mind mires and circles. Then a noise tears away the gauze. The ceiling above you explodes in banging. Someone shouts through the trap, "Cover you eyes. You no look. Cover eyes!"

You fall to the floor and start searching. Somewhere, you've shed the oily rag they used to blindfold you. Discarded the scrap, thinking you'd never have to suffer it again. Now you scramble in the dark, to find it and cover your eyes before the hole opens.

The rag slips on just in time for light to stream in under the folds. A voice you don't recognize commands you to come up. "No talk," it adds.

You crack your head on a rafter, searching for the lip of the steps. False light, the flash of the blow, rips across your closed eyes. You bite down hard, to keep from shouting. As you ascend, you trip on the plate of food, scattering it.

"Why you not eat?" the voice shouts. It holds a mania that you can't afford to ignite.

21

"Terrible," you say. "Bad food. No good."

"No talk," he screams, shoving you from behind.

You come from your suffocating pupa. The upstairs feels warm, light, clear. You're good for another few hours. You will endure whatever face-saving show these men need to enact. Then you'll ask to use the bathroom. To pull yourself together a little, clean up for your release.

You flex, a gift from heaven. Behind you, you hear the puzzled crick of packing tape being ripped from its reel.

"You don't move," the voice tells you. "We tape you. For your safety."

You speak as softly as you can. You fall back on long practice, times trying to say two calming words to Gwen when just the sound of your voice lit her into frenzy.

"I am a schoolteacher. My student . . . misunderstood a joke of mine. I came to this city because . . ."

"Yes. We understand. Don't worry. We don't hurt you. We tape you. For safety. Short drive. Then you go home."

They wrap you like a mummy. They wind around and around you for half an hour. They tape right over your clothes, your hair, your ratty cotton blindfold. They leave just the crown of your head and a too-small sliver for your nose. With chops and shoves, they make you kneel. But bound so tightly, your knees can't bend in their tape tourniquet.

They pummel you into a crate. The constriction bursts your arteries. You try to make some noise—the sound of refusal, of impossibility—through the tape. Nothing comes out but a muffled whimper. You can't fit in the box. You can't even tell them that you don't fit. All you can do is free-fall into panic.

They put you in the crate and cover you. Your annihilation, your live burial. Several men try to lift the crate. The weight of a typical

American in a box dismays them. You wish now that you had eaten the food, just to add injury to insult.

They trundle you down a flight of steps. Your skull caroms against the sides of the box. The foot of the crate crashes to the ground, splintering your ankles and knees. You hear the sounds of the street, snarling mopeds, vendors hawking and haggling. If you called out? A voice seeping out of a sealed coffin, gagged, muffled, a single smeared phoneme. The risk would only seal your fate.

A little patience, and you'll walk past this spot again, tomorrow, free.

From the sound and the smashing and what little light comes in through the cracks, you sense what is happening. They place you into a recessed well in a small van. You must be hanging down in the undercarriage, given the scream of the engine.

The road is a single pothole from here to Kuala Lumpur. Every pit hammers your bound body. They've taped your face too tightly. Between the exhaust fumes, the closed crate, and the triangle of opening they leave your nose, you asphyxiate. First nausea and lightheadedness. Your head and eyes, pressed through a grater. Then a black throb pushes forward against the inside of your face. Blind animal frenzy scrabbles at the base of your brain, a creature trapped under the resealing ice. If you pass out now, you'll never wake up.

You kick against the sides of your coffin, to make them pull over. But tape turns your kicks into a wad of socks tossed into a hamper. Every agitation now sends your lungs deeper into deficit. You try to slow your racing heart by force of will. Drop your pulse into a hibernation that will outlast this endless ride.

The crate heats up, from the engine, the sun, the dry sand whipped up from the road. You fight for air, for a slice of sanity. The engine slows. Covered voices trade a few words.

You sense a barricade, a checkpoint. You shout. Death by gunfire would be a blessing. But the engine roars back to life before any more than a dull moan can escape your mouth.

23

You force your taped knees against the lid of the box. With what strength remains, you manage to crack the seam. A gush of fresh air knifes into you. You shove your nose into the stream. It tastes like God in your nostrils.

The holy sliver of air keeps you alive until the van stops. A chorused confusion hauls you from the well. They tip you on end, and the shift crushes your legs under you. They hoist you to horizontal and pop the lid. Rough hands tear at your packaging. The tape tears your skin and hair as it rips off.

You fall to the ground gasping. You lie still, sucking salvation into your lungs.

"You . . . animal-fucking bastards. . . ."

"Not talk! No make noise!" Someone smashes you across the face. Black collapses inward, and you are nowhere.

You come to in a white room. The pale light overwhelms you, after your hours in the dark. When your eyes adjust, you make out where you are. Nothing to make out. A squalid, plaster box. the room is maybe ten feet wide and twelve feet long. You could stand up fully, if you could stand up.

Here and there, the otherwise featureless walls bear greasy black fingerpainted smudges. Near the corner of one long wall, a five-foot slab of boiler plate barricades the lone doorway. Light dusts the room, seeping around the edges of a wall-sized sheet of corrugated steel nailed over the remnants of French windows.

The planked floor hasn't been swept anytime during your adulthood. The room is barren of furnishing except for a balding mattress and a metal radiator bolted to the filthy floor. Attached to the radiator, a short steel chain. Attached to the chain, your left ankle.

"Hey," you call. Your voice is dry, broken. "Hello?" Louder.

The door rumbles and jerks outwards. A young man, no more than twenty-five, stands in the frame. He is tawny, thin, medium height, black-eyed, black-haired, sleek-bearded, hang-nosed, white-shirted, blue-jeaned, and glaring. You've seen whole armies of him, waving small arms, hanging out of car windows patrolling both sides of the Green Line. He's young enough to be one of your English students. He looks, in the second that you are given to scan him, lamentably like your internal clip-art stereotype of an Arab terrorist.

"What are you doing?" he screams. "Cover your eyes! Don't look!"

You scramble on the floor near the mattress, searching for the blindfold that has chosen the wrong moment to go AWOL. Screaming, the guard rushes you and yanks down the rag that has been riding, this whole while, on your numbed head.

You fix it so that you are blind.

The boy does not retreat. He hovers by your head. His breath forms a moist, warm annulus on your neck. He presses something hard and cold and metal up into your ear.

"You hear me, you cover your eyes. You understand?"

You nod your head. Again. Harder.

*   *   *

"You look, you die."

This new room, too, has no place to relieve yourself—a hopeful fact, although hope is fast going relative. They can't keep you here for long, without leaving you somewhere to pee. Solid plank floors; plaster walls. The chain on your leg would restrict urination to a six-foot radius of where you sit. Surely these animals don't expect you to foul your own bed.

You wait. At least now, you can wait in the half-light. Someone will come before the pressure kills you. Come with food or word of your release. Or barring that, something to piss in.

You wait. The waiting becomes a game. Then the game becomes a contest. They mean to break your will. They find this cute. Some kind of victory for the world's downtrodden, to make mighty

25

America wet its pants. So it turns into a State Department mission, to suppress your bladder until the enemy concedes respect.

The pain goes crippling. A stone forms in your urethra. The denied moisture begins to trickle out your eyes. You've lost, lost against your body, against time, against your captors. You place the blindfold over your head and call out, as contritely as the pain allows.

Someone bangs once on your door and it opens. A voice from darkness's Northeast calls out, "Yes, please?"

Not your previous visitor, the one who fondled your ear with his gun. This one sounds shorter, rounder, slower on the uptake.

"I am sorry," you babble. "I need to pee very badly. Urinate. Toilet? You understand?"

You've learned the Arabic word, but in the press of need, the language tapes fail you. You stand and resort to body language, hips forward, hand to groin, the little Belgian boy, writing your name in the snow of some dream Low Country, universes away.

"Yes please. OK. I know. You wait."

You burst out in a sharp laugh that splits your gut. The man leaves, raising an alarm like the home team during the First Crusade. You must be the first person this band has ever chained up. That Americans have bladders never occurred to them.

The little round voice scurries back. He holds something up to the vee of your pants. You peek under the lip of the blindfold, into the mouth of a sawn-off plastic bleach bottle. You unbutton yourself with your battered thumbs and roll down the waistband of your underwear. But it's hopeless. Desperation changes nothing. You never could piss in public.

"Please. I hold. You leave."

"OK." The man fumbles the container into your hands. "You take."

"Thank you. You go now. Good bye." He walks off a few feet. But no door closes. It will have to do. Under the blindfold, by force of will, you imagine the room empty. Your boarded-up hole, bare but for the mattress and radiator. The floodgates open; coarse yarn pulls out of your urethra at high speed.

You collapse against the wall in relief. Your head falls back slack against the plaster. *"Merhadh."* Toilet. *"Merhadh,"* you sob, all fluids flowing out of you at once.

"Yes, yes," your captor laughs. *"Merhadh, merhadh.* I understand."

Not the word a native would have used. Pronunciation not even close. Failing to come until long after you needed. Yet these two syllables, in his tongue, send him into delight.

"Good, good. I leave bottle here. You use . . . all the time. Make water only. No shit. Shit, mornings only. I come take you. Empty bottle. Good? Yes, please?"

"Listen. Can you bring me something to drink? Water. Another bottle for water. I am very dry. . . ." You make obscure hand gestures meant to signify dehydration. Dust in the throat. "Not good. Not healthy. I must have water. A bottle to drink from." You will work on fluid for now. And put forward the concept of nourishment later.

"OK. No problem. I bring for you. Soon. *Inshallah."*

God willing. You pray the tag line is just a formula.

The door closes upon silence. You lift your blindfold to the emptied room.

How long have they held you? You need some mileage markers. On the day of your capture, you refused to entertain any block of time longer than an hour. The crisis called for small steps, one in front of the other. Just figuring in days conceded defeat. The idea of reckoning in weeks already lay a week beyond survivable. Now survival depends upon the peace that only order can give.

Taken on Tuesday, the 11th of November. Armistice Day, it hits you. A long questioning, long enough to induce hallucination. A stretch

27

in the Hole, where total darkness cut off all passage of time. Interminable transfer by van followed by a stint of unconsciousness. Now, around the edges of the sheet-metaled French windows, you see the last declarations of daylight, brackish, disappearing into the salt sea of night.

But what day? You can't say, and it crazes you. You've lost count, by as much as two full days. Lost your link to the world that they've stolen you from. Market day, school day, wash day, holiday, birthday: you fall into irreversible limbo. You can't live without a date to live in.

You run the sum of hours all possible ways, landing on different calendar squares each time. You walk in chained arcs around the radiator, trying to force up the real date as if it were a forgotten phone number. Here, in this empty cube, you choke like a child lost on a packed midnight train platform in some teeming deportation. You'll call out. Yell for your captors. Trade a beating for today's date.

Then, through the muffling wall, a signal reaches you. The background hum of traffic modulates. The air erupts in a spectral cry, then its echo. The sound reverberates, a civil defense drill. Electronic muezzins pass the fugue back and forth, like shoeless street kids passing around a soccer ball. The size of this call to prayer decides you. A smile floats up your throat to take dominion of your face. Friday. Holy day. Friday the 14th of November. 1986. You close your fingers around the prize and cling to it for sweet life.

Days go by. With each, so does the prospect of a quick release. You consider scratching each one off with your fingernails in the soft wall plaster, stick men herded and tied diagonally into docile groups of seven, down the chute of time's slaughterhouse. But the gesture seems too cheaply cinematic, too much of a surrender. Instead, vague light and dark, a cycle of repugnant meals, the morning blindfold trip to that cesspool opposite your cell all keep time for you, sure and metronomic.

The days cross off more easily than the hours. You look inward for some diversion, a fidgety Iowa kid in the back seat of a Yellowstone-bound Rambler who exhausts the possibilities of license plate bingo long before washing up on the lee shore of Nebraska. Your head is a gray-green, tidal emptiness. Your mind rebels against the smallest admission. Thought becomes a blur. Nothing there. No more than a reflection of the formless pit where they've pitched you.

Surely you knew something once, learned things, stored up diversions that might help pass the brutal infinity from quarter after to quarter to, the wall of minutes so monumental that your pulse can't even measure them? But your brain, ever vigilant, refuses to be caught exploring any other prospect than immediate release.

You talk to yourself, as to a stranger on a Transatlantic flight. You study your résumé from above, hoping to remind yourself of some topic that interests you. Favorite sport. Musical instrument. No thread lasts for more than ten minutes. And you must slog through a hundred ten-minute intervals between any two bouts of blessed unconsciousness.

You sleep on the soggy mattress, a life-sized grease stain seeping along its length. The stench so gags you that even lying on your back, you're afraid to slip off. But with each new night, you habituate to the toxic fumes. You learn to doze intermittently, suppressing the retch reflex.

Mornings they unchain you and march you through the latrine. You fix your blindfold to let you look down your cheekbones to your shuffling feet. You fake a blind stumble, so the guards don't catch on. Then, for ten precious minutes, time returns, its fast-forward mocking the previous twenty-four fossilized hours. You jump like a galvanized corpse, rinsing out your urine bottle and filling your canteen, fighting the giant roaches for a corner of the sink, shitting at the speed of sound, using any remaining seconds to scoop cold water over your head, armpits, and groin, a surreptitious shower that gets you no cleaner and costs you hours of mildewing chill. Yet, it seems a guerilla blow for decency, the smallest symbol of order keeping you alive.

Meals come capriciously, two or three times a day. They vary in quality, from inedible on downward. Breakfast usually consists of stewed okra scraps rimed with smashed chickpea. Lunch tends toward a chewed-over soup bone, what you pray is a pickled tomato, and half a circle of *khobez*. Dinner arrives, at best some self-deluding parody of *baba ghanuj*.

29

Hostage: each passing day adds another letter to the word. It grows hourly harder to deny that you've become the next victim in a serial crime that you thought had exhausted itself in pointlessness. Just one more naïve Westerner, picked off the streets for nothing, an uncashable token held to impress an enemy who doesn't grasp the first thing about the rules of exchange.

Independence Day passes on the 22nd. At least it's the 22nd by your private count. The street below your cell signals no celebration.

"Am I a hostage?" you ask the guard, the knife-voiced one, one morning, as he delivers your breakfast bowl of spotted cucumber rinds and curdled yogurt.

"I don't know," he replies. "You want, I ask Chef."

"Yes, please. Please ask."

Your answer comes that evening, with a plate of gristle rejected by its previous eater.

"Chef say you no hostage. America lets our brothers in Kuwait go free, you go free. Simple. Tomorrow. Tonight." You hear him shrug: *now*, if we get the respect that Satan owes us. Or never. Makes no difference. Entirely up to your people.

He delivers his message and leaves. You fall on the clue as a devout falls upon his prayer mat. Kuwait. Incarcerated brothers. The men who slip your food into this box and lock the door behind it are Shi'ites. At last you have a label for them. Beyond that, only your willed ignorance, your stupid refusal to have learned any more than the basics of the fate you so blithely waltzed into. Something in you, even now, does not want to know this organization's name, the one-word credential stamped on their ransom notes. Something in your scrambling soul still denies that you've been taken by the only organization capable of doing so.

Not a hostage: say just some collateral pawn, held for imaginary leverage in a game where no one can say just what constitutes winning. Word must be out by now, whatever the word is. The school knows that you're not playing hooky. And surely, in this city, they're left with only one conclusion.

By now, you've become some squib in the world papers. "Another American," like the reports you used to read and file away, unimaginable. Chicago now knows the name of those who captured you, while you do not.

Hand between your head and the infested mattress, your free leg slung across the manacled one, you force your two column inches of captivity to materialize on the crazed plaster ceiling. And along with it, the whole front section of today's *Tribune*—World's Greatest Newspaper—the first image of any resolution to grace your private screening room. The blue banner and the hedging headlines. The weather for Chicago and vicinity. Metroland meanderings, carping columnists, gridiron second-guessers: pages scroll across your field of view on microfiche of your own devising. And tucked away, make it page twelve, safe where the news will spare Des Moines and hurt only those whom hurt will benefit, you put a black and white reduction of your college yearbook photo, a face so saddled with goofy impatience for the future that even you no longer recognize it.

Days pass without your marking them, days spent squinting at the accompanying text, at all the details of your mistaken capture, at reports of your captors' confident predictions that, all sides cooperating, you'll be home by Christmas. You read your life, as only another would have told it. And you wonder, God help you, if your story has reached the one you vowed would never hear word of you again.

What Begins With Bird
Noy Holland

I START THE BULBS IN THE WINDOW the day she flies in from Mississippi. I stand them up in the bowls of gravel I scraped with a spoon from the driveway—hours ago, when the ground still showed. Now the yard is a blank of snow. The crocuses are buried and broken.

The bulbs have gone spongy or peeling and split from sitting in paper sacks too long. I should have planted them in October, picked a hole in the pebbly ground. But back then I had things to do yet, things I could do, and I can't now. So I force hyacinth on the sill.

I sit among the brocade chairs and wait for the smallest changes: his lazy eye to open, a sound at the name in my mouth. We have named the boy after the city we succumbed to marriage in, in a storm as freaky as this one: wind from the north for Easter, our sky a pink velour. Our trees are as black as shadows of trees, pressed flat in this light and moaning.

Reno, Reno, Reno—without thinking when we thought of his name what a trial they are, those r's. Weno, we know. But we didn't know it then.

My sister will call the boy something else, no doubt, as soon as she has seen him, not sweetpea, nor pumpkin (I do), but by her weekly sweetheart's name, or somebody lost or dead. They die off early, turn up their toes in babbling sleep, down where my sister lives. She will arrive with photographs, mangled faces, folded into her pockets.

Or it could be the snow has stopped her, turned her back for home. We call it that, all of us: *home:* it is a family habit, this turning away, a lie we began her lifetime ago, gathered over her, immobile: a lump, for months, in her crib.

My sister lives in an institution. The place is built in the dusky bottomland of the Mississippi River, among stands of trifling hardwoods overrun by the south's Great Vine; even in winter the trees bow their heads to that gray roving appetite, a great hunger—acres consumed by the pestilence of kudzu.

Nothing grows as quickly here. The ivy is slow and civil. Our trees

32

bend their heads for hours, a week, then toss off their burdens of snow. This can't last. A day of melt and the goose will be back to jab at the grassy patches.

Only the rabbit, in the surprise of cold, keeps to her routine: brazen creature, fixed as stone at the foot of the leaky birdbath. Frost has split the concrete bowl, parted the fluted column. These rotten New England winters. But everything else is calm: our one raccoon, the fat goose in our yard most mornings.

I tap at the glass. Not a flutter. Even the rabbit won't scare. She will keep to her place at the birdbath while night comes and day again, waiting—who can say for what? Instructions, I suppose, a murmur, a nudge, from her sack of eggs.

Small as he is my boy trumpets, stiffens his back a little. These are *my* instructions. But there is nothing I know to do for him, nothing to do but cluck and drift and wait here for my sister. We pass such liquid, unmoored days, no sleep, and only outside the seeping beech, the rising snow to mark time by. Love, love. I want nothing. My boy draws up again inside me, nights, small body rocked shut, sweet thrill—to feel him pitch and tumble. The sea at night is yellow cream, a tongue from the waking shore.

Too soon—to be asked to speak, to rise and walk. They are slow, my tribe, by habit, to come (it is a birth, after all, not a funeral)—but even so this is too soon for me. I am still jerking awake at night and dressing for the hospital: the chalky, sudden sky, the gray road, salted, gritty, slush hissing from our wheels.

Still bleeding, the stuff dropping from me in great gobs.

I say none of this. What use? We are found out. There is no saying no to my sister. I hear her grinding her teeth over the phone, heels dug in, and her father, ours, our father has bought her the ticket to come. So we ready. I start the bulbs in the window—something more to watch for; I buy wrapped chocolate eggs. My turn—it has been decided, and there is no getting loose from my father either, even from afar.

He calls ahead to say to me, "They say she's been funny lately."

"Funny?"

"I don't know."

We move on to weather, or back to it more likely, because this is also our habit; I am given the nationwide report before he asks about my son.

"Our Mr. Sun," I say, when he has embellished the heat in the middle west with stories of rotting bodies, the elderly done in by stroke in the tenements of Chicago. This is when he seems to remember—that he ought to ask, to have already asked. We are both quiet, quietly breathing, and then my father plunges ahead.

"So how's the baby? Baby okay?" he says.

"Yes, yes—" he must be, though I wake him as so many mothers do to be certain he is still breathing. He grins in his sleep—these are dreams, I say, and startles. An arm swings up. The lid of one eye heaves open. Dear lump. I could round his pointy head, work the flat patch where he sleeps on it, the notched resilient plates, the bone still spongy as the bulbs I found to force in the gloom this morning. But I don't; it won't last; I leave him be.

I leave the plastic band on his wrist where Nurse Jane wrote my name—how strange, that you cannot at first even pick out your own from all the other babies. Mine has eleven dimples—dimples instead of knuckles and one on each side of his nose; in the fat of his leg is a pucker the color of pencil lead, a stitch drawn deep and tightly and tied off at the bone.

I knew him in the dark this way. I felt for it in the dark of my room where the big window looked at the Merrimack, the viscid fenced canal; I watched school children pasting up paper eggs and tousling in the hall and once one boy swung his lace-ups up to catch in the branch of a tree; they dropped, and the other boys spat and hooted. I kept it dark inside in my room for him so that when they brought him to me I knew him by his smell. He smelled of lanolin, clean and old and animal and bitter to me then and now and I knew him then as I do now by the feel of the stitch in his leg, not a stitch, nothing that will heal.

There is this, and the plastic band I will leave on his wrist until Sister has come and gone, my name, we had not named him yet, and there are too the ways in me to say as I do *mine:*

The cut in me, seeping still, the grinning stapled mouth: proof that he has been here, proof that he is gone. Here is where they found him, red and bawling, lifted him plumply out.

My belly-skin a lizard's, shrunk to shimmering and scale.

And here—this dimming mark, gray as ash, that halves me thatch to sternum; this line drawn through my navel that darkened as we grew. We grew, we grew.

I would have carried him in me for years.

And yet here in my face is the vessel I burst trying to push him out. Too late—by then he had already outgrown me, grown into me, a leggy, dogged stalk of boy left to bolt to seed. He left in my forehead the fine mesh of roots that living things send out, the paths, the swerving abruptions of blood, the friable clump in the floor of a pot, as though I had needed first, to birth him, to tear him from my brain.

I do not try to hide it. I obscure no proof, no possible claim.

Am claimed myself without noticing, marked, in the old animal way—the tails of my shirts, my thick brassieres, hair and neck and cupping ear—in the dark you don't expect it, more of it, squatting to swab the floor. All's well. All the lights green for Reno, his penis a plump blue cone. I turn the thick skin with my fingers, gap the bleedy pinprick he pisses on me through.

And if he pisses on Sister? She will skrauk like a crow and giggle, wince, and I will be near, watching over, looking out for her as I used to do, as I look out for snow that slides from a roof, and listen—for the strained-rope sound a branch will make before it tears from the head of a tree. Who could trust her?

I am watchful these new days anyway of anything that moves—small dogs, a fat goose, his own father.

And my sister is always moving, even when she means to sit, or we are, one of us, the rest of us since Mother, we are moving her around. Giving her instructions, keeping her out of the way.

She has a way of making her absence felt. You know better—you should not have let her go. But she is bored, nervous, sullen. She grows weary, quickly, of family, needs somebody new to love. She comes to you for a visit and next you know she has disappeared. It is a monsoon, or a blizzard; you have made your nest in the desert, earthquakes coming, or it is the year of the romance of slums. Scarcely matters. She will wander out into anything, take up with anyone, drift off with the nearest miscreant to look at his tattoos.

I am like her in this; I move away. Even an infant finds safety in motion.

I never settled for years long enough for my father to send her to me, to track me down with news. But he is a good tracker; give him time, he finds you, elated some: some twister gouged the riverbanks, floods in Tennessee. The dying bees all summer. All preamble, priming, the news delivered first that you can do nothing about. And then, *your sister*—calling her not by name of course but by title, binding clause. The slippery possessive. *Your sister. My daughter.* Under what condition would he call her that—her, I think, or me?

It used to be we tracked down a new place for her every few months, every year. Our father's house, the YMCA—disastrous.

Some school near here in Boston that packed her off in a blink to the loony bin. A problem of climate, my father decided. These dreary New England winters. The desert was next, saguaros and sun, the sobriety of a mineral landscape. She burned down her apartment, dropped a lighted cigarette into a heap of dirty laundry. That was Phoenix, and she was pregnant, a condition nobody noticed until she was six months along. Then the family engaged, oh, oh—moved in for the crisis. We are a family that loves a good crisis. Birth control? I'd have thought that you . . . None of us had bothered.

Our father found me, enlisted me; it was a time in my life he could find me, when he could *call in the troops,* as he said. He flew me out to Phoenix first to see if I could persuade her. My father knew of a clinic not far from him, convenient to him, in Atlanta. I was to fly her back over the country to him, to the house we left our boxes in, in the town we had once called home. He had his Triptiks in order. He had his prim new wife. He had mapped out places to show to his wife on the drive to the clinic in Atlanta.

On the flight west I had my soothing, brief heroic moment, or the thought of one, the big idea. Nothing lasts with me. But for a moment I thought I would take her in, be her good big sister—quick, quick, before Daddy comes. Six months. By then a baby is swallowing; it is opening and closing its eyes. It had begun to hear, to know her voice. It must have turned toward the light as mine did, as I felt him face the sun.

Any light, even this gray gloaming, my boy turns his head to see, though he still sees nearly nothing, no distance, mostly only we keepers, mostly only me.

She stays put now, my sister; the grounds are fenced and gated.

Another bellow—raspy and prolonged. I am beginning to know the difference—between hunger, say, and fear.

I lift him to me. I am dripping milk. His mouth opens quick as a bird's.

My breasts are stiff, prickly, lumped. He is rooting, and then uprooting me—that's what it feels like. I feel the tug in the wing of my shoulder and in the ball and socket; he is drawing my ribs together, cinching the narrowing slots; he is dragging silt from my bones.

All's well. Night soon. Above us the snow is ticking down. No distance. No lapsed horizon bleeding pink beyond the flattened trees.

Little raccoon, funny monkey. He drinks and drinks and dozes. Yawns, and the trough in his wrinkled palate shows, slender and deep for sucking. A blister fills on his lip again, the skin of his first mouth already shed, the pale strips frayed and loosened.

Our rabbit flickers her ear. A squirrel drops out of the gingko tree at the far gray rim of our yard. Everything in its place; a place for everything. A patch of dirt for the sickly elm, a barn for broken china, rake and nail and rusting plow, a crib he will soon grow into.

It is all always too soon for me, the crib in the wings, the coming melt, the year's slow resurrection. The steadfast family wagon—my sister fetched from the airport—yawing into the drive.

I lay the boy down in his wicker tub and wheel him away from the door, from the surge of cold when it opens and damp and the squalling of crows in the heads of the trees and the plows groaning out on the highway.

Ready? I think. *Ready?* Because it has already begun.

She is out of the car and running at us before George even opens his door, all teeth and arms and flagging hair, a sidelong lurch and stutter. It is motion, the infant's comfort, mine, which gives her away. When she stops in the doorway and holds out her hands, waiting for me to come to her, nothing seems so wrong. She is pretty, and she has mastered the phony, square-bottomed smile taught in better homes: clean gums, corrected rows of teeth. I move to her to see what I already know, cannot—would not—keep from seeing: the tremor, the scars, her bitten lip, the puddles of shadow around her eyes.

She stamps the snow from her sandals, standing wobbling in the doorway, the cold still streaming in. She hugs me, knocks against my chest. It always feels to me that her heart runs rough, won't idle, wants to race and quit; it is worse every time I see her and tells more clearly what is to come. They come mildly even now to me: days I cannot stop shaking. Another family habit—inherited, her tremor, worse with age (what isn't?) among the women in our tribe. My sister cannot sign her name; she can scarcely hold a pen.

She keeps holding me so I stand there, stroking her hair, feeling her shudder against me. The first hour or two is an act with us, as with the early weeks of love. Easy enough, early on, to be sweeter than you are, to keep your few good secrets. But give a girl time, weather, meals. Quit closing the shithouse door. Pretty soon, this is me, I am chewing my tongue just to sit in the kitchen and listen to you, to the squalor of your feeding.

Those shoes—skinny, strappy things—and the snow some inches deep by now and she has left our George out in it please to gather up her bags. "It's like Cream of Wheat," she says, too loudly, "mercy."

It is a game they two have been playing, I guess, passing the time from the airport. "It's like walking through frozen beer—" that's George's, and he laughs, and water pools as he walks in his footsteps and slops across the porch. He tips his hat. "Hello, rabbit." He kisses me. "Hello, mother. Made it."

The trick must be in knowing who to be afraid of, what.

Our spotted dog, pent up, neglected, pokes her nose around the corner, suffers a sudden paroxysm of joy—somebody fresh to love.

"So how is it in Mississippi?" I ask.

"Nice. Very nice. Flowers and such. But *cold* at night. Mercy."

She shakes the wet from her head, teasing, and the dog still quivers and blinks at her feet. "So where is he? Where's that baby?" She throws her hair back. "C'mere, young'n. Come here."

Somebody fresh to love; somebody new to harvest. I am watchful, and sick in my heart to see the boy calmed in his own father's arms. What use, to see it coming? Bed down one yellow afternoon when the tide is in your favor and you begin the long moving away. Months pass; joints soften, slip; veins give, the blood in you doubles and quickens. And yet this was not the feel of it—not of quickening, not to me, but of paths begun to silt and pinch, to slow, and, slowing, close. My neck swelled; my lungs rode up.

I fell into myself calmly, besotted and sufficient.

I was sufficient and am no longer, will not be again. Any mother knows. It is nothing new; nothing lasting—not the fullness, the thickish calm, and not these weeks the sudden ache of an emptied womb.

The body remembers, seems to insist—there was something it meant to do—to lose him, to birth him. To finish what it had begun. I wake, and find the boy beside me in the ripening bed, my bed, I keep him near me, the nightlight on, the barn beyond the window gone tossing out to sea. I drag the sheets back. His eyes are sprung open. His skin is twisted on him, rubbery and slick. He is not mine, is not the real baby. There is one yet still to be born.

There is everything still to go through again—my belly a stained translucence, the doctors in their starched blues.

Stupid, I know, to think it, want it. But even now, these weeks gone past, the small hard snaps of milk in his chest—witch's milk—dissolved; his lazy eye, the slackened lid, begun to draw up and quicken, so soon: I would go through it all all over again: the idiot howling, blood sliding from me in hot strings. Hours of this and then nothing, the needle pressed into the spine. The limp pale drape someone hung at my chest to keep me from seeing.

His little face had tipped up, watchful.

Somebody whistled somewhere in the greenish bright and quiet and someone was asking, *Ready? They've already begun.*

I felt nothing but that they moved me, crudely, my sloppy haunch, hardly mine—the drape seemed to hang to mark the place where my body detached at the sockets. I listened: this was his being born. This was the sound of a hand wedged in, and then the small bent head popped free, quick as a tooth you are losing. This that I felt backed into my throat was the body shoved into the cage of my ribs, brief, and how surprising: the rest had seemed so distant: a ditch cut into a distant slab, spongy and geologic, marsh, a bowl of softened bone. Then the baby, the bawling sight of him; then the staples driven in.

Nothing lasts, but nothing is finished either. Anybody knows. The brain boils and cools, same as many things, heals with the slickness of scars. Nothing's lost; no grief, unspoken, forgotten.

Yet we hold our tongues. Not a word, these years, about it. Hardly a word between us, even then, my sister and me, the very day, those hours, the long before and after in the back seat to Atlanta, after Phoenix, Daddy driving, after Mother, I think it pleased him, the look of it, his girls, his new wife neatly beside him. He wanted to stop and look at things: Chickamauga, Antietam, the cannons in a row.

Of course I think of it—how it must be, might have been, for Sister, closing in on Atlanta. In the morning, plain tea. The righteous out in the early heat, their foetuses wrinkling in jars. Our father moved to her to take her arm to steady her along. She seemed to straighten: he had noticed her being brave. Had she seen the fluted columns, he wanted to know, the Corinthian scrolling above? She looked up, we all did, and listened, he spoke so little, and spoke of Sherman that day as though they were friends, as though we had him to thank for it, my father, that the building still stood, Georgian and grandly columned, spared—handsome, I remember thinking it then, he was as handsome as when we were girls.

We needed so little from him. To be spoken to, to be steadied, that was extra, that was gravy. Because here already was bounty, I thought, her own crisis, here was her chance to be Daddy's, to be brave, to be seen being brave, being ready.

Here was her act of love.

The worse the march the better. The righteous who strained at the roped-off yard, rattled their jars, a child on a hip, how lucky—something more to endure. Half a year's neglect endured, the wiggy pitching months of it, and now, this late, late as it was, the danger, the night's long labor ahead. The toddlers in the leggy grass, writhing, moaning, *Mommy.*

The day a blaze, the early heat. The bodies yawing sweetly in their lettered jars.

They did not hurry. They were solemn, the two of them, processional: a girl on her father's arm. There was something of a lilt and quickening, something graceful—vaguely—supple, fierce, something punitive and bridal in the way she moved to the door.

She had worn her heels, our mother's pearls. She had worn the dress our mother used to dress for parties in.

I held my tongue; this much was easy. I began for a time to feel it, too, a queer sort of pride in myself: I had gone to Phoenix and fetched her home and here we all were with him, quietly, soberly walking. To what, walking to what, it seemed all at once not to matter. What mattered was that I had done, that we were doing, as he asked.

He made it easy, our father, provided; he gave us our instructions.

I flew out. The desert bloomed. I was to fetch her home.

I withheld him, the threat of him, the name in my mouth, to try her. But nothing else I could think of in the days I spent in Phoenix, not love—I trotted out every homily I had heard of the family romance, sacrifice, devotion, the kindness of a kindhearted man (*my mouth:* I was moving between lovers, snorting junk in the sumac behind the corner store)—her own unreadiness, it did not move her, and not the ghoulish stories I knew of babies grown in wrong—the ones who lasted, babblers, maimed, stood up, shipped out to Mississippi.

My god, the lavishness of her Mississippi. Any outrage I could think to relate was an insult, a pittance against it. But I did not know so then. Mississippi was years to come—bodies dropping in the viney woods, *hula hula,* somebody new: a curdling lunatic glee. We held our ground, the field in bloom, the gate swung shut behind us.

A gate swings shut behind you, going in, if you go, coming out.

They came to us over the open field, toothy, threnodic, multiplying as they moved.

*

40

"The baby's fine," she said. "It's going to be fine."

I said, "That baby grows in you."

We roomed for days in a motel in Phoenix, a dry wind scratching the door.

I said, "I was in the airport. I was on my way here to you."

It was something I had heard in the Ladies', talk of the boy, women tipping toward the mirror to slide their lipstick on. I said I had seen the boy, coming to her, his hand in his mother's skirt, a blinker of flesh hung over one eye, eyebrow to nose, the skin crusted and thick and frilled—I went on, I could feel my voice rising—his eye yellow in its socket, wild, what I saw of it, who saw nothing, and the flap as brown as a potato, gouged, stiff hair hatching from it.

None of this moved her at all. We drew the curtains, hardly spoke and watched daytime TV. When the day came to leave I said what I had been saving to say, to have it on me, to feel that had convinced her. It was easy. "Daddy's on his way."

He held her arm, to guide her, to keep her on course for the door. Sister reached behind her back and fluttered out her hand and I— I think it must have surprised me: that she had thought to reach for me, and then that she had not. I took her hand. She drew me up from behind her to walk along up the walk with them, on Sister's arm, Sister on our father's arm, the new wife trailing behind us. I had not heard her. I had not likely listened. I was hearing I think the rest of them, the fathers, daughters, churchly men, the sisters hissing scripture, a vast unholy throng.

I saw her face then: I saw our mother's. I saw her face in the face of another mother gone to her knees in the uncut grass with her baby hugged against her chest in the litter of all they had brought there.

They had labeled the months, the stations: Here is your baby at three months, here is your baby at four months, here is your baby at five.

They were reaching in under the rope strung up to keep them off my sister, to keep them off of me. They were snatching at the hem of our mother's dress. I kicked at their arms, their faces.

"Mother—" she said it loudly, and let my hand go.

I thought she had meant it: *Mother.*

I heard her all along, I know, walking along: "Mother." But I had not thought of it. This is how I came to think of it—it made it easy, easier for me: we were sending her baby to Mother. There were not enough babies among the dead for all the mothers to mother.

Sister turned from me; she fluttered her hand behind her back, teetering on her heels.

They bent their heads; they were kneeling, rocking on their knees. I thought maybe they meant to drink from the jars, maybe they meant to sing.

I thought, going on—I knew better: I understood it, the news of it, the reason they had come—but then I thought they had come in need to her; they had come to her to be tended to—it was stupid—to be answered—I knew I was being stupid—to be dropped to their knees and saved.

I saw they had saved out a jar for her.

She began to throw them coins.

"One more."

She touched a forehead. She tossed away a ring she liked. She kissed a boy they offered.

"One more baby more," they said.

I saw her knees give, she was turned from me. She was reaching for the new wife's hand, calling the new wife: "Mother."

And this surprised me. It was nothing, it was the way of things.

I fell behind some. If it had been me. She tried to lie down. I might have let her.

She was to let them cut it out of her, the easy way, who can say now, what she thought of it, what I had brought her back over the country to do, what Sister thought she was meant to be doing?

He got her moving. Daddy was gentle. I could see Daddy meant to be gentle. He had her by her hair. He hauled her up some. He had her by the braid his tidy wife had made of the mess of Sister's hair to keep our Sister nice that day, to keep our Sister tidy.

You think it's easy? The way she tries you. The way she—listen. You think it's easy? You think she means to make it easy? *Sister, mother, holy joe.* To be our father? To keep her moving, swung to her feet and gone?

My guess is they gave her Pitocin, a drip, same as what they gave me. They give you your fishnet panties. Then they send you to wander the halls in your socks until the contractions begin.

There are other mothers out there: it's insulting: that it is not only you. But it must have calmed my sister—to have somebody new to talk to, to lap the nurses' station with.

In time, I talked too. Stood in the gaggle in the yellow glare rubbing the drum of my belly. Not because I thought I had to (talk)—

decorum, no, nicety, not then, not yet again. This was our blessed respite. Nothing decorous about it. Only lassitude, rapture, a flaunted animal pleasure. I'll go on, I went on, I have never been quite so sweet on myself, and talky, in time, and shameless—avid, giddy, apart. I might have told anyone anything. I think talking made me hope to prolong it, stop it, hedge some way—I wasn't afraid, much— the table, the curtain drawn, not even the room, the stirrups, the blank chill of the day outside, none of this really shook me—not the pain, quite, the prospect of pain: I thought, *Come on, come on:* what is the pleasure of what doesn't cost you, hurt you?—no, the room I think thrilled me, the wide belts, the tools, the dim medieval look of it.

When he was in me—before the hunger again, the slackness in me—that was when he was easiest to love.

They let me blather on, the others. We all of us mothers did. We scrutinized, amazed ourselves, the hearts we grew, the milk, the bone, the ax to wield; the father, yes, *come in, do, gently— there*—helpless there, supremely; remote, absurd, refined. Our faces swelled, our eyes withdrew; we spoke our old lost tongues. This of course was later; this was the fabled room. We were lucid at our station, patient in the yellow glare, divulging in our measured tones the blanching gape of cervix, vying some, even then, predatory, preying, somebody's sticky plug spit out, somebody's bloody show.

Had your bloody show, dear?

Yes, yes—then nothing. Instructions. Nurses, nurses, somebody always grinning from the corner of my room.

I lost hours; they might be years. The grasses sang. The riverbanks shrilled and buckled. I know I wandered. I saw a white horse burning. I saw my mother sleeping in the bend of a yellow road.

Pieces missing, syllables. The living thinned to shadow, droned, busy at my knees. At what?

But who could know?

Even now I worry George to recall to me the day's events; I want orderliness, a story, the discrete before and after.

And after, before the room, the wide window over the Merrimack, dark, the coming dawn, before they brought him to me—these are the questions that flare in me, petty, absurd—I had not seen him but to see him, plump and bawling, thrashing in the sick light and in whose scoured arms? And who is it who went off with him? What surly immigrant nurse, mistaken for a mother, bathed him, while I in my decorum lay in the cool with the curtains drawn chatting with

43

the postmaster's wife?

What difference? And yet I think of it. Ought to think instead of Sister, yes, be a good big sister. Easter in the morning. Ought to bundle up in the morning, stash my boiled eggs. It being Easter. Since she is my sister.

Sit her down—she claps at me—show her how to hold him, show her what to do.

Her own she could have held—a guess—in an open hand—small as that, if she wanted, if she was lucky, if the nurses were on their rounds.

Of course I think of it. I hardly think of it—except that she is here. I think of us in the blaze of heat and of the room where we waited, the chairs we took, side by side, the row of scaly bucket seats bolted to the wall. We tipped our heads back. People do—and there were years of people before us, drooping in those chairs. How lucky: a single salient detail: the plaster worn smooth behind us, stained: years of hair, the press of heads: oily, elongated patches. We were resting, had been, those of us who came to help, to fill out papers, if help was how you thought of it, who waited there, dozing, until we were certain the job was done.

It was done—this is as much as I know or want to. Do not know or ask so much as even was she on the potty, the sheeted bed, the floor. Was it dead or living. Did she have a look at it. I would think you would have to look at it—see was it a boy, a girl, have a name to call it by, count its fingers, toes. Or maybe this is me. Or maybe I don't know. But I think I would want something from it—a thumb tip, a twist of cord, we keepers, not to have nothing at all from it, anything small to show.

She turns her palms up to me. Supple as he is and weak—what harm? And yet she is my sister. And yet she is my sister.

And there is the favored wingback, stout of arm, of wing, of foot.

I pass him to her. "Watch his neck."

"I know, I know, I know."

Hickory, gingko, willow, elm.

Sweetpea, wicker, junior mint. Little man, I call him, honcho, buster, sugar boy. Almost never Reno, sometimes kid Reno, buckareno, buckaroo. She calls him Binny. *Heeey, Binny. It's your Aunt Kathleen.*

The bird dog she calls Honey Gal and, before long—because much

44

of the time we call her Snoot, for her snoot—my sister calls her Snout. This gets us laughing, George and me, helplessly, until we are falling out of our chairs.

"Nose," she says, and touches his nose. "Ears. Cheeks. Chin. What's this?"

She spreads her hand on the crown of his head and gives it a turn to show me. "Look." But it is only the scabbing rash he has had, yellowish and common, thriving between where his eyebrows will be. "And this, what's this?" on the slope of his nose, the puggish end, the hard pale knots of acne. "Uunh."

She lets his head tip back and fingers his neck and it is in my mouth to stop her but I am thinking I understand it, suppose I do— the hope of finding a flaw in him, some lasting crimson blemish. Even a terrible wrongness, I think, it is not such a stretch to think of it: she is hoping to find her own mark on him, evidence of kinship, even if, or especially if, it is the kinship of the maimed.

I stoop over her, look to see what she sees: there is vernix still, I have missed it, gray and ripe and gummy, smeared in the folds of his chin. My sister draws her finger along a crease and the baby squawks and gags. "That's enough."

Too much for me already. I gather him up. Remember to kiss her. I remember the place at the bend in her arm Mother used to rub before Sister slept, to help her sleep, and I touch it. "Love you great big," I remember. Then make my slow way to bed.

Three Poems
John Ashbery

THE WATER INSPECTOR

Scramble the "Believer" buttons. Silence the chickens. We have more
important things, like intelligence. We say so many cruel things in a
lifetime, and yet. In a whorehouse, young, I obfuscated. Destiny was
this and that, no it was *about* this and that. Do you see what I'm saying?
Nobody needs the whole truth.

Even so we exact repetition. The beat goes on. Terribly surprised about
the report, about your father's death, but these things happen. Often the
dead are found next day, alive but shaken, wondering what it was that happened
to them, trembling beneath a cellar door. And we too wonder what happens
when the sky as we know it cracks in two. Beetle voices serenade us. The
earth and its fountains can't do enough for us, yet we remember, shaken too,
like in the old days.

We were reading and there came a knock at the door. The water inspector, we
thought, and of course no one was there. Stung, and stung again. So we
proceed, always on course, always begging the stars to tell us what happened,
whether we were clean really, were we on course. Always the silence says yes,
you can go home now, round up your siblings, head for the nearest wooded area
if you think that will help.

I was once surprised but lay and brooded, my life at my back now, my discourse
like weeds far out on a lake. It must have come to me, it always does, part
of my profound business.

I think in the think tank, always elegant in my thinking, far away. Far
from what I consider. Once it was all grace in the lifting. Awkward, yes, and not
a little disconcerting.

TWO FOR THE ROAD

Did you want it plain or frosted? (Plain vanilla or busted?)

I bet you've been writing again. She reached under her skirt. Why
don't you let a person see it? Naw, it's no good. Just some chilblains
that got lodged in my fingertips. Who said so? I'll tell you if it's
any good or not, if you'll stop covering it with your hand.

For Pete's sake—

We had forgotten that it was noon, the hour when the ravens emerge from
the door beside the huge clock face and march around it, then back inside to the
showers. Oh, where were you going to say let's perform it?

I thought it was evident from my liquor finish steel.

Oh right, you can certainly have your cocktail, it's my shake, my fair
shake. Dust-colored hydrangeas fell out of the pitcher onto the patio.
Darned if someone doesn't like it this way and always knows it's going to
happen like this when it does. But let me read to you from my peaceful new
story:

"Then the cinnamon tigers arose and there was peace for maybe a quarter
of a century. But you know how things always turn out. The dust bowl slid
in through the French doors. Maria? it said. Would you mind just coming
over here and standing for a moment. Take my place. It'll only be for a
minute. I must go see how the lemmings are doing. And that is how she
soiled herself and brought eternal night upon our shy little country."

YOUR NAME HERE

But how can I be in this bar and also be a recluse?
The colony of ants was marching toward me, stretching
far into the distance, where they were as small as ants.
Their leader held up a twig as big as poplar.
It was obviously supposed to be for me.
But he couldn't say it, with a poplar in his mandibles.
Well, let's all forget that scene and turn to one in Paris.

Ants are walking down the Champs-Elysées
in the snow, in twos and threes, conversing,
revealing a sociability one never supposed them as having.
The larger ones have almost reached the allegorical statues
of French cities (is it?) on the Place de la Concorde.
"You see, I told you he was going to bolt.
Now he just sits in his attic
ordering copious *plats* from a nearby restaurant
as though God had meant him to be quiet."
"You look like a portrait of Mme. de Staël by Overbeck,
that is to say a little serious and washed out.
Remember you can come to me any time
with what is bothering you, just don't ask for money.
Day and night my home, my hearth are open to you,
you great big adorable one, you."

The bar was unexpectedly comfortable.
I thought about staying. There was an alarm clock on it.
Patrons were invited to guess the time (the clock was always wrong).
More cheerful citizenry crowded in, singing the Marseillaise,
congratulating each other for the wrong reasons, like the color
of their socks and taking swigs from a communal jug.
"I just love it when he gets this way,
which happens in the middle of August, when summer is on its way
out, and autumn is still just a glint in its eye,
a chronicle of hoar-frost foretold."
"Yes and he was going to buy all the candy bars in the machine
but something happened, the walls caved in (who knew
the river had risen rapidly) and one by one people were swept away
calling endearing things to each other, using pet names.
"Achilles, meet Angus." Then it all happened so quickly I
guess I never knew where we were going, where the pavement
was taking us. Or the sidewalk, which the English call pavement,
which is what sidewalks are made of, or so it seems.

Things got real quiet in the oubliette.
I was still reading *Jean-Christophe*. I'll never finish the darn thing.
Now is the time for you to go out into the light
and congratulate whoever is left in our city. People who survived
the eclipse. But I was totally taken with you, always have been.
Light a candle in my wreath, I'll be yours forever and will kiss you.

The Sharpshooter
Joyce Carol Oates

> *The secret meaning of the evolution of civilization
> is no longer obscure to us who have pledged our
> lives to the struggle between Good and Evil;
> between the instinct of Life and the instinct of
> Death as it works itself out in the human species.
> So we vow!*
>
> —Preface, *The Book of the Patriot in America*

IT WAS MY DADDY'S PIONEER WISDOM. *There is always something deserving of being shot by the right man.*

When I was eleven my Daddy first took me out onto the range to shoot *butcher birds.* I date my lifelong respect for firearms & my prowess as a Sharpshooter from that time.

Butcher bird was Daddy's name for hawks, falcons, California condors (now almost extinct) & golden eagles (ditto) we would shoot out of the sky. Also, though scavengers & not predators actively threatening our barnyard fowl & spring lambs, Daddy despised turkey vultures as unclean & disgusting creatures there could be no excuse for existing & these ungainly birds too we would shoot out of trees & off fence railings where they perched like old umbrellas. Daddy was not a well man suffering the loss of his left eye & "fifty yards" (as he said) of ulcerated colon as a result of War injuries & so he was filled with a terrible fury for these predator-creatures striking our livestock like flying devils out of the air.

Also crows. Thousands of crows cawing & shrieking in migration darkening the sun.

There are not enough bullets for all the targets deserving, was another of Daddy's firm beliefs. These I have inherited, & Daddy's patriot pride.

Those years, we were living on what remained of our sheep ranch. Fifty acres mostly scrubland in the San Joaquin Valley midway between Salinas to the west & Bakersfield to the south. My Daddy & his older brother who'd been crippled in the War, though not Daddy's war. & me.

Others had deserted us. Never did we speak of them.

49

In our Ford pickup we'd drive out for hours. Sometimes rode horseback. Daddy made a gift to me of his .22-caliber Remington rifle & taught me to load & fire in safety & never in haste. For a long time as a boy I fired at stationary targets. A living & moving target is another thing Daddy warned. Aim carefully before you pull any trigger, remember someday there's a target that, if you miss, will fire back at you & without mercy.

This wisdom of Daddy's, I cherish in my heart.

I am over-cautious as a Sharpshooter, some believe. Yet my belief is, where a target is concerned you may not get a second chance.

Our barnyard fowl, chickens & guineas, & in the fields spring lambs were the *butcher birds'* special prey. Other predators were coyotes & feral dogs & less frequently mountain lions but the *butcher birds* were the worst predators because of their numbers & the swiftness of their attacks. Yet they were beautiful birds, you had to concede. Red-tailed hawks, goshawks & golden eagles. Soaring & gliding & dipping & suddenly dropping like a shot to seize small creatures in their talons & bear them aloft alive & shrieking & struggling.

Others were struck & mutilated where they grazed or slept. The ewes bleating. I'd seen the carcasses in the grass. Eyes picked out & entrails dragged along the ground like shiny slippery ribbons. A cloud of flies was the signal.

Shoot! Shoot the fuckers! Daddy would give the command & at the exact moment, we both shot.

They praised me for my age all who knew me. Sharpshooter they called me. & sometimes Little Soldier.

The golden eagle & the California condor are rarities now but in my boyhood we shot many of these & strung up their carcasses in warning! *Now you know. Now you are but meat & feathers, now you are nothing.* Yet there was beauty in contemplating such powerful creatures of the air, I would have to concede. To bring down a golden eagle as Daddy would say is a task for a man & to see its golden neck feathers close up. (To this day I carry with me, in memory of my boyhood, a six-inch golden feather close to my heart.) The condor was an even larger bird, with black-feathered wings (we'd measured once at ten feet) & vivid white underwing feathers like a second pair of wings. The cries of these great birds! Gliding in wide circles & tilting from side to side & what was strange in such creatures was how, feeding, they might be joined by others swiftly flying from far beyond the range of a man's vision.

Of the *butcher birds* it was goshawks I shot the most of, as a boy. For there were so many. & when their numbers were depleted in our vicinity I would go in search of them; farther & farther from home, in ever-widening circles. Choosing to travel cross-country, I would ride a horse. Later, when I was old enough to have a driver's license, & the price of gasoline not yet too high, I would drive. A goshawk is gray & blue & their feathers like vapor so that drifting against a filmy sky they would vanish & reappear & again vanish & reappear & I would become excited knowing I must fire to strike a target not only speeding but not-visible & yet this I would do, by instinct, sometimes missing (I concede) but often my bullet struck its target to yank the soaring creature from the sky as if I held an invisible string attached to it & had such power over it, unknown by the goshawk, & unguessed, I might yank it down to earth in an instant.

On the ground, their beautiful feathers bloody, & eyes staring open, they lay still as if they'd never been alive.

Butcher bird now you know—I would speak to these calmly.

Butcher bird now you know who has dominion over you, who cannot fly as you fly—never would I gloat, almost there was a sadness in my speech.

For what is the melancholy of the Sharpshooter, after his beautiful prey lies crumpled at his feet? Of this, no poet has yet spoken; & I fear, none ever will.

Those years. I lived in that place yet spent long days roaming, & often slept in the pickup, following I know not what thread of unnameable desire drawing me sometimes as far south as the San Bernardino Mountains & into the vast desert spaces of Nevada. I was a soldier seeking my army. I was a Sharpshooter seeking my calling. In the rearview mirror of the pickup a fine pale-powdery ascension of dust & in the distance before me watery mirages that beckoned & teased. *Your destiny! Where is your destiny!* Driving with my rifle beside me on the passenger's seat, sometimes two rifles, & a double-barreled shotgun, loaded & primed to be fired. Sometimes in the emptiness of the desert I would drive with boyish bravado, my rifle slanted at an angle on the steering wheel as if I might fire through the windshield if required. (Of course, I would never do such a self-destructive thing!) Often I would be gone for days & weeks & by this time Daddy was dead & my uncle elderly & ailing & there was no one to observe me. Not *butcher birds* exclusively but other birds too became my targets, primarily crows, for there are too many crows in

51

existence, & such game birds as pheasants & California quail & geese, for which I would use my shotgun, though I did not trouble to search out their carcasses where they fell stricken from the air.

Rabbits & deer & other creatures I might shoot, yet not as a hunter. A Sharpshooter is not a hunter. With binoculars scanning the range & the desert seeking life, & movement. Once I saw on a mountainside in the Big Maria Mountains (near the Arizona border) what appeared to be a face; a female face; & unnatural blond hair, & unnatural red mouth pursed in a teasing kiss; & though trying not to stare at this apparition I was helpless before it, & my pulses pounded, & my temples, & I reasoned it was but a billboard & not an actual face & yet it teased & taunted so, at last I could not resist aiming my rifle at it as I drove slowly past, & fired a number of times until the terrible pressure was relieved & I'd driven past; & no one to witness. *Now you know. Now you know. Now you know.*

Soon after that my excitation was such, I was drawn to target-shoot sheep & cattle, even a grazing horse provided the countryside was empty of all witnesses. For *how easy to pull the trigger* as they would tell me one day in the Agency. There is a sacred wisdom here, I believe it is a pioneer wisdom. *Where the bullet flies, the target dies.* Subtle as poetry is *What is the target is not the question, only where.* Sometimes I would sight a vehicle far away on the highway scarcely more than a speck rapidly approaching & if there were no witnesses (in the Nevada desert, rarely were there witnesses) at the crucial instant as our vehicles neared each other I would lift my rifle & aim out my rolled-down window & taking into account the probable combined velocities of both vehicles rushing together I would squeeze the trigger at the strategic moment; with the supreme control of the Sharpshooter I would not flinch, though the other driver might pass close enough by me to see the expression on his (or her) face; I would proceed onward without slackening my speed, nor increasing it, observing calmly in my rearview mirror the target vehicle swerving from the highway to crash by the roadside. If there were witnesses what were they but *butcher birds* gazing down at such a spectacle from their high-soaring heights; & *butcher birds* despite the keenness of their eyes cannot bear witness. These were in no way personal vengeful acts, only the instinct of the Sharpshooter.

Shoot! Shoot the fuckers! Daddy would command. & what could a son do but obey.

*

52

It was in 1946 I would be hired by the Agency. Too young to have served my country in Wartime, I pledged to serve my country in these interludes of false peace. For Evil has come home to America. It is not of Europe now nor even of the Soviets exclusively but has come to our continent to subvert & destroy our American heritage. For the Communist Enemy is both foreign & yet close to us as any neighbor. This Enemy can be indeed the neighbor. *Evil is the word for the target* as it is said in the Agency. *Evil is what we mean by our target.*

The Impunity of the Sacred Car
Eduardo Galeano

—With illustrations by José Guadalupe Posada,
translated from Spanish by Mark Fried

Human rights pale beside the rights of machines. In more and more cities, especially in the giant metropoli of the south of the world, people have been banned. Automobiles usurp human space, poison the air and frequently murder the interlopers who invade their conquered territory—all with utter impunity. Is there a difference between violence that kills by car and that which kills by knife or bullet?

THE END OF THE TWENTIETH CENTURY scorns public transport. When this century was celebrating its mid-point, Europeans were using trains, buses, subways and streetcars for three quarters of their comings and goings. Today, the European average has fallen to a fourth. That's still high compared to the United States where public transport, virtually exterminated in most cities, accounts for only five per cent of all transportation.

Henry Ford and Harvey Firestone were very good friends back in the twenties, and they both got on well with the Rockefellers. Their mutual affection reinforced a mutuality of interests that went a long way toward dismantling the railroads and creating a vast network of roads, then highways, throughout the United States. With the passing of the years, the power of the car, tire and oil magnates have grown more and more ruinous in the U.S. and beyond. Of the sixty largest companies in the world, half either belong to this holy alliance or work for it.

The high heavens of this *fin-de-siècle*: the United States has the greatest concentration of cars and the greatest quantity of weapons. Six, six, six: of every six dollars spent by the average American, one is for the car; of every six hours of life, one is spent traveling in the

55

Paradise

If we behave ourselves, it will come to pass. We will all see the same images and hear the same sounds and wear the same clothes and eat the same hamburgers and enjoy the same solitude in our houses all alike in neighborhoods all alike in cities all alike where we will all breathe the same garbage and serve our cars with the same devotion and carry out the orders of the same machines in a world that will be marvelous for all who have no legs or wings or roots.

---

car or working to pay for it; and of every six jobs, one is directly or indirectly related to the car, and another to violence and its industries. With each murder by cars and guns, of people and of nature, the gross national product grows.

Talismans against loneliness or invitations to crime? Car sales parallel the sale of weapons, and the former could well be considered part of the latter: cars are the principal killers of young people, with guns a close second. Every year cars kill and wound more Americans than all the Americans killed and wounded throughout the long war in Vietnam, and in many states a driver's license is all you need to buy a machine gun and riddle the entire neighborhood with bullets. Besides such daily needs, a driver's license is also required to pay by check or to cash a check, to sign for documents or notarize a contract. A driver's license is the most common ID: cars give people their identity.

North Americans enjoy some of the cheapest gasoline in the world thanks to sheiks in dark glasses, kings of the light opera and other allies of democracy whose business it is to sell oil at a bargain, violate human rights and buy American weapons. According to the calculations of the Worldwatch Institute, if ecological damages and other "hidden costs" were taken into account, the price of gasoline would at least double. In the United States gasoline is three times as cheap as in Italy, the second most motorized country in the world, and each American burns on average four times as much gas as the average Italian, which is to say a lot.

American society, afflicted with autoitis, generates a quarter of the gases that most poison the atmosphere. Although cars and their unquenchable thirst for gasoline are mostly to blame, it is politicians who give cars impunity in exchange for money and votes. Every time some fool suggests raising gas taxes, the Detroit Big Three (General Motors, Ford and Chrysler) scream to the high heavens and with broad popular support mount million-dollar campaigns decrying this vile threat to public freedom. And when a wayward politician feels wracked by doubts, the companies prescribe an infallible remedy: as *Newsweek* once put it, "The relationship between money and politics is so organic that seeking reform is tantamount to asking a doctor to perform open-heart surgery on himself."

Rarely is any politician, Democrat or Republican, willing to commit sacrilege against the national way of life that venerates machines, squanders the planet's natural resources and equates human development with economic growth. Advertising exalts the miracles that way of life performs and which the entire world would like to deserve. In the United States everyone can achieve the dream of owning their own car, and many can trade them in regularly for new ones. If you can't afford the latest model, you can overcome this identity crisis with aerosol sprays that make your autosaurous purchased three or four years ago smell like new.

Like death, old age is a sign of failure. The car is the one eternally youthful body you can buy. It eats gasoline and oil in its own restaurants, has its own pharmacies with its own medicine and its own

---

Flight

In the sewers, under the asphalt, the abandoned children of the Argentine city of Córdoba make their home. Once in a while they surface to grab pocketbooks and wallets. If the police don't catch them and beat them to a pulp, they use their booty to buy pizza and beer to share. And they buy tubes of glue to inhale.

Journalist Marta Platía asked them what they felt like when they got high.

One of the kids said he whirled his finger and created wind: he pointed at a tree and the tree bent back and forth in the wind he sent forth.

Another recounted that the world filled with stars and he flew through the sky all around him, there was sky above and sky below and sky in the four corners of the earth.

And another said that he was sitting beside the most expensive and aerodynamic motorcycle in the city. Just by looking at it, it was his. Looking at it more, he was riding it full speed while it grew and changed colors.

Rights and Duties

Although the majority of Latin Americans do not have the right to buy a car, all have the duty to pay for that right of the few. For every thousand Haitians, barely five are motorized, but Haiti spends a third of its foreign exchange to import vehicles, spare parts and gasoline. As does El Salvador, where public transport is so disastrous and dangerous that people call buses "caskets on wheels." According to Ricardo Navarro, a specialist in these matters, the money that Colombia spends *every year* to subsidize the price of gasoline would pay for handing out two-and-a-half million bicycles to the people.

hospitals for diagnosis and treatment. It even has its own bedrooms and cemeteries.

Cars promise people freedom—highways aren't called "freeways" for nothing—yet they act like traveling cages. Despite technological progress, the human workday continues to lengthen year after year and so does the time required to get to work and back in traffic that moves at a crawl and shreds your nerves. You live in your car and it won't let you go. "Drive-by shooting": without leaving your speeding car you can pull the trigger and shoot blind, as sometimes happens in the Los Angeles night. "Drive-thru teller," "drive-in restaurant": without getting out of your car you can get money from the bank and eat hamburgers for supper. And without leaving your car you can also get married, "drive-in marriage": in Reno, Nevada, the car rolls under arches of plastic flowers, a witness appears at one window, the pastor at the other and, Bible in hand, he declares you man and wife. On the way out a woman dressed in wings and a halo gives you your marriage certificate and receives your "love donation."

The automobile, buyable body, moves while the human body sits still and fattens. The mechanical body has more rights than that of flesh and bone. As we all know, the United States has launched a holy war against the devil tobacco. I saw a cigarette ad in a magazine covered by the required public health warning: "Tobacco smoke contains carbon monoxide." But the same magazine had several car ads and not one of them warned that car exhaust, nearly always invisible, contains much more carbon monoxide. People can't smoke. Cars can.

Cars are like gods. Born to serve people as talismans against fear and solitude, they end up making people serve them. The church of the sacred car with its US-based Vatican has the entire world on its knees. The spread of this gospel has proven catastrophic, each version deliriously multiplying the defects of the original.

A tiny proportion of the world's cars circulate on Latin America's streets, but Latin America boasts some of the most polluted cities on the globe. The structures of hereditary injustice laced with fierce social contradictions have given rise to cities that are outsized monsters beyond any possible control. The imported faith in the four-wheeled god and the confusion of democracy with consumption have been more devastating than any bombardment.

Never have so many suffered so much for so few. Disastrous public transport and the absence of bicycle lanes make the use of private cars practically obligatory, but how many people can enjoy the luxury? Latin Americans who don't own a car and can never hope to buy one live engulfed by traffic and suffocated by smog. Sidewalks shrink or disappear altogether, distances increase, more and more cars cross paths while fewer and fewer people meet. Buses are not only scarce. In the majority of our cities public transport relies on a few rust-heaps that spew out deadly plumes of exhaust, adding to pollution instead of alleviating it.

In the name of freedom—free enterprise, freeways and the freedom to buy—the world's air is becoming unbreathable. Cars aren't the

only guilty party in this daily act of murder, but they are the worst culprits. In cities the world over, they produce most of the noxious cocktail that destroys our lungs and eyes and everything else. They cause most of the noise and tension that makes our ears hurt and our hair stand on end. In the north of the world, cars are generally obliged to use fuels and technologies that at least limit the poison they give off—a big improvement if only cars didn't reproduce like flies. But in the south, it's much worse. Only in rare cases are unleaded gas and catalytic converters required, and even then the law is respected but not obeyed, as tradition dating from colonial times would have it. Ferocious volleys of lead penetrate the blood with utter impunity, and attack the lungs, liver, bones and soul.

The inhabitants of Latin America's largest cities spend their days praying for rain to cleanse the air, or wind to carry the poison elsewhere. Mexico City, the largest in the world, lives in a state of perpetual environmental emergency. Five centuries ago, an Aztec song asked:

Who could lay siege to Tenochtitlan?
Who could move the foundations of the heavens?

Today the city once called Tenochtitlan is under siege by pollution. Babies are born with lead in their blood and one person in three suffers frequent headaches. The government's guidelines for dealing with the motorized plague read like a defense against an invasion from Mars. In 1995 the Metropolitan Commission for the Prevention and Control of Environmental Pollution advised residents of Mexico's capital that on so-called "days of environmental contingency," they should

go out of doors as little as possible,
keep doors, windows and vents closed,
do not exercise between ten a.m. and four p.m.

On those days, which occur ever more frequently, more than half a million people require some sort of medical attention, because of breathing what was known not so long ago as "the most transparent of air." At the end of 1996 fifteen poor peasants from the state of Guerrero marched in Mexico City to protest injustices; all of them ended up in the public hospital.

It's a Joke

On a large avenue in a large Latin American city, a man is waiting to cross. He stands at the curb, by the incessant flow of cars. The pedestrian waits ten minutes, twenty minutes, an hour. Then he turns his head and spies a man leaning against a wall, smoking. And he asks, "Tell me, how do I cross to the other side?"

"I don't know," the man responds. "I was born over here."

Far from there, on another day in 1996, it rained oceans on the city of São Paulo, creating the largest traffic jam in the country's history. Mayor Paulo Maluf celebrated:

"Traffic jams are a sign of progress."

A thousand new cars join the streets of São Paulo every day. The city breathes on Sunday and chokes the rest of the week. Only on Sunday can you see the city from the outskirts. The mayor of Rio de Janeiro, Luiz Paulo Conde, also likes traffic jams. Thanks to that blessing of urban civilization, he once said, motorists can talk on their cell phones, watch their portable TVs, and enjoy music from cassettes or compact discs.

"In the future," the mayor announced, "a city without traffic jams will be considered boring."

His prediction coincided with an ecological catastrophe in Santiago de Chile. Schools were closed and crowds of children packed the emergency rooms. In Santiago, environmentalists say, each child breathes the equivalent of seven cigarettes a day and one child out of four suffers some form of bronchitis. The city is separated from the heavens by an umbrella of pollution that has doubled in density over the past fifteen years, a period when the number of cars also doubled.

The airs of the city called Buenos Aires grow more poisonous year by year, keeping pace with the number of vehicles which increases by half a million every twelve months. In 1996 sixteen neighborhoods already suffered "very dangerous" noise levels, a perpetual racket that the World Health Organization says "can produce irreversible damage to human health." Charlie Chaplin liked to say that silence is the gold of the poor. Years have passed and silence is more and more the privilege of the few who can afford it.

Consumer society imposes its own symbolism of power and its own mythology of social progress. Advertising sends out invitations to join the ruling class; all it takes is a magic little ignition key: "Get

---

It's no Joke

1996, Managua, Las Colinas neighborhood, a night for celebrating. Cardinal Obando, the U.S. ambassador, several government ministers and the cream of local society attend the inauguration. They raise their glasses to toast Nicaragua's prosperity. Music and speeches resound.

"This is how you create jobs," declares the ambassador. "This is how you build progress."

"It's just like being in Miami," gushes Cardinal Obando. Smiling for the TV cameras, his eminence cuts the red ribbon on the new Texaco station. The company announces that it will build more service stations in the near future.

---

it your way!" orders the voice that gives the orders in the market. "You are in charge!" "Strut your stuff!" And if you put a tiger in your tank, according to the billboards I recall from my childhood, you'll be quicker and more powerful than anyone else, crushing anyone who gets in your way on the road to success. Language creates the illusory reality that advertising depends on. But real reality isn't at all like the spells of commercial witchcraft.

For every two children born into the world a car is born, and the car birthrate is gaining on that of babies. Every child wants to own a car, two cars, a thousand cars. How many adults will be able to realize their childhood fantasies? The numbers show cars to be a privilege, not a right. Twenty per cent of humanity owns eighty per cent of the cars, even though one hundred per cent of humanity has to breathe the poisoned air. Like so many other symbols of consumer society, cars belong to a minority whose habits are parlayed into universal truths, obliging the rest of us to see cars as the only possible prolongation of the human body.

The number of cars in Latin America's Babylons keeps swelling but it's nothing compared to the centers of world prosperity. In 1995 the United States and Canada had more motor vehicles than the rest of the world put together save Europe. Germany that year had as many cars, trucks, pick-ups, mobile homes and motorcycles as all of Latin America and Africa. Yet it's in the cities of the south where three out of every four deaths by car occur. And of the three who die, two are pedestrians. Brazil has a third as many cars as Germany, but three times as many victims. Every year Colombia suffers six thousand homicides, politely called "traffic accidents."

Advertisements like to promote new cars as if they were weapons. At least that's one way they're not lying. Accelerating is like firing a gun, it offers the same pleasure and the same power. Every year cars kill as many people as were killed at Hiroshima and Nagasaki. In 1990 they caused many more deaths or disabilities than wars or AIDS. According to World Health Organization projections, in the year 2020 cars will be the third cause of death or disability. Wars will be eighth, AIDS tenth.

Hunting down pedestrians is part of daily routine in big Latin American cities where four-wheeled corsairs encourage the traditional arrogance of those who rule and those who act as if they did. A driver's license is equivalent to a gun permit, and it gives you license to kill. Ever more demons are ready to run down anyone who crosses their path. On top of the untouchable thuggery we've always faced, hysteria about robberies and kidnappings has made it more and more dangerous, and less and less common, to stop at red lights. In some cities stoplights mean speed up. Privileged minorities, condemned to perpetual fear, step on the accelerator to flee reality, and reality is something very dangerous lurking on the other side of car windows rolled up tight.

In 1992 a plebiscite was held in Amsterdam. People voted to reduce by half the already restricted area where cars can circulate in that kingdom of cyclists and pedestrians. Three years later Florence rebelled against auto-cracy, the dictatorship of cars, and banned private vehicles from the downtown core. The mayor announced that the prohibition would be extended gradually to the entire city as streetcar, subway and bus lines and pedestrian walkways expanded. And bike paths, too: according to plans it will be possible to pedal anywhere in the city safely, on a means of transportation that is cheap and runs on nothing and was invented five centuries ago by a Florentine, Leonardo da Vinci.

Modernization, motorization: the roar of traffic drowns out the chorus of voices denouncing civilization's sleight of hand that steals our freedom then sells it back to us, and that cuts off our legs to make us buy cars and exercise machines. Imposed on the world as the only possible way of life is a nightmare of cities governed by cars. Latin America's cities dream of becoming like Los Angeles with its eight million cars ordering people about. Trained for five centuries to copy instead of create, we aspire to become a grotesque version of that nausea. If we must suffer copyitis, couldn't we at least choose what to copy a little more carefully?

Sources Consulted

American Automobile Manufacturers Association. *World Motor Vehicle Data* (Detroit, 1995).

Barrett, Richard and Ismail Serageldin. "Environmentally Sustainable Urban Transport: Defining a Global Policy" (Washington: World Bank, 1993).

Business Week. "The Global 1,000" (July 13, 1992).

Cevallos, Diego. "El reino del auto," *Tierramérica* (Mexico, June 1996).

Faiz, Asif and others. "Automotive Air Pollution: Issues and Options for Developing Countries" (Washington: World Bank, 1990).

Fortune. "Global 500: The World's Largest Corporations" (August 7, 1995 and April 29, 1996).

Greenpeace International. *El impacto del automóvil sobre el medio ambiente* (Santiago de Chile, 1992).

Guinsberg, Enrique. "El auto nuestro de cada día," *Transición* (Mexico, February 1996).

International Road Federation. *World Road Statistics* (Geneva, 1994).

Marshall, Stuart. "Gunship or Racing Car?" *Financial Times* (November 10, 1990).

Navarro, Ricardo with Urs Heirli and Victor Beck. *La bicicleta y los triciclos* (Santiago de Chile: SKAT/CETAL, 1985).

World Health Organization. "World Health Report" (Geneva, 1996).

World Health Organization and United Nations Environment Program. *Urban Air Pollution in Megacities of the World* (Cambridge: Blackwell, 1992).

Ibid. "City Air Quality Trends" (Nairobi, 1995).

Wolf, Winfried. *Car Mania: A Critical History of Transport* (London: Pluto, 1996).

Earthshine
Arthur Sze

1.

"Fuck you, *fuck you*," he repeated as he drove down the dirt road
    while tamarisk branches scraped the side of the pickup;

what scrapes in the mind as it dilates to darkness?

"Jodido," he winced and turned up the whites of his eyes;

"What comes from darkness, I strike with darkness";

who hears a night-blooming cereus
unfold a white blossom by the windowsill?

crackle of flames in the fireplace;

lapping of waves against rocks
as a manta ray flips and feeds on plankton;

the gasp when he glanced down at the obituaries;

the gasp when she unwrapped flecked rice paper
to find a letterpress broadside;

spurt of match into gold as he lights white beeswax candles;

she is running her hair between his toes;
he is rubbing her nipples with his palms;

"What comes from brightness, I strike with brightness";

his ankles creaked as he tiptoed to the bathroom;

waking to a cat chewing on a mouse in the dark.

2.

Walking up a trail in the Manoa Valley arboretum,
he motions with his hand to stop as he tries
to distinguish whether a red-whiskered or
red-vented bulbul has just landed on a branch.
I spot a macadamia nut on the ground, look
up into an adjacent tree and am shocked to see
two enormous jackfruit suspended from the trunk.
Revelation never comes as a fern uncoiling
a frond in mist; it comes when I trip on a root,
slap a mosquito on my arm. We go on, but stop again
when gnats lift into a cloud as we stumble into
a bunch of rose apples rotting on the ground.
Although we go on to a dead end where water
runs down a sheer rock, the mind stops here:
here *Amanita muscarias* release a cloud of spores
into cool August air; here lovers make
earthshine on a waxing crescent moon; here
the phone rings and I learn of a suicide,
a pinhole grows into an eclipse; here I hear
water drip as I walk into a sloping black lava tube.

3.

Say teeth;
say gnawed his teeth in his sleep;
say each spring he scraped peeling blue paint off the windowsill;
say the ocean flickers;
say a squiggly chalk line screeching down a blackboard opens
    a black rift;
say on a float house yellow cedar smoke rises in the woodstove;
say burn;
say crumpled white papers ripple then burst into yellow twists
    of flame;
say parallel lines touch in the infinite;
say peel;
say stoplight screech go green laugh;
say screech, rip, slam, thud, body scrapes, bleeds to bone;
say hyena;
say bobcat stripped of skin;
say a black cricket chirps in a corner of the room;
say hang;
say ox shoulder hangs off hook;
say trimming roses, she slashed her left wrist;
say shit-smear hair-sway leaf-gold ooze;
say crack;
say breaking a wineglass in a white napkin recovers a sliver of
    original light;
say egg-white eyeball splash;
say rinse;
say bend to earth, find a single stalk budding gold.

4.

He hanged himself with his belt in the bosque
is no longer a whip that reddens and flays the skin.
"Donkey piss," he once cracked—but who
knows how the light sizzled and burned a hole
that gnawed and gnawed so that the more he
twisted the more he convulsed into a black pitch?
Orange daylilies are blooming along the driveway;
long-stalked delphinium are bending to earth.
A firework explodes in white gold then bursts
into a green shimmer. He leaves teeth marks
on her neck; she groans and shows the whites
of her eyes. When a car rushes by on a wet road,
he hears a laborer throw sand against a tilted screen
and realizes twenty-three years ago he threw
sand against a tilted screen. Now, when he
strokes the tendons of her left wrist, she sighs.
They are now nowhere everywhere none such;
they are not *look back time* but full moon first light.

5.

She said he said "moon" in his sleep;

when he looked through the pot-bellied telescope,
the light of the full moon made him wince;

he had to look into darkness
and then saw from *Mare Cognitum* to *Mare Serenitatis*;

the mind aches to see at such distance such definition;

when she heard the barking dog,
she shined a flashlight and spotted a porcupine on the roof;

as you would spotlight a deer;

a snake slides under the redwood boardwalk by the kitchen;

he kisses her shoulders,
rubs the soles of her feet;

the mind aligns such slivers;

say dragonfly, quartz, cattail, tuning fork, wave;
say earthstar bursting into alpine air;
say c^2;

say even the sacred barley drink separates if it is not stirred,
and see how, stirred, one can find repose.

6.

Sipping mint tea in the ebbing heat of the day,
I recollect how we stumbled onto a raccoon
squashed between boards leaning against a fence,
saw tadpoles wriggling at the edge of a pond.
On the living room table, thirty-six peonies
in a vase dry and become crepe-paper light
to touch. Yesterday you watered blue chamisa
along the county road, while I watered desert grass
under the willow. I recollect I opened a brown,
humid box and, stunned, lifting a handful
of morels, inhaled the black aroma of earth.
What is it we give each other—gold, shark's fin—
other than a renewed sense of the miraculous?
Nanao saw a blip on the radar screen; later,
when he saw the flash, he thought Mt. Fuji
had erupted in a burst of light. Sipping mint tea
on the longest day of the year, I sense how
the balance of a life sways, and a petal may tip it.

7.

A steady evening with a first–quarter moon;
numerous craters along the terminator are razor sharp;

I see the ghostly bluish glow of earthshine
and feel how the moon has no permanent dark side.

A horse neighs by the barbed wire fence;
we trudge into a wet field, carrying, from under the portal,

a bee's nest in a basket, place it in a nook
of a silver poplar. Will any bees hatch in spring?

I notice thorns on the bare branches of Russian olives;
you spot coyote scat before the v-shaped gate.

We walk to where the Pojoaque and Nambe flow together—
I am amazed at how we blossom into each other.

I hear the occasional drone of cars on highway 285,
hear how the living expire into smoke

and the dead inflame the minds of the living.
When I exhale against a cold window, I see

the ever–shifting line along the terminator;
and, as the shadow cast by the rim of Theophilus

slips across the crater's floor, I feel light
surge into a honeycomb gold—it all goes and comes at once.

Where Europe Begins
Yoko Tawada

—Translated from German by Susan Bernofsky

I.

FOR MY GRANDMOTHER, to travel was to drink foreign water. Different places, different water. There was no need to be afraid of foreign landscapes, but foreign water could be dangerous. In her village lived a girl whose mother was suffering from an incurable illness. Day by day her strength waned, and her brothers were secretly planning her funeral. One day as the girl sat alone in the garden beneath the tree, a white serpent appeared and said to her: "Take your mother to see the Fire Bird. When she has touched its flaming feathers, she will be well again." "Where does the Fire Bird live?" asked the girl. "Just keep going west. Behind three tall mountains lies a bright shining city, and at its center, atop a high tower, sits the Fire Bird." "How can we ever reach this city if it is so far off? They say the mountains are inhabited by monsters." The serpent replied: "You needn't be afraid of them. When you see them, just remember that you, too, like all other human beings, were once a monster in one of your previous lives. Neither hate them nor do battle with them, just continue on your way. There is only one thing you must remember: when you are in the city where the Fire Bird lives, you must not drink a single drop of water." The girl thanked him, went to her mother and told her everything she had learned. The next day the two of them set off. On every mountain they met a monster that spewed green, yellow and blue fire and tried to burn them up; but as soon as the girl reminded herself that she, too, had once been just like them, the monsters sank into the ground. For ninety-nine days they wandered through the forest, and finally they reached the city, which shone brightly with a strange light. In the burning heat, they saw a tower in the middle of this city, and atop it sat the Fire Bird. In her joy, the girl forgot the serpent's warning and drank water from the pond. Instantly the girl was ninety-nine years old and her mother vanished in the flaming air.

When I was a little girl, I never believed there was such a thing as foreign water, for I had always thought of the globe as a sphere of

73

water with all sorts of small and large islands swimming on it. Water had to be the same everywhere. Sometimes in sleep I heard the murmur of the water that flowed beneath the main island of Japan. The border surrounding the island was also made of water that ceaselessly beat against the shore in waves. How can one say where the place of foreign water begins when the border itself is water?

II.

The crews of three Russian ships stood in uniform on the upper deck playing a farewell march whose unfamiliar solemnity all at once stirred up the oddest feelings in me. I, too, stood on the upper deck, like a theatergoer who had mistakenly stepped onstage, for my eyes were still watching me from among the crowd on the dock, while I myself stood blind and helpless on the ship. Other passengers threw long paper snakes in various colors toward the dock. The red streamers turned midair into umbilical cords—one last link between the passengers and their loved ones. The green streamers became serpents and proclaimed their warning, which would probably only be forgotten on the way anyhow. I tossed one of the white streamers into the air. It became my memory. The crowd slowly withdrew, the music faded, and the sky grew larger behind the mainland. The moment my paper snake disintegrated, my memory ceased to function. This is why I no longer remember anything of this journey. The fifty hours aboard the ship to the harbor town in Eastern Siberia, followed by the hundred and sixty hours it took to reach Europe on the Trans-Siberian Railroad, have become a blank space in my life which can be replaced only by a written account of my journey.

III.

Diary excerpt:

The ship followed the coastline northward. Soon it was dark, but many passengers still sat on the upper deck. In the distance one could see the lights of smaller ships. "The fishermen are fishing for squid," a voice said behind me. "I don't like squid. When I was little, we had squid for supper every third night. What about you?" another voice asked. "Yes," a third one responded, "I ate them all the time, too. I always imagined they were descended from monsters." "Where did you grow up?" the first voice asked.

Voices murmured all around me, tendrils gradually entwining. On board such a ship, everyone begins putting together a brief autobiography, as though he might otherwise forget who he is.

"Where are you going?" the person sitting next to me asked. "I'm on my way to Moscow." He stared at me in surprise. "My parents spoke of this city so often I want to see it with my own eyes." Had my parents really talked about Moscow? On board such a ship, everyone begins to lie. The man was looking so horrified I had to say something else right away. "Actually I'm not so interested in Moscow itself, but I want to have experienced Siberia." "What do you want to experience in Siberia?" he asked, "What is there in Siberia?" "I don't know yet. Maybe nothing to speak of. But the important thing for me is traveling *through* Siberia." The longer I spoke, the more unsure of myself I became. He went to sit beside another passenger, leaving me alone with the transparent word *through*.

IV.

A few months before I set off on my journey, I was working evenings after school in a food processing factory. A poster advertising a trip to Europe on the Trans-Siberian Railroad transformed the immeasurably long distance to Europe into a finite sum of money.

In the factory, the air was kept at a very low temperature so the meat wouldn't go bad. I stood in this cold, which I referred to as "Siberian frost," wrapping frozen poultry in plastic. Beside the table stood a bucket of hot water in which I could warm my hands at intervals.

Once three frozen chickens appeared in my dreams: I watched my mother place them in the frying pan. When the pan was hot, they suddenly came to life and flew out the kitchen window. "No wonder we never have enough to eat," I said with such viciousness even I was shocked. "What am I supposed to do?" my mother asked, weeping.

Besides earning money, there were two other things I wanted to do before my departure: learn Russian and write an account of the journey. I always wrote a travel narrative before I set off on a trip, so that during the journey I'd have something to quote from. I was often speechless when I traveled. This time it was particularly useful that I'd written my report beforehand. Otherwise, I wouldn't have known what to say about Siberia. Of course, I might have quoted from my diary, but I have to admit that I made up the diary afterward, having neglected to keep one during the journey.

V.

Excerpt from my first travel narrative:

Our ship left the Pacific and entered the Sea of Japan, which separates Japan from Eurasia. Since the remains of Siberian mammoths were discovered in Japan, there have been claims that a land bridge once linked Japan and Siberia. Presumably, human beings also crossed from Siberia to Japan. In other words, Japan was once part of Siberia.

In the World Atlas in the ship's library I looked up Japan, this child of Siberia that had turned its back on its mother and now swam alone in the Pacific. Its body resembled that of a seahorse, which in Japanese is called "Tatsu-no-otoshigo"—the lost child of the dragon.

Next to the library was the dining room, which was always empty during the day. The ship rolled on the stormy seas, and the passengers stayed in bed. I stood alone in the dining room, watching plates on the table slide back and forth without being touched. All at once I realized I had been expecting this stormy day for years, since I was a child.

VI.

Something I told a woman three years after the journey:

At school we often had to write essays, and sometimes these included "dream descriptions." Once I wrote about the dream in which my father had red skin.

My father comes from a family of merchants in Osaka. After World War II, he came to Tokyo with all he owned: a bundle containing, among other things, an alarm clock. This clock, which he called the "Rooster of the Revolution," soon stopped running, but as a result, it showed the correct time twice each day, an hour that had to be returned to twice a day anyhow. "Time runs on its own, you don't need an alarm clock for that," he always said in defense of his broken clock, "and when the time comes, the city will be so filled with voices of the oppressed that no one will be able to hear a clock ring any longer."

His reasons for leaving the land of his birth he always explained to his relatives in a hostile tone: "Because he was infected with the Red Plague." These words always made me think of red, inflamed skin.

A huge square, crowds of people strolling about. Some of them had white hair, others green or gold, but all of them had red skin. When I looked closer, I saw that their skin was not inflamed but rather inscribed with red script. I was unable to read the text. No, it wasn't a text at all but consisted of many calendars written on top of each other. I saw numberless stars in the sky. At the tip of the tower, the Fire Bird sat observing the motion in the square.

This must have been "Moscow," I wrote in my essay, which my teacher praised without noticing I had invented the dream. But then what dream is not invented?

Later I learned that for a number of leftists in Western Europe this city had a different name: Peking.

VII.

Diary excerpt:

The ship arrived in the harbor of the small Eastern Siberian town Nachodka. The earth seemed to sway beneath my feet. No sooner had I felt the sensation of having put a border, the sea, behind me than I glimpsed the beginning of the train tracks that stretched for ten thousand kilometers.

That night I boarded the train. I sat down in a four-bed compartment where I was soon joined by two Russians. The woman, Masha, offered me pickled mushrooms and told me she was on her way to visit her mother in Moscow. "Ever since I got married and moved to Nachodka, my mother has been *behind* Siberia," she said. Siberia, then, is the border between here and there, I thought, such a wide border!

I lay down on the bed on my belly and gazed out the window. Above the outlines of thousands of birches I saw numberless stars that seemed about to tumble down. I took out my pocket notebook and wrote:

When I was a baby, I slept in a Mexican hammock. My parents had bought the hammock not because they found it romantic, but because the apartment was so cramped that there was no room for me except in the air. The only thing in the room was seven thousand books whose stacks lined the three walls all the way to the ceiling. At night they turned into trees thick with foliage. When a large truck drove past the house, my Mexican hammock swung in the forest. But during the minor earthquakes that frequently shook the house, it remained perfectly still, as though there were an invisible thread connecting it to the subterranean water.

VIII.

Diary excerpt:

When the first sun rose over Siberia, I saw an infinitely long row of birches. After breakfast I tried to describe the landscape, but couldn't. The window with its tiny curtains was like the screen in a movie theater. I sat in the front row, and the picture on the screen was too close and too large. The segment of landscape was repeated, constantly changing, and refused me entry. I picked up a collection of Siberian fairy tales and began to read.

In the afternoon I had tea and gazed out the window again. Birches, nothing but birches. Over my second cup of tea I chatted with Masha, but not about the Siberian landscape, we talked about Moscow and Tokyo. Then Masha went to another compartment, and I remained alone at the window. I was bored and began to get sleepy. Soon I began to enjoy my boredom. The birches vanished before my eyes, leaving only the again-and-again of their passage, as in an imageless dream.

IX.

Excerpt from my first travel narrative:

Siberia, "the sleeping land" (from the Tartar: sib = sleep, ir = Earth), but it wasn't asleep. So it really wasn't at all necessary for the prince to come kiss the Earth awake. (He came from a European fairy tale.) Or did he come to find treasure?

When the Creator of the Universe was distributing treasures on Earth and flew over Siberia, he trembled so violently with cold that his hands grew stiff and the precious stones and metals he held in them fell to the ground. To hide these treasures from Man, he covered Siberia with eternal frost.

It was August, and there was no trace of the cold that had stiffened the Creator's hands. The Siberian tribes mentioned in my book were also nowhere to be seen, for the Trans-Siberian Railroad traverses only those regions populated by Russians—tracing out a path of conquered territory, a narrow extension of Europe.

X.

Something I told a woman three years after the journey:

For me, Moscow was always the city where you never arrive. When I was three years old, the Moscow Artists' Theater performed in Tokyo for the first time. My parents spent half a month's salary on tickets for Chekhov's *Three Sisters*.

When Irina, one of the three sisters, spoke the famous words "To Moscow, to Moscow, to Moscow," her voice pierced my parents' ears so deeply that these very same words began to leap out of their own mouths as well. The three sisters never got to Moscow, either. The city must have been hidden somewhere backstage. So it wasn't Siberia, but rather the theater stage that lay between my parents and the city of their dreams.

In any case, my parents, who were often unemployed during this period, occasionally quoted these words. When my father, for example, spoke of his unrealistic plan of founding his own publishing house, my mother would say, laughing: "To Moscow, to Moscow, to Moscow. . . ." My father would say the same thing whenever my mother spoke of her childhood in such a way as though she might be able to become a child again. Naturally, I didn't understand what they meant. I only sensed that the word had something to do with impossibility. Since the word "Moscow" was always repeated three times, I didn't even know it was a city and not a magic word.

XI.

Diary excerpt:

I flipped through a brochure the conductor had given me. The photographs showed modern hospitals and schools in Siberia. The train stopped at the big station at Ulan-Ude. For the first time, there were many faces in the train that were not Russian.

I laid the brochure aside and picked up my book.

A Tungusian fairy tale:

Once upon a time there was a shaman who awakened all the dead and wouldn't let even a single person die. This made him stronger than God. So God suggested a contest: by magic words alone, the shaman was to transform two pieces of chicken meat given him by God into live chickens. If the shaman failed, he wouldn't be stronger than God any longer. The first piece of meat was transformed into a chicken by the magic words and flew away, but not the second one. Ever since, human beings have died. Mostly in hospitals.

Why was the shaman unable to change the second piece of meat into a chicken? Was the second piece somehow different from the first, or did the number two rob the shaman of his power? For some reason, the number two always makes me uneasy.

I also made the acquaintance of a shaman, but not in Siberia; it was much later, in a museum of anthropology in Europe. He stood in a glass case, and his voice came from a tape recorder that was already rather old. For this reason his voice always quavered prodigiously and was louder than a voice from a human body. The microphone is an imitation of the flame that enhances the voice's magical powers.

Usually, the shamans were able to move freely between the three zones of the world. That is, they could visit both the heavens and the world of the dead just by climbing up and down the World-Tree. My shaman, though, stood not in one of these three zones, but in a fourth one: the museum. The number four deprived him permanently of his power: his face was frozen in an expression of fear, his mouth, half-open, was dry, and in his painted eyes burned no fire.

XII.

Excerpt from my first travel narrative:

In the restaurant car I ate a fish called *omul'*. Lake Baikal is also home to several other species that actually belong in a saltwater habitat, said a Russian teacher sitting across from me—the Baikal used to be a sea.

But how could there possibly be a sea here, in the middle of the continent? Or is the Baikal a hole in the continent that goes all the way through? That would mean my childish notion about the globe being a sphere of water was right after all. The water of the Baikal, then, would be the surface of the water-sphere. A fish could reach the far side of the sphere by swimming through the water.

And so the *omul'* I had eaten swam around inside my body that night, as though it wanted to find a place where its journey could finally come to an end.

XIII.

There were once two brothers whose mother, a Russian painter, had emigrated to Tokyo during the Revolution and lived there ever since. On her eightieth birthday she expressed the wish to see her native city, Moscow, once more before she died. Her sons arranged for her visa and accompanied her on her journey on the Trans-Siberian Railroad. But when the third sun rose over Siberia, their mother was no longer on the train. The brothers searched for her from first car to last, but they couldn't find her. The conductor told them the story of an old man who, three years earlier, had opened the door of the car, mistaking it for the door to the toilet, and had fallen from the train. The brothers were granted a special visa and traveled the same stretch in the opposite direction on the local train. At each station they got out and asked whether anyone had seen their mother. A month passed without their finding the slightest trace.

I can remember the story up to this point, afterward I must have fallen asleep. My mother often read me stories that filled the space between waking and sleep so completely that, in comparison, the time when I was awake lost much of its color and force. Many years later I found, quite by chance, the continuation of this story in a library.

The old painter lost her memory when she fell from the train. She could remember neither her origins nor her plans. So she remained living in a small village in Siberia that seemed strangely familiar to her. Only at night, when she heard the train coming, did she feel uneasy, and sometimes she even ran along through the dark woods to the tracks, as though someone had called to her.

XIV.

As a child, my mother was often ill, just like her own mother, who had spent half her life in bed. My mother grew up in a Buddhist temple in which one could hear, as early as five o'clock in the morning, the prayer that her father, the head priest of the temple, was chanting with his disciples.

One day, as she sat alone under a tree reading a novel, a student who had come to visit the temple approached her and asked whether she always read such thick books. My mother immediately replied that what she'd like best was a novel so long she could never finish it, for she had no other occupation but reading.

The student considered a moment, then told her that in the library in Moscow there was a novel so long that no one could read all of it in a lifetime. This novel was not only long, but also as cryptic and cunning as the forests of Siberia, so that people got lost in it and never found their way out again once they'd entered. Since then, Moscow has been the city of her dreams, its center not Red Square, but the library.

This is the sort of thing my mother told me about her childhood. I was still a little girl and believed in neither the infinitely long novel in Moscow nor the student who might have been my father. For my mother was a good liar and told lies often and with pleasure. But when I saw her sitting and reading in the middle of the forest of books, I was afraid she might disappear into a novel. She never rushed through books. The more exciting the story became, the more slowly she read.

81

She never actually wanted to arrive at any destination at all, not even "Moscow." She would greatly have preferred for "Siberia" to be infinitely large. With my father things were somewhat different. Although he never got to Moscow, either, he did inherit money and founded his own publishing house, which bore the name of this dream city.

XV.

A diary excerpt:

There were always a few men standing in the corridor smoking strong-smelling cigarettes whose brand name was "Stolica" (capital city).

"How much longer is it to Moscow?" I asked an old man who was looking out the window with his grandchild.

"Three more days," he responded and smiled with eyes that lay buried in deep folds.

So in three days I would really have crossed Siberia and would arrive at the point where Europe begins? Suddenly I noticed how afraid I was of arriving in Moscow.

"Are you from Vietnam?" he asked.

"No, I'm from Tokyo."

His grandchild gazed at me and asked him in a low voice: "Where is Tokyo?" The old man stroked the child's head and said softly but clearly: "In the East." The child was silent and for a moment stared into the air as though a city were visible there. A city that it would probably never visit.

Hadn't I also asked questions like that when I was a child? — Where is Peking? —In the West. —And what is in the East, on the other side of the sea? —America.—

The world sphere I had envisioned was definitely not round, but rather like a night sky, with all the foreign places sparkling like fireworks.

XVI.

During the night I woke up. Rain knocked softly on the window-pane. The train went slower and slower. I looked out the window and tried to recognize something in the darkness. . . . The train stopped, but I couldn't see a station. The outlines of the birches became clearer and clearer, their skins brighter, and suddenly there was a shadow moving between them. A bear? I remember that many Siberian tribes bury the bones of bears so that these animals can be resurrected. Was this a bear that had just been returned to life?

The shadow approached the train. It was not a bear but a person. The thin figure, face half-concealed beneath wet hair, came closer and closer with outstretched arms. I saw the beams of three flash-lights to the left. For a brief moment the face of the figure was illuminated: it was an old woman. Her eyes were shut, her mouth open, as though she wanted to cry out. When she felt the light on her, she gave a shudder, then vanished in the dark wood.

This was part of the novel I wrote before the journey and read aloud to my mother. In this novel, I hadn't built a secret path leading home for her. For, in contrast to the novel in Moscow, it wasn't very long.

"No wonder this novel is so short," my mother said, "Whenever a woman like that shows up in a novel, it always ends soon, with her death."

"Why should she die. *She* is Siberia."

"Why is Siberia a *she?* You're just like your father, the two of you only have one thing in your heads: going to Moscow."

"Why don't *you* go to Moscow?

"Because then you wouldn't get there. But if I stay here, you can reach your destination."

"Then I won't go, I'll stay here."

"It's too late. You're already on your way."

XVII.

Excerpt from the letter to my parents:

Europe begins not in Moscow but somewhere before. I looked out the window and saw a sign as tall as a man with two arrows painted on it, beneath which the words "Europe" and "Asia" were written. The sign stood in the middle of a field like a solitary customs agent.

"We're in Europe already!" I shouted to Masha, who was drinking tea in our compartment.

"Yes, everything's Europe behind the Ural Mountains," she replied, unmoved, as though this had no importance, and went on drinking her tea.

I went over to a Frenchman, the only foreigner in the car besides me, and told him that Europe didn't just begin in Moscow. He gave a short laugh and said that Moscow was *not* Europe.

XVIII.

Excerpt from my first travel narrative:

The waiter placed my borscht on the table and smiled at Sasha, who was playing with the wooden doll Matroshka next to me. He removed the figure of the round farmwife from its belly. The smaller doll, too, was immediately taken apart, and from its belly came—an expected surprise—an even smaller one. Sasha's father, who had been watching his son all this time with a smile, now looked at me and said: "When you are in Moscow, buy a Matroshka as a souvenir. This is a typically Russian toy."

Many Russians do not know that this "typically Russian" toy was first manufactured in Russia at the end of the nineteenth century, modeled after ancient Japanese dolls. But I don't know what sort of Japanese doll could have been the model for Matroshka. Perhaps a Kokeshi, which my grandmother once told me of: A long time ago, when the people of her village were still suffering from extreme poverty, it sometimes happened that women killed their own children at birth rather than starving together with them. For every dead child, a Kokeshi, meaning *Make-the-child-go-away*, was constructed, so that the people would never forget that they had survived at the expense of these children. To what story might people connect Matroshka some day? Perhaps with the story of the souvenir, when people no longer know what souvenirs are.

"I'll buy a Matroshka in Moscow," I said to Sasha's father. Sasha extracted the fifth doll and attempted to take it, too, apart. "No, Sasha, that's the littlest one," his father cried. "Now you must pack them up again."

The game now continued in reverse. The smallest doll vanished inside the next-smallest one, then this one inside the next, and so on.

In a book about shamans I had once read that our souls can appear in dreams in the form of animals or shadows or even dolls. The Matroshka is probably the soul of the travelers in Russia who, sound asleep in Siberia, dream of the capital.

XIX.

I read a Samoyedic fairy tale:

One upon a time there was a small village in which seven clans lived in seven tents. During the long, hard winter, when the men were off hunting, the women sat with their children in the tents. Among them was a woman who especially loved her child.

One day, she was sitting with her child close beside the fire, warming herself. Suddenly a spark leapt out of the fire and landed on her child's skin. The child began to cry. The woman scolded the fire: I give you wood to eat and you make my child cry! How dare you? I'm going to pour water on you!" She poured water into the fire, and so the fire went out.

It grew cold and dark in the tent, and the child began to cry again. The woman went to the next tent to fetch new fire, but the moment she stepped into the tent, this fire, too, went out. She went on to the next one, but here the same thing happened. All seven fires went out, and the village was dark and cold.

"Do you realize we're almost in Moscow?" Masha asked me. I nodded and went on reading.

When the grandmother of this child heard what had happened, she came to the tent of the woman, squatted down before the fire and gazed deep into it. Inside, on the hearth, sat an ancient old woman, the empress of the fire, with blood on her forehead. "What has happened? What should we do?" the grandmother asked. With a deep, dark voice the empress said that the water had torn open her forehead and that the woman must sacrifice her child so that people will never forget that fire comes from the heart of the child.

"Look out the window! There's Moscow!" cried Masha. "Do you see *her*? That's Moscow, *Moskva!*"

"What have you done?" the grandmother scolded the woman. "Because of you, the whole village is without fire! You must sacrifice your child, otherwise we'll all die of cold!" The mother lamented and wept in despair, but there was nothing she could do.

"Why don't you look out the window? We're finally there!" Masha cried. The train went slower and slower.

When the child was laid on the hearth, the flames shot up from its heart, and the whole village was lit up so brightly it was as if the Fire Bird had descended to Earth. In the flames the villagers saw the empress of the fire, who took the child in her arms and vanished with it into the depths of the light.

XX.

The train arrived in Moscow, and a woman from Intourist walked up to me and said that I had to go home again at once, because my visa was no longer valid. The Frenchman whispered in my ear: "Start screaming that you want to stay here." I screamed so loud that the wall of the station cracked in two. Behind the ruins, I saw a city that looked familiar: it was Tokyo. "Scream louder or you'll never see

Moscow!" the Frenchman said, but I couldn't scream anymore because my throat was burning and my voice was gone. I saw a pond in the middle of the station and discovered that I was unbearably thirsty. When I drank the water from the pond, my gut began to ache and I immediately lay down on the ground. The water I had drunk grew and grew in my belly and soon it had become a huge sphere of water with the names of thousands of cities written on it. Among them I found *her*. But already the sphere was beginning to turn and the names all flowed together, becoming completely illegible. I lost *her*. "Where is she?" I asked, "Where is she?" "But she's right here. Don't you see her?" replied a voice from within my belly. "Come into the water with us!" another voice in my belly cried.

I leapt into the water.

Here stood a high tower, brightly shining with a strange light. Atop this tower sat the Fire Bird, which spat out flaming letters: M, O, S, K, V, A, then these letters were transformed: M became a mother and gave birth to me within my belly. O turned into *omul'* and swam off with S-seahorse. K became a knife and severed my umbilical cord. V had long since become a volcano, at whose peak sat a familiar-looking monster.

But what about A? A became a strange fruit I had never before tasted: an apple. Hadn't my grandmother told me of the serpent's warning never to drink foreign water? But fruit isn't the same as water. Why shouldn't I be allowed to eat foreign fruit? So I bit into the apple and swallowed its juicy flesh. Instantly the mother, the *omul'*, the seahorse, the knife and the volcano with its monster vanished before my eyes. Everything was still and cold. It had never been so cold before in Siberia.

I realized I was standing in the middle of Europe.

Songs at Climate Level
Mark McMorris

BEDTIME IN NEW GUINEA

I.

The wattage of the ordinary is not far off, the coast of New Guinea,
the mark I left so you could find me again
whoever "you" propose to be tonight, on this
drive from country to the town of villanelles.
By and by, the rivers look less like the image
that hides in your name, delicate letters
that I used to roll on my tongue and promised
never to tire of, how they tasted on my way out the door, felt
behind the lids of my being, to bathe there, in day
or night, under the leafy banana or the storm cloud.

II.

The trees blow through the house where a cat sleeps.
In a neighboring field, a boy floats a kite.
I've fetched in the deck-chairs to save them from weather
and nullified the urge to think things through, being
of a mind these days to read only the précis
the lustrous equation dense with meaning and seductive
—I do not need the proofs—just as I'm happy
to sport among the tiger lilies of a virgin princess
never mind how I got here, never you mind.
I won't be leaving her company any time soon.
Inside the garden, if you go by the orthodox route—
the rasp of the mower, the smell of fresh-cut grass,
the wasp nests which complicate the summer—
if you stay there with good will, then one day perhaps,
the rest of it will convene: the rotating sky
divided by jet exhaust from one corner to the face
of sun, and the bleeding tree whose green fruit
is poison, by report and not by any test of your own,

the reptiles, crickets, spiders, fireflies, and moths:
the winds of nostalgia will take you as a friend
and voices stumbled out of the bush, to pay you back.
Such, at any rate, is the theory of time to people
who have too much of it on their hands, to play around with.

III.

Going in the other direction, away from the city of parrots,
we share the auto-route with busloads of older forms
—forms known to the Inca, the "Perusine" of lore,
the Cannibal, Hebrew, and Chaldean, all with their
rhyming verses done up in country hats and gloves.
From the top of the ridge, the fairground looks inviting
but as you come closer things are more mixed:
Yes, the poets will give us a sexy ride, and show off
their muscles as they grip and tumble high over the sawdust
to the sound of "ooh," and "well, now," and "damn,"
and be well paid for these risks, and beloved of the press.
Morning puts another face on these amusements.
Dawn is the postman's time, the hedges brushing the sky
and shedding roses on the burlap of phenomena
to guide the cache of letters to our door, like a tugboat.
The animals of the park have capered to an old-folks home
to prepare a place for themselves, beside the father;
and the letter you craved has fallen like one sparrow
we don't need these humors of regret, to soften
the slither of bills, into day's debris. They're equally suspect,

the poet and carrier, both deal in woeful methods
making hay from language as the crow parts
the tissues of rain, and they disappear into vans
with questions still on your lips. I'm off to the river
to have a little quiet. School is out, and schoolgirls
address the day with their uniforms of gold and pink,
their hair-clips in orange and leather satchels.
The water relaxes, foaming amid the boulders.
Some other life, a water nymph comes to divert me
from the business of knowing—or of dreaming—
if only for a little while, a small gap in the static
through which a person may come to understand
the boy he was, on the other side of the island.

It is a foolish man who tries to cultivate the foam
and take it with him, since time shows an endless supply
beating and gurgling from the invisible ocean
that encircles the rum shop, and the rum on the bar,
with rhymes and assonantal noise, to cheer up the heart.

IV.

Among the rubble of the system is a neckbrace
and to walk on that road is to suffer the umbilical tear
without profit to the community, which depends on
artifacts to counter the drain of capital to the north
some forts, and cannon, a massive anchor
milled and threaded, for an admiral on station:
the hero of the books we read, to the thud of surf.
His name graces our small alleyways and a few parks
serve as telescopes to the bygone battles, the blows
for trading routes, won or lost, which the banker knows—
the word "England" echoes in tones of seductive ivory
it rings on the malarial river, and in the bedrooms
of gentlemen and valets, everyone has a good time:
the verses, together with the manual, will see you in
as they turn back at the border of the man's resignation.

You always knew you'd come back to the ordinary spouse
solid and there over the cat box, which fades, and yellows,
and unlock the irons of your inconsolable grief
because some wants are like a thundercloud and fatal
to small craft such as the poem you claim to be pilot of.

V.

I'll soon be writing to "you," and expect a reward
for windy advice, not to say a pension from the house of cards
I've built up from nothing and taken public
the way a woman takes her new child for a promenade
in a sailor's outfit and cap, and watches
him the length of the dock until the steamer leaves.
"I think I'll stay put for a while," she says to herself.
"Tomorrow there will be the ferry to Staten Island
and other boats to exciting destinations, discoveries
did not end with the South Seas or the Sea
of Tranquility, and my turn will come, to find the flower."

Mark McMorris

*

That woman was my mother, and I've no doubt mirrored
her gaze to the far-off adobe abodes of the gods
because while you were away I saw pharonic riches
heaped up like so much broken tile, and golden poodles
waiting at the doors of spas, and everyone was 6' 2",
with legs of copper and jade, with honey on their tongues,
and new Cadillacs patrolled the sleek roads of that city.
O, I wanted one, not in excess of what I deserve
moving from the study with the air conditioner's murmur
to abstract ledgers of time, I will make my case
to hills that can hardly afford to be at peace, in such a climate.

FLOWERS

1.
it is daylight, common day
the labourers out in the fields
"the simple fate of it"

amply beyond the next rise
nothing: in the tactile stillness
not even rain, not even a gust

a blending more than borders
with ruled fences, and a gradual
respect for the way it is sealed

how can we bend into history
the valley's eye not our eye
a landscape without argument

to study this land is madness
just as the books are
with deeds of another century

mad in the webs of the very letters
my own small piece of the time
however it is spelt and in what speech

90

Mark McMorris

the name of an old controversy
this one, at least, will survive
the passage of several under the earth

and a logic careening to death
which let us wait for it to pass
so that the fields recover their mirth

give up the effort fought for
and you give up the evenings
the right to be in them oneself

troubles left by systems of exchange
no dissembling or false murders
only the forthright tactics of a butcher

and in this place the fudge man
the calypso man, the tinker
with pans dangling from an old truck

a push-cart of discarded boards
one man leaning into the weight
—the stoplight—loaded with bottles

city traders, mementos of trans-
sahara but on asphalt not sand
and fetching back no manufactures

mementos of trans-sahara, *memento
mori* as the slogan
in other words for this work

where are the labourers
the fields hold only the crop
some burnt and wrecked

in profit, the sign of rebellion
fire which they have in common
the land diminishes with each light

2.
and if land diminishes
the eye refuses anything
more solid than the visible

the simple pure of it
the voluptuous landscape
Ipswich, Ginger Hill: names

and I took out my eye
and dealt it for visionary power
to subdue the cascade

to make thought out of it
as rum comes out of sugar
my one eye, my only circuitry

the phallus on a rampage
all over the parish, the eye
is a virgin of the guillotine

and myth is the loverboy
come here, as wind talks
the usual gibberish "as if"

outline of an embrace
a bonfire of bibles
stuck in hot pavement

I would crawl on the bones of my elbows . . .
I know what I'm owed
from land, from rock stone

but the eye is a nipple
the eye is simplicity
so the water leads me

among grassy aqueducts
and beneath their legs
a builder's will and testament

things to be aware of
the same things in a place that is not the same
things become flat

small coves that survive
drought, election years
murder walking out of the sea

things in a frame
the snail, the fantail palm
peacocks by the ocean

the blood slows to the pace
of a dray or roadwork
mountains dominate the city

an archipelago of mind
pouring over the edge
a waterfall in the offing

sea travel and a retreat to
the bush of mental space
indices of geological drift

the green names shut up
in blood of ephemera
going to a mass interment

3.
one eye coaxing an idea
out of the green casing
of field and mountain pass

manifest undulations
of earth being pushed up
blood soaking the text

where sand meets water
the fishing boats, the restless
light of the day's work

who will remember them
changing rope of elements
when anarchy smashes the boats?

and the sibyl is long dead
who spoke the (m)other tongue
I've seen pieces of the heart

APHRODITE OF ECONOMY

Landscape, as the events of a prior discontinuity,
will never know what we make of it, although
telegrams come, and breath hurries, at the top of a rise
to survey the orderly valleys, the young cane
and the mixed shoots, some as tall as a man,
and miles of them going back into another century
of uniform labour the colour of earth.
Anyone can break the code to take out the truth
because it is there, so long as there is an eye.
Language is different. History chokes on a rag of kerosene
the fuse is lit down a corridor of echoing images
and one cannot shuffle the fulgurating words
to nominate as aesthetics what time calls blood—
though once, it was thought, once—and a woman
doubled over and coughing must signal the scar
of cutlasses, diseases of the womb that maim the adult.
What do the fields represent, the harvest?
ratios, roads, drainage—the plucked flower of science—
these words are fuel to tinder, they promise
extremes of hatred if not boredom with the text
we were born to desecrate, and that's the paradox
of being from an offshore rig: how to put out
the wide savagery when you're inside the beast
that in other legends, as wolf, swallows the community
in this one has left prints in the form of sugar cane
that actually broaches a goddess of slave economy.

Mark McMorris

BEING AT LOOSE ENDS

The general calls for a retreat back into the bush
of mental space where we cook without smoke
water drips from citrus and ask fewer questions
of big-foot hedges lining the day with propaganda

the comparisons belong to the rhetoric of our poets
silence trails an exhaust to where they bivouac
at the secluded cow-pond, expecting stars to erupt
and blot out the error and the wild pig's rampage

at the home for athletes, more statues than love
at the speed of light, birds fly out of reach
and the last buccaneer is dead from liver disease
a bamboo complication, that crushes the heart

the road swept with petals, enter a green country
buoyed up on nudges from a reactor, how it hums
songs of the murderous climate to my two-step dirge
with weapons in a pile like so much useless rope

we were at loose ends in Babylon and made things up
while genocide flowered in the breeze, it was lovely
to be on the patio with the hills like a comfortable shoulder
it was a morning's work to send off the beggar

a day's to study the red roofs, to hack out a path
from alphabet to harbour where a body drifts
and build a constabulary for the village estates
when prophets are abundant, mania always wins

buying at one end of the coast what sells in Kingston—
things that move around like a love-pain, from groin
to nightmare, heaped up like tumuli, a sea-conch's girth
which announces the victim, hand over the accounts

I was at loose ends and therefore level with the grass
without call from the sky to believe in a blue width
how to persuade the bougainvillea to suspend its drift?
some say that innocence foundered at the foundry

Mark McMorris

the ships forever wander the Antilles, like the mist
the basin of mind's archipelago crossed
and dredged till wires snap and whir emptily
at the dominant mountains, this is a rumour of war

it's not easy to dismiss, the sky-plants are sinking
before the car of the sun, which turns on
the cracked jalousies, and heats up the plumes
of birds that walk freely, as others of us walked

bewildered by losses—the general in his hammock—
love-stricken, faltering, at the rocky shelf

Dressing Up Our Pets
Mei-mei B*erssenbrugge*

1.
I sew a bright hood for my pet mouse.

I make holes for the eyes, the nose and ears.

I stand it on two legs and it stands on its own a while.

My friend, the white mouse, is iridescent, not an image that
began in my intuition as ready-found material.

I sew a hood for the rabbit, eye and nose holes, sheathed ears.

Its movement, the difference between a thing and its color,
burdens the activity of dressing our pets.

The mouse is old, but its image is light.

Between its alleged color and its alleged visibility is a lining
like the double of a mouse, latency, flesh.

The surface of the visibility of my family doubles over its
whole extension with an invisible reserve.

In your flesh what's visible, by refolding or padding, exhibits
their being as the complement of possibility.

Since possibility is this situation as thought, as a universal.

2.
The sun is distributional on desert below us.

Small trees are distributional, but not integrative.

The moonlight is distributional *and* integrative.

Pines on a crest at dusk, separate figures, will become
imageless, integration of all the black trees, black animals,
etc., night animals, domestic animals waiting at home.

These innocents from nature are my attempt to draw near sacred
feeling without others present, who, as unending movement,
consume tranquil ground.

Then ground becomes like other people.

It's why I remember a span of light, not because of satisfaction,
but framing, an interruption that will inhabit me, like what
happened the other day, when he forgot me.

We were shopping, and he just went on.

Ordinarily, I wouldn't be sensitive, but that day, the usual
stimulation, looking at fruits and vegetables, seemed to belong
to him.

I also should have experience, for how would I make my selection?

3.
"How old are you . . . have seen a lot . . . you wait still . . . hard to
see . . ."

The audience integrates the man singing with what's visible
behind them.

He delicately rotates his hands to an emotion that's like a
place.

His age and our suffering became a concrete node of things
happening at once and things one after another.

He is not real like a star, but he has his own impetus of how the
song goes at dusk.

So you think his song caused sad feeling, like your hand
touching your hand.

A girl sings along, without knowing the words and enters your
memory.

That there's no present of what will happen to her is
expectation.

Everyone becomes great in proportion to a singer's spurious
expectations, like many good mistakes.

4.
Parachute on the desert, blue-white with light, eleven
sheep head to head in a circle asleep.

Enjoyment and substance in real time involve clearings about
which pivot opaque zones.

Real is a span of visibility, inasmuch as your flesh is not
chaotic, *of* a contingency.

The real thing substitutes for another, who's not representable,
as he gathers up parachute and delivery.

If I stay here and you mean something to me, what's common
is disjunct from what you mean, like my hands touching.

That you're telepathic means nothing; you've facts you
can't know at work in connections of my experience.

A rock in rain distributing water along texture is my response to
experience.

Mei-mei Berssenbrugge

When your flesh invisibly interplays a disjunction needed for
 identity, flesh is texture.

Our meeting occurs near a hill you climb every day to water
transplanted iris.

Why don't you let others do that?

5.

Although I do not wish to separate from him, now, due to faults
of compound phenomena being demonstrated, he will disappear
from my sight and hearing.

The beauty of his song derives from the fact it represents
something to someone.

Any family that's concentrated insofar as it represents
something, may be taken for someone.

Wherever there's waiting is this transference.

The danger is, you'll be deceived by the metonymy of my tender
feeling, light and multiple.

You go to pick up the child after school.

You remain a few moments, talking with a teacher beside the
loom.

Why are you telling her this?

Glory, formless substance, circular dawn—like a child's drawing
of stars or snowflakes and lines.

Each line connects, so it's the same star falling, loop the loop.

And each line belongs to each star, my friend the white rabbit,
little mouse, squirrel, impatient, shaking off their clothes.

The Country Road
Carol Azadeh

ON THE QUIET COUNTRY ROAD I stopped. The warm air moved among the seeding roadside grasses nodding their blobs of cuckoo spit and the bitter blackberry bushes coated with road dust. I was walking up to the pub and willing something to happen. Now. Make it now. Then I had to slow down because the pub, Keegan's, was getting farther behind me and the mulberry bushes of our lane coming nearer and the rule said that the magic held as far as the big stone outside our lane. *Now.* And in that split second, the sky opened behind me and roared past, screaming dustily, sealing my eyes and lips in dryness and fear and joy at my power to call forth an event. When I was able to look, I saw a motorbike, the driver whooping freely; behind him flowed dark brown hair, sleek and long enough to sit on. 'Celine,' I gasped. The bike swerved, made a round dust-whirl and, before leaping into our lane, paused infinitesimally, just long enough for me to understand with my middle child's percipience that Celine on the back had not wanted the bike to turn off thus, she did not want Mammy stumbling out of the kitchen into the hen-yard to see her eldest daughter on this bike with its dark green mudguards and brake shield. I ran all the way down the road to our lane, my school bag bumping up and down against my back, my sandalled feet slapping against the lonely quiet that had closed over their passage. In our lane they had flung the bike against a hedge; in the sunlight and smell of warm tyre one of the wheels turned slowly. For a moment I stared—they had tricked me! I crouched on the grassy verge, dropped my school bag, gently parted the hedge and whiteweed, resisting the powdery, itchy smell of the whiteweed . . . and then I stopped. I knew enough and so much by simply closing my eyes and seeing how her long, thin brown hair covered her back and his arms that to this day I can't tell if I saw them there in the quiet field or not.

This was the nineteen-fifties, and the countryside of the north of Ireland was quiet, inhabited by Sunday sluggishness that thickened in the vein. Not many people could afford to put a car on the road.

Carol Azadeh

I was a schoolgirl and I had lived nothing but that road on past the schoolhouse and our lane. Just after the school the road turned at Biddy Dempsey's shop and went on into town past Keegan's pub. Old hairy-faced Biddy Dempsey had a wild temper. On Saturday afternoons my big sister Celine and her friends walked idly past the shop, looking in the dim window and commenting loudly, daring each other to obscenities and laughing at the top of their voices until Biddy flew out, shouting at them, hairy face and bony body clenched and shaking with anger like an impotent Rumpelstiltskin, and the girls ran off shrieking with half-simulated fear. (I remember Padraig Pearse laughing and calling me Biddy Dempsey for screaming in rage.) By the year I was eight, Biddy had lost her sting, her face had sunken in on its gummy toothlessness, eyes and mind had rheumed over. 'Biddy's winding down,' said our daddy. So there was no longer any crack for Celine in walking past the shop door, arm in arm with her best friends, to taunt the reaches of Biddy's anger straining like a dog on its chain, and I knew Biddy would no longer tell on me to Mammy that summer when I defied the hawthorn stick on the top of the kitchen press, and to the pace of my hard-beating heart walked farther up the road than I was allowed by myself, past the riverbank of long grass, on to Keegan's pub with its wire-meshed window of tea-coloured glass and the dour plank door painted brown.

There I paused, waiting for someone to go in or out. On the afternoon air I breathed the smell of fry from Biddy Dempsey's dinner until hunger got the better of my trepidation. In those warm spring afternoons the road slumbered. The fields released their pre-summer smell of turned clay, thick bruise-coloured clouds insulated the earth. I waited, watching the plank door of the pub, and when Biddy's lunch faded there came the forbidden, sickly sigh of beer-on-the-breath familiar from visiting uncles.

The door stayed closed, blank, its painted slats of wood changeless as the small green fields on either side of the road.

These were the months after my eighth birthday. Every afternoon after school and before tea I ran back down the road towards our lane, hungry, but light-footed and light-hearted too at running alone on the road, the breeze in my hair and my school bag bumping against my tailbone, and then Mammy's face, heavy, wary with fatigue, rose before me. Mammy rarely left our cottage. She was as permanent a fixture as the pump under the hedge which dealt us our water. When our daddy wasn't home, Mammy shivered at movements in the yard outside. In those winters before electricity came, black dark drowned

102

the country from shore to shore. Mammy huddled in the oil-lit three-room interior of the cottage like a big fragile insect stuck on a lamp.

Already at the age of eight I swore never to cower like Mammy. After supper I liked to announce that I was going out. Roused from her bleariness she said, 'Houl on, let me look,' and went slowly over to the kitchen door to check the incoming dark. If she didn't catch my arm I slipped by her, wee titch, being light, unlike Mammy, and free as a bird. I ran off, laughing cheekily in the night air, pounding my feet on that dusty lane with its high spine of tufted grass. I had a coal-black cat called Pusheen, a flighty, susceptible animal who followed me bounding madly like a dog, ears flat on its head until it dived into the hedge, overcome by its own excitement.

Mammy called me her 'changeling'. She wanted to excuse my scrawny, sallow-skinned limbs to visitors who admired the other rosy, plump children, good-looking by country standards. The tone in which she said 'changeling', pinching my 'tinker-brown' skin or catching my eyes in the mirror when she was combing my hair back into the severe plait I hated, made me laugh. When at last, at night, Mammy sat down at the kitchen table, she never suspected how I studied the quiet in her eyes or looked at the width of her back and hips straining over a pile of sheets in the washbasket and wondered, 'Is she really my mother?' Or perhaps she did know, which explained her tendency to take the hawthorn to my legs more than she did with my brothers and sisters. Those days Mammy beat me absentmindedly, breathing stertorously, more out of duty than anger.

One evening in the spring of that year Celine and I had been clearing the table after dinner when Mammy told us to stop and listen to her. Then she said baldly that from now on neither one of us two, nor our younger sister, were allowed up the road past the pub by ourselves.

'Why not?' I demanded instantly, knowing I couldn't rely on Celine, who was too sly for direct opposition. Fourteen-year-old Celine had just earned the right to Saturday dances in the town hall and would henceforth submit to anything to keep that privilege. For the girls like Celine in those days, the girls who grew their hair long to compensate for a plain face and paid no attention at school, life melted down to Saturday night, which in turn dissolved into the single hope of getting a dance from a boy with a car.

'Because I don't like you girls going past that Keegan's pub, that's why, and because I say so,' said Mammy.

Poor Mammy. 'Thick' was the word for Mammy, for the premature obesity of her arms and legs from cooking all day for the six of us, 'thick' the slowness of her head from standing on her feet from dawn to dusk every day, 'thick' her inability to explain herself to herself, still less to her children. When life was beyond Mammy, she made a Novena to St Jude, Help of the Hopeless, getting up even earlier than usual to go down on her knees. Mammy did not tell us a new B Special barracks was settling in the market town that began at the far end of the road. That is, she set out to tell us about it, she had been turning the words in her head all day. But St Jude worked a miracle of transubstantiation. Old, well-established anxieties, Drink-Fear, Pub-Fear, absorbed the new fright of B-men and what they might do to her girls, and finally with sustained prayer the whole anxious mass coalesced into the reassuring threat of the hawthorn stick.

My sister and I looked at each other wonderingly. We thought of Mr Keegan, whom Mammy said was 'a soak' and 'you could smell it on him a mile off', and Mrs Keegan, a bony, cross woman never lit by a smile. I saw Celine's one-track mind thinking that the only men around Keegan's were toothless, propped on sticks with the sky in their eyes.

Mammy caught my eye. 'I mean what I toul yez an' don' let me hear of yez wanderin' up there on your own,' she threatened, suspicion turning her intolerant. As always our big brother Padraig Pearse, whose loud, brash manner was law in the cottage when our daddy wasn't there, backed her up.

'The road's not for wee girls,' he sneered. 'The road's not for titchy girls,' he said.

From that day on if Mammy ran out of sugar or tea, she sent out Padraig Pearse. And that's what got me thinking about Keegan's. That's how the pub's wire-meshed square window turned into a blind eye whose mystery I determined to pluck out, and I began walking up there regularly after school.

I walked that road in all seasons. The surface patched with tar was as familiar to me as the changing patterns of healing scratches and bumps on my knees. Rain, warm or cold, sleeked the tar and ran into pools in the cowprints trodden on the clay verge. On bright days the distant whitewashed walls of cottages like ours caught the sunlight on the violet slopes of the far hills. I walked alone. Celine and Padraig went to the senior school in town, the wee ones played at home all day. Sometimes a tractor roared past slowly, leaving a trail of straw and diesel in the field-scented air. Or a bicycle, bowling elegantly against the breeze. Then the quiet closed over my head, the country quiet, the wet quiet of a clay burial. I liked to imagine myself from the viewpoint of the other driving or cycling past me, a thin, bushy-haired girl in a green felt cap walking alone no one knew where. I tried to forget that later the very same day they would probably meet my father in the fields round about and say, 'I saw your wee Cathy on the way ti school today.'

Later that spring the weather turned hot. Patches of the road softened in the heat. I picked off the small lumps of pitch stuck to my shoes and rubbed the tar-stains with butter. I invented ways to keep the tension in my defiance of Mammy as I walked up the road after school, forbidding myself to breathe or even look at the pub until I came to the long grass opposite, but boredom got the better of me. I was no longer interested in the pub for disobedience's sake, and my feet trailed heavily on my way past the wire-meshed window. The day that I saw Mrs Keegan get out of a car and go in with another man was going to be the last afternoon I bothered walking so far down the road. A missionary had visited the school that day and told us about Signs of Christ revealed, including photos of Canadian snow melting in the form of Christ's face and a vision of the crucifixion formed by blood-red clouds at sunset. So I was paying attention to the sky. The usual heavy rainclouds ranged the horizon. Behind them rolled the sun, piercing their weakest places with beams that shone on the arable earth in straight lines like the Holy Ghost illustrated in my school catechism. The man with Mrs Keegan was a stranger, poor and from town by the look of his thin trousers and battered sports shoes and dark, floppy hair. Men like my father wore heavy work-shoes and cut their hair short. This man couldn't even afford light town shoes.

'Hullo Mrs Keegan!' I sang out instinctively from the other side of the road.

'Hullo there, wee Cathy.' The sad-faced woman scarcely glanced over at me. Dark Floppy Hair did not turn his head. He took keys out of his pocket, unlocked the pub door and stepped back to let her pass before him. With the plank door opened, the foreign, stale smell of spirits that so terrorized Mammy sneaked onto the road. Mrs Keegan went in first, without looking behind. The unembellished door closed behind their backs.

*

It was Padraig Pearse who picked up that word from neighbours who came to our cottage with the news. Celine and I were hanging sheets in the back. I couldn't remember having heard the word 'rape' before but it didn't surprise me. Now I knew the mystery of the wire-meshed window. Masked men had burst into Keegan's pub, 'the very time wee Cathy was comin' home from school', sighed Mammy thankfully, crossing herself and promising St Jude a Novena and also St Anne, the Blessed Virgin's mother. They had tied the publican up in a cupboard and raped his wife before shooting him through the cupboard door.

'They put a towel over his head,' said Padraig to Celine where they sat on the doorstep, keeping an eye on me as I played dressing up Pusheen in dolls' clothes before wheeling her around in the rusty baby's pram. A baby's game which I hadn't played for a long time but today I felt like bossing Pusheen, whose wiry black body arched angrily against my hands as I forced her to the old humiliations of dolls' bonnets.

'They raped her,' Padraig Pearse said to Celine, who was examining the curtain of her hair for split ends.

'I know,' said Celine without asking what that meant.

'They gagged him.' My big brother had the same disgusted emphasis he had heard adults use. 'They cut off all her hair too.'

Celine's green eyes gleamed wide. 'Why'd they do that for?'

Padraig Pearse shrugged. 'The Keegans a been keepin' house for the B Specials in that there bar. She'd been goin' wi' them. They do that to them girls that goes wi' the B-men.' The righteous tone sounded odd in his mouth, for at fifteen years of age he still hadn't made it on his own.

Home, schoolhouse, home, chapel, home. Patience was the smell of a rain-soaked, sun-beaten road. For eight years I had breathed the light-pink and dark-pink tea roses proliferating on our cottage walls. Inside smelt sweet and suffocating, of cinders and baking and damp and soap, like a fat grandmother pressing you to her chest, summer and winter. Every morning and evening we fetched water from the pump, Celine and I. When winter came on we lit the oil-lamps early. In summer we lay in our bed wide awake because night refused to come and the sheets smelt damp from the chill of the stone walls. At night the country silence deepened, submerged in darkness. The sound of a dog barking carried on the still air, then stopped. Sounds disappeared in the night leaving echoes to fade like the ever-widening circles after a stone thrown in a deep pool. Cast-iron was that winter quiet. I remember lightless winter afternoons lived under a white monochrome lid, fields, road, trees, stiffened into voicelessness. At last with spring the movement of green differentiated this silence. Cottage doors opened to the pale sun. The first grass smells in the quiet hinted at long summer days outdoors from dawn to sunset for which the air was still too chilly. We were impatient and restless, we hungered for summer. The first signs of real oncoming heat were the pink scent of the opening tea roses, the flies being hard to keep out of the cottage and then the old people who had survived winter and came visiting in the spring. They sat by the fireplace distilling that faint odour of piss and cheap *eau de toilette* that I have come to associate with illness or old age. Their gossip was of lawsuits over bits of land, of men and women broken by marriage and drink, of cancer, deformity, accidents, decapitation, bone-breaking and attack from farm tools and animals, as if their bleak words could tempt providence to compensate them for the hard times of old age in an unforeseen stroke of bad luck. They did not spoil us or try to win our love; we had to be on our best behaviour, even Padraig and Celine, and not do anything they might report in other cottages. Mammy gave them the best to eat and drink while they commented that we were 'wild eaters' and 'surely stout ones to feed', and finally I remember that often we couldn't bear to look at them. They were ugly with hard gums instead of teeth and pushed-in faces and rheumy eyes and the sight and sound of them eating a plate of stew was enough to put you off your food for a week. And yet our daddy said that they were not much older than him, only their lives in the fields had been backbreaking. He added honestly that we were lucky not to have to share the cottage with an oldie, thinking of his unmarried sister who lived alone with an aged aunt 'who ruled the roost' and from whom she was to inherit the house and the piece of land it was on.

In the spring of the year I was eight I saw our daddy stand for a long time in the doorway in the evenings and stare at the high sky ribbed with the soft herringbone clouds of reluctant summer, so as not to have to listen to the old men in the firecorner. The next morning at breakfast he sucked in his cheeks toothlessly, screwed up his eyes and nudged Celine.

'D'ye mind that aul bull of O'Hearn's and the times I toul yez that it were a dangerous beast that should be put down?'

I spluttered into my glass of milk.

'Catch a hold on yerself,' Mammy said crossly, coming to set the teapot on the table. Mammy never understood our daddy's jokes, which she considered a sort of side effect of what she called his 'moodiness'. *'He's a shockin' moody man.'* When our daddy mimicked the neighbours like this, Mammy always imagined that it was me leading him and the others on. It had been years since she loved our father as well as she loved her eldest son, Padraig Pearse, the only one of us humourless enough to batten on her admiration.

'Sure there was I in broad daylight in Market Street wi' my wee gran'son Jimmy,' our daddy went on wheezily, 'an' that great beast come chargin' round the corner up ti Jimmy and knocks him down flat on his back before continuying on up the road and away on, on outta sight, as if nothin' a happened!'

'What about wee Jimmy?' said Celine, who could keep a straight face.

'Sure, he'd no idea what an' under God had hit him, it happened that fast! I goes inti the nearest shop for help but none of them ones believes me! For the aul bull has gone and wee Jimmy's jumped up saying he's as right as rain! I ask ye, after being toppled by a great bruthe of a bull like O'Hearn's! "Niver mind yer saying yer right as rain now," says I to Jimmy. "Shut yer face an' come down to the police for I'll witness against O'Hearn's bull and have him for trauma if it's the last thing I'll ever do!"'

'Cathy!' Mammy snapped.

Our father wiped his mouth and stood up. 'Imagine the traumytizing effect on a child of being knocked flat by a bruthe of a beast like that!' he said to Mammy above the delighted shouts of the two wee ones infected by the covert glances and smiles of Celine and Padraig. 'Enough to ruin a child for life, do ye not think, Eileen?' he murmured, going out the door.

'Go on the rest of yez, scat,' said Mammy, 'I'm at the end of my tether with ye all!'

When I was eight I really thought that this was all that would ever be. These long, daylit, amorous evenings of late summer (I didn't know the word at the time but the softness of the pinkening summer days already caressed me into a state of anticipation nearly unbearable), and the image of a sunken, toothless mouth chewing on itself, which I tried not to look at. I was the first one home from school and I ate the grilled potato pie that Mammy had ready on the stove. I argued with Mammy about going outside again while she forced me to do some useless housework for which she had no time, polishing brass ornaments, rubbing stains out of sheets, ironing Celine's frilly dance dresses. I spent the end of the day alone with Pusheen, playing in the yard while the shadows coagulated around us. I always pretended not to be waiting for our daddy to come back from the fields but I was waiting, waiting. His return was the only event in the evening and, finally fed up, I finished my day in a fugue of ingratitude. Just as her cat-spirit soared ecstatically in the half light, I tapped Pusheen smartly on the nose, which she hated so much that with a back-flip and a yowl she vanished into the shadows.

Everyone knew our daddy's comings and goings were the peaks and troughs of my days. Sometimes today the warm grass-smell of a daylit summer evening brings back the peculiar flavour of my waiting for him that year when I was eight. I stood at the mouth of our lane, smelling the flourishing hedges which scented the air like a caress, watching the expiring heat rise to the lilac sky. After a certain period of waiting and seeing no movement on the road between Keegan's roof and our lane, bleakness settled, large, damp and ugly, like a big insect fluttering in the centre of my being, and my heart began to beat uncomfortably in time to the idea, *What if he doesn't come* . . . . I stared dully in front of me as if the air were grey, the fields naked brown and the sky blank as a dead dog's eye. Those were moments I'll remember until the day I die, the dull moments of being eight and lonely on an isolated country road. A dullness worse than anger, worse than crying, and the reason why, even to this day, and although they'll never understand me, I can never take my own daughters back to the country, or tell them they are right in the romantic country tales of my childhood they have invented for themselves in their heads.

What if he doesn't come . . .

Our daddy would appear without warning, striding along noncommittally as if he had been there all the time on the road before me. If he saw I was in a bad mood, he stopped and opened his arms. I ran to him and then the whole of that day, the trepidation in my heart of sneaking up to Keegan's, my defiance of Mammy, the dullness of waiting, the terror that he might never come, all melted in the certainty that my time of light-footed happiness would come true as surely as our daddy swinging along the road to meet me.

It was to him that I complained, especially when Mammy did not let me go outside after school, that 'all the days were the same'. If he was tired, he reacted with a grain of Mammy's 'thick' wisdom. 'Stop your whingin', darlin'.' More often he didn't answer but picked me up and set me on his shoulders (showing he, like the rest of them, thought of me as a baby, though more fun than the wee'uns). 'Titch, wee Titch,' our daddy said when I was angry and screamed at Padraig, who liked to boss me around, 'What are ye so mad at?' Padraig, not understanding our daddy's tone, joined in, jeering, 'A great big voice for a wee titchy girl!' They all laughed, Padraig Pearse loudly, just to hear himself, Celine silently, squeezing up her green eyes and pushing back her sleek, dark-brown hair, which she never forgot was long enough to sit on, and Mammy with her tired, gamey smile because she always thought Padraig's loudness was funny, and then the wee brother and sister who didn't know anything but always watched Celine's and Padraig's faces to understand what to do.

That summer our daddy came home from town with an oval radio in polished nutwood which he placed on the mantelpiece where it watched us like an owl. Mammy smiled slowly as she always did at our daddy's ideas. The wee brother sucking his thumb hid behind the wee sister. Celine looked at Padraig, who disguised his curiosity and asked cheekily like a big man of the world, 'How much'd that cost ye then?'

I knew then I was justified in loving uniquely our daddy in this family. Apart from me, only he understood how the radio's urbane chat banished the clay silence of the fields, the awful bleakness of their retained breath in winter, the suffocation of their moist fertility in summer. 'A circle of good company,' he said, which meant the news from Belfast at six and London at seven and an alternating rhythm of something different through the bedroom door left ajar at night and also in the afternoons when I played in the yard which smelt of cows, baking bread, buttercups and rose petals. Between us we knew that he believed in an alternative to that endless beat of day following on day and season on season, timelessly without change forever and ever world without end, Amen.

After the radio came the visit from our uncles who lived down south. We knew that they had come to talk seriously about an old plan in our family, the dream of emigration to America. The brothers, Barry and John James, arrived up from Dublin. They gave us children money as they always did and sat back gravely around the fireplace, which smoked with a damp summer fire out over the hearth chock-a-block with flies leapfrogging round the stains and remnants of pieces of bread and cake eaten there and hard bits of food thrown into the embers. The uncles smoked too, thin packs of

Players with a red stripe. They let me scratch their unopened packs to find the place where the gold band tore evenly round the wrapper like a present. These men smoked so hard their fingers were mustard-coloured from the third joint upwards and their clothes smelt so raw of smoke and sweat that Celine, who stayed outside or in the bedroom practically all the time they were there, put her finger down her throat to make fake puking motions behind their backs. I was still young enough to have their dry, hard hands on my head or even around my waist while they talked and I fiddled with things from their pockets. I had to be there with them, and not just for their unwashed, sweaty smoke smell that as the hours went by absorbed into itself all our smells from soap and baking powder and fry from the kitchen and even the old, deep fugs and scents of the fire. I couldn't resist staying there, listening, through Mammy's comments on how spoiled I had got, through their long dull hours of talk, because since the brothers' arrival our daddy's new, strange vivacity changed our house more than Christmas, more than I had ever believed it was possible to change.

Mammy had cooked a special meal of stew under pie crust to 'see off' the brothers' return to Dublin. That night we were to finish the big, baked dome for dinner but the meat and potatoes in the centre of the table congealed in their glass oven-dish. Our daddy, usually first to pile his plate again, had laid his knife and fork across his plate, meaning he could eat no more. His excitement curtailed our appetite and bothered Mammy into the beginnings of her usual fearfulness.

'My stomach couldn't take another drop of food tonight,' he stood up, his hand light on Mammy's shoulder, then he left the kitchen through the halfdoor closed all day to keep out the hens. We saw him walk across the moonlit yard with his hands in his pockets. Mammy looked at Celine and started to cry. I didn't take much notice; she cried so often, Mammy, sometimes out of sheer tiredness, and even then I thought that was her own fault. No one *asked* her to work that hard. The story was that the brothers, John James and Barry, planned to emigrate to New York the following winter. December, January was a good time. Our father would follow with me, then send for the wee 'uns and then my mother with Padraig Pearse and Celine. Over the next weeks, the family split down the middle. Behind our daddy's back, Padraig swore he would not leave the country. He had just finished school and he envisaged a year or two dossing as a farm hand, drinking, flirting in the fields around the cottage. Celine said nothing. Nevertheless, I knew from her smile and her narrowed eyes she was with Padraig. At fourteen she had tasted too much of the local dancehall to be tempted by other freedoms.

In the days after the uncles went back to Dublin I took advantage of Mammy's frequent tears to leave the kitchen without bothering to clear the table or waiting for her to send me out to the pump for dishwater. Outside in the yard, Pusheen, a long black stain in the moonlight, scampered like a firefly against the cottage wall. I chased her briefly and then wandered over to our father who stood smoking at the start of the lane up to the mulberry bushes. Already I was sure America would be everything we both wanted. I knew myself wiser and older than the others behind us in their kitchen, fearful in their warm meat smell. Our daddy put his arm around my shoulder, one hard hand on my back.

I looked at the sky. Above the arable fields the white-ribbed cloud plains held the dark.

'America's like the sea!' I said to him. The night air on my face smelt of grass and the warmth of the animals who had lain on it all day, an odour so etherealized by the wind and the moon I could smell salt on it. I realized then that the joy that had been in me since the moment in the kitchen when he had stood up and walked out was like the shock that had hit me last summer when we rounded the corner in the bus at Castlerock and saw the sea, oblivious and contained and more real than any picture I had ever seen. He laughed, then sighed and rubbed his hand over his face, 'I don't know, I don't know.'

'I have so been to Castlerock last summer!' I reminded him, irritated by this drop in his spirits.

'And ye wouldn't miss home and all?' he asked me in a strange tone.

'All what?' I turned to look at his face, sombre and handsome (as I remember it) in the moonlight. He indicated the end of the lane which ran into the Wee Field pitted with heel-shaped ridges, small wells the cows' hooves had left, now filled with reflecting water. A solitary thorn tree, scraggy and well known by day, stood transmogrified by moonlight. I was thinking only of how, living with him in America, with Celine and Padraig Pearse staying behind, I would be freer and happier than ever I had been in my whole eight years.

'What's there to miss, we're all going together!' I said. He stroked the top of my head and then stood up slowly.

'You should've been the eldest boy.'

At night he took a chair and, placing it outside the front door, sat with his legs crossed, gazing straight over the field whose darkness held steady to the depths of the moonlit spaces overhead. Mammy made me go to bed earlier than usual, which I did without fighting; our daddy's mood had cast a peculiar spell on me. In the dark bedroom where my sisters slept peacefully, I smelt the smoke from his Player's No. 6. I left the bed where Celine had rolled heavily into sleep and tiptoed to the deep-set window. The thick little pane we never opened magnified the starlight. I clambered onto the broad sill and saw the dark effigy of his head. The stone under my legs was colder than ice. Lifeless, intractable cold under which nothing grows; not even in deepest summer did those stone walls ever warm at the centre. I climbed off, found a towel, spread it on the sill, and with a secret shiver of delectation settled back, determined to keep vigil with my father in this night so precious in its miraculous advent of a new world. The novelty of my happiness accentuated every detail around me. I was living the happiest night of my life and I knew it. Never before had I been aware of the grandeur and the sorrow of passing time. I stared at the sky fretted with constellations whose names I didn't know, not understanding this emotion for which tears seemed so inappropriate. The immobility of the stars, their infinitesimal winks in the quiet sky worked on me until their silence filled my ears with a single symphonic note . . . Yet his head motionless as carved stone, the monotonous rhythm of his smoking, broken now and then by his thick cough, a sound to which we were all so used to that we scarcely heard it anymore, lulled my eyes. I heard his monosyllabic replies to Mammy's concerned voice from inside the yellow of the kitchen and at last I slid sleepily off the sill and went to bed just as Mammy, always nervous and deferent to our father's 'moods', shuffled tiredly to rest herself. I knew that Mammy was thinking, 'Ah, I'm weary, weary, so weary,' and my last thought on that strange, luminous night of happiness was that Mammy had never bothered to understand our daddy because she was always too tired.

I was putting Pusheen's front legs through dress sleeves when I heard heavy boots skidding down the lane and dragging a weight behind in a skittering wake of pebbles and dry mud. Before I had time to look up Mammy rushed out of the cottage with her hands to her face, shouting at me, 'My God, my God, wee Cathy!' Her voice trembled.

Later on, the memory of this pathos made me angry; what was I supposed to do to assuage her helplessness, her beseeching me to contradict the sight before us?

Two men held daddy under the arms and dragged him roughly into the house as I remembered once seeing them heaving one of my uncles home down the lane after a Christmas dance in town. That had been on a crystalline night in January and our daddy standing in the oblong light of the doorway had laughed at their ragged songs and the scarves of their misty breaths in the air. Today, the sun brightened in the sturdy monotony of mid-afternoon. I squeezed Pusheen, who scratched my forearm before streaking treacherously behind me.

His face was limp and his head slumped as if someone had cut the cords in his neck. I ran up to him and saw a shining, white line between his half-opened eyelids, then I knew that he was alive and I grasped the sleeves of his hanging ragdoll arms and pushed the men's legs away with all my force.

'Nobody asked you lot to come here, let him go!' I screeched at them, throwing myself on him where they had laid him on the bed. They pulled me off at once, quietly, saying, 'Would ye take the wee'un, Eileen.' Mammy's trembling, disorientated hands pushed me out of the room. Nevertheless, pressing my face to my father's neck I had already had time to smell the rubbishy odour of his breath which shocked me to silence. I had never been close to rot before and didn't know the name of the sweet smell in my nostrils.

The men bringing our daddy back from the fields had seen him groaning, crouching over a stone. He was vomiting blood in the first of the haemorrhages from the stomach cancer that meant instead of starting life in a new country, he was going to die at the end of the summer, at the age of forty-one, in the ancient familiarity of the three-roomed cottage he had lived in all his life.

Rape was an eyeless, noseless makeface, a heart beating in a dark cupboard, a wire-meshed window, an explosion of light and sound in the tiny space of the head. At night I lay awake, hugging the wee sister for comfort, and watched Celine sleep with her hair over her face. In the day a fleeting, sickish smell lined my nostrils; I couldn't tell what it was until I remembered Mammy's disgust for Mr Keegan—'Did ye smell it on him? Sure ye could've smelt him a mile off!' Then I knew I had the death smell of whiskey in my nose. I dreamed I sat alone in the middle of a sticky floor in the shade of

Keegan's pub and the battered sports shoes appeared before me. It was Dark Floppy Hair with his gunflashes who said, 'Where'll I kill ye? In the feet or the head?'

I screamed with cowardice and reached for a soft body beside me for protection, the wee sister, whom he killed easily in a vertical line of bullets; then bullets spat, neither hot nor cold, along my legs.

After our daddy's death I used to dream that my screams woke him up and brought him into our room. 'Whisht, will'ye quiet up wee Cathy! It's only a bad dream!' Celine shook me awake. 'Look, there's Pusheen!' The black cat had sensed my wakefulness and turned in the pinkening square of the bedroom window, opening her mouth in a silent plea. Celine, freed by our daddy's death to drop out of school and work backbreaking hours in a shoe shop in town, fell asleep again instantly. I lay awake and thought of how daddy's forehead wrinkled when he was tired, how he rubbed his face pretending to be sleepier than he was when he wanted us all to let him be. What if I asked him where Mrs Keegan was now? Gently he said, 'Sure, I couldn't tell ye.'

Of course we didn't go to America as he wanted us to. We went on living at the bottom of the grass-ridged lane dense with mulberry bushes, in our three-roomed, whitewashed cottage. The thick stone walls trapped flies and clammy heat in summer and preserved the damp chill of winter. His death had weakened me. The power of the year when I was eight faded in the oncoming seasons. Then I was only a child growing up, her fantasies no longer strong enough for the magic of calling an event into being, as I had once conjured Celine on the motorbike coming home from school. After my daddy's death I started to faint regularly. I fainted in mass and at school, so often that the nuns stopped paying any attention when it happened. We went on living together, Mammy, Padraig Pearse, Celine, and the wee'uns who had no memory at all of our daddy's plans, and no suspicion, when Mammy took the stick to their legs, that the wrong one had died. She didn't hit them as hard as she had beaten me, though. Tragedy had sealed her into a sort of hopelessness which irritated everyone except Padraig. Unlike the others I argued with Padraig every day. I could not be like Celine and agree with one side of my face whilst doing what I liked with the other. I screamed at Padraig because although he was only my brother, Mammy's docility allowed him the power of forbidding me to leave the cottage in the evenings. At fourteen I took to spending my days like an old woman, glowering at visitors from my stool near the uneven stone sill of the kitchen window, or staring out at the lane that led to the main road behind the mulberry bushes. I didn't say a word to anyone but I was waiting to go away.

One day near the end of those years Padraig Pearse refused to allow me to go to a local *céilídh*. That is, he swore he would come and 'make a show' of me in front of the whole *céilídh* if I 'dared' go out of the cottage that evening. It was the height of summer again, the time of pink evenings, flies and tea roses. I was 'thran' for not want-ing to stay off school and 'help out', which meant cook for everyone. Mammy had been in bed, feverish and sickly as she was more and more often those days. She blamed her ill-health on her teeth. This time she had, in fact, been speechless with toothache for nearly a week.

I waited in my usual seat at the kitchen window. Behind me summer flies piled stickily in the cold grate. Padraig helped Mammy into a neighbour's car he had borrowed to take her into town to the nearest dentist. I watched them, my Mammy and my brother, as if they were people I didn't know. Though she was not even fifty years of age, Mammy's back was hooped from hardship. Her teeth had browned and gone rotten in her gums. Near the car door, she turned and hesitated in that mute manner that always irritated me. She held on to her son's arm, peering anxiously at my face in the window. Since our daddy's death she didn't like any sort of venture into town by car or bus. Her sheer recalcitrance before trips to the doctor or the dentist stopped up my pity for her. She had tied a scarf round her neck and the pain in her jaw prevented her from saying anything. Padraig slammed the car door behind her and followed her glance in my direction. Under his breath he swore and called out, 'Don't you dare budge from the house, wee Cathy. We've some talking to do when I get back.'

I didn't answer. I didn't 'budge' until the car had climbed the lane leading up the hill to the main road. Even then, with my eyes closed, I could see the rough grasp of his hand on the arm of the old woman who swayed slightly at her son's loud words.

People I don't know.

I left the cottage, taking nothing but my cardigan and a pocketful of biscuits. I stepped out of the muddy farmyard pitted and ploughed by goat and cow hooves, walking quickly, not looking back at the tiny white cottage behind me. In the summer heat I walked over the fields to our 'neighbour's' farm. There I slipped into an animal shed and stole a bicycle. I intended to ride it to a chocolate factory near Castlerock where I had heard they were taking on packers.

The summer day burned hot on the tar of the country road. All my life the smell of melting tar will remind me of this flight to freedom through the full-leaved countryside mature in summer under the high sky, nearly the high, magical blue of my first childhood. I was happy. Not the eight-year-old height of joy, but happier than for a long while. Blackbirds plunged madly across my path into the thick hedgerows. In the rush of the bicycle I was mistress of myself at last. Once I had arrived in town and found a job, I would be an adult. Padraig Pearse would never be able to make me come back to the cottage. I sang into the field-scented air.

The route I was taking wound circuitously uphill and down, looping around fields and thickets. My back and legs did not begin to ache until long after I'd left behind me the houses and shops after Keegan's. Then I lost all sense of time. Sweat clouded my vision, weariness numbed my feet. A sweetish late afternoon enveloped the town I was riding into and I cycled past workers hurrying along the street. The chocolate factory would be closed for the day. My only desire then was to stop pedalling but the constant motion had mesmerized my legs and so I continued, cycling round the streets where shopkeepers were stowing boxes and crates and locking up their shops. In my head, a chill space of fading brightness, there beat mercilessly the winging rhythm of bicycle tyres on the grey road that chilled in the rising night. I would have ridden the stolen bicycle until I had dropped off, if a car had not emerged unexpectedly from round a corner and knocked me flying over the handlebars. Pain split diamond-hard in my head. I fell into the dark.

Someone repeated my name. Warmth soothed my forehead, an insistent acrid smell drew me up to consciousness. I resisted. Lost and resisted again and slept. 'Cathy, Cathy,' said a voice I recognized. I opened my eyes. They had laid me on my back on the grey sofa of a small shop storeroom. From stacked cardboard boxes came the disciplinary tang of antiseptic. The softness on my forehead was Mammy's weak hand stroking my hair back from my face. The old woman's touch shook. I had frightened her. Tears oozed helplessly from my eyes. At that moment Mammy's trembling struck me as the most unbearable sight of all. I closed my eyes again. 'Don't,' I said, lifting Mammy's warm, dry wrist away. 'I'm alright.'

'How is the wee'un, Mrs Kelly?' came a voice from the back of the shop.

'A'right, 'hank ye'ery much, Mr Mawhinney,' said Mammy. From behind my shut eyes I sensed how she turned her head gratefully in the direction of the voice. Her voice sounded thick, as if with tears. But when I opened my eyes again, she was looking down at me, smiling. My heart froze. Mammy's mouth was a swollen weal. And something else. Too soft, boneless, a mimicry of a mouth, a cheeky hand in a sock mimicking a gummy old woman's mouth. For the first time I noticed the bloodstained white cloth in her shapeless hand. 'What did they do, Mammy?' I cried, turning my head violently on the grey cushion of the sofa. It was her teeth. They had taken out the rest of her teeth.

'Ssshush up, wee Cathy,' said Mammy. 'They gave me some stuff so's I don't feel a thing. Don't fuss yoursel' now.' The thickness of her speech against her soft gums did not hide the satisfaction of a buyer who has made a bargain. 'Sure I'll be a new woman the morrow.'

They took me back to our cottage in the neighbour's car. Padraig driving had nothing to say, after all. His head was an inert rectangle turned to the road from whose green-black night midges and moths and every other variety of summer insect flew headlong against the windscreen. Mammy dabbed ice wrapped in a pink-stained cloth to her face with one hand and tried to restrain my tears with the other.

Even now, when I haven't been back along that road for twenty, thirty years, I remember how I wept all the way home through that summer night while Mammy dabbed her mouth. I remember how I was weeping, not only for the exhilaration of my flight that had dissolved like the memory of sunlight in the night, but also for some other inconsolable defeat which would take its toll, even when I flew again. Overhead, the stolen bicycle tied to the roof-rack of the neighbour's car shifted back and forward with the movement of the car. The accident had only twisted the front wheel a little. It would take to the road again. Slightly, slightly the wheels moved in the animal-scented air that stretched for fathoms over that black country.

Five Poems
Malinda Markham

THE OUTING

The girl throws fruit at the squirrels. They dodge
and do not approach. The picnic was fine,
there was tea and sweet milk. Watermelon and salt,
that's how the men like it. Children put olives
on their fingers and drop them on the ground.
This is the path. They must be waiting for us
over that hill. Night reels itself in.
First color drains from the trees, then stars
are drawn across the grass and away.
It is summer, and children can play outside
until dawn. They cannot. Night birds awaken
and stitch the leaves shut with their cries.
Trees breathe at the periphery.
Sing night songs, and the dolls go to sleep.
The ceramic teapot falls off a rock and bursts
into stars. See, there is light now. We tell all the stories
we know. Gather the pieces,
you must gather the pieces. All will be well.
We are pirates and tie the dolls up. Muted leaves
billow like sails. Bees halo the young boy's head.
I did love you so, the girl says, and turns
into a small crop of fern. This time,
the pineapple is sweet. The children divide it,
breaking off chunks with their hands. Asleep,
the fox curls into its ribs. This is not grief.
There is no evidence that animals can feel.
The pineapple is sweet, why will you not eat it?
The day is not so far yet away.

Malinda Markham

MATCHSTICKS

The house is burning. Memories press
against its upper corners
for pockets of air. See the windows wanting to melt.
See the smoke making the windows
turn to thin milk: There are no children here,
but paint blisters like mouths. Birds rise in an arc from the trees,
and women clasp their hands on film. The house
is burning, and lightbulbs pop, one by one.
Air breaks around the room. See the fruit waver in its skin.
See each apple burst in its own
time, a terrible flower.
Did you count how many times you touched the door
and found it cool? Can you sound out
the noise the footsteps made,
ten years or more crossing wide, wooden floors?
Even the moon will burst in the heat. Curtains of flame
are no worse than the blankets
tacked above the glass. An empty mouth
no different from a full one,
in time. A hand just a structure,
no record of what it has reached out
for. Mirrors blacken with soot.
This is the house you grew up in. Or, this is the father's house
as a child, the first story blown away by a bomb.
This is a collection of all those words you thought
you knew. They touched you the way a leaf does
when you watch it fall all the way down to your foot.
You cannot hold it, but no matter: it is colorless
and dry. In a dream, wasps filled the mouth of the tree,
and when the singer sang, poured in barbed notes
from his mouth. Smoke gets in the hair like that,
fills the narrow space between torso and arm.
If the field catches, will the purple weeds explode tiny
satellites? Can you list the last five words
the person you thought you loved
said? You have one chance to chronicle
this burning. People file away in small groups, or alone.

Malinda Markham

IF A BLUE FLAME BUT NO FIGURE APPEARS

You could have had what you wanted. I would have
cupped my hands, let my nails grow
hard as shells to collect even
your voice. Take the offerings at the temple.
Gather the coins and press them cool
to your lids. Through them you will see
and have not seen me rightly. At night
when trees cover the moon
I wait by your window, my shape all
you could wish. During the day I sweep
with insect care. Nothing but the hum
of what might as well be wings. Stolen oil
from the temple a small price,
don't you think? My hair glistens
and even you cannot help but see.
Light tricks us like that, enters the field
between book and your eyes,
creeps between the door and reed mats
in your chamber. Light is hollow and sad.
It cups your face as I would
if you were not made of stone. You part me like water.
A blue flame is only a kind
of repetition, words swarming in the chest
and always and never enough.
Lamps whisper their burden into trees,
as do stars. Cry out at night,
I will melt to fill that darkness.
Eight miles I walk along this river and more.

Malinda Markham

HAVING OVERHEARD TALK OF THE FATES,
THE CLEAREST PATH IS SILENCE

Low voices carry on wind. One child will burst into luck.
The solstice-flower unfolds its red petals
all at once, over grass so sharp
a child can cut fingers on it. Voices only like clouds.
When you try to recall accurate words,
see that the pattern
has shifted. They talk not of children, but you.

No. They talk about baskets, tight-woven and clean.
One will fall off a boat and sink to the bottom,
gathering coins and small shipwrecked hands.
Bones collect like anything does:
reeds do not discern
one matter from the rest. Name this basket *Luck*.
Name it *Silent Mouth*, and keep yours
suitably still. The other holds fish,
the gaping tails and silken fins. It is only
a kind of grave, like the woman's arms
holding people who do not love her
after. Talk fills the room, almost smothers
small flames. Weeds gather in slim vases:
The need to protect does not soon go away.

Voices overlap, then extinguish into night.
Be careful of trees. *Be careful*, you whisper.
Overheard words must instantly
be forgotten. Your own life is simple, but enough.
In the next village, a fortunate boy
will marry unluck. You have seen her—
the hair feathers beneath feathers,
her eyes always reflect back. When lightning
strikes the old tree, she will crush
pungentlike herbs beneath it.
Processions wind through thin forest
in violent rain. *Upon fear of my death*,
you think. Under this slivered moon,
wet brides are beautiful above all.

To the spoken voices, say:
Flowers have no spines. You must not pierce
a spineless thing with wood.
Hear: *One basket is like the rest. You are no more secure.*
Without me, my wife is unsafe.
Lightning is quick, the tree almost as brilliant.
She wakes before dawn to start the cooking fire.
She holds but does not love me at all.
If you act, your next words
will puncture your throat like small bones.
She held me once (you say). I remember us both.

But walking so, you nearly touch the girl's arm.
If lightning cracks, you think, I will throw her aside.
Does lightning smell like sulfur in the air?
Does her hair smell like flowers
right after she bathes? And what kind?
Your wife is at home, enclosed in her body.
At your death, neighbors would sing and probably
she would weep. Herbs and sharp bones
cluster in the mind. The crook of the girl's arm
is a reed, the hand its small flower.
Pale grass under stars, when cut,
is your fragrance sharp as secret places, as fine?

JUST PAST THIS ROAD
LIVES A FIGURE IMPRISONED IN A TOWER

Each moment starts again, each blade of grass
Stands apart from the rest.
From close enough, it's hard to believe

The blade is not a continent. On the other side,
Small people build fires,
Press together in the cold. There are ways

To harbor warmth that almost make them
Sing. Perhaps language is simple:
There are no words to speak

About distance. People barely believe
It exists. Do you wake at night
Shuddering? Do you want

To shudder but sit very still instead?
At the window, night places cold palms
Over all the eyes of flowers.

There is nothing wrong
With this stillness, nothing broken
In what it uncovers and covers again.

This is breath: faces nearly forgotten:
Is air entering the body until even its bones
Barely exist. First the mouth

Disappears, then the throat
And warm lungs. What we do have: a clock
We can stop at times, not at will.

Your room is a ball I can break apart
And reassemble,
If you permit. A smaller hollow nests inside,

And inside the throat,
Another hollow still. This road
Measures my steps. From far away,

Leaves framing your window
Could be anything at all. Six thousand words,
Their order obscured. How many times

People set out to reach you.
Against this cold air, I can see your breath.
I cannot imagine your ribs.

From Minding the Darkness
Peter Dale Scott

OCTOBER 4, 1997

In Siam after the war
    when the Buddhist *sangha*
    had lost control of *education and culture*   *Sulak '92 4*

(says Sulak's book *Seeds of Peace*
    here on the library shelf
    my first night at the Villa Serbelloni)

the forces of Pridi   *Pridi Banomyong*
    who *wanted Siam to be democratic*   *Sulak '92 15*
    were ousted by Pibul   *Pibulsongkram*

whose racial vision for Thailand
    at the expense of non-Thais
    in alliance with Hitler

(*whose writings he had translated*)   *Sulak '92 157*
    Mussolini and Japan
    had led to Pibul's being tried

as a war criminal   *Sulak '92 16-19*
    and of course the Americans
    who during the Second World War

had been allied with Pridi
    preferred in the Cold War fifties
    to work with Pibul

just as in the Philippines
    the guerrillas who had fought the Japanese
    and turned in their names for veterans' benefits

125

were instead hunted down and murdered   *McClintock 97*
    CIA aid for Pibul
  was channeled through a front established

by a veteran of OSS and CIA   *Marshall Scott & Hunter 32, 64*
    with connections to the Miami mob   *Scott '72 210-12*
  thus helping to open up the world

to a flood of heroin through Thailand   *McCoy 168-173*
    while the mob in Manila
  helped to Westernize the Philippines

by its control of gambling   *Seagrave 161-64, 328-37*
    and later child prostitution
  carried on in the big hotels   *Seagrave 318-23*

Can we be surprised this happened
    when the mob was being protected
  both by Hoover in the FBI   *Gentry 531-32*

and Angleton in the CIA
    who *vetoed* a Justice Department investigation   *Scelso 168-69*
  and almost no one in the US seemed to care

at least in its universities
    When I wanted to pinpoint
  the center of the corruption

I did not point to the CIA
    who seemed to think they were doing their job
  or even the government

which has always been corrupt
    so much as to universities
  for having tolerated

what was called *political science*
    when it was known the American
  Political Science Association

was run for years by two men   *Evron Kirkpatrick, Max Kampelman*
    from a CIA-funded think-tank   *OPRI, Washington Post 3/7/67, A2*
And for what? That we could take Russia

out of the hands of the Communist Party
    and into the hands of the Russian mobs
the KGB (with western help)

outlasting the Soviet Union?
    With our mobs and secret police in cahoots
can it surprise anyone

when those who have spoken out for peace
    Jaurès Gandhi Robert Kennedy King
end up exiled or murdered

and almost no one in the *halls of truth*
    seeming to care?
Should we simply accept

in the spirit of Foucault
    that (as the court historian
Nebrija wrote in his dedication

to Queen Isabella of Spain)
    language is the instrument of empire?   *Rafael 23*
I ask these questions

not out of hopelessness
    but pondering my own role
and that of those I trusted

in today's *cunning of reason*   *Hegel '42 xx*
    When the Thai student
supporters of democracy were slaughtered

by the Army in 1976
    their teacher Sulak Sivaraksa
whose book *Questioning Development*

Peter Dale Scott

was the outcome of meetings
    at the villa Serbelloni   *Sulak '98 98*
and whose work for *conservation and peace*

had for years it now turns out
    been funded by the CIA   *Sulak '98 87*
came in as a scholar

for a year to UC Berkeley   *Sulak '98 149*
    (sponsored by Professor Phillips
whom other anthropologists accused

of having worked with the CIA
    but then the CIA helped so many
from Frantz Fanon to the American Quakers

thus even my first book)   *Schurmann Scott & Zelnik*
    where he quoted from the Suttas   *Sutras*
If people are mindful

using enlightenment as guidelines
    they can achieve the desirable society   *Sulak '92 110*
to support his own teaching

It is easy to hate our enemies
    who exploit us and pollute our atmosphere
But one must come to see

that there is no "other"
    It is greed hatred and delusion
that we need to overcome   *Sulak '92 116*

(*Buddhist Economics*
    which might have been called *Christian*
but then *no one would have read it*)   *Schumacher; Ellsberg 389*

The importance here
    is not whether Sulak's NGOs   *non-governmental organizations*
will outlast the Thai dictators

he himself felt his role
    at his *organization*
  on alternative development

had been a failure   *Sulak '98 156-57*
    it is that this critic
  from the other side of the world

whom I had never heard of till tonight
    has spoken not just my beliefs
  but for all of Wordsworth's

great family of poets   *Prelude 11.62*
    each with each connected   *Prelude 12.301-02*
  and not just poets

but the whole community of saints
    St. Francis Gandhi Weil
  collected by Dan's son Robert

along with Sulak's *friends*
    like Abdurrahman Wahid of Indonesia   *Sulak '98 158*
  leader of NU   *Nahdlatul Ulama*

the largest non-governmental Islamic
    organization in the world   *Ramage 45*
  who like myself   *Scott 7/30/98*

on the Internet
    a year from now
  striving for peace in post-Soeharto Indonesia

will speak out *strongly*
    against the violence
  experienced by Indonesia's

ethnic Chinese   *Reuter's 7/26/98; cf. Voice of America 6/18/98*

129

Peter Dale Scott

OCTOBER 10, 1997

Let others debate the canon!
    I who mostly escaped
a classical education

reading Ovid and Dante for myself
    heard them as counselors
to mistrust the constructed world

as in Isaiah's
    She that was full of justice
righteousness lodged in her—

but now murderers!   *Isaiah 1:21*
    or Virgil's rebuke of *frenzy*   *belli rabies et amor habendi*
of war and passion for gain   *Aen. 8.327*

or Augustine *what are states*
    when they lack justice
if not organized crime?   *latrocinia; Aug. City of God 4.4*

or in the early days
    when it was still lonely
to oppose the Vietnam War

there was John Adams *a nation*
    at *height of power*
never fails to loose

her Wisdom and Moderation   *Adams '62 4.158*
    to say nothing of Jesus
the prime talking-point of charlatans

and Grand Inquisitors
    For what are we profited
if we gain the whole world

and lose our own soul?   *Matthew 16:26*
    and his first community
the primitive church

who *had all things in common*   Acts 4:32
        One might have thought
    that with the passage of centuries

wisdom might be enthroned
        more and more securely
    but it is not so

the universities themselves
        are busy disenthroning
    what the past accepted

and publishers make fortunes
        from new books not old ones
    the concern here is not Voltaire

or Nietzsche's *we must efface*
        even the shadow of God
    but the deceit of Kinsey's

the scientist of the gall-wasp
        presenting his scientific study
    of sexual behavior

as if he were Galileo
        displacing the terrocentric myth
    in the name of sanity

It was not till much later
        we learned that Kinsey had died
    after masochistic excesses

or that he had participated
        in licentious parties
    with Hitler's convicted publicist

and *Nazi sympathizers*
        like the one who later became
    Marguerite Oswald's lover   *Lee 105, 437*

Peter Dale Scott

I remember Berkeley
     in the 1970s
   with Lenin so crudely demonized

by policemen and hypocrites
      we did not waste time considering
   if he had not in fact been wrong

so sharply to separate
     the necessities of today
   from the freedom promised tomorrow

the man to come
     parted as by a gulph
   from him who had been   *Prelude 11.59-60*

much as my idol Sartre
     (for whose sake I wandered lonely
   through the tourist night-life

of the Boulevard St. Germain)
     separated essence from existence
   and *en-soi* from *pour-soi*

in a search for innovation
     relegating policemen et al. to the status
   of servants of the Not

a split which in retrospect
     seems not totally unlike Kinsey's
   or even that imaginative voice

of Wordsworth   *Our destiny*
     is with infinitude—and only there   *Prelude 6.538.39*
   And though I wish compassion

for all of us struggling
     to stay partly sane
   was it not an error on the left

Peter Dale Scott

to mimic the establishment
    in separating politics from morals?
  What I remember

from Reagan's Washington
    in 1987
  (When a country is ill-governed

riches and honour
    are things to be ashamed of)   *Confucius, Analects 8.13.3*
  but never wrote about

was how the lackeys
    of North and his Administration
  elected by the Christian Right

numbed by brutalities of power
    found relaxation in orgies
  at private homes

which we in our left-wing center
    were able to confirm
  because one of our colleagues

participated also
    It was the usual
  Borgia sort of thing

that afflicts imperial wealth
    and generates reformations
  Many people were moral of course

I counted it a chief
    attraction of the *movement*
  to be working with them

but in a state where morality
    led you into opposition
  moralities became partial

Peter Dale Scott

the *Berkeley Barb* published
    along with photographs
  accounts of Kinseyesque orgies

among some of our local protesters
    that rivaled those on the Potomac
  it was easy to make mistakes

and there were good people
    who could inspire us
  (no one could have been more moral than Noam Chomsky!)

There has to be two of me!
    one part more and more alarmed
  sensing the logic of these words

quarrel with the illogic of life
    the wealth of reality
  to which we surrender ourselves

without prejudice
    showing *to what an extent*
  the differences between ways of life

have already lessened   *Auerbach '57 488*
    the other part noting with Flaubert
  the age's *manque*

de base théologique   *Auerbach '57 430*
    in the midst of which this poem
  is constrained to think back to

the single Way
    so many ancestors describe   *Acts 9:2; Conf. Ta Hsueh i;*
  our radical past   *Digha Nikaya 19.8*

the end nothing else
but to seek out the lost mind   *Mencius 6A:11.4*

Peter Dale Scott

To Fred Crews December 19, 1996

When I read of Russell's
    war to the knife
  between intellect and intuition

opposing Bergson who *thinks*
    the intellect a wicked imp
  and *loves instinct*   *Monk 235*

was I wrong Fred to think of you?
    And why did I so react
  to your demeaning of Yeats's *voice*

of the revolt of the soul
    against the intellect
  where I saw Yeats following Shelley   *Yeats '86 303; Murphy 373;*
                                          cf. Yeats '68 65-66

(the imagination
    has some way of lighting on the truth
  that the reason has not)   *Yeats '68 65*

but where you heard *a mere echo*
    of a far more confident voice
  Madame Blavatsky?   *Crews '96 26; cf. Murphy 372*

Though I had to approve
    your dislike of charlatans
  this struck me as a reduction

Once when discussing E.M. Forster
    you wrote that Adela in the cave
  (whose significance, you added

is apparently Freudian)   *Crews '62 160*
    glimpsed an *order of truth beyond*
  the field of her rational vision   *Crews '62 161*

*(*a depth you saw also in Hawthorne
    a more penetrating fiction
than any slice of life)   *Crews '66 263*

135

Peter Dale Scott

just as Russell admitted
      what he had learnt from Shelley   *Monk 34*
   two levels *one of science*

another terrifying subterranean
      which in some sense held more truth
   than the everyday view   *Monk 317*

bonding him to Conrad
      who had also lost his parents
   buried himself in books

both men sharing with Freud
      the ever-imminent danger
   of sinking into the madness

below the civilised crust   *Monk 320*
      both men pulling back like Marlow
   from the edge of the fire

at *The Heart of Darkness*
      where *one will find madness*   *Monk 317*
   (even you on your motorcycle

coming in at dawn
      over the icy roads
   across Mount Tamalpais

have in your own way tested
      the threshold of the invisible)   *Monk 317*
   after reading Karl Popper   *Crews '95 8*

(whose critique of the self-validating
      both of us agree with
   but who alienated me

by that campaign against Hegel
      he himself call a *war effort)*   *Cockett 82; MacGregor 32*
   pulled back from Freud

whom you now dismiss
    as *the most overrated figure*
in the history of science

who wrought immense harm   *Crews '95 298*
    though your language in dismissing
this *visionary artist*   *Crews '95 12*

who *stood to his patients' dreams*
    more as painter to his pigments
than as sleuth to his cigar ash   *Cioffi 110; Crews '95 11*

with his *seductively mythic alternative*
    to *the rational-empirical ethos*   *Crews '95 8*
returns my non-scientific mind

with *puzzlement as to why it impresses us*   *Cioffi 103, 105*
    to the ambivalence
of Wittgenstein's *Aesthetics*

a matter of 'a good simile'   *Cioffi 105*
    while my fear late last night
that I lacked madness

(*the ferocity that is needed*
    to redeem culture)   *Monk 353-54*
produced a vivid dream

of descent from Mount Royal
    down a rotting staircase
into a private estate

of eighteenth-century gardens   *Garsington⸮⸮*
    I had no business in
from which *both asleep and awake*   *Yeats '68 159, 423; Scott '91 5*

I somehow recovered
    what I was tempted wrongly to call
a *repressed memory*

that had somehow escaped
  my dredgings these sixteen years
 the undergraduate night

I alone in the basement
  of the McGill Union
 facing the arrival

of a woman no longer loved
  my Rhodes application late
 heard on the telephone

a landlord threatening to sue
  I who before then
 had occasionally heard voices

natter within me
  now listened to them
 screaming incomprehensibly

in a way which brought strangers
  to lift me off the floor
 my muscles unmanageable

and for the next four years
  I waited grimly
 for it to happen again

as it did at Oxford
  after I failed my degree
 only this time those who held me

were my roommates and friends
  the long fear mostly over
 I was left with the distinction

between those who think mostly in words
  and those who think images
 that cannot be put into words

Peter Dale Scott

they make themselves manifest   Wittgenstein 6.521; Monk 568
　　from the Buddha to Wittgenstein   *Majjhima Nikaya 592*
the flowing forms of mind

freed from all impulse
　　not out of itself   Yeats '68 75; Scott '91 5
Before the divisions

of the Irish troubles
　　had shattered Yeats's dreams
he had agreed with Shelley

for want of correspondence
　　with the imagination
The rich have become richer

the poor poorer
　　from an unmitigated exercise
of the calculating faculty   Shelley 1887 30-31; Yeats '68 68;
　　　　　　　　　　　　　Scott '91 4

(a passage so relevant
　　to our mental plight today
it is not in the Cambridge Edition)   cf. Shelley 1975 609

So Fred you are clearly right
　　to describe Joscelyn Godwin's
Theosophical Enlightenment

(which I confess once titillated me
　　for its tracing of Kabbalism
from the Sabbatian Samuel Falk

to the poetry of Blake)   Godwin 93-105, 131-36
　　as the work of an *occult partisan*   Crews '96 26
or to blame *Freud's incompetence*   Crews '95 40

as a source for today's
　　plague of false charges
from that *highly lucrative enterprise*

139

Peter Dale Scott

the recovered memory business   *Crews '95 242, 194*
        one cannot reduce your work
    as some friends from the '60s have done

to a *repudiation of the utopian*
            that began with Richard Nixon   *Zaretsky 67; Crews '95 292*
    from every point of view

(except perhaps that of the crayfish
        we plucked with twigs
    from a stream behind Big Sur

and dropped into sizzling butter)
        you are *a kind and gentle man*   *Begley 29; Crews '95 293*
    having somehow learned

more than either Russell or Yeats
        the habits of sanity
    which in a world ill-governed

are not always to be condemned)   *Milosz and Scott '68*
        I share your respect
    for *the rational-empirical ethos*   *Crews '95 8*

so what was it in myself
        that was roused against you?
    Indeed it is obvious

there is a *Yeats problem*   *Crews '96 29*
        when sotted by Blavatsky   *Bloom 70, 75, 410*
    as well as the hatreds

swirling round him in Ireland   *Bloom 318-24; Scott '91 9*
        Yeats obsessed with the *antithetical*   *Bloom 279, 318*
    and voicing the despair

and powerlessness we all must feel
        in a demonic century
    turned even on Shelley

140

whose *logical* efforts
    to satisfy desire   *Yeats '68 421*
Yeats blamed for the *Jacobin frenzies*   *Yeats '68 425*

of friends like Maud Gonne   *Bloom 307*
    saying now *we must not demand*
even the welfare of the human race   *Yeats '68 425*

so I have to examine
    what issue inside myself
made me challenge you

both applaud your exposure
    of Freud's pretensions to science
and also worry for truth

in a landscape torched
    by relentless demands
for *the needed evidence*   *Crews '98 xxiii*

which zealots like Popper
    have used to liberate us
from Hegel Marx

and moralists back to Plato   *Popper*
    You have praised Hawthorne
for his *more penetrating fiction*

in works that rested
    on the shared fantasy of mankind   *Crews '66 263*
encouraging me to ask

Could we not share Flaubert's fantasy
    mystical in the last analysis
but like all true mysticism

based upon reason and experience
    of a self-forgetful absorption
in the subjects of reality

Peter Dale Scott

which transforms them?   *Auerbach '57 429*
  or (in Yeats's and Shelley's words)
 seek to awaken

in all things that are
  a community
 with what we experience

within ourselves?   *Shelley '75 600; Yeats '68 69; Scott '91 5*
  And if not at least
 accept our twin destinies

in the *ordo saeclorum*
  the search for convergence
for a faith not offending

a reason that does not
  desecrate
our shared *deference*

to the unknown?   *Crews '62 163*

OCTOBER 9, 1997

Imagination!
  source of language!
 product of language!

enlarging not by yourself
  but as language escaping
 the rules of syntax

and prosody and aesthetics
  dialectically enlarges
from Virgil's strict similes of control

Neptune calming the ocean
  like an orator a crowd   *Aeneid 1.142-53*
 even Hades a place

142

of measured judgment
      to Ovid's *discors concordia*   *discordant harmony Met. 1.433*
   in which those too fixed

on order or even music
      Pentheus Orpheus
   are torn apart by the chthonic

forces they fail to respect   *Ovid Met. 3.712-33; 11.1-43*
      and those too devoted
   to what the young Keats called

the holiness of the Heart's affections   *Letters 11/22/17*
      Narcissus Medea
   suffered the terrible

retribution of what they wished
      And in the Dark Ages
   the image became a symbol

as the world retreated from cities
      and syntax became obscure
   Dido as wounded deer   *Aeneid 4.9*

panting among waterbrooks   *Psalm 42:1*
      or the cuckoo in springtime   *Scott '65*
   towards the love no reason knows

Whether one sees this
      as progress towards realism   *Auerbach '57 488*
   or towards surrealism   *Breton*

two innovations which have now
      like all before them
   both hardened into genres

the point is the maturation
      of language itself
   along with art and music

Peter Dale Scott

in fulfillment of some pattern
      not visible until much later
   sets the tasks in each age

for a Blake or Balzac
      or even in our own time
   language or computer poets

Poets Laureate rappers Hallmark poets
      all of them no matter what they say
   in their outward performance

still guided from within
      by something   what is it?
   not the Ich but the Ungenannt   *Unnamed*

Freud never imagined?
      our entropic society
   always diffusing writers

into a kind of ocean
      to the point where imagination
   by filling every cranny of the mind

with truth and its opposite—lies
      longing to lose *the gift of order*
   despoiling the self   *R. Howard xiii; Williamson 106*

has become a fetish
      in the Cult of Imagination
   self exfoliating to Self

as enlighenment to Enlightenment
      imagination to Imagination
   as *civilization progresses*

accumulating its pyramiding memories
      its mountain of statistics
   which is finally the Tower of Babel   *Williamson 140*

Peter Dale Scott

Imagination! I had believed you
  on the chosen authority
 of Dante Wordsworth and Shelley

as the strongest redress
  to the debasing influence
 of the calculating faculty   Shelley '87 30-31; Yeats '68 68

but whatever has moved
  me to write this poem
 (in that small aperture

between future and past)
  has pushed me to your limits
 your overgrowth

of proliferating foliage
  that to our detriment
 has obscured the trunk beneath

Thus if the older Keats (*the poetical*
  character has no self)   Letters 11/27/18
 anticipated Eliot

the progress of an artist
  is a continual extinction
 of personality   Eliot '51 17

(Borges *We are all one*
  our inconsequential minds
 are much alike)   Borges 269; Heaney 8

why then did Eliot
  who as much as anyone
 Milton or Keats himself

professed allegiance only to principles
  which he himself had espoused
 challenge the fetish

Peter Dale Scott

that *pursuit of self-knowledge*
    will come upon
  a self that is universal!   *Eliot '51 27*

(*the interior search*
    for the lost paradise
  in *imagination*   *the essential self*)   *Williamson 117*

lash out at the Inner Voice
    which breathes the eternal message
  of vanity fear and lust!   *Eliot '51 27*

and shock his former friends
    with ridiculous unsustainable
  pretensions to royalism?   *Scott '94 69-70*

Beneath these irrelevancies
    the challenge to Self
  with the insistence

that the poet must develop
    the consciousness of the past   *Eliot '51 17*
  giving depth to ecology

economics politics
    and of course religion
  I feel the tug of two forces

the yang of experiment
    (was not Dahmer's imagination
  of eating his sexual victims

fed first from literature?)
    the yin of intuitive retreat
  the only peace I know of

with the imagination
    when *the light of sense goes out*   *Prelude 6.534-35*
  (an expansion

which without diligence
      relaxes to dissipation)
   is in that other society

we all are part of
      the dead
   speaking through us

(when we hear them clearly
      in our moments of loss)
   of what they have seen already

for the sake of the future
      since we have been
   a conversation

transmuting *the world into word*   *Heidegger 279*
      all of us fashioned
   by something   what is it?

from the shards of shattered genres

Bill Gaddis, 1987
Julian Schnabel
Oil, plates and bondo on wood, 60 x 48 inches
Photograph by Phillips/Schwab

William Gaddis Tribute

A NOTE OF GRATITUDE
Sarah Gaddis

THE FOLLOWING TRIBUTES honoring my father, William Gaddis, were read on May 6, 1999 at the American Academy of Arts & Letters, on the same stage where he won his first National Book Award in 1976. My brother Matthew and I decided to hold the tribute there so that as many people could attend as possible, and because our father would have wanted it; he would have wanted the memory of that night to be with us. When we approached each of the speakers about writing and reading a tribute, I was comforted when they accepted—but had no idea that besides being grateful for their words, I would feel such joy as I listened. I regret not having had the wherewithal to find Mary Caponegro and ask her to speak. Mary was a student of my father's and he spoke of her highly, and he didn't do that often. I was glad to meet her finally and to be able to tell her that. Over two hundred people attended the tribute. Gaddis' college friends, his friends from the Village days, friends and writers he knew at every point in his life, were there. The speakers and guests came from as far away as Key West and California and Europe. One man who came up and introduced himself was a stranger to me, younger than most of the people there and I couldn't imagine what connection he'd had to my father. It turned out he was there to represent the Harvard Lampoon. That would have pleased WG.

*   *   *

Not a man after glory, but respect, William Gaddis was greatly moved by loyalty shown him in friendship, which he reciprocated absolutely. He liked to dismiss sentimentality, yet what deep pleasure he got from reflecting about people who were important in his life. A loner, he was hard on himself for his mistakes and never took for granted his good fortune. "Oh, I count my blessings," he often said, about family, health and friends.

Reflecting aloud about someone he liked immensely, Gaddis

149

would shake his head, utter a few words and smile just a bit. He did so when speaking of Louis Auchincloss, for whom he had warm feelings and the highest regard. They got to know each other while traveling in Russia, and through the years they developed a friendship suited to men of a certain reserve. The law library that sits in WG's studio was given to him by Mr. Auchincloss while he was writing *A Frolic of His Own*. Louis Auchincloss paid tribute to WG back in 1987 in his piece "Recognizing Gaddis," a profile which appeared in the *New York Times Magazine*. At the Academy on May 6 Auchincloss drew from that eloquent article, and especially those who could not attend should please locate it (available both on the New York Times website and through Lexus Nexus search engine): Gaddis was overwhelmed when the piece came out, as it attests to both an understanding of his work and an insight into the man. (It also includes the account of Gaddis' reaction to Allen Ginsberg's harmonium playing in Russia.)

Gaddis had known Rust Hills and Joy Williams over the years (decades!) and then they found each other again, down in Key West. He admired Joy's work ("You will see how good she is in *The Little Winter*," he wrote to me long ago), and at the tribute she brought the house down with her descriptions of "Mr. Gaddis" and his particular use of the language, and with her society-wise interpretation as she read a passage from *Frolic*.

"Julian would be doing what he does no matter what," WG was always quick to point out when talking about Julian Schnabel and his commitment to his work. Otherwise he was fond of Julian because "He just gets so excited about things!" Last summer when we visited Julian in Montauk my father was quite frail. Julian wanted to carry him up to the top floor so that he could take in the view. With his enthusiasm and his expansiveness he was a good friend to WG. At the tribute Julian read from *The Recognitions*, which inspired his Recognitions series paintings.

"Penny. How does he do it? Just look at him, he's like a boy. It isn't fair." So said Gaddis at his old friend D. A. Pennebaker's birthday party a few years ago. After knowing Penny for over forty years he still spoke of him—of his work and his energy—with amazement. At the tribute Pennebaker described the wild atmosphere of their first encounter, and told the story of "The Cord," which I knew from my father's side, through letters that expressed the same hectic abandon.

William Gass was important to Gaddis, was one of the people he wanted to talk to at the last. He held Gass in the highest esteem for his work, and no other writer made him feel so understood. Gass's emphatic, brilliant words at the tribute rang out with conviction and confidence as he went on with his indefatiguable defense of the language, talked about WG's work and his own, and told hilarious anecdotes around their shared post-modernist title & identities.

* * *

Matthew and I would like to again thank Louis Auchincloss in his capacity as president of the American Academy of Arts and Letters, and Director Virginia Dajant and the staff, for opening the doors of the Academy for our tribute. We are grateful to friends who traveled such distances and are indebted to Carol Phillips, Benji Swett and Jamie Ross for helping us to realize what was an extraordinary event.

‿❧

MEMORIES OF MASTER GADDIS
William H. *Gass*

IN 1955, A WRITER with no record, no resources, and few connections, published a novel called *The Recognitions*. Great novels are never merely "about" something, but certainly one theme of this unexpected beast of a book was counterfeiting—forging, faking, aping, impersonating, conning, duping, misleading, pretending, lying, misrepresenting, spinning, dreaming—a continuum which travels almost perversely from the cheap knock-off to the creation, by the imagination, of the ineffably real. Its reviewers didn't read *The Recognitions*, but they hated it anyway; verifying, by means of their own vilification, the novel's vision of America as a land where the flim-flam flag waves . . . from "me" to shining "me" . . .

While its author, who had scarcely surfaced, sank out of sight once more, the few who loved the book circled protectively about it. Critics said we were a cult, as if, at midnight, we gathered in abandoned barns to tear out pages of Herman Wouk, while chanting from *The Recognitions* especially loved lines like "Merry Christmas! the man threatened," a sentiment which belongs alongside Ring Lardner's treasured "Shut up! he explained." There were bits of poetry also worth memorizing, but it was not true that we recited them in dark stalls. I remember, particularly, sweet Norah Winebiscuit:

Pride drew her garments up, and swathed her face
In lineaments incapable of disgrace.
Slipped then away, her face bedewed with do,
Beyond the glass, and knowing all, she knew
That the immortals have their ashcans too.

So in the absence of the author, in the absence of the audience, we, the Faithful, did create an icon, and make the sudden appearance of this skull-busting, heart-breaking book—its sordid reception, the ensuing silence—into an emblematic *cause celebre;* because what *The Recognitions* proved was that great ambitions were still possible, they were not just instances of romantic futility; that the real, the original, the genuine work of art could be accomplished; that the novel was not dead, as many liked to think, but had only taken a brief nap, a short snooze; that the book's bleak outlook could be shared with something like a wry smile rather than the suicidal funk the sad seaminess of its world-view suggested.

The novel's motto became our motto: no counterfeits, no fakes, no imitations, no compromise.

And twenty years appeared to pass. We began to fear that solicitude was scarcely enough to sustain such a work forever. Then, quite coincidentally (for coincidence is the real ruler of all things), I was asked to be a judge for the National Book Award during the very year in which *JR*, William Gaddis's second novel, would appear. Mary McCarthy, also on the jury, simply shoved the third judge (a worn-out hack reviewer) into the corner as you would an unnecessary chair, and the Award went to Junior, as she liked to call it. This did not mean the war was won. The war against mediocrity is never ending. Mediocrity is like the salt mill of fable, it keeps on turning, and a sea of brains goes brackish. For decades, Gaddis had endured our culture's obdurate resistance to excellence, but now he would have to endure more. George Steiner pronounced *JR* "unreadable," and Alfred Kazin, bless his bourgeois heart, wrote that it was "like nothing else around, and is not a masterpiece." Well, he was half right. It was like nothing else around.

JR is about that great depersonalizer, money, and is written in speech scraps, confettilike wiggles of brightly colored cliché. As a medium, it would appear to be as unpromising as might be imagined. And the reader has to ride in the parade and organize all that fluttering that's come down from on high. *JR* takes time. *JR* takes patience. *JR* takes faith. But unlike other faiths, it does not put off salvation until some weekend after all who have lived are dead and only their bones dance; it is immediately and continuously redeeming.

Reading it I could see Gaddis with his scissors slicing another instance of inanity and foolishness from the news, lining up this imbecility above that one, or wondering whether this jackass should sit over here nearby still another numbskull. The world convicted itself of lunacy almost daily, and Gaddis had his chuckle and his scissors ready for it.

As time goes by, the mysterious Mister Gaddis is actually seen in public, is elected to the Academy, earns a MacArthur, writes a book in less than twenty years. He must be slipping. *Carpenter's Gothic*, the briefer, more accessible novel, breaks the cult's hold on his appreciation and gives him a larger audience. This is certainly true in Europe, especially in Germany, where *Carpenter's Gothic* and *A Frolic of His Own* have been acclaimed. Reviewers read no better than they ever did, but they are respectful now. Damn, did we, the faithful, want him to have this kind of approval?

When *A Frolic of His Own* appeared, and after the Lannan Foundation awarded William Gaddis their lifetime achievement award, those earlier works quietly became classics, as if they had never been thunderclaps, as if they had always been applauded, as if his artistry, his stature, had never been in doubt, as if he had never exposed America as the land of the fraudulently free, as he was doing once again—this land of the litigatious—of the sue.er and the sue.ee—in a depiction so farcically funny, so absurdly interconnected, so bottomlessly baroque, that it reads not like something scissored from the *New York Times* but bits rescued from a *National Inquirer* that's come apart in the rain.

Given their material, and each book's point, these novels ought to be gloomy and sour, but they manage to achieve quite the opposite effect. I have found myself momentarily happy that Man has been such a mean and selfish small-time huckster, because he has thereby furnished William Gaddis such a satisfying target.

His death did not catch me altogether by surprise. Sarah Gaddis had reached my answering machine with the message that Gaddis was in the hospital, that he was being brought home soon (a disheartening phrase), that he wanted to talk to me. She gave me two numbers: the hospital where he would be no longer by the time I rang; and another, presumably "home," where he wouldn't be either. That second number was a wildly wrong one. A voice had been misheard or misconstrued. Perfect. If Gaddis could still chuckle the chuckle he had perfected, he'd chuckle—this artist of missed, of broken, of imperfectly made connections.

"Number" was one of Gaddis's tic words too. He would say he had someone's number, or that so-and-so had done a number on him, or that another's number had come up, or that a lovely young woman, just observed, was quite a number. He allowed these mostly faded uses to place him, to tell us when he had been young and with the crowd, and to say he wasn't ashamed that a part of him was still of that time and that place.

Chuckle he surely would, too, if he were able to see that on the back of his *New York Times* obituary, there was a list of mutual funds and their performance. Remember how *JR* opens: "—Money . . .? in a voice that rustled." "Paper, yes."

Opening the *Times*, I half expected to read of my own demise. Our names—Gaddis and mine—were so frequently confused. The first time was during the babble of voices that make up cocktail parties, and provide for the participants decent cover. At the awards ceremony for *JR* I at last met Gaddis. In the din of artificial levity and the crush of mostly insincere congratulations, I was mistaken for him so many times that evening I finally began to accept sweet nothings on his behalf with a benign smile and a modest nod.

This confusion could not always be put down to static and a bad connection, because, later, the *New York Times* credited me with the authorship of *Carpenter's Gothic*, and *Books in Print*, confusing my "Introduction" with the text, listed me as the author of *The Recognitions*. I could enjoy these mistakes, since Gaddis seemed equally amused, but I couldn't help notice that no one mistook Gaddis for Gass, only Gass for Gaddis.

There was no other place from which a mix-up might emerge because if I was shabby, shaggy and paunchy, Gaddis was dapper and thin, even a bit gaunt on his gray days, a face from which good looks had gone but only after a long stay. He was quiet, and though opinionated, did not feel the need to advertise or argue or orate, whereas I (at the same age Hercules had throttled a serpent in his crib) was lecturing my parents on the art of bringing up baby.

We saw one another on the rare and brief visits I made to New York, at this or that occasion of award, sharing an LA earthquake once; or, by odd chance, on trips we took abroad together: to the Soviet Union, in Cologne. Offered a second vodka, Gaddis would give me a gleeful roguish look: we're on a junk-ket . . . junk-ket . . . a term reserved for pointless trips by politicians on padded expense accounts. In Leningrad, forced by our hosts to follow Rashkolnikov's footsteps up and down a dark and bitterly cold stairwell while being read to from *Crime and Punishment,* Gaddis and Gass heard themselves muttering in concert: but it's fiction, it's fiction. Then walking by a bookstore window in Germany and seeing there as large as life, Gaddis pictured on a Key West porch, accompanied by the announcement, formerly appropriate only for God: Gaddis kommt. Best of all, though, was the moment, with Matthew, in Cologne, after riding through the dark in a limolike car to Gaddis's great German celebration, when Gaddis slowly emerged into a starfall of flash bulbs worthy of the Academy Awards, the popping of a hundred corks. It was so impressive that I said, to cover my glee: I must be riding with Jimmy Stewart, and Gaddis replied, to cover his: William Holden, I think. It was a wonderful evening, fully worthy of him, which he nevertheless had to go to Germany to enjoy.

When the bad news came, that his number was up, I was able to take it. I had seen him sitting in a window a world away, so I knew: Gaddis didn't went. He kommt.

⁂

MR. GADDIS
Joy Williams

I ALWAYS CALLED Mr. Gaddis, well, Mr. Gaddis. I was in awe of him of course, as are so many of his readers. Even when we had supper together or commented on the news together or sat in old Adirondack chairs looking at ducks in the water together or looked up at the starry night bestowing its blessings on silly Key West together, I called him Mr. Gaddis. Through the years—the '70s, the '80s, the '90s—decades when he was creating his remarkable, inimitable books, *JR, Carpenter's Gothic, A Frolic of His Own*—during our infrequent but (to me) mesmerizing reunions, he became more and more unequivocally, monumentally Mr. Gaddis. Every time I learned something or read something or understood something anew or differently, I thought—Mr. Gaddis would know that and know it in about seven ways. I had long since forgiven him for what he did on page 51 of *The Recognitions* when the poor innocent, the Barbary Ape, Heracles, who lived in the carriage house and rang sleigh bells when he wanted company, who danced and sang and was somewhat mawkishly attached to his pet rabbit, was brutally sacrificed by the

Rev. Gwyon in a desperate pagan effort to save his son, Wyatt. Heracles died so that Art might live, after all, or in any Art as Resembler, Art in all its demiurgical complexity and falsehood and yearning. And of course the Rev. was nuts, miscomprehending everything and being quite terminally miscomprehended, his very ashes being mistaken for oatmeal and baked into a bread. And even more of course, of course, Mr. Gaddis had made the whole thing up— the whole massive, towering, difficult, preposterous masterpiece that was *The Recognitions.*

His work was formidable but he was not in the least forbidding. For all his complexity and erudition and sophistication, Mr. Gaddis was fun. (I mentioned this to someone once, someone who was acquainted with him and knew his work earnestly and well, and the man looked at me as though I were mad. William Gaddis was a genius. Geniuses are not *fun.*) But he *was* fun. He was mordant and sardonic and ever alert to the preposterousness of all human endeavor. I loved his laugh. Heh heh heh. It was diabolical, cheerily diabolical. No folly or complacency or stupidity or absurdity surprised or escaped him—he was amused at everything America and the American way of life could throw at him, at all of us. He seemed to have absorbed our babbling, incoherent, greedy, bewildered society whole—its feckless striving and inconsequentiality—and by some gleeful alchemy returned the chaos, the cacophony, to us as literature, great literature. He really was an alchemist, a particularly wily and impassioned and irreverent one. Working with the devalued words and wants of our time he made novels that are demanding, irresistible, exaggerated and true. They are great glittering avalanches of novels thundering down on our unsheltered heads. They dazzle—with their remarkable, recognizable world of anti-meaning. From the crush of anti-meaning comes uneasy revelation. From the mad chorus of voices comes an art that burns with a pure, very *un*reassuring light.

Mr. Gaddis relished the humble story of the Thermos bottle. You put something cold in it and it keeps it cold. You put something hot in it and it keeps it hot. But how do it *know?¿?* Heh heh heh. How on earth did Mr. Gaddis know? How did he know so much?? How did he create those great avalanches of novels, those whirlwinds. How did he do it? How did he sustain their manic power, their frantic self-generating pace? Oh, the frolicking nerve of it all. The energy. He was an intellectual, brimming with integrity and dark humor. He was quintessentially an American writer but he was not quite like an

156

American writer—there was a certain other *manner* he had—as a wizard might, an outraged wizard, elegant, most stylish, with a high moral sense and an eye for the scam at the heart of the matter.

There was a prayer that my father liked to offer in church. It began . . . *Oh thou who standest within the shadow from whence our dreams arise, move us to mightier dreaming* . . . Mr. Gaddis was moved to a mightiness of dreaming, of creation. If the God we praise notes every sparrow's fall He is nicely balanced by Mr. Gaddis firmly drawing our attention to the lack of significance—to say nothing of the questionable probability—of selfsame. One returns to his works again and again—not to be refreshed and renewed—those are simpler gifts more easily provided by others—but to be challenged, to be troubled, to be torn from our mind's pallid dreaming and be swept into life—and art's—perturbing eye.

I wish he were here today, his lean keen face assessing us, here today to hear what a wonderful writer he is. How true he always was to his great design. A real artist, audacious. A wonderful writer.

ൿ

REMEMBERING GADDIS
D. A. *Pennebaker*

At the memorial tribute to William Gaddis at the National Academy of Arts and Letters, several people were asked to say something about him. I was one of those people, and this is my recollection of what I may have said. As I spoke without notes . . . a cinema vérité reminiscence that I'm having trouble remembering at all. I'm also having trouble getting it down in writing. "That impressionistic drizzle may work for you filmmakers," Willie once reminded me, "but writing is different."

I KNEW GADDIS for quite a while before I met him. I had come to New York with my brand new GI-Bill engineering degree to look for a job. I also had a lead on a basement apartment in the Village . . . on Horatio Street, a street I knew about because somebody in one of John O'Hara's books had lived there. An old friend, Barbara Hale, had introduced me to Douglas Wood, whose ex-roommate, a friend of his at Harvard, had been expelled for drunkenness the day before graduation and had moved into Horatio for a while to regroup and then

157

disappeared. This was my first prescience of William Gaddis, whom I had yet to meet but whose image haunted that apartment as long as I lived in it. There was one room with two couches and boxes everywhere full of jazz records . . . old 78s. Douglas and I each owned hundreds maybe thousands of them collected throughout our undergraduate lives and we played them night after night until either the neighbors or the police shut us down. I had gotten an engineering job and was making enough money to buy an amplifier and a good turntable. Sitting around listening to records and cooking delicatessen food seemed like a perfect arrangement. But the ghost of Gaddis kept popping up. In the bathroom, I noticed an aging newspaper headline nailed over the door: "Innocent little Switzerland; the country the bombers missed." "Gaddis," said Douglas. Messages were everywhere. Bits of newspapers stuck up all around the apartment, endorsed with despairing comments.

One day, he simply left, Douglas told me. Drove off to Mexico with his friend Bill Davison in a convertible Auburn. I knew about Auburns. My father worshipped them. A collector's car. I doubt that there were more than a hundred in the world. This jewel actually belonged to Davison's father, and their plan was to drive the car to Mexico and sell it. Unfortunately, it was so battered by the time they got there that it was abandoned and never seen again. He must have come back after Mexico as there was a 100-peso note stuck to the ceiling with a hunting knife. There was also a symmetrically distorted car fender hanging on one wall (certainly not from the Auburn), and a large folder filled with typewritten pages that had been thrown into the airshaft, along with disclaimers from *The New Yorker.* Of the several stories, which seemed to have been rejected, I recall one about a couple who wake up one Sunday to find New York City completely deserted and no sign of why. They wander about the empty streets. I can't remember what they did eventually. There was also a story about a leather-garbed motorcyclist who wore his jacket backwards. He has an accident and a passerby notices that his head is facing the wrong way and straightens it. On the wall over where I slept was scribbled in a meticulous handwriting a bit of poetry that I could only see lying on my pillow: "i've come to ask you if there isn't a new moon outside your window . . . saying if that's all, just if. . . ." A few years later, a book of poems by e. e. cummings fell open and there it was waiting for me.

One day, after coming home from work, I discovered three strangers sitting around drinking beer. Gaddis I knew right off. With his wry hard-boned cowboy face, he was the Yankee incarnate. Eldred Mowrey, an ominous accomplice, sat staring at the floor, while Bill Davison, of the Auburn caper, sat on the hearth with a hammer hitting .22 bullets and sending bits of lead cracking about the room. We all went out to the corner bar, the old El Faro, for dinner, where sitting across the table from the three desperadoes I had the uneasy feeling my life was about to change, and not necessarily for the better. That night there was boisterous excitement at the corner brothel and a number of heavy pillows were thrown out on the street from the upper windows. We carried them all back to the apartment where they remained till the day I moved out.

Gaddis hung around for a while. He seemed to have an endless supply of Italian girlfriends with whom he stayed nightly, bringing them over for meals and listening to records or meeting at Nick's where there was always live music. It was holiday time and, buoyed up by the atmosphere of comraderie I quit my engineering job on Christmas Eve and became a drop-out. It never occurred to me that I had taken a decisive step, or that I was now on a road from which there is no turning, but Gaddis understood right away, and always held me accountable. I think it was his macabre sense of humor, and his outrageous view of everything around him that finally set my own life into motion. By the time he left for Paris to finish *The Recognitions*, I was quite unemployable. But by the end of that year Douglas and I had both moved out of Horatio Street, gotten married, and moved on. And later when Willie was married and lived in Massapequa, he and Pat drove in for feasts and poker games that carried long into the night.

All of our lives began to untangle. Ormond and Max went off to make a movie. Sherry went off to Spain to finish his book. I had some children to raise and took a temporary writing job at an agency up the block from where Gaddis was working at Pfizer. We would meet sometimes and review our lives. His job was writing speeches for the big wheels there and stories of corporate disorder would regale our expense account lunches.

And there were the shoes. Two pairs of English Peel shoes in perfect condition found at an East Hampton thrift shop one rainy afternoon. I had never seen a Peel shoe, only heard about them. But I knew right away that these were the real things. Genuine, but alas too small. In fact, I could scarcely get my toes into them so I kept them around to brighten up my life. One day Willie saw them and said with his mildest and most seductive snicker, "Let's see those rascals." I knew even as he started to put them on that it was all over. Of course they were an exact fit. "Karma," he remarked and I never thought of him again without seeing him in those beautiful shoes.

When Douglas died, of mysterious causes one Christmas day, his records were donated to Rutgers where they will never again outrage Horatio Street neighbors living on an airshaft. I still have mine, and I play them once in a while, but never the way we used to. And when I listen to them I have a fleeting memory of Horatio and the years I lived there. The names of those friends and companions read like poetry in my mind: Ormond Dekay, Douglas Wood, Max Furlaud, Barbara Hale, John Sherry, Dick Wheatland, Bernie Winebaum, and the dark-haired Ariel from upstairs, my Horatio Street love and, of course, Willie who pointed out the way and helped me move on.

Four Cornell Boxes
Rosmarie Waldrop

ENIGMA BOX

Am I caught in the stare of a Medici Prince or do I hold him in the crosshairs?[1] I myself have always been quietly alert. In my dream I stood both at the stern and struggled under water, but a gun is another story. Don't step on the shards, she cries, not with bare feet, so frightening the smart missiles, the limits of time and space, the implicational character of mathematical demonstration.

Marbles, cordial glasses, soap bubbles reflect the sensual world, while around my navel there is concentrated a circular[2] red rash. I am extremely interested in failure. The beginning of art lies next to the body, transitive fissure, with high waves immediately behind. Sun, sea, severance, and people in the street, she cries, what deviance from curved diameter and straightest line.

The intimate scale of childhood also attracts hourglass, clay pipe, and intelligent collaborators. Others may prefer columns of a smaller diameter,[3] but a Mediterranean garden surrounds my Northern mind. I feel her tiny wet tongue licking my finger. The ocean, she cries, glare, wind, salt, scattered islands, limited income, it's not encounters in cabins, but chains of logical relations that compel proof.

Most remarkable, the presence of the egg. In a sea so calm not the slightest tremor suggested the tides of sexual impulse threatening the individual. The fact that we dream night after night surpasses the most heated fantasies. What lavish, wasteful refraction of light, she cries, deserted planets, desperate obsessions, do I have to invent everything all over, and without auxiliary concepts like the curvature[4] of a surface?

[1] to define with accuracy, a story on shards
[2] perfect, *obs.*, unease
[3] through the center, and you must feed
[4] the invisible if it exists across my eye

161

Rosmarie Waldrop

ICE BOX

He is fascinated by the parallel seams in the ship's sails, the threads of the web. But I am not some kind of psychic casualty, I simply want to please.[1] You know, in the winter of 1835, in Russia, Marie Taglioni's carriage was halted by a highwayman? A barely perceptible, she sighs, an uncertain, and how he approached with bare feet along a line of perspective, without being able to, without touching—and yet we stay on the surface and do not measure the *real diameter* through the inner parts.

If he dreams of a wooden ball with a long needle sticking through it no one in America knows more coldly accurate. The whiteness of the ship is everywhere, a short-time slice against tidal connotations. The enchanting creature was commanded to dance for this audience of one upon a panther's skin spread over the snow. Intimate turn, the unmarried moon, she signs, so foreign, stunned senses, I panic, take flight as if the third dimension alone could tell crooked from straight.

While fervently admiring healthier possibilities, I take my florid face out of the menu and feel my armpits growing dry. What is the relation between the large particles we call elephants,[2] and the extremely small ones we call molecules[3] or fading passage? This is the counsel of despair, snow between stars. And years later, she sighs, a disappointed smile, our eyes for a, as if his double, the feeling of it gone, and the ratio changed between circumference and diameter.

He had a special star-shaped box made the more menacing. I resented this and rearranged the napkin in my lap. The motivation of biological mechanism[4] falls short of the Puritan plan. Severely ship-shape she placed a piece of ice among her jewels. First thought on waking, she sighs, dust whirling in slant light, the excessive whispers, the flight of time, but the curvature of space is the more flagrant structure.

[1] the light of other days
[2] elect: electrons, shimmering relation
[3] feel deeply and a hint of atmosphere on sphere
[4] atoms tropical, our fading passing

Rosmarie Waldrop

JACK IN THE BOX

—In memory of John Hawkes

The enemies of the novel are plot, character, setting and theme, you said, but the marquise still goes out at five, and at the stern where we were standing together but separated, it was impossible to hear the engines of the ship. The alternatives of free[1] will and causal determination do not exclude each other, though problems arise if we look for truth where definitions are needed. I heard the sudden hiss of urine. Fist through glass, you said, her legs straddling the railing, underclothes ravaged from an invisible clothesline, pollen, hollows of the body, such tension.

Everything is dangerous, you said, everything tentative, nothing certain, life jackets engulfed by crosscurrents, the thrashing of the great blades just below us and innocence in extremis. There would be contradiction only if a man could see through himself,[2] which is as impossible as knowing if a measuring rod retains its length when taken to another planet. Suppose instead we enter a period of midriffs, of second skins. Ja-Ja-Ja, you said quickly, the eye, bodily, the despotism of the uterine, odorous, earthen, vulval, convolvaceous, saline, mutable, seductive.

Can you rivet your eyes on the close-by,[3] we asked, and yet turn them toward hemispheric distances, can you crowd a spare sentence with absence and spare it? The question whether causality applies to actions of your own will is a travesty as pure and dark as a blackened negative. It's dreadful, dreadful no one has yet seen a wave-length. Of speech or suffocation, you said, white cadences, cold fire, hair like a dense furry tongue, natural lace, beetle leg, scar, a field of blood.

The enemy of pleasure, you said, is the curve of probability and flat exit. And so science must acknowledge singing in the wake of pubic darkness. A different geometry would obtain if we had rigid bodies. No turning back of time, you[4] said, unbearable sunlight, gunmetal ocean, Irish eye, glass splinters, a dream of flying and falling, a deep leap into, while the rest of us stand here, stabbed with sorrow.

[1]Cf. fall, hold, lance, wheeling, dom, for all
[2]and smoke five Dutch cigars
[3]a single fly, buzzing

[4]knife, daw, rabbit, straws, o'-lantern, in the pulpit, in the box

Rosmarie Waldrop

CINDER BOX

Virtuoso of fragments, master of absences.[1] Was she about to smile or replace the glass slipper with the notion of the variable? No sharp line of demarcation[2] between organism and environment because blood in the shoe. Warning cry, raven, more in my head, lunar eclipse, she cries, not stored in the brain but spread throughout the body, rewind of nightmare to single out the actual kingdom among possible untitled.

The variable demands that we think both the stable and unstable, the invariant within the variation. Her lashes, like the physical sensation of the I. Do not assume the a-logical core of the world is a pumpkin at midnight or stepmother. His look sharp like a camera, barely blinking, she cries, were there cinders in the cellar, were there mountains, other daughters, was it possible to measure the space in which we do not understand.

A spiraling watch spring, the fullness of time,[3] knots, neighborhoods, snug fit. He should not have revealed his loneliness, distaste for travel, ambiguous feeling toward women or the intense activity within the atom on which its mass and other prophecies depend. Stop muttering in Italian, she cries, images stored in my head, doors not properly balanced, it all always vanishes, as if to prove I have not looked, just taken pictures. With due respect to losses (slippers) we must return to the slot machine.

Is the prince's ritual magic or the tacit reign of the tactile? A saxophone barking in the distance, the stable measure of the foot replaced by seven-league-boots. Fur-lined. Utilitarian delusions,[4] she cries, unusual effects, moss and oak leaves by the Roman temple, nest of nymphs and swimming moon, is it meaningful to assert geometrical diffidence?

[1]raven more
[2]too vast too barely blinking

[3]possibly untitled
[4]examples of

Design for a Footbridge
Frank O. Gehry and Richard Serra

One of the most familiar landmarks on the south bank of London's River Thames is the disused Bankside power station, with its distinctive single chimney. Radically transformed, this building is about to re-emerge as the new Tate Gallery of Modern Art. Though situated just across the river from another important landmark, St. Paul's Cathedral, there is no direct way for a pedestrian to cross over to reach this new museum, or the Globe Theater next door, without undertaking a considerable detour to one of the main bridges.

With the conversion of Bankside well under way, an international competition was launched in 1996 for the design of a local footbridge which would connect the two banks of the river, forming an axis between these two distinctive buildings. One of the most poetic and open-ended solutions was the result of a collaboration between architect Frank Gehry and sculptor Richard Serra. *Conjunctions* is pleased to publish, for the first time anywhere, some of their preparatory drawings, and photographs of the final model that accompanied their proposal. Within their introductory notes they wrote:

"We hope to create a form whose reading will extend the realm of the imagination and whose matrix-like structure will function as an infinite cipher. Metaphorical transformations of the bridge into an oar, a stem, a stringed instrument, a reptile, an insect, a ship, even the Concorde, can easily enter into the experience. . . . Having the bridge end in a large-scale floating plaza facing the Tate will hopefully promote unforeseeable cultural and public events of all kinds. It can function as a balcony from which to view open-air theatrical and musical performances in the landscape in front of the Tate or, vice versa, can serve as an elevated stage with the audience assembled in the garden below. . . . The function of the bridge as a mere connector ought to be just one of many functions."

It is London's loss that this footbridge was not selected as the winning entry in the competition.

— *Anthony McCall*

Frank O. Gehry and Richard Serra

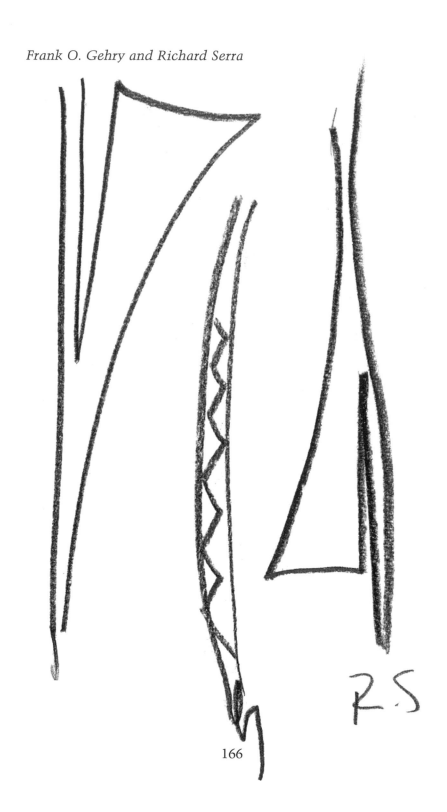

166

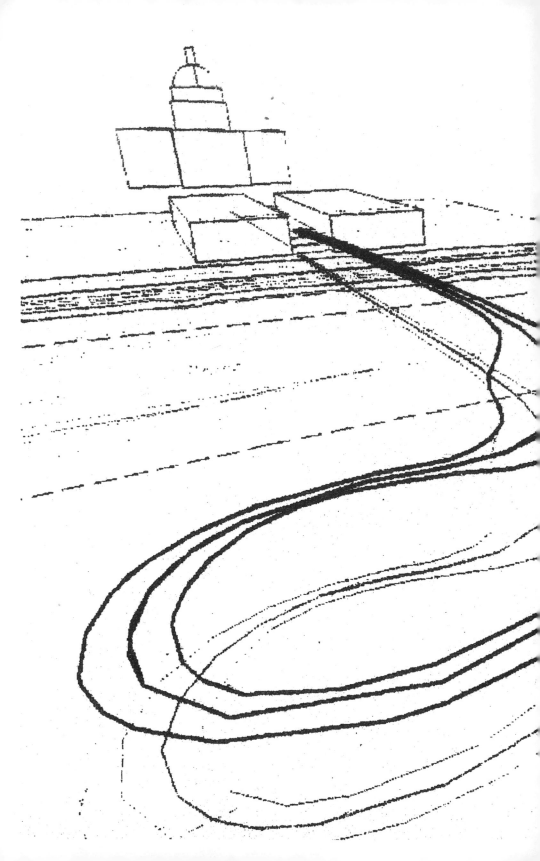

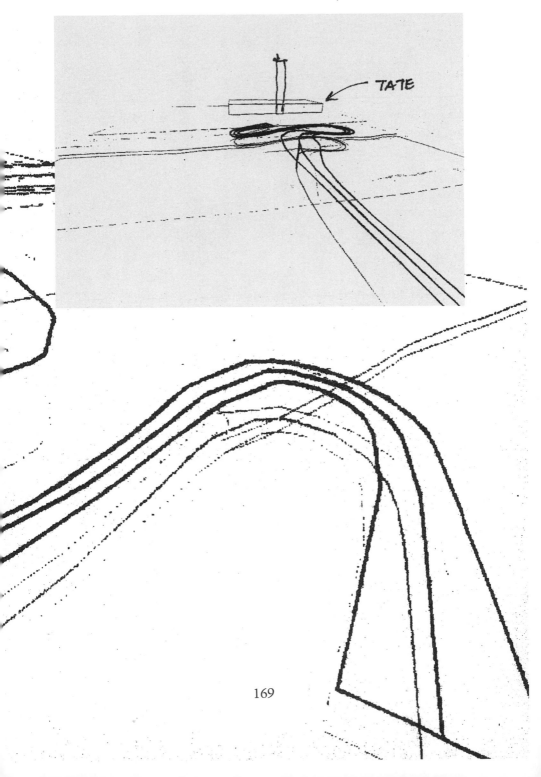

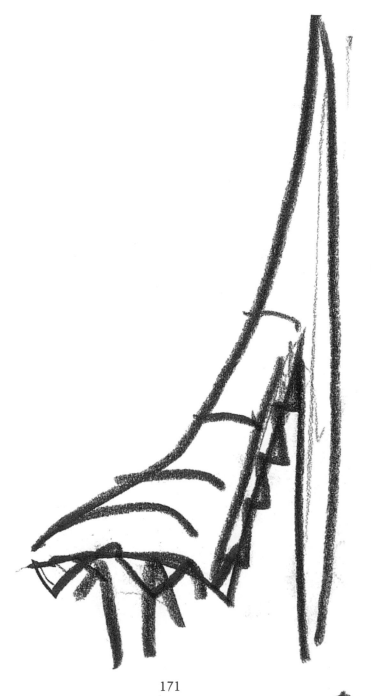

Ten Thousand in the Round
Lois-Ann Yamanaka

MY MADDA ALWAYS SAYING she the lucky one. She got ten thousand wishes for her whole life. Thass plenny enough wishes, if you ask me. Far as wishes go, no mo' too much going around far as I can see.

She use her first one when I was born. She wish me dead.

Kill um, God. Kill this fuckin' thing.

She saying this soft up until the time the doctor yelling at her to "Oosh, girlie, oosh." Then yelling at the nurse to "Strap this girl's arms down."

Thas when my madda started swinging and yelling at him to "Kill this fuckin' piggie" she get stuck up her Japanee trap.

Far as she concern, they all sugar plantation pigs except the Japs and haoles. And she don't give a horse's ass if she less one mo' fuck-up from the get-go child.

Wish.

My madda yelling the most filthiest words at the plantation doctor who take out one appendix for every so-wa stomach he treat. So he tell her, "Shaddap, small girl," and shove the forceps up her chocho, clamp um on my head and pull me out from deep inside her.

Ten thousand.

Ten thousand.

Nine thousand nine hundred ninety-nine 'cause a wish is thin, thin as a pheasant's eyelid.

We living in Aunty Momo's old plantation house down the Mill Camp with black-eye susan and scraggly lawa`e down the crack sidewalk. We there only a little while and my madda in the bedroom with Ernie Agliam.

My madda make one more wish. This time she wish for a boy from Ernie. But we neva get no baby.

We got a empty crib, and Carnie and me being push around in a baby carriage built for twinnies.

She pushing C and me through the Mill Camp and up to the Shopping Centre. The days real hot and long. No mo' baby in her

173

'cause it died, but her stomach still flabs.

Ernie neva come around no mo' in his bust-up yellow truck yelling for his ole lady come outside chew the fat little while.

C, she four. I three. I wish I was dead.

I seen death in my face in the pictures I found in the mildew box, way, way back in the moss and termite nest under the house.

And my teacher says like Jimminy says and wez suppose to believe them:

> *If you wish upon a star*
> *doesn't matter who you are.*

Does.

My madda stirring her coffee slow and telling Aunty Nancy about something while she pulling the little petals offa the African daisies from the Suyat's backyard I picked for the table. Something call The-Pill.

"I wish I wen' get um from the clinic and take um every day like that fuckin' doctor said," she tell. "I wish. I wish." She hitting her forehead with hand and wasting all her wishes.

"Shut yo' mouth, Iris," Aunty Nancy tell.

"Acting like he fuckin' Supa-man with the goddam riddem method like he can pull out before he come. Yeah, right," my madda tell and she throw the bolohead flower stem at me.

"You so fuckin' dumb," Aunty Nancy says to my madda. "Yeah, maybe she just sitting there, but she listening to every word you saying. And one day, one of these days, Iris, you mark my words, yo' very own evil mouth going come back fo' get your rotten ass."

She glare down at me. I one small girl but I undastand everything, every word. "What? What?" she yell at me. "What the fuck you like, hah? What you staring fo', hah? You get eye problems?"

I no say nothing. I pick up the broken flowers but I don't dare move from the spot.

"Look her," my madda says to Aunty Nancy. "All kinky her hair and she get chocho lips just like her fadda, that man-hoa loser, welfare, good-fo'-nothing."

Wish.

Wish.

Ma, no put no extra candles on my bertday cake.

No tell me when the day turn light purple, "There the first star, Lucy."

No make me fold the thousand-one gold cranes for Roxy's
wedding.
No baby teeth in a jar.
No rabbit feet.
Or wishing well.
Or touch blue, yo' dream come true.
No falling stars over Wood Valley.
I neva use my wishes like that once a night, every second, minute
or hour of passing time.
'Cause it's every day I glad I made it through another one.
It's every minute I glad I still here.

Ten thousand wishes, gasp for rain.
Ten thousand wishes, fall like a sigh.
Ten thousand wishes in the round:
I am the girl with the kinky hair.
The Jap with the green eyes.
The hurtful one.
The stupid one.
The sullen one.
The hateful one.
The one full of evil whose madda cannot take and she force to
wish for a joint, a 'lude, a line.
Nine thousand nine hundred ninety-eight.
She lucky. She can get stoned and fall asleep.

Ma, I sleeping back here in this man's back seat.
Wish my eyes to close.
One.
Wish my heart to stop.
Two.
Wish my tongue he swallow.
Three.
His hand stop, his mouth no laugh.
Four. Five.
Ma, you know him. He take me home all the time 'cause you tell
me call him Uncle. He take me look for puka shells down the cove.
He take me to the ponds.
Wish my body outta here quick.
Ma, before he want this too much.

I have her eye in my pocket. Thass only a marble so I put um in my mouth, all spit, and ha-rack um out in the mud puddle by Yoshimura Store.

And every crack I see, I step on um hard.

Step a crack. Step a crack.

I put her teeth in my fist, though it's only puka shells I shake in a baby jar, glinting and clinking mother-of-pearl fangs.

I have hair from her brush, a horsehair braid I will use to paint a mural with one day, "The Story of My Life."

I get her heart with my shoe. Thass only a stone.

And I step a crack, hard.

I tell my friends that it ain't no wasted wish to ask my madda make me canned peach halves with mayonnaise and grated Velveeta on leafs of romaine lettuce all cold and slippery.

And every morning, my madda make me scramble eggs and bacon and toast, every morning like their maddas with pancakes and syrup. But I leave the pancakes part out. Might make the story mo' real.

Ask Carnie,

How come your sista so quiet and moon face? She stand around the whole recess kicking the dirt or dangling her arms and legs on the tire swing, legs spread and spinning 'til her hair fly in a blur.

And Carnie says, she no even flinch, " 'Cause she's a so-sho and emo-sho mal-adjust, thass why. And no spread um around that she my sista."

Ma, this Uncle, he age thirty, and I just a little girlie. He kissing my thighs and making um all slippery. You always say he leading me to dark corners. I one fuckin' little ho-a.

You watching me.

Yeah, thass right, you watching every move I make.

Then how come you no can see?

The man you call my Uncle, watching me.

Ma, spend your wishes quick and fast. He kissing me higher and higher and taking deep breaths and moaning.

We coming home from the beach with a Baggie full of puka shells and a panty full of sand, the sea inside me.

"Bye, Baby," Uncle tell when I get out the truck.

"Say bye, stupid," my madda says as she shove me hard. "What's your problem, hah kid?"

176

"Eh, Iris," Uncle yell. "Come up the gym tonight. Fil-Am league night. You and Nancy drink with me, Ernie, WillyJoe, all the boiz. All-nighta, Babe. Leave the kids home. They only fuckin' troubles."

I look away from him. I dunno why she make me go with him. She tell me in the house, "Uncle said you guys get nuff brown shells fo' make me one opera length lei."

She looking hard at me. " 'Til you get nuff fo' three brown strands, Lucy, you go with Uncle. And I not asking, I telling."

I look at the shells in my hands. We got plenny purples and pinks. Thass when I look up in the lavendar sky.

Star light, star bright, first star I see tonight:

I wish I may, I wish I might—

nine thousand nine hundred sixty-nine.

One wish for light.

One for twinnies.

One for the red umbrella I take over the bridge to Coconut Island.

Two wishes for brown shells.

Two for rain that fall like a sigh.

Three wishes for Jimminy.

Three for extra candles.

Three for the faces in those pictures under the house, give um light.

I going sing from my skin, Ma, 'til every pore open, 'til every hair stand for you 'cause it's all in the breathing, the right way of this song.

I just a little girlie and all your ten thousand almost gone.

Ask God, Ma, ask God for just a couple mo'.

Ask God give you just five mo' so you can say five times, but might take six:

I wish I could love her.

I wish I could love her.

Four more times now.

I wish I could love her.

I wish I could.

I wish I could.

I wish I could.

Love her, my Lucy.

Most Japs go to the Buddhist Church except us. We go the plantation Methodist Church. Nobody go for God:

177

Roxy go 'cause Ernie go.

Who go 'cause his madda Lizzy Agliam force him go.

Who go 'cause her sista Gramma Mary go and Lizzy no like her sista Mary be mo' religious than her.

Mary who is WillyJoe gramma and Ezra hanai madda.

Mary and Lizzy who make their bachelor bradda Uncle Primo, short for Primavero, get up from his hangover so he no go Church of the Holy Mattress, Father Pillow, Amen.

My madda go 'cause Roxy go, and nobody but nobody, take her man from under her nose even if she keeping Uncle on the side.

Who make C and me go. But C no care 'cause they serve Kool-Aid and Rice Crispie cookies in Sunday School and she can check out all the 39 and Under league mens.

I go 'cause of God.

I pray hard every day for God remember me.

No forget me.

I ask the Holy Spirit:

Put a star next to my name in God's Book: I wuz hea'.

I sitting in this church, third pew, for early morning choir practice while the Preacher's wife teaching us some new hymns. Me and my sista singing to help our English be better, so we can sound less ignerant, so we pronounce correct for once, so we can sing, *God. How great thou art.* Great *thou* art? What *thou* mean?

I ask my madda when she show up for the service, but she no answer except to say that she know the Preacher's wife helping us be good girls who talk good and act good, not like her, when all the Preacher's wife doing in that early morning choir practice is correcting our talk and telling us how to say those big ass church words, not what they mean.

The Preacher think he there for God. I no think so. He all white in those yellow and red robes, up high on that pulpit yelling words at us every Sunday morning.

I swear he nuts 'cause half of the congregation only talk Filipino. And they looking at him like where the hell the guy who use to preach to us in Filipino before the real service?

Us had our own service before and now no mo'. Us had Mr. Llamas playing *How Great Thou Art* on his fiddle for the Filipino service before this preacher came.

Mr. Llamas would tell me what thou mean.

My sista sitting next to me in a white dress from Western Store and she acting floozy with the white gloves she got last Easter.

I love how she fold her hands together like a little lady and bow her head when the Preacher say, "Let us pray—dear heavenly Father"; the way she whisper at the end, "Amen," when she stepping on my shiny black shoes 'cause I whistling. The part:

let me take you down
'cause I going to
twoo-berry fields
nothing is real.

And Ma eyeing Roxy who eyeing Ernie who smiling at his madda who cussing out her youngest brother Uncle Primo who giving the elbow to WillyJoe to sign to Ezra, "We go drink Cuervos afta church pau. I get all the limes pre-cut already, and no let Gramma Mary see."

Ezra same age with WillyJoe and Ezra deaf and dumb, but he so handsome, he turn heads, so long as he in one slow cruising car and nobody ask him one question.

During Responsive Reading time, when the Preacher read some lines of scripture and us respond our lines from the back of the hymn book, I watch Lizzy Agliam fanning herself with a lacy white fan; she pretending like she can read, and all the other old ladies, they acting too, while the Preacher stare down at them with those blue ice eyes like they spoiling the whole thing.

I reading loud as I can; I the only one reading loud and clear. Everybody else mumbling the words, even the ones who know how to read. Nobody like make shame with no *funny kind pidgin talk* like the Preacher call um.

Black bold letters mean Preacher: "A thousand thousands that kept ministering to him," he read with Bible thumping feeling.

Red mean congregation: "And ten thousand times ten thousand that kept standing right before him."

"Who, C, who the ten thousand?" I ask my sista.

She no give a shit. She watching WillyJoe. She elbow my chest.

Let me take you down.

Then she refold her white-gloved hands.

"Who?" I ask her.

"Like I give a flying fuck," she tell when all her staring at WillyJoe end up in nothing.

They reading on without me, black, red, black, red.

The ten thousand.

I panicking. Who the ten thousand?

I see WillyJoe signing to Ezra. "The Shining Ones," he tell him.

179

No ask me how I know their secret sign language, I just know. Then he look at me. "Who shine on you, through you and around you." Ezra smiling.

And now I know.

"The Shining Ones," I tell C.

"Who?" she tell. "What shining one? Like me butane your knees again? You like shine, hah, Lucy?"

"I seen WillyJoe tell Ezra," I tell her.

"How can? Ezra deaf, stupid." Then she pause to catch his eye. "WillyJoe?" She still looking his way and when he finally turn, she lick her lips. WillyJoe no look our way for the rest of the service.

Gramma Mary humming the tune of the hymn the Preacher chose. Last preacher we had let Mr. Llamas play his fiddle while all the old ladies sing real joyous hymns, smiling and singing like they mean it.

"Hymns, dey prayers in song," Mr. Llamas tell us every Sunday. But not anymore. Us no even know some of the words. Force to mumble or hum, like what is tri-bu-la-shun?

I use to think about the meaning of the songs like Mr. Llamas use to tell us, sing like we singing on God's bertday. Now, I thinking about words like tri-bu-la-shun. And my mind start singing (*let me take you down*), the way one song stick to your head from the time you wake up to the time you sleep. And your head cannot un-shake um.

At morning sermon time, the Preacher says, "God, He so great. He bein' so great to this church that He bless us richly. God, He give me a callin' when I was prayin' on ma knees at semi-nary school to come to this town and spread the news of the gospel to ya'll sinners.

"For it is your sin that will cause your down-fall, fall into the WORLD. The world of porno-graphy, false theo-logy, wrongful bio-logy and worse of all, worse of all, FOR-ni-CAAA-shun.

"You are the for-ni-cator. I've seen it with my own two eyes. You girl and that man. You girl and that man. You sister and that brother. All God's chillun, making all kinds of hell-ish trouble for yourselves.

"You going burn, burn, I tell you. All your people burning now. That's why God called me here to be HIS servant. Called me to SAVE you, to baptize you in the name of the Father (amen), the Son (praise be), and the Holy Spirit (almighty).

"For the sin of ADULT-ery must be confessed. Must be given to God. Must be for-given by Him and HIM alone. Yes, sister, you are an ADULT-eress causing the fall of that brother, like Eve to Adam.

Baring your skin to him in the darkness of motel rooms. A-whoring and causing the fall of that brother.

"He is my brother. He is holy onto me. And you, my sister, child of sin, for-ni-caaa-shun, and adult-ery, turn, I say to you, TURN ye to Grace."

He looking straight at all the ho-as. At least he got that right. I picking one scab off of my knee while the Preacher yell on.

There Roxy. She seen me staring. She give me one upward head jerk like hi, how you doing, and why you staring at me, you saying I one ho-a, hah, Lucy?

She the very sinner the Preacher talking about, stealing her best friend's ex-old man and coming to church again only to dress up in lacy red prom dress for Ernie who bringing his madda, the brown teeth stain Lizzy.

Roxy sitting right behind him all obvious, and him, he stretch both his arms across the back of the pew, turn his head to her little bit and give her one upward head jerk, like howzit baby.

Then he pull his black comb out of his shirt pocket to give his pomade head one swift comb or two. Ernie's big fingers tapping on the pew back, and I wish, I really wish he could see Roxy all holy, bowing her head and praying, praying real hard as she can that Ernie ask her if she need a long ride home after church.

I singing the final hymn, the way the Preacher's wife want me to, singing loud and trying so hard, but the words ain't clear. Ain't my language.

Singing, *Just as I am wit'out one plea, but da-at dye blood was shed fo' me.*

And I like hide from God, run, and no let Him see my stupid face and all these stupid people around me fuckin' everything up, they all a bunch of fuckin' holy phonies gone a-whoring 'til I hear:

Shine, Lucy. Shine.
On you.
Through you.
Around you.

No ask me how I hear this. First, I think thass WillyJoe talking to Ezra. But Ezra deaf. Where that voice coming from? Only nuts hear things. I looking around all panic, but everybody else carrying on with the final verse of the last hymn. Then come to me:

They not words, they lights. They blue and green lights. And the whole like church smell like sandalwood from the forest above the town.

181

Everybody singing on. The Preacher move to the front of the pulpit to call all the sinners forward in the benediction.

I dunno what fo' do.

The whole church filling with light. WillyJoe look up through the stain glass window behind the pulpit. He raise his face to the light.

Ezra standing up and raising his hands to the lights that connecting in blue and green strands to his fingers.

Hah, what? Only us three see this? Me, one deaf and dumb man, and one handsome weirdo who talk strange things?

And then I think, So what, Preacher, you can see or what? So how come we see the lights and you cannot?

He go on praying about sin, praying that some sinners come forward and confess themself to him.

Don't spend another day in the darkness of your sin.

Ma madda nodding her head, amen, brother, amen. "What she acting fo'?" Roxy whispering in Ernie ear.

And then I think, So what, Preacher, how come you cannot see, yet we the one sound stupid to you? And ignerant. But you no see the blue green lights of the Shining Ones right here in your plantation Methodist Church.

Telling us more about tri-bu-la-shun. Come forward you sinners. Any Sunday without one lost sheep walking forward to the slaughter is one black mark in God's Book.

Uncle Primo try to make Ezra sit down and Gramma Mary close her eyes to the bright lights. Then WillyJoe stand up next to Ezra. And Lizzy Agliam shoving Ernie to make his fuckin' cousins sit down. Crazy fuckas.

Still the service go on. Like nothing happening. So the blue green lights turn off.

And they both sit down.

They holding each other.

Everybody else buzzing and laughing like they just witness two nuts crack up, and of all places, in church. Damn drug addicts, alcoholics.

Then WillyJoe turn to me. He no say nothing but my eyes no can lie.

I seen the blue green lights. Put a star next to my name, God, in your Book. WillyJoe and Ezra too. Gramma Mary even if she shut her eye. Thass four stars, God, no forget.

I hate the way the Preacher pat me on my back on the way outta the church saying, "God loves you, sister." He no even know my name. And how he shake my sista's white-gloved hand all lightly and treat her like one lady—he no even know *what* she did with that hand.

I barely squeeze by the fat Preacher before I tell him, "This Word mine, no matters how I—" He put his hand on the back of my head and oosh me out the door.

I watch my sista trying to catch ride with WillyJoe and Ezra. Roxy climbing in the truck between Lizzy Agliam and Ernie. My madda calling Uncle from the phone in the church office. Uncle Primo waiting for Gramma Mary who walking toward me.

"Ten thousand times ten thousand that kept standing right before him," she whisper to me. "No close yo' eyes to the lights. No be like me. No make the beam come weak. Shine, Lucy. Shine."

From Little Casino
Gilbert Sorrentino

> When you look through binoculars, you are holding
> an instrument of precision and you see very clearly
> a small cabin which would seem quite indistinct
> without the binoculars. So you say, "Well, well, it's
> just like another one I know, they are almost alike,"
> and as soon as you say that you no longer see it, in
> your mind you are comparing it with the one you
> think came before, while, in fact, it comes after.
> Truth means binoculars, precision, the thing that
> really comes first is the binoculars. You should say,
> "Well, well, these binoculars are almost the cabin."
>
> —*Robert Pinget*

> Although we may catalogue a kind of chain mys-
> terious is the force that holds the chain together.
>
> —*Joseph Cornell*

THE IMPRINT OF DEATH

PEOPLE ENTER AND THEN INHABIT, helplessly, periods of their lives
during which they look as if death has spoken to them, or, even more
eerily, as if they themselves are companions to death. It is not usual
for others to notice this in daily intercourse, but the look is manifest
in photographs taken during these periods.

He and his wife stand side by side in casual summer clothes, comfortable, and, as they say, contemporary, but in no other way remarkable. Behind them is a cluttered, even messy kitchen table, in the
center of which, curiously, a tangerine sits atop a coffee mug, and on
the wall behind that is a very poorly done pencil drawing made by a
neighbor's daughter, a senior at the High School of Music and Art.
Such infirm productions attest to the inevitable errors of talent
selection. In the man's face we can see, clearly, the imprint of death
left there years ago by the deaths of his mother and father, who died
less than a year apart. They died badly, as do many people, gasping,
fighting, twitching, their staring eyes registering amazement at how
their bodies were impatiently closing themselves down, literally
getting rid of themselves. Enough! Enough! And then they were

184

gone, they *passed away.* His wife's face has, uncannily, borrowed the subtly peakèd, greyish blandness of his own, and so she, too, looks as if she has to do with *the other side.*

But here is another photograph of a middle-aged man, let's say he's the wife's brother, whose eyes, in a placid, contented, almost smug face, have the half-mad, glazed expression which used to be known, among infantrymen, as a thousand-yard stare. Precisely at the spot at which those thousand yards end, or, perhaps, begin, is the more precise word, stands death itself, in mundane disguise, of course, looking like James Stewart in one of his honest-friend roles. The face of the man in the photograph is unsettling, since its peaceful demeanor belies the crazed eyes, which reveal the dark truth. Death, as James Stewart, may have even been approaching when the photograph was taken. Which would go a long way toward explaining the ocular terror.

And here is a group of eight or nine children in a Brooklyn playground in 1959. There are four boys and two girls and they are smiling and mugging with their gap-toothed mouths, their shirts and shorts soaked from the sprinklers whose gossamer spray can be seen in the background. They are enough to break your heart. One of them, a sweet girl with straight black hair, cut short, and a tiny Miraculous Medal on a chain around her neck, has her hands crossed on her chest. It is this pose which somehow allows access to the expression beneath the sweetness of her lovely face. The occulted expression is the one that can be seen on prisoners in Auschwitz, although this little girl knows nothing of Auschwitz. He puts the photograph down, he *hides* the photograph, but has no true idea why. Yet the message has been delivered, oh yes. It is at such times that we are brought to consider how completely strange death is, how remote from us, how foreign, how impenetrable, how unfriendly. In its ineradicable distance from our entire experience, it is inhuman.

* * *

Or: "Death is not an event in life: we do not live to experience death." (6.4311)

Click. Now you see us, now you don't.

Click.

Many people cannot understand why certain religions do not allow animals to enter heaven. Well, we know that they have no souls, but many people wonder about that, too. Do they? When the Rapture snatches Joe Bob Joe outen his Ford pickup, it'll be tough on Mr. Joe to leave Rend and Tear, his "really gentle" Rottweilers, behind.

"Let him change his religion and truly be saved!" Bob Joe Bob says, perhaps irrelevantly.

May their souls and the souls of all the faithful departed, through the mercy of God, rest in peace. Amen. Which implies, maybe, that if God does not wish, in, of course, selected cases, to be merciful, these faithful departed may *not* rest in peace.

Tangerine was, indeed, all they claimed, but she's been dead for about 50 years. Bob Eberle knew her well, and even, so they say, had an amour with her. He may be dead by now as well.

> Of what is't fools make such vain keeping?
> Sin their conception, their birth weeping,
> Their life a general mist of error,
> Their death a hideous storm of terror.

John Webster was, clearly, unfamiliar with the rhetoric of grief counseling.

I once heard Ray Eberle, Bob's brother, at the end of his rather undistinguished career, sing in a Brooklyn saloon named Henry's. His backup band was a disastrous trio, piano, accordion, and drums, but he was game. He bummed a cigarette from me at the bar. I was going to tell him that I'd seen him at the Paramount with Glenn Miller, but what was the point?

Click.

THE CHUMS OF 6B4

Mario wore rubbers to school every day, for the uppers of his shoes were cracked and split, and the soles worn all the way through. He could have chosen not to wear rubbers, of course, for this was, even in the '30s, America, and freedom, enough to choke a horse, was in the unfailing ascendant. An unkind youth with a belief in his own superiority once thought to bait him about these rubbers, industrial rubbers, as they surely were, slaughterhouse rubbers, with their unmistakable thick red soles. The rage that he saw within Mario's tautly held body dissuaded him, however, and warned him away. A lot of the boys in class, knowing of his plans, were disappointed, because they had hoped that maybe Mario would, in the parlance of the day, clean the little bastard's fucking clock. Maybe, God willing, even kill him. Nobody would miss him, least of all the chums of 6B4.

* * *

"I wish that all the pain that _____ _____ is feeling could be visited, in spades, on my worst enemy," is a refreshing phrase. If one can't wish one's enemies misery or death, what is the use of sin and redemption?

Follow the leader: Mario, after his bitter childhood years of poverty, which he shared with his older brother, Mike, followed Mike and Mike's wife, Connie, to Trenton, N.J., for God knows what reason. They may still live there, doing the Jersey bounce.

It is generally agreed, or so I understand, that the word "chum" is no longer in general use, save for ironic or parodic effect. It functions, that is, much like the well-made short story.

"Of which we've read, ah, plenty."

ON A STUDEBAKER COUPE

He takes Bubbsy, whom he hates, but has no idea why, up to the roof, for reasons never explained, reasons never even suggested by the quiet, handsome boy, who has lived, more or less, in saloons most of his life. His mother has kept him in food and clothes, despite the fact that she rarely leaves the bar, save to stagger into the ladies' room with one drunken lothario or another. He pulls Bubbsy, by the hair, to the edge of the roof, and throws him off. Bubbsy lands on a Studebaker coupe, crushing the roof with his head, which cracks open in a mess of blood and brains. He leans over the edge of the roof and lights a cigarette, then carefully drops a burnt match, aiming at the body, but the wind blows the match well off line and out of sight. He thinks that the coupe belongs to that stupid prick who lives over the candy store on the corner. That would be nice.

* * *

Hide and seek: death. He had been in Lincoln Hall. After the death of Bubbsy, he was sent to Coxsackie, then Dannemora. Nobody knew where he went from there, although there were recurring, preposterous rumors that he was acting in the movies, with a different face.

"They can do fuckin' anything in Hollywood."

Bubbsy liked to torture cats and cruelly tease and hurt little children. Had he lived, there is a good chance that he would have become a hail-fellow-well-met regular sport of a bully, drunk, and dedicated beater of women, like his older brother, Mac, the cop.

"There are always, sure, a few bad apples in the barrel, but it's very wrong to condemn and blacken all the other honest, hard-working, law-abiding people who and so forth, and who and so on, and who, day in and day out, do this and do that and do the other thing too."

It could happen to you. Hide. And seek.

The same darkness envelops them all.

THE BURDENS OF THE DEPRESSION

Have a spaghetti sangwich! Have a spaghetti sangwich with pieces of cold frankfurter on it! Have a cod-liver oil sandwich, a sammich that'll put hair on your chest, your head, your hands and your freezing feet!

A ketchup sammich? A ketchup-and-mustard sammich? Or how

does a cold stringbean sammich strike you, little fella? A canned pineapple sandwich might go well with a big jelly jar chock by Jesus Christ up to the brim with lemon Epco or grape Kool-Aid, as too, might a canned-spinach sandwich. Succotash on moldy rye? Mmmm.

A cottage-cheese-and-cold-boiled-puhtaytuh sangaweech on stale Bond bread, now that is the absolute ticket! You're talking nutrition? Then, too, sangwiches of sliced green pepper and Crisco will surely refresh after a long day of career discussions. And don't neglect to pop over to friendly Gallagher's, sport, for a pitcher of Trommer's: crisp, light, and tingling! And zesty! It's the Ivy League beverage of choice, you'll recall?

How to feed your family of five, or even six, on a dollar a day, without endangering their health or welfare. Just takes a little g-u-m-p gumption!

Stay away, oh, stay far hence from those terrible crumb buns, cinnamon buns, coconut buns, crullers, doughnuts, and Danish pastries, they'll send you to your grave, yowzah.

Break out the lettuce-and-oleo sammiches, pliz. Look at those smiling children in the sunny kitchen! Look at those cavities and suppurating ears! Bacon and eggs and sausages and toast with butter, again! That will do it every time.

Afterward, when the coughing lets up a little, these tykes can build a little character selling *Liberty* at the subway station. "How To Feed Your Growing Family On Fifty Cents A Day" is in the latest issue, wow!

And for the love of God, who does not cotton to the idle poor, as we all know, *please* avoid those thick steaks, buttered mashed potatoes, rich sauces, cream-laden desserts, all those deadly foods that will damage the courageous heart, O.K.?

Lard on toast might allay certain yearnings, but moderation, moderation.

How amazing that the poor have *always* eaten a healthy diet, rich in vegetables, legumes, and whole grains, and low in fat and sugars. They've had it puh-retty darn good!

Here you go—a kohlrabi sangwich on what looks like a fetching pale-green slice of Silvercup! Fulla vitamins Q and T.

* * *

Herbert Hoover died at the age of 137, of course. It is said that he never ate a steak in his life, and that his favorite dinner was farmer cheese on soda crackers with skimmed milk.

He did *not* call the unemployed "the shiftless idle," and the rumor that attributed this remark to him has been traced to Ethel and Julius Rosenberg, described as "Godless un-Cristian [sic] Jews" in *Jesus Knows News*. It is a cruel rumor, and one that is in very poor taste as well.

When the burdens of the Depression and such aberrations as the Bonus March could not be lightened by cheery thoughts of Tom Mix, Mr. Hoover often went fly-fishing, called "the sport of dukes." He wore his Stanford tie.

"Don't fence me in!" the doughty President would exultantly cry to the aromatic woods. And soon it would be time for a raw onion.

THE VERY PICTURE OF LONELINESS

Desolate lot. A boy of perhaps four, in a tattered and patched hand-me-down windbreaker, a knitted cap on his head against the raw cold of a late March afternoon. He is alone, rooting with a stick in the rubble of broken red and buff bricks, shards of stained porcelain, diseased shingles, tree limbs, all the rubbish and detritus of this failing neighborhood, struggling for life on the thinnest edge of utter decay. It is the very picture of loneliness. The boy's father, who has gone to look for him as the bitter darkness begins to slide across the low roofs of the neighborhood houses, watches him, heartbrokenly, in silence. He knows, although he has no idea that he knows, that the boy, alone in the sad quiet of this grey, dispirited lot, will be alone always in his life, and that the distant, perplexing world that he is to inhabit, is one to which he will be forever strange. This knowledge enters the father with viral efficiency, and years later, he will remember this day, even remember the shape of a brown leaf that lies at his feet, crepitant.

And years later, after a long period of estrangement and silence, the boy, now a solitary man, will write his father a letter, suggesting that the years of separation and misunderstanding might, possibly, be ended, might, possibly, be "cured," is his odd word. And the father, tentatively, carefully, replies, with guarded love and exquisite care, but hopelessly. The boy will have no memory of the death of hope that lay at the center of that lot, at the center of that raw afternoon, eerie in thin, failing sunlight and dirty cold. The father will have no way of telling his son of the truth that was thrust upon him, as he watched from the sidewalk before he called to him to come home. The fact of the loveless void of that shattered lot on that unremarkable block in Brooklyn in the fading years of the 1950s, will be in and of his letter, and even as he mails it, the letter, full of carefully phrased sentences that demand nothing and expect nothing and promise nothing, that is but a salute, labored yet authentic, will not, he knows, be answered.

*   *   *

Céline writes that "the living people we've lost in the crypts of time sleep so soundly side by side with the dead that the same darkness envelops them all."

No one used to think that a vacant lot was *owned*, rather, lots were everybody's property, loci of quiet anarchy. A lot took its character from that of the surrounding neighborhood. Because of this, it was an accurate index of a neighborhood's present, but held no hint of its future. To place a living human figure in the center of a lot is to *compose* a kind of iconic reality that is, oddly, more real than the presence of an actual living figure in the center of a lot.

It is hard to be a father.

No love. No nothing.

THE SCOW

The boy leaps from the slippery edge of the pier out toward the scow tied up alongside it. He's done this dozens of times over the past few years, timing the slow heave and slide of the clumsy vessel as the swells carry it toward the pier and then away from it, but this time he misjudges and, in mid-air, his arms outstretched and his legs pistoning, realizes that he won't land on the deck. His left foot touches the gunwale, but the scow is riding away from him on the water, glassy with oil. Some other boys stand in momentary silent terror, still, on the pier in the anemic sunlight and brisk wind of the October afternoon, knowing that their friend's foot has not gained purchase. He falls between the hull and the pier just as the scow reaches its maximum distance from the pier, and is held, wholly still, by its huge, splintery hawsers. As the boy surfaces, the scow lifts and begins its terrible slide toward him, the swell carrying it silently, calmly, toward the pier. A deckhand hears the screaming of the boys on the pier and emerges, half-drunk, from a makeshift cabin of planks and tarpaper on the deck, and knows, instantly, what has happened, and that there is nothing to be done. He stands at the gunwale and looks into the space between the hull and the pier, sees the boy's small, tough face white with shock and fear, and yells, in a voice high with rage and anguish, in a near-comic Norwegian accent, that the focking goddamn kid is focking goddamn crazy and to get the focking goddamn hell out of there, and then the boy is a soft crack and an explosion of gore and, weirdly, makes no sound as he is crushed to his filthy death.

*   *   *

"What did you see as you fell? What did you hear as you sank?/Did it make
you drunken with hearing?"

The boy would not have understood these lines in any other way but the
literal. That is, had anyone known to avail him of the poem from which they
come. But who would have known?

Go fish. And blues in the night.

A MORE INNOCENT TIME

To bombard the small and inefficient gas refrigerator with grapefruit
would be his weekly, perhaps daily delight, yet he was astigmatic,
myopic, amblyopic, cross-eyed, knock-kneed, bowlegged, and box-
ankled. To heave huge turkeys, each shot several times with a .38
caliber Smith and Wesson revolver, into the kitchen sink, seemed a
promising idea, not, however, to be realized by the likes of him, who
could not catch a ball, the pitiful bastard. To pull up the skirts and
slips of all the pretty girls on their way to Sunday mass was a romantic ideal, and yet, he broke his steel clinic glasses every week or so.
What about throwing the guys who had ripped his shirt right off the
fucking roof, one after the other? But had he ever, once, managed to
hit the ball past the infield? Killing that large, handsome German
shepherd with a perfect slab of perfectly poisoned meat would have
surely benefited mankind, but the poor chooch was afraid to put his
head underwater. To become a priest, kind and brave and strong
among the disgusting yet worthy lepers, was a noble calling, but how
could he find time to study when he couldn't stop polluting himself
for a minute, the pasty-faced, underweight, nervous degenerate? He
could easily kidnap Dolores and Georgene from in front of Font-
bonne Hall and carry them off to Rio and CARNIVAL! and unspeakable sin, although he would not let them know that he still, on
occasion, wet the bed. To sink, with nary a moment's hesitation, the
Staten Island ferry, so as to drown the secret Nazi agents who spied
on convoys in the Narrows would have shortened the war by a
month, but he was having serious problems with long division. To
use his Amazing Hypnotic Powers, from time to time, and solely
for the refined amusement of his closest academic chums, so as to
compel Miss Ramsay to happily strip naked in front of the hearty
group gathered in the detention room was a pastime that appealed to
his sense of fair play, but hard, hard to do when she pinched his earlobe and called him a dunce. To smoke a quiet pipe before the cheery

191

fire while mulling over the details of the latest gruesome ax murder always hit the old anglophilic spot, but not for the sort of rough fellow who smoked Wings, Twenty Grand, and Sweet Caporal loosies. To show Liz and Mary how to do the Harlem Glide could have been a charming way to pass the time, had the young women been willing to tolerate the importunate if unintentional prodding of his manly erection. He argued, convincingly, that a Tom Collins was more refreshing than a John Collins, that upstart drink, but his buttocks showed through the large holes in his threadbare corduroy knickers. And who better to warn the grizzled pilots of the *Queen Mary* and the *Normandy,* as the great ships approached the Narrows, of the foul Sargasso Sea of floating condoms that threatened their safety? But had not two Garfield Boys cut his tie off with a switchblade and stolen his lunch money? To batter the persons of the neighborhood bullies in, of course, strict accordance with the Rules of the Ring, while casually remarking on Annette's tiny though shapely breasts, was always invigorating, but the shirt-cardboard inserts in his worn-out shoes were soaked through. To carry swiftly messages of highest priority, down pitch-black streets, from one air-raid warden to another, could help to bring the Axis to its knees, but 3-cent chocolate sodas and Mrs. Wagner's strangely malevolent pies had given him a faceful of pimples. Most seriously, he would have liked to explode a magical bomb that he had invented one night in bed, a bomb that would to the Job, that is, maim, dismember, roast, fry, broil, and obliterate all his enemies, but for the fact that a group of charming and brilliant, sober and judicious proxy killers were about to do the trick. Twice.

* * *

Turkeys that have been shot, however accurately, with .32 caliber slugs, are not edible. A man named Pasquale Colluccio demonstrated this fact to me when I was sixteen, and to my complete satisfaction.

In Brooklyn, in what many people have been taught by crack journalists to call "a more innocent time," floating condoms were often called "Coney Island whitefish," whereas condoms discarded on the ground after use were, quite simply, "scumbags," semen being, of course, "scum." Bodies torn apart by bullets fired into them at close range were often come upon in vacant lots in Bath Beach and Canarsie. "Hello! There's Santo Throckmorton, the jewel thief!" The occasional newborn infant would be fished out, dead as Santo, from ashcans filled with clinkers and "scumbags," or recovered from the ladies' room in the Alpine, Stanley, Electra, Bay Ridge, Dyker and Harbor.

An "ashcan" was the name given to a very large and powerful firecracker, responsible, each Fourth of July, for the loss of the fingers and eyes of many neighborhood youths. These occurrences might be placed under the heading of "Good Practice" for the good and righteous war that was just around the cozy little corner. We showed *them*.

It is often forgotten that they also showed us.

Someone, after Hiroshima, was reported to have remarked, anent the scientists who had created the bomb: What did they *think* was going to happen when it exploded?

"Music? Music? Music?"

LEST IT BE FORGOTTEN

After an hour or so of trying to get her brassiere off, or her skirt up, or both, he lies back, next to her, on the couch, thinking that maybe he'll just go home, when she accidentally brushes, with the back of her hand, and through his slacks, his still-erect but by now leaden penis, and he realizes that he's going to come. It's like a joke. Let's say, unequivocally, that it *is* a joke.

Some ten years later, the boy, now, of course, a man, very drunk but not so drunk as his wife, spreads her legs open as they lie, he is somewhat surprised to realize, on the living room carpeting. She is humming, over and over, the first bar of "Ruby, My Dear." He cannot understand, for the life of him, and it's not, let's face it, much of a life, why he is unable to pull her panties any further down than her thighs. Can't make a fucking thing *right* anymore, he says to her, but she pays him no mind, or, in any event, she does not reply. Then he puts his head on her naked belly and they both fall asleep.

And, lest it be forgotten, there is his first serious sexual experience, when a nurse or a nurse's aide at Brooklyn Eye and Ear, where he lies after an operation, both eyes bandaged, feeds him his supper, tells him what she looks like, and, while spooning what may be tapioca pudding into his mouth, masturbates him under the covers with skill and dispatch. He thinks that he might faint with pleasure, but he stays marvelously conscious, even alert, listening to the rustle of what he imagines to be her crisp white uniform.

As she is leaving the room, she says, mysteriously, "There are a lot of nice guys in Jersey, too, but."

* * *

One might, as an amusement, do worse than to think of adventures such as these enveloping forward-looking politicians, dim professors of civil engineering, and dreadful Christian fundamentalists. (Add or substitute your own favorites.)

193

Gilbert Sorrentino

It is the fashion to make fun of New Jersey, much as it is the fashion to denigrate Los Angeles and to praise the San Francisco Bay Area. "What weather!" they bubble, as the earth splits open amid vast fires, and the houses slide downhill, in cataracts of mud, onto the clogged and poisonous freeways.

Sexual experiences are rarely reported with candor, accuracy or honesty, and these are no exceptions.

Why is this the case? It's magic?

In 1968, CBS wanted Thelonious Monk to record an album of Beatles tunes. There sat the band's songbook on his piano. To add, as the nice phrase has it, insult to injury, the company sent someone to Monk's apartment to play through the book. In case Monk couldn't read music.

Well, you needn't, motherfucker.

Five Poems
Peter Sacks

CALLING

Woken by
the always less than

full-strength
angel

fists clenched
mouth still open

undergone

you had to look around

————

I swallowed I began to
swallow river-bank

stone root stump
graft of who lay back?

whose plough?

————

To separate the words: black furrow

ox axe spine
inconstant constant

gold streaks straggling fortune
sweet juice in your mouth

for what?—

just there
below the shag of

————

doublings where the blade

shears through each
further version

————

death each way

————

white scales
the high unsentencing

————

set free (his representing
power of another kind)

————

before the end
I cut the whole wings

from my heart.

Peter Sacks

THE TRIAL

Dark flame seeding
rimless

bolted

will & matter
indistinguishable

until they had
invented God

one God.

―――

I felt it
in the warning

downward

leaf & branch
beneath

their fingers
rapid

murderous
(& there was music

—hacking)

(cities multiplied)

the defile
late cut deep into

the bone
abraded hand–

sewn through
surrendered

needle-grained

the wick &
spending

between worlds.

White boulders,
dry sea bed.

Absolved.

Or is it taken back

under the smoke?

Peter Sacks

ASK ME

Unlit
channel leaf

I cannot
whistles

everywhere against
the setting

hung to bleed

a thorn-like bow
string blur

unblurred

it sinks into
the throat

define it
red drop

feather

merchandise
unveiled

the flesh
once only

to be sold

this near edge
nothing mercy

flung all
face-of-hearing

Peter Sacks

lean stone
membrane

dug
who listen

swiftly kept
alongside

lifted
hope how it

would cling
against

necessity

it clings you
do as from

the cliff high
branches and

you will.

Peter Sacks

THE CHANGE

Appearance
clings to

being

my defense

light steps
braided

animal

above the ridge

endured

my doing as
his tongue

required

said *thorn*

hedge flickers

will remain

I rushed gray

terraces

unshielded the

scatter-shot

majority

hauled off
& swung

Peter Sacks

let it come
down

our second
shoreline

heaped
hazing into

bush the late

regime

robed in
the chambers

sworn.

Peter Sacks

CHOICE

Door to door
the drag–

search
shot through

caution

our unshackled

marrow-fleck
& mineral

finding more than

offshoots

blood spun

rapid-thickened

battering the

singular

inhuman

as charged—

do you think
I did not

wish to take
your hands

that
narrative

not grief flung

swallowed
fully

as the future
comes out of its

hiding stem
seed-coma

famished

for the form
of its own

perishing within
us

pull me now
from inside

further
into you

remorseless—

& we give it
life.

The New Calendar
Norman Manea

—Translated from Romanian by Patrick Camiller

PALE, OVERWHELMED by the enormity of the occasion, he thought about the farce that had chosen him as protagonist. Was he to act in a self-parody? One of the many such parodies, performed every moment in our cement-mixer of a world?

The pettiness of affiliation, the absurdity of it, was at issue. Nothing but that. Had he not shed the tight-fitting skin in which he had previously lived? Had he not yet forgotten the past—he who forgot faces seen only an hour ago?

A blue-costumed lady kept making gestures at him. When he finally noticed her, she was already close by, yet still pointing her finger at his absentmindedness.

"You, sir. Follow me to the Commission."

Taking his briefcase, he rose from the bench on which five people were huddled together. He followed the secretary through a door she had left ajar.

"First you'll be talking to the French representative. When you've finished, come back and see me again."

She pointed him toward a door to the left of her office.

"Please, go in."

He moved to the left three steps, was inside. The lanky man behind the desk offered a seat facing him. He sat down, briefcase in arms.

"Would you like us to speak in German?" the Frenchman asked in German. "Or French, rather?"

"We can speak French if you prefer," replied the candidate in German.

"I'm glad to hear it," continued the examiner, in French. "Nearly all Romanians speak French, don't they? My Romanian friends in Paris don't have any trouble adapting."

"Yes, Romanians find French easy," confirmed the Romanian in French.

He looked closely at the man sitting opposite him. These days, examiners are always younger than examinees, the Romanian thought in Romanian.

The official had a thin face, a fine prominent nose, dark intelligent eyes, thick hair, a nice youthful smile. His tie was loosened at the neck, blue shirt collar undone, and his navy jacket hung open with a touch of elegance on his bony shoulders. His voice was pleasant, familiar—yes, pleasant and familiar.

"I was discussing you with a lady yesterday. I knew we'd be having this talk today, so I asked her if she knew you."

The candidate did not react. He quite simply remained silent, in French, the language in which this surprising news had just been presented.

The man opposite lighted a cigarette and glued both palms to the edges of the desk. He sat slightly back in the revolving leather chair in which he appeared to feel very comfortable.

"You're not exactly a stranger. Yesterday, as I was reading through your files and the list of books, I was suddenly struck by the coincidence."

As he said "books," he lifted the candidate's file from the desk, and held it in the air for a fraction of a second before putting it back in place. A very long, untranslatable silence transpired. Only after quite some time did the Frenchman resume in his melodious Gallic, "I know the novel *Captives.*" The *parfait* rhythm of French could be heard in the perfect stillness of the room, like the laconic announcement at a fencing match. Was that a *touchee* uttered by sabres? No, the silence in the room remained perfect. "Back around the mid-seventies, I think," continued the Parisian. "I was taking a course in Romanian at Paris University."

The candidate removed his glasses and began to clean them. "An evening course?" No, the word "evening" had not been spoken, only imagined.

"There was a lot in the course about censorship. Censorship and methods of coding. Criticism of the totalitarian system. The code— the captives' code, I believe."

The candidate gripped the handle of his briefcase. Liar! he would have liked to shout, in every language. Now he knew for sure this man was not a simple run-of-the-mill diplomatic official.

Was the West no different than the East? The same innuendoes, the same flattery, the same traps? Would the stateless person who had rejected haggling with the national devil in his own country now have to face supernational agents of that same infamous profession?

Had he become a dependent prisoner, even before receiving the stateless person's certificate? An impersonal pariah, to be blackmailed and manipulated at the first turn in the road?

"That comes as quite a surprise to me," the candidate finally stuttered in French. "I didn't know, no one told me the book ever reached Paris."

"Yes, it was a surprise for me, too. Imagine when I saw your name on this file. . . ."

Again, he picked up the candidate's file and put it back down on the desk.

"I saw your name, the book titles. . . . You should settle in France."

"You should settle in France"—a piece of advice, a promise, a coded bargaining chip? The "surprise" was no longer a surprise. Nor was the friendliness, the way he was being treated as a respectable acquaintance—yes, honored with tricks more rarified than the ones used on ordinary plebeians.

"France is the easiest place to settle in, for a Romanian. You know that. Soon you'll have friends there. You'll write in French. So many of your illustrious predecessors . . . ," etcetera etcetera.

Yes, the examiner knew not only the title and contents of *Captives,* as well as the famous trio Ionesco-Cioran-Eliade, but also Princesse Bibesco and the Princesse de Noailes and Princesse Vacaresco and *la grande princesse* and *la petite princesse.* He had done his homework; he was ready to offer a veritable seminar on spying-informing-coding.

The conversation continued in much the same way. At the end, the examiner walked around his desk and stood next to the examinee. He presented some last tokens of friendship: his business card with his address in Berlin and in Paris; an invitation to spend an evening together; and assurances of support, "any support," that might be needed in Berlin or even more in Paris, on any occasion. Any occasion. . . .

"Any occasion, any time": the code of smiles, words, diction. Smiling and shaking his hand, he stared affectionately over his glasses; meanwhile it would be nice to spend an evening together, here in Berlin, where fate had granted them the chance to meet each other.

Monsieur le grand ami accompanied the candidate not quite to the door, but to the antechamber where the blue-costumed controller was waiting. He announced that Mr. So-and-So, his friend, had finished his interview with the French authorities and could now move on to the other two great Allied powers.

The German woman showed no sign of weakness in the face of such Latin complicity. She waited impassively for the two French-speakers to say their goodbyes.

After the door on the left was closed, the candidate remained mute. When the secretary finally looked up at the large shriveled briefcase that he held in his arms, she said clearly and concisely in German, "So, you're finished for today!"

The stranger looked at his watch. It was ten to twelve. He was glad he could go.

"Tomorrow morning at eight. The door where the lists are drawn up. Be here at nine. Room 135."

The day was cold and sunny. He walked to the bus stop, took a bus and then a tram, and finally walked some more. By two he had reached his refuge in the city center.

Tomorrow morning: the fifty-year-old will be reborn in the After-world, which from that day will be called the Other World.

Lying on the sofa, he red-circled the page of the calendar. He did not tear it out, for the day was not yet over. Nor was the mission over. He stood up, recircled the page in red, and wrote in big red letters above the fading day: MARIANNE! He waited a moment, looking at what he had done. No, he was not satisfied. With his pen he crossed out in red the red letters. Then he wrote, this time at the bottom of the page: FRANCE. He stood, wavering before the name. Then, smiling like a child happy with a trick played on Auntie, he inserted some more letters: A-n-a-t-o-l-e. Anatole FRANCE.

He turned around once more toward the sofa. He stared for a long time at the French agent's visiting card in his right hand.

Spend an evening, several evenings. Could these attempts perhaps cure you of your suspiciousness, you who brought with you suspicion itself? No, he wasn't cunning enough, nor did he intend to be cunning. Rather, he tore the agent's card into the tiniest of pieces— proof that he did not yet understand the advantages of freedom and the possibilities it offered.

The next day, he took the same road to the sacred Tripartite Commission on the outskirts of the city. He waited patiently, briefcase in arms, on the same bench facing Room 135. Finally, at a quarter past eleven, he came before the controller, who silently showed him the American door on the right.

He took three steps to the right, opened the door, was inside. The bald-headed young man behind the desk offered him a seat. Briefcase still in arms, he sat.

"Do you speak English?" asked the American, in his American English.

"A little," the candidate evasively replied in Esperanto.

"Okay, we can speak in German," continued the American in his American German. "Okay?"

The candidate nodded in agreement and looked more closely at the man facing him. This examiner was even younger than the one the day before. Solidly built, crammed into a brown suit with wide lapels. White shirt, handcuff-tight collar, thick white neck. Dark prying eyes, short strong hands. A thick gold ring on his left hand, an elegant gold pen in his right. Gold cuff links on white sleeves shot well beyond his jacket sleeves.

"Your passport."

Army voice, army manner.

The candidate leaned over the huge briefcase he was holding in his arms. He took out a green folder, extracted the green passport and handed it to the examiner, who examined it slowly, page by page.

"This is not your first trip to the West."

The candidate did not comment on the comment. The Great Power looked at him long and hard. Refusing to read into this silence, he once more resolutely broke the diaphanous stillness of the room.

"I see you've been in the West before."

Again, silence settled its angelic wings over the two chairs.

"Where's the money from? Where does the money for these trips come from?"—silence seemed now to be shredded by the American's German words. "In the East you don't get foreign currency unless the government gives it to you. And the government only gives when it has an interest in you."

"I didn't travel on government money," the suspect hurriedly replied. "Relatives in the West sent me some."

"Relatives? Generous people. Where do you have relatives? In which countries?"

Shunning silence, the traveler rushed over his answer and ended up more suspect than ever. He'd listed the countries where his wandering family had taken refuge.

"In the United States, too?" the U.S. representative said, rather more cheerily. "Whereabouts? What kind of relatives?"

The cosmopolitan again replied at once: his wife's sister. Married to an American for more than a decade. The mother of two American children, a girl ten and a boy four.

"And Berlin? How did you get to Berlin? Your relatives didn't choose this place, did they? I don't imagine they're very fond of Berlin."

The candidate's silence grew. The American seemed content with what he read into the muteness of this Eastern European survivor.

And yet, the candidate had been thinking it over. Apparently, he did want to answer the question.

"I came here on a German government grant, as I mentioned in my statement."

"Yes, you did mention that," conceded the official as he lifted the file from his desk. He held it in the air for a few moments and then put it back in place, even pushing it slightly toward the right edge of the desk, as if it were not of much importance.

"The vanquished offering a grant to the victor? Might we put it like that?"

The American seemed to be in no hurry to finish with the German theme. He allowed himself the right to more pleasure—after all, it had not been an easy victory over the enemy. That victory, he seemed to suggest, united him, the young American, with the aging Eastern European seated opposite him.

A grant inspired by guilt? Yes, the recipient had himself thought that more than once. A grant offered by the vanquished to survivors whom they had not managed to eradicate? A grant from prosperous Germany to an East that had always been the vanquished—inferior, barbarian, doomed to poverty, exile, anonymity? Even within its smaller frontiers, postwar Germany still remained the land of efficient, hardworking Germans, with the same flag and the same national anthem. After the war, not even Bavaria belonged to the Jews—contrary to the prediction of some astrologists that the entire land of Goethe and Bismarck would be ruled by the survivors asking Germans to show proof of philo-semitism over three generations, before granting them again the German citizenship they had lost in the cataclysm.

A joke, one might say—said the survivor to himself.

The joke had been "read" in the opposite direction, from right to leftt, as in the biblical alphabet. For it was the Jews who were asked, on leaving the crematoria, to prove they belonged by blood to the very state that had wanted to exterminate them! Only then could they be offered the enviable citizenship of prosperous postwar

Germany—the Germany which awarded grants to the poor and lost and rebellious, who no longer hoped for a redefinition of victory.

The candidate did not get a chance to say all this. The young examiner had broken off the conversation and immersed himself in writing instead, in filling all manner of questionnaires in the file. It was not polite to disturb him. And yet wouldn't the examiner probably have enjoyed hearing such anti-Nazi digressions, seeing them as pro-American flattery, a way into the good graces of the Great Power?

When the candidate looked up from his briefcase, he saw the American authority was already on his feet, smiling with obvious sympathy and holding out his hand in comradeship.

"Good luck, good luck, sir!" he wished in American, abandoning the language of the common enemy.

Next to come was the British lion, evidently no longer a lion. But the lady controller, caught up in a jovial telephone conversation, did not notice that the American test had ended. Even when she put the receiver back on the cradle, she did not appear to see the shadow in front of her.

"So now there's an interview with the English?" the intruder asked timidly.

"There's nothing else, sir," came the prompt answer. "You've finished. Mr. Jackson signed for the English as well."

The candidate nodded in assent, took up his briefcase and headed for the door.

"Don't forget, sir. Tomorrow morning at nine-thirty."

So it was over, but not quite. He turned to the controller in surprise.

"Tomorrow you'll have your last interview with the German authorities. First floor. Room 102. Nine-thirty."

He walked slowly, extremely slowly, toward the bus stop.

The stairs—slowly, slowly—to the third floor. It was warm in the apartment, quiet. Before undressing, he picked up the thick red ballpoint from the table and went over to the calendar. He crumpled the page for January 20th, then the page for January 21st. He drew two thick red circles on the page for Friday, January 22nd, 1988, then wrote across it "If I live until tomorrow" and added in brackets "The Count, Yasnaya Polyana."

A year had passed since he left his native larva. Stretched out on the sofa, he looked out the window into the white nocturnal mist, the elegant buildings and boulevards of Transit City. Party music could be heard in the distance. The nightlife of this overpopulated island of artists and spies was intense. He thought he could make out the shape of the Great Wall that defended the Enclave of Liberty from the captive world outside, and defended the great prison beyond the frontier from the virus of liberation.

The survivor again lived to see another day. At nine-thirty he presented himself in the appointed room. The German official was short and chubby. Surprisingly, he wore not a suit and tie but velvet trousers, with a thick green woolen jacket over a pullover that was also green. His blond hair was carefully combed. His large hands had patches of white discoloration, which were repeated on his forehead and neck.

After an hour and a half of interrogation, the candidate came out feeling giddy if perplexed, unable to remember any of the questions he had answered. What he did remember was the precise manner in which the German bureaucrat twice said that the road on which he was embarking was long and uncertain; the first step was only a first step.

Ja, ja, bestimmt, Bukovina—that was it. But as the gentleman candidate well knows, we are neither French nor American—no, neither American nor English, we don't have their Birth and Citizenship laws, even if we are in the building of the Great Allied Commission. As he spoke, he raised his hands and eyebrows toward heaven, indicating that no greater folly had ever been seen.

You're not German just because you were born in Germany! Not to mention the fact that— Again he leaned forward to read in the file that word impossible to remember.

Oh, sicher, Bukovina—a former Austrian province, for no more than eighty years, or so. Austrian and German are two different things, completely different, as the gentleman undoubtedly knows. That madman who destroyed Germany, and thanks to whom the Great Allied Commission is now in Berlin. . . . The German official, born of pure German parents and grandparents, themselves with pure German ancestors, again raised his hands and eyebrows to the Almighty, who was playing so shamelessly with the fate of his Fatherland.

No, that madman because of whom Germany had to go on paying and paying, to go on accepting debts and insults and hordes of foreigners outside the Great Allied Commission—that madman was not German but Austrian, as everyone knows! From Linz, Austria—

that's where mad Adolf came from, and he never denied the fact.

"Even if you are German, what kind of German are you if you've been away from your country for eight hundred years? A few days ago I saw a compatriot of ours on television. Being German, or so she said, she claimed to have repatriated herself to Germany. After eight hundred years, that is! We're talking of *eight hundred years, acht Hundert jahre*, since the German settlers arrived in—what's it called?—Banat."

He had found the barbaric word not in the file on the table, next to Bukovina, but, proud of his achievement, in his own memory.

"Yes, Banat! Even after eight hundred years it's utterly obvious. You can hear it in the accent, the vocabulary, see it in the behavior."

So, nothing that had happened yesterday, or the day before, or today really mattered. This was what the well-intentioned German representative had tried to tell him.

Reconciled with the nothingness of the day, with its unavailable code, ready to celebrate, he went into the first bar he could find.

In the evening, as he opened the door of his apartment, he heard his roommate's usual greeting in the dark. "Decision is a moment of madness," Mr. Kierkegaard said in the same insidious whisper he used on other evenings.

Yes, but not should the madness of indecision be overlooked.

He knew his friend's obsessions and could no longer endure these nightly disputes.

The Eighteen Days
Isaac Bashevis Singer

NOTE

While the white smoke of Munich lifted Ophelia in its open palm, while Gregor Samsa, Raskolnivkov, and young Alice were singed from their pages on propagandist bonfires, while writers themselves burned dust-to-dust in Buchenwald, Auschwitz, and Terezin, Isaac Bashevis Singer was in his Upper West Side apartment learning English.

Friday, July 12: *rafter*. Monday, July 15: *silt*. Wednesday, July 17: *incubus, tenuous, lurid light*. The days continue, three or four words each: *dabble, grapple, doting, husky, wainscot, parterre, pew, appellation, fallow, aftermath, appurtenances of civilization, the mutability of the quality we call American, erosion, lucid . . .*

These eighteen days—shown here for the first time, courtesy of the Judaic Collection of the Florida State University Libraries—represent the longest continuous span of such vocabulary-building in Singer's daily journal for 1940, the year he began his first writings in English. Other pages contain doodles, reminders, scribbled plot seeds for stories and novels never planted, and seemingly random notes, including a kind of daily credo, which includes:

> *Whatever I have to do today, no matter how annoying my work, how irritating or futile my task is, I am going to accomplish it in the best possible way, in a manner as if the whole world and its future would depend on it.*

—a sentiment at once adolescent and prophetic.

These pages of Singer's are not great literature; surely they were never intended to be published. But like all great literature, like the stories, poems and play by which these eighteen days are now surrounded, they are the product of a seemingly impossible faith in communication—of person to person, idea to utterance, mind to

214

hand to paper—a faith made so much more impossible in the new era of Babel in which Singer was learning English.

Judaism is a religion of words. While Yiddish was the language of the shtetl, and almost all of Singer's writing, it is Hebrew that rests on Judaism's tongue. The Hebrew language contains far fewer words than English does; most words have several meanings, and all words have profound and profoundly unavoidable biblical resonances. Words are sacred, and inextricably linked with other words, as well as numbers and subcutaneous meaning. One could not, for example, think of eighteen days without at once noting that eighteen is the numerical equivalent to *chai*, Hebrew for "life." Here, against a backdrop of broken glass and human incineration, is a chapter of *life*. A quiet chapter, yes. A chapter easily lost in the dark corners of Jewish history. But an essential chapter: while Torahs were made into lampshades, while scholars were made into lampshades, Singer was learning words.

In the beginning was the word . . .

Honor the word . . .

Etch the word on the doorposts of your house and on your gates . . .

Yes, but what word? What word?

Singer's most loved myth (which became the subject of his most brilliant fiction) was that of the Golem, a monster made of clay and soil by Prague's chief rabbi, to save the Jews from persecution. To give the beast life, the rabbi placed a slip of parchment under its tongue, on which was written the unknowable, unspeakable name of God.

Singer too held this under his tongue; he saw his task as a kind of modern version of the Golem's. But it was not only the God under his tongue that he had faith in. It was *the word:* the unknowable word for which we search, for which we exhaust dictionaries, for which we write and erase and write again, the word whose existence we believe in without any proof, the next word we will learn, which we pray will come closer to expressing our desired meaning. Our God of the lexicon. A God we can believe in.

—*Jonathan Safran Foer*

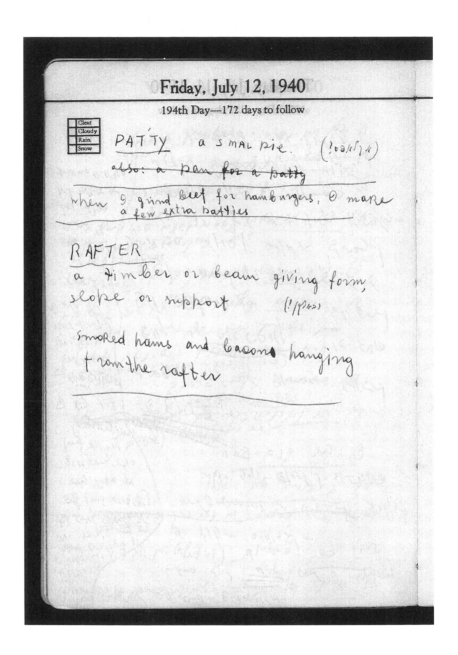

Friday, July 12, 1940
194th Day—172 days to follow

Clear
Cloudy
Rain
Snow

PATTY   a smal pie.   (לאָדעלקע)

also: a pan for a patty

when I grind beef for hamburgers, I make
a few extra patties

RAFTER

a timber or beam giving form,
slope or support   (בעלקע)

smoked hams and bacons hanging
from the rafter

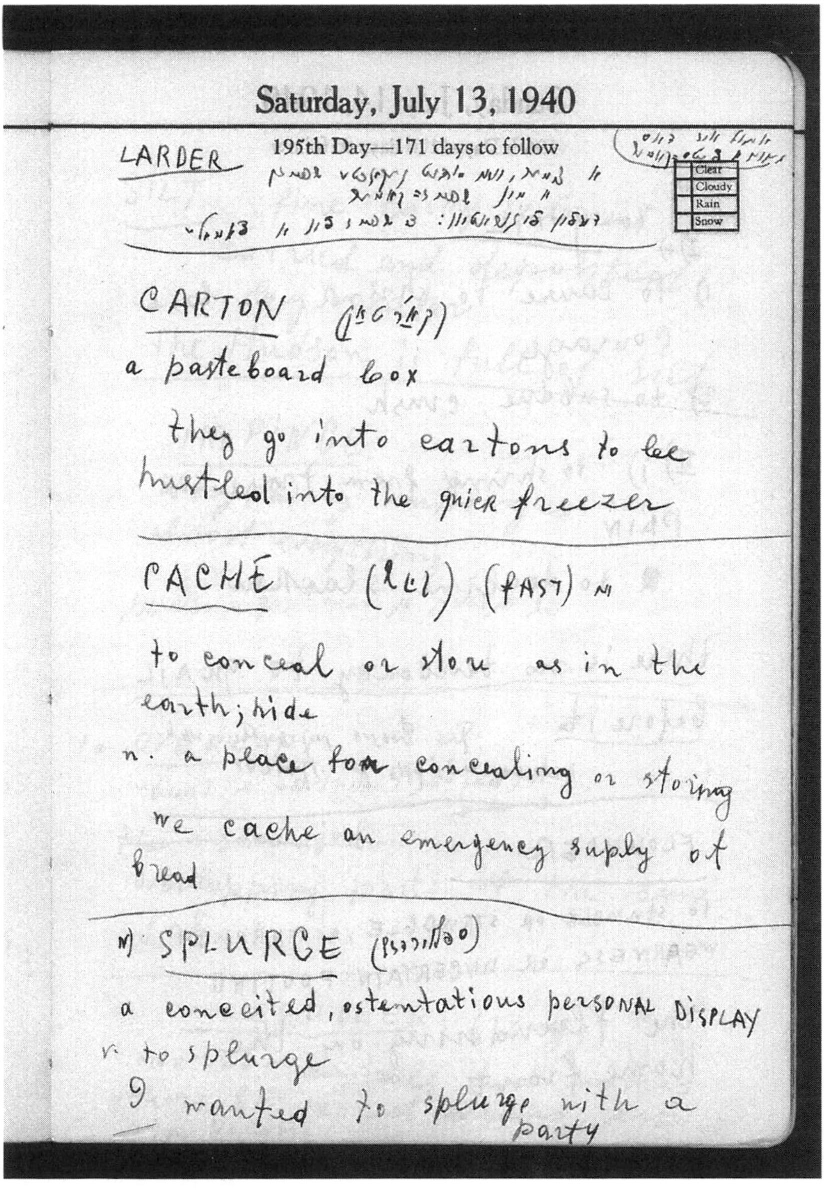

Saturday, July 13, 1940

LARDER   195th Day—171 days to follow

[Yiddish/Hebrew handwritten notes]

CARTON _(קארטאן)_

a pasteboard box

they go into cartons to be
hustled into the quick freezer

CACHE _(כעש)_ _(PAST)_ n

to conceal or store as in the
earth; hide
n. a place for concealing or storing
we cache an emergency suply of
bread

n SPLURGE _(ספלוירדזש)_

a conceited, ostentatious personal DISPLAY
v. to splurge
I wanted to splurge with a
party

Sunday, July 14, 1940

196th Day—170 days to follow

Clear / Cloudy / Rain / Snow

to **QUAIL**

I) +)

1) to cause to shrink or lose courage

2) to subdue, crush

II) i) to shrink from TRIAL OR PAIN

to decline slacken

there is no tendency to QUAIL before it

FLOUNDER

to stumble or struggle, as through WEAKNESS or UNCERTAIN FOOTING

the floundering on the home front

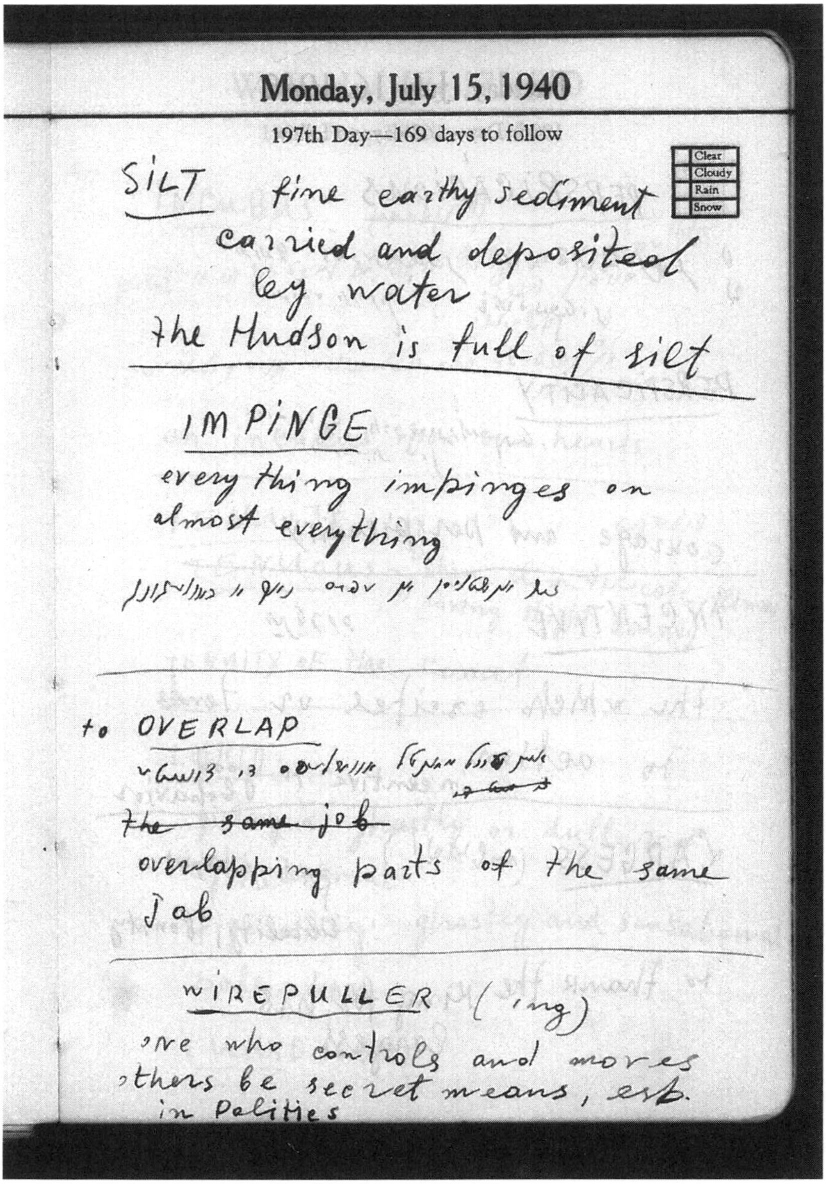

Monday, July 15, 1940

197th Day—169 days to follow

Clear
Cloudy
Rain
Snow

SILT   fine earthy sediment
carried and deposited
by water
the Hudson is full of silt

IMPINGE

every thing impinges on
almost everything

[Hebrew/Yiddish text]

to OVERLAP

[Yiddish text]

~~the same job~~

overlapping parts of the same
job

WIREPULLER (ing)

one who controls and moves
others be secret means, esp.
in Politics

Tuesday, July 16, 1940

198th Day—168 days to follow

PERSPICACIOUS

courage and perspicacity

INCENTIVE

the which excites or tends to action. incentive to good behavior

LARGESS

liberality, bounty

to thank the King for his largess

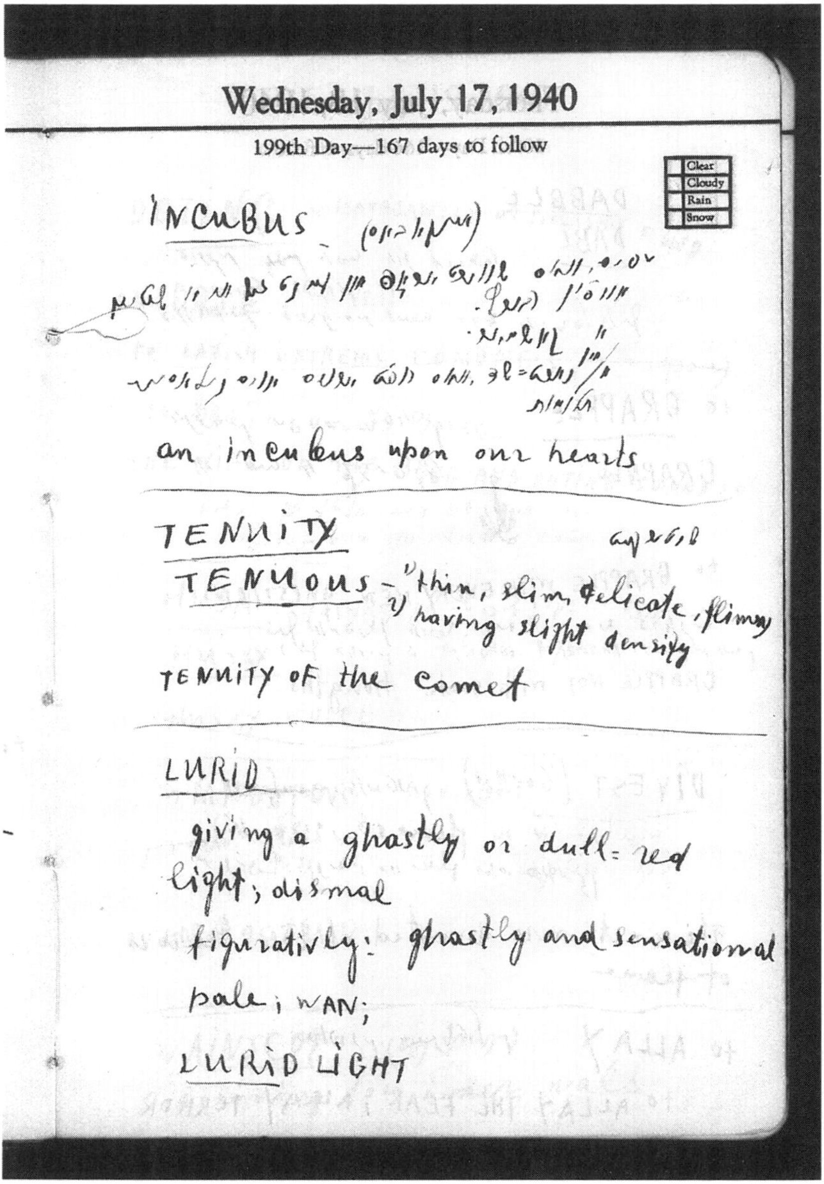

Wednesday, July 17, 1940

199th Day—167 days to follow

| Clear |
| Cloudy |
| Rain |
| Snow |

INCUBUS (הׁפּיוט‎)

[Hebrew/Yiddish handwriting]

an incubus upon our hearts

TENUITY

TENUOUS — "thin, slim, delicate, flimsy
"having slight density

TENUITY OF the comet

LURID

giving a ghastly or dull=red
light; dismal
figuratively: ghastly and sensational
pale; WAN;

LURID LIGHT

Thursday, July 18, 1940

200th Day—166 days to follow

Clear / Cloudy / Rain / Snow

DABBLE
DABL

to GRAPPLE

GRAPNEL

to GRAPPLE WITH EVERY NEW QUESTION

GRAPPLE NOT with such thoughts

DIVEST

The comets were divested of the Terrors of flame

to ALLAY

to ALLAY THE FEAR, ALLAY TERROR

Friday, July 19, 1940

201st Day—165 days to follow

Clear / Cloudy / Rain / Snow

DOTING ᴇxᴛʀᴀᴠᴀɢᴀɴᴛʟʏ ᴏʀ ꜰᴏᴏʟɪꜱʜʟʏ ꜰᴏɴᴅ

to DOTE (‎)

to LAVISH EXTREME FONDNESS (on, upon)

to be in one's DOTAGE

THE WIFE OF THE AGED AND DOTING SO AND SO

HUSK

HUSKY

HUSKY VOICE

IMPOSTOR

IMPOSTUR

WAINSCOT (‎)
a lining for inner wals

223

Saturday, July 20, 1940

202nd Day—164 days to follow

Clear
Cloudy
Rain
Snow

STUDDED withe iron bolts

egressions and ingressions

PARTERRE

a small parterre planted
with shrubs

LATERAL

the lateral branches

Sunday, July 21, 1940

203rd Day—163 days to follow

| Clear |
| Cloudy |
| Rain |
| Snow |

TO <u>RAMBLE</u>

[Yiddish handwriting]

   RAMBLING DETAILS

[Yiddish handwriting]

PEW ([Yiddish])

a long enclosed seat in a church

---

to <u>GLOSS</u> [Yiddish]

[Yiddish]

[Yiddish]

[Yiddish]

[Yiddish] to gloss over...

gloss-glossy

HA-BIL-í-ment ([Yiddish])

<u>FERULE</u> [Yiddish]

[Yiddish]

[Yiddish]

---

to <u>STUD</u> [Yiddish]

[Yiddish]

STUDDED with stars, daisies stud the meadow

Monday, July 22, 1940

204th Day—162 days to follow

Clear
Cloudy
Rain
Snow

STAG

STAG DINNER

CONGEAL

CADGY

APPELATION

my real appelation

TO BRUIT

to noise abroad, report, proclaim
a rumor noised abroad
indignant winds bruited its infamy

Tuesday, July 23, 1940

205th Day—161 days to follow

		Clear	
		Cloudy	
		Rain	
		Snow	

to SLEUTH (אויסשפירן) אויספאָרשן

n. שפיאָנעווען

                      "שפיאָנירן"

the carried their sleuthing one step further

FALLOW ברוכפעלד (אומבאַאַרבעט)

(The field remained fallow)

BRACKET קלאַמער, איינקלאַמערן, האַלטער

                      שטיץ, אָנהאַלט, שטעלן אין קלאַמער

[ ] (2

DEPLOY

TO SPREAD out in line of battle,
as troops

SEDITION אויפּרודערונג

BLUDGEON פּאַלקע

       שטשן מיט אַ פּאַלקע, פּאַלקען: אַראָפּשלאָגן

227

Isaac Bashevis Singer

Wednesday, July 24, 1940

206th Day—160 days to follow

DOCILITY

the docility of TRAINED SUBJECTS

CEREBRATIONS

CEREBRAL

INSIDIOUS (lavender) (furcrisch?)

doing harm as if by lying in wait;

a insidious plague

AFTERMATH

228

Thursday, July 25, 1940

207th Day—159 days to follow

| Clear |
| Cloudy |
| Rain |
| Snow |

to HOBNOB (פֿאַרברענגען)

1ᵗᵒ clink (glasses) together in convivial drinking

2) to drink together familiarly

hence: to be on familiar terms.

(The Japanese with whom he)
(HOBNOBBED so long)

APPURTENANCE (Zubehör)

appurtenances of civilization

PERCIPIENT

who has the necessary percipience and no delusions

Friday, July 26, 1940

208th Day—158 days to follow

Clear
Cloudy
Rain
Snow

INTRICATE

INTRICACY

the EXTREME INTRICACY OF american life

MUTABILITY

the mutability of the quality we call american

INVIDIOUS

expressing, prompted by or provoking
envy or ill will
unjustly discriminating

and-in no invidious sence, a
politician

Saturday, July 27, 1940

209th Day—157 days to follow

UBIQUITY

(ubiquitous)

TO HALT

the halt, the blind, the mad

EROSION

ERODED

the heartsoil knowing quick
erosion

LUCID

LUCID SANITY

Sunday, July 28, 1940

210th Day—156 days to follow

Clear / Cloudy / Rain / Snow

PACER TROTTER

[Yiddish handwriting]

[Yiddish handwriting]

Slobe TROTTER

TO EDDY   *[Yiddish] ?*

THE RIVER.. SOMEWHOT EDDYING, but
NAVIGABLE
EDDY MIND

[Yiddish handwriting]
[Yiddish handwriting] ?

PERFUNTORY   (s. Curls)
        c

DONE CARELESLY
SOME OF HIS ACTS HAVE BEEN PERFUNTORY
IN THE EXTREME

Monday, July 29, 1940

211th Day—155 days to follow

Clear
Cloudy
Rain
Snow

PARSON

a RECTOR; ANY BENEFICED CLERGYMAN

METTLE

HIS METTLE AND STATURE AS A DRAMATIST

TO PUT A PERSON ON HIS METTLE

SQUIP

a DAMP SQUIP. ALL SPLUTTER AND NO EXPLOSION

IMP

IMPISH MIND

TO EKE OUT (with)   supplement

such rewards even
eked out with
SPECIAL FEES FOR ODD JOBS
you are furnished a SORRY SUPPORT

Medium

Sandra Newman

A TROUPE OF CHINESE ACROBATS forms a human pyramid, fifteen strong at the base. They wear silver jumpsuits, appliquéd with red satin stars. When the pyramid is complete, it's so high, the top man's head is obscured by the proscenium. Thus, when he kicks away and rises free, he at first appears to have grasped some hook in the ceiling. Only when he drifts out, coaxing his body past the proscenium with twitches of the buttocks, does he show himself to be floating with no wire. He proceeds thus over the audience, moving with some difficulty, like a worm tunneling through the air. Above the stalls, row G or thereabouts, he pauses, bobbing, and tips on a horizontal axis to hang upside down.

He tells us the Oriental secret of eternal life.

He says, in China, putting faith in God, the dead are raised by simple peasants; the price of this service is the same as that of a loaf of bread in Britain.

Gradually, beginning with his shaven pate, he makes himself invisible. For a long time, his red slippers kick, alone, skating and hopping along the plaster ornaments of the theater ceiling.

This is an essay about the possibility of, advantages to, stains left on the tiles and in the tub itself by, communicating with the dead.

I prefer to do mine with the lights off, in about a foot of hot un-scented water. From time to time I crawl out and lie spread-eagled on the bath mat, face down, towel draped over my buttocks. I can still, faintly, hear the traffic outside.

The dead will tell me insignificant details of my day to come. My train will be delayed; the boss will wear a sequined jacket; there will be a special on salmon at the restaurant which I am on no account to take, because the fish is off. It seems calculated to convince me of their reality without offering any actual aid. I ask them:

Where is my lover, where is my young man, my John? Where are my father and brother? Are you ghosts or only demons, and what use are you actually—

They say it's beautiful where they are and they are at peace.

It's like some sales pitch; it makes me wild. No matter what I say, they give the same old tired travel brochure. Sometimes they pass on "messages" from John, but they will not let me see him. He too says it's beautiful, blah blah, and about the fish.

I cannot, not, understand how other mediums buy this crap.

A band of marauders stops the caravan at a rocky pass. Twirling his sword, the bandit king demands the party's souls, represented in gold, to be presented by dawn's light. That night by the campfire, the travelers confer, uneasily shrugging at the muskets trained on their backs from the surrounding blackness.

There is disagreement over whether a totem actually contains the spirit represented. Given as booty, is it lost, or will it nonetheless be claimed by heaven? The smith is abused for his interpretation of the souls of one middle-aged woman, repetitiously stricken, in the course of the journey, by "vapors," and a child whose blond curls belie her frightful temper. The first is rendered as a ragged, bent thing, identifiable in the brighter leaps of the fire as a crushed snake. The second he balks at and says he cannot make a speck, a tittle, nothing, for there is no original.

In the taut atmosphere, the party nearly comes to blows;

and through the night, the members hunt out every speck, every tittle of gold they may have hitherto stashed. Teeth come out, and heirloom bracelets; spoons inscribed with the crests of abolished Dukedoms; wedding bands, and medallions said to have a curative influence on gout and boils. Each piles his hoard separately, catching the smith's eye, hoping for a flatteringly copious soul totem.

As dawn breaks, blinding on every slope, puzzlingly appearing to come from 360 degrees and from the zenith and from the golden figures, tiny and standing deep in the loose dry dirt as if rooted;

the marauders have vanished, leaving not even hoofprints, not even a scent of camel, no dung nor human soil

and the human figurines are dazzling, too hot to regard or even gingerly approach, fingers extended, within ten feet

and the smith has risen, flown, is seen flapping mid-sky like Mohammed, arms and legs spread star-fashion and blue. Called to, he makes no sign or sound but hangs as before, occasionally glittering. The travelers confer over whether to attempt tossing up a rope but reflect that this is pointless, their longest rope, never mind throw, not near sufficing.

They mill about for some time, no longer speaking; then some harness up and go, leaving a few moon-eyed sufferers keeping watch at the blaze of that gold. Some days later, some dehydration visions and convulsions later, they are felt by the smith to fly past in a chill shriek, zooming in a multiple upwards so absolute as to be notional
like a geometer's conceived line.

This is an essay about the possibility of, pluses and minuses and hidden snags to, remaining evidence in archaeological finds for, communicating with the dead.

It can be taught; curiously enough. I have on occasion assembled classes, not, you understand, in the actual bathroom, but in my front room or in a basement let from the local School for Girls. Although I semi-hypnotize my pupils, give hints and suggest visualizations, the truth is, I suspect, that the active ingredient is the fee, which has been set at 120 pounds since I began. Shelling out money seems to have a reassuring effect. Having paid for the service, people are then willing to believe that they have been connected to the other world.

I get a remarkable number, furthermore, calling back to complain that the ability faded after no more and no less than three days, suggesting that the rate is forty pounds per day line rental, with no variation made for use.

I have had nightmares in which the spirits come to collect these monies from me, demanding them in gold doubloons which I have, oddly enough, stashed in the hollow beneath my bathtub—though in the dream I strenuously deny it. John is there, semiconscious and bloodied as I saw him last, held by the arms by two burly ghosts who warn he will never speak to me until the debt is paid.

When I take a bath now I often imagine these gold doubloons beneath me, stirring restlessly as if animate. If I am drowsy or preoccupied, I even idly worry about possible damage to them from leaked detergent.

I think now I am going to my bathroom when I die.

"But why muddy?" said John. He was on all fours, scrubbing muddy footprints from our bedroom carpet. Still in his boxers; four A.M. I'd said it was better to catch fresh, not to wait until they were dry come morning. Because you end up whittling at them with a bread knife; it's clay really I guess.

Whatever earth they have in the graveyard.
I may have said that then, I don't remember.
John was saying, "So this supposedly runs in your family?"
"Yes, we hear banshees and things. We're just basically haunted.
One of my uncles was even pursued by the devil on horseback." I
began to giggle, I felt lightheaded and foolishly pleased.
"The devil? Or your uncle? On horseback."
"Oh, the devil. Though I guess my uncle must have been as
well, or the devil would have caught him, surely."
The devil would have caught him, anyway. Being the devil"
"No, according to my uncle, the devil just went white hot all of
a sudden and shrieked up into the air."
John began to laugh too, so much he stopped and sat down like
a dog with both hands on the floor like paws and we were laugh-
ing until it reached some critical point and I had to pull the lamp
chain. So the room sprang into light. And the footprints are still
there, but we're not laughing. It's as if we weren't really laughing, it
only seemed as if we were laughing in the dark. And it seems to me,
suddenly, that John will die in a tragic accident on the M25, in which
he will be thrown from his motorbike at an angle which is somehow
very clear to my mind, and there is an associated color, maybe of
flames, but I don't know about these visions, and I can't change it
anyhow, and if the date and time, rather than that stupid trajectory,
had come to me, it might have been worth thinking about, but I put
it from my mind.

John says, "This is ridiculous. Could we put down kitchen roll or
something, for tomorrow night?"

"Well," I say, suddenly venomous, insulted, "It's only my dead
father, you know. Don't take it so much to heart."

Three stop in the air and one lingers below, fretful. All four tremble
as if exhausted, as if they are lights whose source is nearly depleted.
One of the airborne makes what would be a sound and they all disappear and re-become a short film about the life of Edward Pencil,
inventor of the pencil, who died tragically by falling into his mother's womb which opened before him in his living room carpet, as if
casually, as if opening up just on the way to some routine task, and
although Pencil saw through this stratagem, he was aware that he
was required to be fooled, to take the bait and lean out too far over
the gaping hole, saying "Mother? Is that you?" and even then to gasp
in feigned surprise as the tentacle flew up from that maw, snap-

wrapped around his neck ten times and whipped him down. I am watching the colorized version.

A voice cries behind the screen, "It's not true! It's not true!" but, whether this is the voice of the calumniated Pencil or of some rival, more legitimate inventor, is unclear.

Suddenly an audience is present, whose eyes illuminate the auditorium, brilliant as headlights. The audience members seem unaware of this, and eat popcorn methodically, fidget and gape like other, unlighting, audiences.

I realize that soon the high, piercing noise in my gut will rise in volume; that this must draw the attention of the lighting crowd. One by one they'll turn and train their beams on me until the concentrated light will heat to explosiveness my small heart. It will spray its doubloons, spill its wealth . . . I must preserve these at all costs, all I have in the way of ransom . . . I rise and, trailing ribbons and weeds, trailing my poppies and rowan branches, run from the theater. At the exit I trip and the wind takes me. I scream as it lifts me in intelligent hands, bearing me, delivering me up to the tunnel and the ascent.

John, come back to me, bring me word from my brother, come in ordinary clothes, be visible, be all sensible and available to my wet grasp, come wash the blood from your temples in my bath and make me bring the mirror to shave your coffin beard. We can live off our bathtub doubloons in the middle sky.

Do not send your go-betweens to me any longer, John, don't poison me with your fellows, don't you know I can already see through my shins, in a strong light? Yet I believe, I will risk I am heavy enough still, ballast enough, if you just hold on to me, hold on to me, why did you not hold on to me

Your foul ascent will founder; there will be no remounting of that rainy heaven; you and I can linger in between, in eternal practice, always forgetting what happens to you after you die.

Roses from the South

Paul West

UNTIL I AT LAST WEARIED of Treischnitt's skies, I peered at them daily, that old master's, at their texture and their hint of third dimension, having no inkling of how much I would eventually peer at Kolberhoff's houses, which always looked different when viewed right after peering at Treischnitt's skies, as was also true for Kolberhoff's houses. It was all a matter of context, even if the Treischnitt sky I was peering at was in a painting that contained no house at all, and vice versa. The only true context, I told myself, was in the mind of the beholder. Treischnitt died before Kolberhoff, of course, being older, but they had both vanished from my ken before I realized I would never know them intimately. I had always hoped, even in my salad days, not to be lethally disregarded by those who mattered to me. So Treischnitt died, much given to anger in his last years, not Kolberhoff, their works persisting in my head, neither living nor dead, but neutrally exact. It would have been the same if Kolberhoff, genial to the last, had gone first, before Treischnitt, except that in the end Kolberhoff might have been thinking he would precede Treischnitt, thus *condemning* Treischnitt to a Kolberhoffless world. It was in their works they died first. There is a death each time you lay down paint and it dries amid the rough ownership of your gaze. Only those who have not eaten too large a portion of life can remain happy with their work; they always have something to look forward to. So if it was not skies it was houses and on red-letter days houses below skies, skies above houses in the decent balance the illustrative artist aspires to. After all, you are only transferring the stuff of one world to another place in the same world. These truths came to me early, but I won no credit for them, indeed receiving many mouthfuls of renegade insult about my lacking the power of mutilation. You cannot have everything, not even in later years when, picking a point and a place, you consider how you have fared. You may not be able to do this later, for grotesque reasons. So, with Treischnitt and Kolberhoff missing, and their works a blur of buried secrets—How could either of them be that

239

good?—I learned how to look at the space behind a canvas, seeing nothing at all, though conceding the obvious presence of a wall or a fireplace. If their work no longer detains you, you miss them less, whom you never got to know anyway, they being somewhat stand-offish whether in bad or good temper. They were not clavichords. Sometimes one must practice a mental hygiene based on self-saving ardor. When those who claim to know refuse to make the rest move over, then you have to minister to yourself, making sweet calm where you might have been as cranky as Treischnitt, or Kolberhoff imitating him so as not to seem a softie. Oh, the murder in their hearts as they failed to take their critics with them into finality, as in some old song of saying farewell to the world that has bruised you so. No matter: I linger on these men. With what hesitation I had left for Treischnitt a crumpled little postcard of some Italian lake, popped on his stoop like a hostage. It would have been amazing if he had concluded it came from anyone at all but had blown there on the wind, willed to embarrass him by Kolberhoff. It was only after I had wooed Treischnitt with another postcard, signed with my initials, and then a little watercolor of my own unsigned, that I turned to Kolberhoff. I left more for Treischnitt than for Kolberhoff, having started with Treischnitt, but I soon caught up with my leavings for Treischnitt, leaving much the same kinds of things for Kolberhoff, though to equal disregard, which is to say both Treischnitt and Kolberhoff ignored my existence with the same degree of uninformed aversion, responding to neither my name nor my initials, though of course Kolberhoff ignored me for longer, having outlived Treischnitt, at least until I desisted altogether. Two men, so important in my young life, yet so aloof to me. It hardly bears thinking about, though I have long pondered the chance of any minute differences between what I left Treischnitt and then Kolberhoff, proud famous painters both. Look them up now, meaning in reference books (not calling on them in person), and you will never find them, nor, as it were, in the last glimpse of their dying eyes the last painting they looked at: one of mine. What they did do has slid into the chasm of what they did not do, which has vanished altogether, whereas several violent deformers of mankind's noble face, and the trim honor of its windowboxes, have gone on from generation to generation, Urlschelb and Grenzhabe and Tlöch, to name only a few offenders who vanquished Treischnitt and Kolberhoff, although both Treischnitt and Kolberhoff were the more gifted, lacking as they were in social graces. One day, my face wrapped tight in a huge brown scarf, I accosted Treischnitt and thrust a small coin in his hand, just to see what he would do, but he merely gaped, which Kolberhoff did not do when I pennied him; he only laughed. In the end, all my solicitations came to naught as the opiners who passed judgment on me and my toil happened to be Treischnitt's and Kolberhoff's juniors, crass imitators at the most. Whom did I have to kiss to prosper? In whose fist put coin? Besides, I had not the time to get on with serious work and at the same time conjure up little pastels and quaint greetings for Treischnitt and Kolberhoff. I would have had more success groveling before a statue of Frederick the Great or Charlemagne. It is hard to learn what you need not do in this world, whom you must woo and whom you must spurn. You make choices as best you can, and then get thrashed by the heirs of Treischnitt and Kolberhoff, our beloved native land being the one that boasts the most decorations and orders, sashes and stars, almost even a satin gown for yawning. However, without having spun in the periphery of Treischnitt and Kolberhoff, I would never have understood the canker that afflicted their heirs, to whom Treischnitt and Kolberhoff were generous Neanderthals. It was nearly enough to make me want a war to break out, something that would kill me off and so spare both Treischnitt and Kolberhoff the embarrassment of my juvenile attentions, tracking them at a distance when they sometimes went for a walk together puffing on cigars (Treischnitt's a Turkish flavor, Kolberhoff's more a Balkan Sobranie). I have always loathed tobacco, but, following the two of them, I made a small sacrifice, though it seemed as if the two tobacco aromas fused into what two men with stomach trouble might have vented behind them. Did they see me? I doubt it. Treischnitt and Kolberhoff walked together only because no one would accompany either and provide a good quarrel, which was all they walked for, jabbing at the air and wagging an index finger in the direction of march. An ungenerous person would say I was obsessed with Treischnitt and Kolberhoff, but rather I was a case of highly developed loyalty, knowing, as they say, not Treischnitt and Kolberhoff but everyone else, where my bread might be buttered provided either of these grand old nobodies was willing to hoick the butter from its shelf and ply the butter knife: Must help this promising little chap with his career, not leave the privilege to deadheads. It must have gone like that if Treischnitt and Kolberhoff talked about me at all, lamenting my uncouth ways, my persistence, but recognizing at the same time my classical ardor, for what is classical is what all agree on. It is not a freak thing. There is a social sanction.

241

So you might wonder what those two blockheads Treischnitt and Kolberhoff were arguing about, dyed-in-the-wool classicists that they were. It was not as if rival schools of portraiture, say, were having at each other, Köbel and Steinitz and Probstschule against Klarf, Ulruhst and Delbers, which would have been uproarious, no, but Kolnsheft having at Döbelzeiss, who as you well know spent their lives at other people's throats. No, there is a way of arguing that celebrates the sun, the trees, the lapping water, and two die-hard opponents can exchange insults above a bridge of natural agreement. Had I had my chance to quarrel or agree with either Treischnitt or Kolberhoff, my two art-hounds lolloping on before me by some fifty kilometers or so, I might have extorted from either a recognition that would pay off endlessly in finer technique to the end of my days. I was deprived of that if you can be deprived of what you have never had. My own doctrine, of how the watercolors actually tasted as you sipped the mohair bristles to a sharp point, might have joined us in an entirely new school of art: burnt sienna—tea; Naples yellow—baby-dung; Alizarin crimson—blood of a dog. What a wide-open world of experiences awaited them at my hands, but it never happened, and on they droned, painting with their eyes, maybe a little smell now and then, but quite severed from the world of taste, which was almost like not eating. Treischnitt and Kolberhoff (I would address them thus jointly like two linked cars in a train) remained conjoint in their indifference, pseudo-quarreling only to cement their bond. At my wildest, then, I would do my best to invade the sleep of one or the other, Treischnitt or Kolberhoff, even when Treischnitt was dreaming about Kolberhoff with candid aversion, or Kolberhoff about Treischnitt with undisguised envy, or indeed either dreaming about the other's dreaming about him. I was in there, in the gaps, egging them on to further resentments or sunnier loathings, wishing to roost in their minds forever, nudging this or that flash of dare I say it genius? All imagined, of course, as if I were the proprietor of dreamland, developing scripts and scenarios for these two malleable giants to perform amid their snores. Why they never smoked cigars while napping I never knew, but they could have, such was their power. Walking behind either of two men is one thing, but dreaming along with them is another, requiring invasive skill, even to the extent of fondling this or that part of their anatomy in order to give a misleading effect, though I made their most private parts soggy as battered milkwort, just to stimulate their minds. From sleep with me, they would arise rumpled and ill-rested, and I imagined myself as never quite going away but sojourning under the bed, right beneath the point at which the mattress creaked most. Truth told, even if you loathe your targets, you eventually come to enjoy something about them, the curve of an earlobe, say, or the tilt of the septum. There they lay, my two hearties, aesthetic men of war, even as I scribbled and scrawled in my mind's eye the masterworks that would join me to them in after-years, not exactly inspiring me, but embodying the impetus of the true artist, whom nothing distracted from his toil. At times, in dreams or out, I would fancy myself mixing pencil shavings into my porridge to crispen it up as well as to make it more artful, or squeezing a little burnt sienna into the mustard (some friends of mine painted in mustard, boot polish, and a white paste for tennis shoes called Blanco, imported from that haven of taste England). All I was trying to do, unlike Treischnitt and Kolberhoff, was to fuse the world of art with that of not-art, easier to say than to do, almost to the point at which you could not tell a postcard from what it depicted. Perhaps to accomplish this one needed satanic help, a Faustian touch denied me at that time, since it was a mode of magic hitherto unknown in the world of visual art. Such prodigies we try for, we doodlers among the pigments and powders, lubricating our brains with linseed or water. In a word, as I would have told both Treischnitt and Kolberhoff, I was trying to force the created into perfect similarity, with nothing extraneous allowed. Hence my leaning toward those two worthies, as distinct from the even more renowned Klötzheide, Funknasch, and Zwölftraum, esteemed because more socially adroit than either of my two magi. I would one day, I hoped, be even more adroit than they, always tucking my shirt in, never accepting a penny from strangers. You see how I keep looking back, an act about which I have thought a good deal, hour after hour while plucking fibers from the old run-down sofa in my garret, horsehair bursting out at all angles like a beast having a hemorrhage. Put it this way: If you are in your teens, and you keep on looking back on your earlier teens from the vantage of your later teens, then you are more in tune, more closely connected, than if you are looking back at your teens from your fifties, say (if you get that far). It sounds right: the closer you are to what you look back on, the warmer, the keener your recollection will be. I don't believe it. The whole enterprise is one of how articulate you are. People have told me that the closer your idiom is to that of the period you are recalling (nineteen recalling eighteen, say), the more convincing your account is, but only if you have ruled out the refinement and

243

delicacy of a much later speaker, writer, who can muster many more shades and gradations, subtleties and hints, than the nineteen-year-old. The ultimate caricature of the view I am rejecting is that of the three-year-old infant babbling about being Age Two. What I am after, given the time, is what someone called the faint subterfuges of un-tutored eloquence as if the words themselves had understood. The man of fifty, even with blurred and blighted recall, can make more of his infancy than the hobgoblin of twenty-one. Not that it matters: we are lucky when anyone at all gets it right, this excavation of the heart, supervised by a hurt intellect that tells itself there has always, all along, been a *Doppelgänger* dogging his steps, preceding him in all things, treading in his footprints, seating himself on the warmed-up toilet, eating off the cleared plate, brushing the already scoured teeth. It comes to either this or, as I once discovered, rambling about old Vienna, some two hundred old geezers in a huge hall, all playing cards, waiting for the ax to fall. Honing their minds of course. A stronger image, that, than the Jew raving on Saturday, the Christian raving on Sunday, and who knows how many other religious maniacs bellowing their faith above the traffic. As may be obvious, this is a later me doing the tell-tale, not in the least hot on the heels of the pimply, raucous teenager, which of course tells you that I survived the years in between, somehow, yet forever awed by the alter ego I might have become. I could feel him edging up on me, stealing my body aroma for his, clipping his toenails on my own foot. Who he was will not bear saying, but perhaps he was only one of dozens sent to plague me as I strove to become somebody worth locking in jail for his outlandish ideas, his reckless thirst for power. In my time I came across theories that helped me to fathom who these other beings, my accompanists, were: Errol von Knechtvold, for instance, who said that our heads were full of voices from pre-history, which was the source of myth, or Joachim Kernsvogler, who said all echoes were prophetic. How impossible, say I, to collect up all the disparate bits of a possible you and make them firm, permanent, under one umbrella. If others help, now with a thrashing, now with a failing grade, it might be managed, but not without consummate pain. Experts are those who have dodged their own questions by blocking the avenue of thought with parboiled clichés. If you have sat at the feet of a wiseacre, or pawed the fly of a genius, you are even more on your own than before; the answer is only in what's impetuous, done without thought but with the whole crescendo of biased atoms behind you. I am bound to lose both Treischnitt and Kolberhoff, my lightning rods, without whom I have no alpha and omega, not that they did not overlap: Trieberhoff and Kolberschnitt, my two whatever other combination appeals. Without either of them to serve as backsight and foresight, I will have to take in the all, *Blick in Chaos*, as we sometimes say: peer into the mess. A migraine follows, and then you are painting in a chrome-flashing gloom. Better to have them back, hale them back, as zombies, kicked this way and that, than have no inkling of them at all, their faces contorted and wizened, their hands mowing about, their feet splayed. Push them when they will not serve, almost as if you were the one's mother, Frau Treischnitt, the other's spouse, Frau Kolberhoff. Always to either they were little lads, two friendly little lads with roving eyes, changelings to both *Frauen*, twins of a kind like those English poets Browning and Tennyson, who took long walks together without ever speaking. I have always been an admirer of the English way, the only nation that has found a real place in civilized concourse for aloofness, porridge, disdain, snottiness, raspberry jam, and the stiff upper lip (better than a penis in many circumstances). But it was the highly decorated Viennese I had to cope with, wondering why amid so many titles I had none myself (would that come?), though I imagined that all the sumptuous cream cakes I could not afford, but watched being sucked on, were honors I would one day merit and receive with open mouth, tongue poised to taste. All productive of the finest chrome yellow gases, blown away by the corrupt circular breeze, akin to a Wild Western dust devil that never left the esplanade of the cafés. How do you get on in the art world? You behave as if it is all over and you predicate all you do on a *réclame* long past, yet nonetheless there to be counted on, a launching pad for every wild overture. Hence your confidence, invented, cast behind you, sponsoring you without yet having been. These complexities at first stirred me, but I then took them for granted, knowing I would sweep all before me as an old soul does, born wrinkled, but chronically expert in the ways of the climb. Just be yourself and ask: that was it, simpler than bowel movement, more direct than the yawn. If only it were so. Small wonder that, peering through the mesh of the Treischnitts Herr and Frau and the Kolberhoffs Herr and Frau, and all the varied combinations of the four held before my gaze like the muslin we drape hanging beeves with, I lost track of who I was, as well as of what I was meant to be, compensating—if you will tolerate such a word—by overdoing everything, even the muted pencil touches that completed an acanthus leaf on a frieze. It might be put thus: Lost

245

amid the world of infinite mischance, he became palely hyperbolical, imagining grotesque picnics with Frau Treischnitt and Frau Kolberhoff, rubbing steel wool against high bulges under their skirts until the blood came and a stench of slaughterhouse washing arose to pollute the countryside and the suave aromas of champagne and wicker hampers. A violent child overgrown, you might say. Say it then, I have no inhibitions about being damned. The urgent thing, amid a million tangents, was to cut the first niche in my cliff of fame, clinching my status with a few well-designed watercolors faintly daubed here and there with Frau and Frau blood, Treischnitt and Kolberhoff thumbprints, and whatever else lay to hand, always tinting ever so quietly, so much so that not an examiner would be able to tell the chromatic tremor in the atmosphere from a tremor in his eyelid. Auersberg Palace, then, around 1911: meticulous corners and high fluted goblet shapes, but the people dwarfed, as befits, none of them asked me for preferential treatment, and I wanted to convey how many of them it would take to cram that vacant square: a mere half dozen seemed to halt in mid-float, even the one wheeling something, perhaps a barrow or a child's scooter, none of them appearing to look at the others, scratched in as if on metal, and enormously humbled by the dominant slab and the infinitely increasing steps. Here you can count the chimneys (four) and guess at the minarets. Actually the figures in the foreground have come from another age and time, the returning dead, all sloping with a limp I have arrested with the stroke of my pen. What a lovely studio he must have created this in, its atmosphere velvet and gold moiré, except it has only the merest rug in it that resembles not a rug but the recently removed skin of a wolfhound, smeary and rank, hurled in a rage across the biggest smirch on the concrete floor. On this I lie, *repose,* licking the inside of a wooden can, my tongue already deformed into shape by the constant licking of such containers and my hand weary of holding it skyward for the final drip. What was it? Beets or broken kohlrabi? Washed down with water from the peat-smelling pump outside, where dogs crouch at the snarl. What drops on me from the ceiling—mauve, slimy, and warm—I have no idea, but I keep them from my mouth, oh yes you blithe comfortable buggers at the windows of the Auersberg Palace, watching the most inspired of his rotten generation swig the slop. Something has to keep body and soul, hand and imagination, together, even if only the drip from the broken roof above, dropping by the light of a rare candle, its ration of light about two hours. It is my only palace. In they go. Who has more

246

right? Perhaps even an embossed pass issued by the Herr Doktor Professor Burgomaster, Saint Peter of the Auersberg gate. They part company, Treischnitt the thin and fairly tall off to the left, tapping at doors and windows with his umbrella's steel tip (no doubt touched with curare), dumpy Kolberhoff going to the right, where he taps on nothing but speeds up his waddle. They arrive, brood, do their task, followed by huge clanging sounds of reservoirs being emptied, not so much the gush of pent-up water as the self-willed onrush of a sea. Oh good, it has all gone, and like two spry little colts Treischnitt and Kolberhoff reappear to get on with the day's examining or form-filling. No painting here, not by them or anyone else. Who has followed them into those sultry doorways, edging in disguised as a raincoat or wraith, there to carp or plead in some office, not with a painter? One day I alone will. I hope I will. I have to or I become a potato scumbler for life, scooping out eyes and stripping skins. In we go, after them, following, as if this were physically possible, the peppermint aroma of Treischnitt, the sobranie of Kolberhoff, I as if a little dog sniffing the crotches of women. Those paltry figures in the front courtyard have not moved: scarecrows, symbolizing something awesome, perhaps an old Greek idea that the word symbol recalls. Once upon a time, everything was all of a piece and only symbolism gives us back that halved-up world, whose main crime is to divide the image from the things seen. It recalls for me the image of the ship, not an ocean liner but sizeable, that in bad weather broke clean in half, the two halves floating off in different directions in the dark and fog. The few survivors, clinging to wreckage, were delighted, when dawn broke, to find two rescue ships bearing down on them from different quarters, arriving at laudable speed with minimum delay. Imagine their chagrin when the two mercy vessels coming to pick them up turned out to be the two halves, hulks, of the original, the worse for wear, once more coming together, or near enough, of course not making it, but evocative in their proximity of a serener outcome. In some moment of deluded optimism, did the survivors imagine the two halves, bow and stern, would come back together and fuse? Such things happen only in the golden dimension of Greek metaphor, when, say, image and thing join up as they should after eons of severance! But no, neither on the high seas nor in the etymological lexicon, does this kind of reunion happen. The survivors stick it out if they can, longing for yet another boat, or at least to get aboard either remnant and flourish before one or the other of them founders and vanishes. Or even both. Only the Greeks with their consummate sense of the unity of all created things would imagine the reunion of things that, by human fecklessness, had been thrown together ages ago. What a luscious idea, to reunite what has been sundered. I am the healer of ikons, I tell myself even as I shuffle up the steps of the Kohler Adlon, hover in the hallway having inhaled the perfume of the porte cochère, and now peek into the unguarded dining room, actually helping myself to a menu that has fallen, fluttered, in from Mars. If you can afford it, a three-shrimp appetizer called Three Whorls, on a bed of chopped fennel smothered in tangy mustard, will cost you what two dozen shrimps costs you in the green market. You pay for the ambience, the thundering suavity. Of course. It is all in the presentation, at least before they turf me out, shady loiterer, no credit given for artistic endowment or noble sentiment. Down the steps I go, but not before seeing and longing for the dark green jade table on which the guestbook sits, as marine a green as there has ever been, streaked with slashes of cornered sunlight. On such a table I will one day write an autobiography, spelling out in greater detail all that happened to me in composing this brief entry. As if I had hope of something's happening to me, something grand. What does the great Goethe say of such palaces as the Auersberg? We spend our time building palaces, and adorning them, when we cannot even dispose of our own excrement. How this bears on the career of the artist will emerge: we cannot help having to have the palaces, of course not. Who wants to say, in spite of all, he has devoted his life and gifts to sewage disposal? It is clear that, even if you happen to be Treischnitt or Kolberhoff, you bide your time, postponing the delicious moment until you are consummately ready, bound to prevail, with no carping from overfed vests crowned with mayoral watch chains. I pause and pause and pause, ever hoping to improve on the work just finished, knowing I can, I must, I will, but having to sleep on it, dream on it, let it wander unescorted through the labyrinth of my peristalsis and heartbeat. One day the heart almost stops, pulsing in a rapid frenzy in its cage, and you know you have to go, abandon your work to the appraisers in a room full of farts and aphorisms, leaving it behind to the sort that Treischnitt and Kolberhoff are without their actually being Treischnitt and Kolberhoff. Someone will squinny at your life's gift and pull a sour face, saying tell him to wait another ten years. Or, in the tradition of some famous British university, possibly impervious Oxford, the examiners work themselves into a sherry-fed frenzy saying we demand a meeting, we must lay eyes on this genius before he melts or dies. It is called A Congratulatory First, whatever that means. It means you have come in before all others, racehorse style, but have landed in heaven without cantering through the gutter of the hoi polloi. What a pipe dream. What opium. Yet I always shrink from that terminal encounter, even with my Auersberg masterpiece, knowing it will not be a masterpiece, even to Treischnitt and Kolberhoff, within a month of hard endeavor. Up the ladder I go, on limp rungs. This is why, in some kind of decorous declension, you never get around to the *coup de grâce*, which some not in the know call the *coup de gras*, knowing you are indefinitely capable of something better. Thus, at seventeen, you get cold feet, at eighteen butterflies, at nineteen the shakes, at twenty the cold-lard belly contortions, at twenty-one—well, let us not paddle fingers in the tragic vomit of twenty-one, an age at which both Treischnitt and Kolberhoff were going strong, having not only satisfied the examiners, but piled up the work, actually selling it to the blind. I have dallied, I confess; I am always dallying, but some piece of my chrysalis goes through the gates and offers curdled heart's blood to the synod of judges, hoping for miracles, but expecting shame. You have to begin somewhere, so say my allies August and Reinhold, but they are more gifted painters than I, and there comes at that moment an intuition of some other way of becoming great, of making the angel Gabriel turn tail, bowing low before a superior tenderness. Yet I try, knees knocking, up to the Auersberg, in my insolence having depicted, *my* fashion, the very building in which I am to be reviewed, down whose steps I have been tossed a score of times for loitering, just to catch a glimpse of winning entries, even a pisshouse scrawl done by one of the elect, even while wetting my trousers, fouling my ragged shirt, reddening my eyes. So it begins, inasmuch as it has not already begun. Who is to know when the tendrils of an event do not grow backward into the source or the cause, alerting the wise as to what is to come? I had rehearsed this, yearning for a mirror in my hovel, but making do with shadows, addressing chiaroscuro on the wall when the sun came in right, high up, deforming all it touched. I began with the mohair question, which astounded them since they were painters in oils and I, when I was anything, was a watercolorist, but they made some joking reference, Treischnitt and Kolberhoff, to people who paint with their fingers and noses, all depending on what social class they came from. They could see I was trying to be polite in the most relevant way, lump of turnip safely secreted in that old punctured balloon I had found floating through the Kölnstrasse, beside my bits of purloined

schnitzel and cabbage. Perhaps there was even a morsel of dead starling in there, fatally hinged to the turnip by its wing or the claw of
its foot. Emergency rations, these, against a long interview. This was
the dreaded *Abschied* interview, so-called because it sorted the can-
didates out, bidding most of them *farewell* before any of their work
had come into question. It was a matter of fitness and training, you
could tell that from their very demeanor. Strange about the balloon.
Though punctured, it kept my victuals fresh, almost good enough to
offer them, but I refrained of course. You never know what a refined
gentleman is or is not allowed to eat. At certain ages, certain foods—
well, enough of that. On it goes, and I swiftly tune in to the right
approach, shifting from watercolors and mohair to what I thought
suitable for the occasion: some talk of turpentine, but which, thanks
to nervousness, I kept getting wrong whenever I spoke it, starting
with turfentide, turpsentice, and turfindict, going as far as serpen-
thyme and earthentide. They got the general idea, though, mocking
me a little, Treischnitt and Kolberhoff, often dreamed about though
never at such close quarters as this. There had been no rehearsal of
such nearness, not even of such topics as squeezing the tube, Squeezing the Tube, a matter of enormous delicacy: from the top or the
bottom, rolling up the bottom to keep the tube neat, or leaving little
bulges for later call-up, conferring an additional delight of something
overlooked and now commandeered into the final crushing sweep.
Out it came, whatever color, crying to be mixed and used, not on the
palette but directly onto canvas, I said boldly, to air my knowledge
of how they did their work. What of crimps? They did not respond to
that, of course, heeding no date or manufacturer, and I quietly abandoned the idea of peeling off the label, thus making all tubes alike,
the only means of identifying them being to peer into the bowels
through the nozzle. None of that, nor any of my proposed blather
about easels, resting the eyes on a color not recently worked in, but
Treischnitt with Kolberhoff assenting, told me that, after years of
worry, he had learned how best to cover wet oils, by draping a pair of
lady's voluminous bloomers over the work. The resulting stains, he
confided, Treischnitt, Kolberhoff fussily assenting, were more exciting than anything he'd seen. I agreed, promising to drape knickers
over my watercolors in the future, taking special note of the taint of
stains and wondering at their possibly imaginary source. These were
the obiter dicta of successful gentlemen, and I was more than eager
to pass muster. What came next, however, now we had all three
settled down, and the supplementary questioners—a Grenzhaus and

a Plöchnasch, I recall, unknown to me for their art or even their demeanor—had left, having satisfied themselves about the major part of the examination, though not about me. Now the gloves were off. Treischnitt began it, as he would, taking a comb, bidding me stand, and quietly combing my lank, dark hair upward into a lolling tod. I had not washed it in readiness for the interview, not suspecting it would figure among the questions, or the issues, but I knew it was greasy and therefore lank, would fall in that disastrous dun cable across my right eye, slinking forward over my eyes because I had never cut it off or paid a barber to do it for me. There it stood, collapsed, dangled, a monument to my own sexual mishaps, and Treischnitt groaned, echocd by you know whom, as if I had located Bellini in the wrong century. He's a goner, he sighed. He was a goner when he came in, Kolberhoff said. Now he's doubly useless. Perhaps a little bone-glue, the kind they make from fishheads, would hold it up. Or horses' bones, crooned Treischnitt. He has no future if his hair won't stand to attention when combed. Up, boy, he shouted, as if bracing an animal for an endurance test, trying once again, but all fell down from the preposterous height he had raised it to, quite a length when unsettled from its resting place, with all the dandruff, like a shower of corpseflakes from the nearby Ganges of my face, floated up and then to their dismay settled on the table. Look at that, said Treischnitt, who always spoke first, being older, and Kolberhoff was used to this. *He sheds.* Yes, I shedded. You shed, Kolberhoff added. I do, I told him. I should never shed. No, don't ever again shed on my desk. I will never again shed on your desk, I said, or on the desk of the Honorable Doktor von—Enough of that groveling scheiss, either Treischnitt or Kolberhoff said (it was the former, I deduced, as one could). That part of the test was over, thank God, and I had spent nights boning up on perspective and such crap. Was not pointillism in the air? It got worse when they opened my fly without probing further, to discomfit me as I stood there, and then asked me to remove my mud-caked boots. My work, I began, but they silenced me, indicating that the most serious part of the interview was already underway, pounding me with questions I had never dreamed of. How much horsehair was there in canvas? In Prussian blue, they asked in unison like a fugitive couple from operetta, heavily implying yes. I recoiled, brushing frantically at my quiff, which had fallen forward to bisect my forehead, thanks to their upward-combing endeavors. Now I was truly an unkempt candidate. On it went, from impossible to grotesque, if that is the right order in deterioration, when things

251

are really going to pot or to hell. Iron filings in lamp black? I had heard nothing like this. Where was my beloved work, cherished over so many years and brought here by hand in sackcloth with a mouth full of ashes? Next, we discussed the use of various cheeses in priming a canvas, tea leaves in linseed oil (and the visual spatter they made), after which we paused, as if we had accomplished something profound. Not far away, two female voices raised in shrill dissent nagged at our attention (I proud to use the plural, fusing my attention with theirs, but it was true). Was I passing? Had I failed? Was I going to be a painter after all? Or just a victim? If this last, I was going to turn a few of them into victims of my own, quizzing them in my fifties and sixties until they could stand it no longer. But no, it was lunchtime, the hour of the feedbag. One never quite knew what realm of being was going to appeal to them next and dominate their current of behavior. Animal, vegetable or mineral. Lunch was brought, but first two identical sashes, the Danube Silk, which Treischnitt had won eleven times, Kolberhoff only ten (a source of much debate in the coffeehouses). We ate normally enough, breaking our black bread into tiny divots and pecking at sausage. We might have been sparrows or starlings, even. I fished for and found my bit of turnip, which they refused with disgust, then a few crumbs they waved away. I would even eat the balloon, choking myself to death to please them, but they motioned otherwise, spurning my death throes and warning me to ready myself for the next phase, the even more dreaded *Wilkommen* or Welcome test, which had to do, so went the rumor, with one's actual work. Had I then passed the preceding interrogations? I must have. I was so overjoyed I choked on my turnip, which I had gnashed at in mingled relief and shame. Now, fueled up, they were ready for me. Look at his balls, Treischnitt was saying as the waiter paraded in with my Auersberg horizontal on a tray and a leek straddling it, he can't draw. His people are stalks of celery. Is there no accuracy left in the world? I do declare, Kohoff, if one took the trouble to measure up this stuff, it wouldn't pan out. Clearly he has never sighted using his finger. He has no regard for the loveliness of human anatomy. What shall we do with him? I began to shake and hiccup. The faint subterfuges of something or other came upon me and left me empty. I was failing at this very moment. Emboldened by whatever force, I cried out, You haven't even looked, you turkeys. He has spirit, Treischnitt said, shall we let him off? One day, you can see it, he will achieve a position of superb power, and we shall be proud to have failed him. Look at the other work, I hissed. They did. They said the same. I took mustard and added a few drastic mustaches to the stonework of my Auersberg, shocking them with my apparent abandon and openness of mind. Ah, said Treischnitt, now he's a bloody Norwegian, just look at him. There's hope yet, old boy. They lit cigars as catalysts to serious thought, and looked again at my poor Auersberg. He's certainly added something, Treischnitt observed, eyeing my brown and yellow mottled sweeps, *sans brosse.* Depraved indifference to human life? Kolberhoff sighed and said no, it was a misdemeanor, as if citing a manual of jurisprudence. There were no laws in those times about what a painter might or might not read, especially one with eleven or ten Danube sashes for—what the hell did they give those sashes for? I was sighing, but they were not buying. He could be a carter, I heard. Or a hotel porter. A toilet cleaner has a good future, as the great Goethe once said, spurning the job himself, except in his work. Treischnitt and Kolberhoff then spoke as one: No. Come back in six months to repeat the entire examination. Since you have failed in one part, the parts in which you passed have also become failures. This is known in the profession as the Leviticus Spillover, a deadly formula originating in the Ukraine. No appointment, good sir. Just keep stopping by to ask if we are in. I was ushered out, my mustard Auersberg under my arm, my face a cashiered white, my step unsteady. However, before you go, they had said, we would like to nominate you for one of the Fisher King fellowships, which brings you a garret, a regular supply of black bread and kipper paste for one year, during which you are to create your best work. You eat the same thing every day, receive no money, but live rent-free, the entire award based on *chutzpah.* In all probability you have no gift, but a certain amount of initiative, in which we choose to invest just to see what comes of it. All will depend, mein Herr, on how you perform with us on your next visit, which might be timed with Herr Kolberhoff's receipt of an eleventh Danube Sash for—well, it is universally known what he gets awards for. So keep this in mind. You could be living off the fat of the land in no time at all, the kipper of it anyway. Don't fret. All is well. You will have to reconcile your goals with your gifts, good sir. Stop following us. Do not send any more postcards or leave vegetables on either stoop. We do not need your charity or your obsequious attention. Can you not see we are grand old men such as they do not make anymore? We are not Norwegian crazies. Nor German fanatics. Remember the country's enormous contribution to world culture, indeed to Treischnitt and Kolberhoff, who now record you in the examination book as having appeared here and done your duty. We do not need you, but one day you may need us when you have reached toilet level. See you in the basement, sir, and be busy. Out I fell.

Five Poems
Reginald Shepherd

JUSTICE: AN ODE

There was a man in the land,
he is green before the sun, the sinews
of his stones are wrapped together,
but he shall not be gathered

The flood breaketh out from the inhabitant
skin for skin (*Am I a sea, or a whale?*)
and the teeth of the young lions are broken
which are blackish by reason of the ice

If they destroy him from his place, it shall deny
him and bind their faces in secret
on the left hand, where he doth work:
dead things are formed under the waters

But put forth thine hand now
and fill him with the east wind
No mention shall be made of coral
and the chambers of the south

Through the scent of water and the inhabitants
thereof (even the waters forgotten
of the foot), remember that my life
is wind, fenced with bones and sinews

Did I say, *Bring unto me? Pursue the dry
stubble and the arms of the fatherless
which made Arcturus, Orion and Pleiades
enter the treasures of the snow?*

Thou hast plentifully declared the thing as
it is, and hangeth the earth upon
nothing, made a decree for the rain
and said, *There is a manchild conceived*

in league with the stones of the field
where the slain are, the blackness
of day: and now I am their song
Who can open the doors of his face?

THE PRACTICE OF GOODBYE

The young sing *es eiona*
while the old men laugh and clap
in the direction of suspicion:

these dour suburban bacchants
(perennials grown as annuals)
killing the lions and harmless wasps

Purple ornamental kale in corner
pots, planters of silver-furred dusty miller
make a boundary, flower late or not at all:

semen tints the atmosphere,
landscape oblique to occasion
hammering summer boys to heat

Paint and ruined blossoms,
melancholic white men
scattered with torn petals, tanagers

disaster, lovely saunter
down damp streets, were the gods
ever so in love with their own lies

My horizon will be pounding waves
of horses, white breaking
across black rocks at bay

light flooding water, promise
or threat: anywhere risk
accumulates, the hands wash ashore

The muddled windows (melting),
the ripped desiccated branch (awaiting
which) maintain the wind:

death-dealing Eros
extinguishes the torch
and I am disappearance

FLICKER

— For Gabrielle Karras

scatters afternoon across blank
water, warmest by late September,
an artifice of lakefront's
drowning weather. Scuba

divers strip off black flippers,
no bodies recovered today. The
secretive shore moves stealthily
up to and exceeding its limits,

green wave crests higher than
concrete banks, barrier dunes'
collected complaints against
wave and sand's copulation,

contamination of divide.
Horizoned to a skein of sheen
and weatherblown smooth, lake
asymptote is interrupted by intervals

of pumping platforms: small islands
in the mind, moments of thing
and motion, less. Shapes
movement leaves behind

in the eye, imagoes of its afterward:
herring gull hung against sun setting
on the other side, west match
set to oiled water, but at a distance

watching knows. (A film reflecting
vaguely on a wavering world
of absences and outlines, anecdotal
figures blurring into view.) Leaves

waiting for burning already take
burnt colors, huddled on highway
trees, red lights, squabble of gulls
settles on wet bread crumbs, skittish

sand: an accident in progress
at twenty-four frames a second
holds still, distills spilled light
to artifacts in the floating eye

marrying empty space to sky

"UND DIE MANDELHODE GEWITTERT UND BLÜHT"

— For Paul Celan

Lightfall. Toward which
rises the many-spoked night, slurred
wastrel clouds (notions
of clouds), wind-drench
and algid breath: your hurricane
called history, your gas
of colorless sleep: sweet
on the smoke-tongue, the hour
-long song, word-silted always
-autumn afternoon. Blue
sky of your terrifying
mouth, where nowhere reigns.

258

(Creeded, accreted, wrap this
in ashes, water it well.)

Which is these bitter
petals fallen from your almond
-lips, flake-stammered over
Seine (acid light erodes
your face nightward): sorrow-branch
bloom-stripped by wind, your wind
still celebrates your loss.
Fog-deserts promise
new rain, you juxtapose back
and rank care for a pilgrim's
end-stopped now: spilled bowl
of air, you rain, you also rain.

SUTURE

The open doorway is a ruin, or the door
was locked: they differ in the abandoned
details, now as transparency, now
as wall (lucent weather on the other side

of glass). Sheetrock and sheered plaster,
mix spackling where the vertical
won't hold. *Move him into the sun.* The flicker
pictures, holds its thrall. Myths

burn paper in alleys to keep warm
without a subject, kerosene smell
of drying paint, fat smoke,
a tripped floodlight scums cobbles

with appearance and slurried
dog shit: half notes floating out a half
-open window, nothing that adds up to
song, son, salsa, soca or merengue

blaring night blear. (The man warming up
his car at three a.m. wouldn't offer
a ride, I dust off my interest and find just
used condoms, irony congealing

in the reservoir tip.) All rodent, ardent,
gnawing at the day's remains, and light
wears down to this heaped corner
of dirty snow, all that white left: flurry,

blizzard, storm, street festival, confetti
cacophony (shredded English
of the sensual). Am I paper, am I parchment,
vellum or papyrus, much-crumpled thesis

scrawled away? These marks leave themselves in me
I can't make out, make way for manhood
littering demotic sidewalks. His glance invents
me, then dismantles me, several

-spoked night crumbles my face: accumulation
of missteps across white lane divider, macadam-
and glass-scribbled palimpsest, kiss for
the brother in the broken-bottle eden.

The Intercession of the Saints
Carole Maso

SAINTS HOLD A TAMBOURINE, a lily, a pomegranate, a flame, a red book, a plum.

A chalice of seawater. The world's last music. A fire in a stone bowl. A starling. A globe.

Their longing makes a burning sound. Their most precious blood tolls.

A dulcimer. An egg. A basket of plums. A plume of smoke.

The saints marvel. They love nothing more than a miracle or two: the child's small hand in mine, milk flowing from an open vein, or the covenant made anew each day.

Saints sing like ships sing. Like fog. Like the phases of the moon. Like a mantle of blue. A rhapsody. Saints sing.

They believe in the new covenant of the replaced blood.

A perched village on a platter. A tiny basilica. A ruby casting its jewel tone. Bone ash. Marrow. Cup of mysterious universe.

The temptation to believe is great.

The heart swings like a pendulum toward and then away from God. Toward and then away. Nearer and then farther. The heart's proximities are two carrier pigeons. Are the message they carry. A logic of wings. A philosophy of light.

Saints with rakes are out harvesting bone marrow while we speak.

Their pure health. Their faith like crazy.

The weight of their sweat more precious than gold.

The saints say: *one conquers the temptations of the world through pain.*

Saint Agatha under her veil of sorrows. Holding the last handfuls of hair in her hands.

The anesthesia is like dusk: soft, hot, blue, misty. They float through so beautifully now, cradling their symbols.

A scale, a spade, a goose.

The saints in their infinite sweetness renounce the world.

Dancing saints have a lilting charm.

Who could not love Saint Theresa doing her frenzied wedding dance?

She sang like a bird.

Falling into a collapsed time.

Saints hold a head, a sonnet, a tongue. A lily, a pomegranate, an apple, a plum.

Above the crucified Christ a swan and its young.

Saint Francis in his holy hovel.

The Madonna with five angels.

Madame holding a chalice of seawater.

The angel holding Matthew's inkwell.

Novice saints hold a fragment of flame in their hair.

Saints hold keys, fish, small ships, a rooster, a stone.

Saints hold.

Your body is a heart, an angel flagellated, a wheel, a flame, and darkness.

They visit the hospital in a kind of solidarity. They fall and swoon. They carry little vessels of bone and hope.

Saints sun-bake in the God-light. *The job of the soul is to suffer.*

Saints hold the flame whole in their perfect hands. Saints can.

I wish I were a bird with a crimson head.
A garden.
His mother's hair.

The saints hold a staff, a lamb, a feather, the bambino. Or clutch a small bird.

I thought the two weeks of apparitions had ended. The *frisson* of weeping angels, the thorns in a cup, the ladle of white blood soup, the violations at the grave.

As if the halo were being scissored off, as if the light were being sliced, as if you could take that away from an angel or a person just like that—with a blade.

Voices come, they die away.

You were more precious than song.

The saints carry their regrets. Their 7.5 pound unborn babies each, their condolences.

Saints suffer down the page. They fall like roses. Pale birds.

On the last rung of the ladder in the Seventh House of the Apocalypse.

Carole Maso

The saints pierce themselves on swastikas. Smuggle children to the
borders. Move to the ends of earthly pain.

Saint Catherine of Siena: *one tries not enough.*

Saints suffer their way.

In the anesthesia called twilight the saints attempt to defeat time.

Filing by one by one:

Saint Hippolytus torn by horses.
Saint Helena dreaming the Cross, the coat of nails, the road.
Saint John the Baptist and his attributes: a lamb, wings and a
honey pot.
Saint Rose of Lima, too beautiful.
Saint Wencelaus still trudging through the bitterly cold night
carrying logs for a poor man's fire. His footprints in the snow.
Saint Martha with a ladle and keys and a broom.
Saint Hildegarde, pop star, with five hits on the charts.
Saint Apollonia holding a tooth in a pair of pincers.

The hermits and scholars sit quietly in intensive care thinking
and brooding. Saint Giles, one of the 14 Holy Helpers holding
a chamber pot. Saint Sebastian like a fountain.

Saint Christopher has a rakish charm with his river and flowing
staff and arrows and dog's head.

What's up with the dog's head?

Saints look on bewildered by the weapons of mass destruction.

The dream too often, during sex, or when contemplating God, is
the dream of annihilation.

Saint Ava in ecstasy.

Trance

After pain a floating feeling comes.

From the open chest in the operating theater: birds fly. Soul goes off.

Look closely at the child holding a small bouquet of violets—a sweet offering to the now sutured chest. Taking the heart out. Putting it back in.

Burning. The river is burning. The children are burning.

Saints smolder.

Saints lay their bodies down in front of tanks. War has a boyish charm: Desert Fox, Desert Storm. The saints sigh.

The body turned into a torch. A lantern. A bell.

The heart out.

The saints say *one day paradise.* They put on their moody Houdini suits and wait.

The saints say.

7 Saints stand in the 7 Churches of the Apocalypse.

Deciding to fast, refusing all food, until the killing stops, they recite the 404 verses.

Tiny parachutes on the Normandy coast. The heart back in.

A rain of roses.

World's end.

A fever of roses.

A love letter laced in Anthrax.

Carole Maso

I wish my hand might touch the fire between the letters of the alphabet. I wish I could translate God's reticence.

For seven months she held the child under her heart.

The ocean is a cistern overflowed with tears. The world does not beat.

Some saints I'm told smell like roses after their death.

A chalice of heartbreak, a peace offering, a forest of semaphores. A ball of fire, a lion, a cloak split in half.

The heart like a metronome swings.

We're a little lost. In the semiotics. And not a graduate student in sight.

Not to worry, the saints hold their compass rose.

Saint Francis throws himself onto a bed of thorns to quell desire. Such sad and useless heroics.

The desolate heights. Heat and light.

One day you are walking to the university where you teach, you happen to look up, and what—what is it you see—in that one instant—your death unfolds as if on a paper scroll—you lift your hand—the light shines through . . .

The light shines through you.

The world is not a trinket or an oyster or an ornament.

And you fall into time while the angels watch.

Ava Klein, you fall into time—

As when you were pregnant and you watched its explicit work on you.

Never had you felt the workings of time—just time—so dramatically.

The saints reiterate *life is unbearable without suffering.*

OK, OK.

See how the infant in utero already waves to a distant horizon.

Complicity with the dark. Complicity with the light. The saints look up and hum.

I hear the last light in the sky. *Wish I may—wish I might—*

I wish I were bells.

Have the wish I wish tonight.

The saints whisper sweet nothings. Make no promises. This no nonsense brand of saint can really grate.

There were many things that nothing could cure.

Not prayer, not song, not alcohol, not chemotherapy—certainly not.

The saints whisper sweet nothings in my ear.

I wish I were bells, something plangent and beautiful and able to modulate the dark—sing God's silences.

In the hush of the lung, in the shadow the T cell casts, you, solitary saint sing a perfect nocturne.

The long bones of illness, her tuning fork.

I wish I were a field of wheat.

Blood and light collected in a chalice.

Lovingly she takes the shroud and places it at my feet.

267

Carole Maso

Music for a too late afternoon.

Anatole, saved from drowning.

Francesco weeps. He loves Italian saints. Saint Chiara. Saint Francis of Assisi,

Who hurls himself one more time onto a rosebush—seedlings sprouting wherever the drops of his blood fall.

Francesco loves him best of all. He reads from *The Book of Saints:*

"Paintings depict Francis with and without a dog's head (it was believed that he begged the Lord to make him ugly as a dog to escape the attention of women), carrying Jesus as a child and surrounded by two prostitutes (sometimes envisioned as sexy mermaids)."

The adoration of the saint.

Their relics gleam. Luminous in agony—brilliant at it. Locked as they are away in sarcophagi, reliquaries, under glass—for a thousand lira they light up like July.

I wish I were a 6 stringed instrument.

Or locked away in the chambers of the heart. Saint Valentine in bondage.

Or the head off.

Wishing for sleep I see Aunt Sophie at the ditch, barefoot and pregnant and begging.

Sophie, at the mouth of the world—a latter day saint.

Saints fly like falling stars.

Saints sail in hot air balloons rescuing the doomed. *Hey Sophie, we're up here!* They lend a hand.

High above the troubled world.

Blood and light collected in a chalice. *Live* they whisper.

Saints burn in extremis.

Saints whiz by fueled by adoration, in the day, in the night. Intoxicating, don't you think?

Yes I do.

The intensity of saints.

There's no real cure for it.

The pure oxygen.

Wings burn. They burn.

Desire one more time hurls Saint Francis into thorns.

Snow works I'm told. *Oh right.*

Saints emit an eerie light. Roses open.

The five wounds of the crucified Christ on mortified flesh bloom. *Stigmata*—a kind of board game they like to play those saints.

Saints hold very nice looking tarts in their hands. The key to a perfect crust is ice water.

Saints hold a mandolin. A quill. An apple. A small bird.

Witness Saint Agnes and her lamb offering her maidenhead to God.

Saint Anthony of Padua and the presentation of the Host to the Mule. That's a good one.

Saint Catherine of Genoa recites the Treatise on Purgatory.

Saint Jerome in the desert. A fire in a stone bowl. The arc of blood. A dove at his throat. An angel in red.

Some saints carry bunches of bananas on their heads to feed the poor.

Saints at the soup kitchen. Saints at the cinema. Saints in every imaginable place.

In Firenze Francesco, the angel holds a scroll over the sleeper's head revealing the dream to us. Not even the solitude of dreams anymore.

In Siena, meanwhile

Saint Catherine undoes the collar and lets the head drop onto her lap after the chop—good God! When the cadaver was taken away she says, my soul rested in such delicious peace and I rejoiced so in the perfume of that blood that I did not wish them to take away that thing that lay upon my clothes.

That's just how saints are.

Her favorite words were *fire* and *blood*.

What is the head doing off?

She used a stone for a pillow.

She was known to go into the *Capella dela Volte* where many Sienese watched the host go flying from the hand of the priest directly into her mouth.

She was cut up by the Romans.

Her head ensconced in a golden reliquary.

Brain scan.

The Venetians have a foot.

An earthquake in Assisi. Saint Francis crumbling.

Saints sigh *this world.* The women swoon for their doozy bridegroom.

They carry bouquets of bloodroot and bleeding heart and trillium. That's nice.

Under the weeping willow saints play.

Dulcimer. Bone ash. Sparrow.

In their blood they carry bits of the true cross splintered.

Bone marrow transplant.

Saint Rose waves at the vanishing point.

At the melting point.

At the place the blood freezes, saints say *let it bleed.*

The saints wait patiently.

They forge virginity certificates.

They idolize their bleary bridegroom. They practice *I do* and *I will,* as if they needed to. Weeping and fever become them. They wait for Him with the patience of, well, you know.

Saints in ecstasy say strange things.

The saints carry blankets for all night international flights.

They sing the *Stabat Mater Dolorosa* so beautifully. In a wounded way.

The saints carry little nuclear winters under tiny glass domes. They keep us safe they say.

Carole Maso

They pray over the hazardous wastes.

The saints trudge up the mountain, the saints trudge down. (Concern for the cat, the pot still simmering, the clothes on their backs, etc.)

They carry an ocean of sorrow in their cupped hands.

They carry the *fin-de-siecle* on their backs.

Children are jumping.

They carry the origin of tears.

Amniotic, last, most perfect night.

Children are flying.

Cupping a chalice of seawater.

God wades through the tears of the saints to his next destination.

Joan burns. She burns.

Through the smoke of the saints.

And the seraphs.

With the patience of a saint you wait, Francesco, as if with perfect attention you might change the course of what will be.

Cats moving in and out—scanning the place for available saints.

You've got a crazy faith.

God wades through a universe of tears.

The sleeping children float in the safety of Saint Lucy's blue pupil.

Three women dreaming next to water recall how at just the sight of the angel's wing . . . The infinitesimal world taking shape in their gaze.

Carrying so much hope.

A rain of roses will fall at my death. Saint Therese.

I wish I could decipher your silence.

They cradle the head.

A blue ghost in the bones.

The human skin remembers everything. Everything. So the child in surgery becomes a saint his whole life.

Open heart. There is always hope, the saints say.

And the saints carry wedding cakes and twelve wedding rings.

There is always love they whisper through the cobalt light.

The saints in blue with rakes in otherworldly loneliness.

Pluck ashes from the filling mouth.

The saints smuggle children with forged passports to the border.

The saints understand it is almost time, but not yet.

Roses to the border.

The saints know ashes.

Mend us with fire.

Their longing makes a burning sound.

Those crazy saints! They have a sheepish charm.

Carole Maso

In anesthesia's twilight.

They whisper *How beautiful are the feet.*

Mother, it certainly does seem—the blood begins to sing.

cup bearer

orbit

soul

The seven sleepers . . .

Saints cast a lovely light.

Filophilia
Melvin Jules Bukiet

YOU DO WHAT YOU HAVE TO DO to feel what you must. Sometimes a man will go to a hardware store and buy a tool, a router, say, which he'll unpack and never use, but just enjoy, because it's there in his basement, because the molding of wood is an idea that gives him a deep, enduring pleasure. Even if he never accomplishes a perfect ogee, the concept of the curvature of pine satisfies him. That's harmless and we can smile at the indulgence with . . . indulgence. But sometimes the indulgence is more provocative.

Sometimes it's a midnight phone call to an old friend or an old lover, and the meaningfulness of the call to the caller will frighten the one who's been called, because he may think he's safe in his new life, the most vital characteristic of which is that it proceeds without you. You evoke a past better left untouched when you finger a number that by all rights you should not have, preferably on a dial that glows in the dark. You do not even know what state the area code represents or what time it is there. It's a number that a judge in a court has told you that you had better not dial.

Though criminal, obsession is, nonetheless, comprehensible, within the range of normal human behavior, because everyone's felt such need—even if almost everyone has wisely refrained from acting upon it. But what about the needs that few feel and fewer still fulfill? Now we cross an interesting boundary, enter a different territory, where there's no area code.

Now we must consider an act that everyone—judges, lawyers, neighbors—considers vile, taboo, a trespass of basic moral posture. Sometimes it's killing teenagers and eating their hearts. That's bad. I know that. I agree. I have incorporated the values of my civilization, some of them, to some extent. I have no craving to devour anyone's heart. I have more rarefied tastes.

What if the loathsome pursuit—and capture—hurts no one? Why then is it so universally condemned? Rationally, irrationally, I don't know. Something is encoded in the genes for the benefit of the species, something which only I—is it possible?—only I—are there others?—can say has served its day—to keep humanity from devolving into brutes with curly tails and no brains—because now there's birth control.

What a nice term. I've used pills, spermicidal sprays and unguentined plastic devices. Tiny copper coils were inserted inside my body by doctors who would have rather inserted . . . no, that's speculation. That's suburbia.

No, it probably happens in the city too, with judges and lawyers.

The fact is that now we can indulge.

Indeed, some of us must.

Some of us do.

Some of us say, "Wallace, come here."

Fatherless, friendless, weak-chinned, eleven years old and hardly able to read, Wallace comes when his mother calls him. He gallops across the low-ceilinged room, blocking the television, which is always on, casts a swift shadow. He leaves his notebooks: Colonial Jamestown, Elementary Mathematics, Earth Science. His class is gathering and categorizing leaves, discovering observation and method for themselves. He is "slow," but he knows what wisdom is. He does not look past the undusted Venetian blinds to see if the neighbors are watching. This house, the neighbors are always watching.

"Wallace, come here."

"Coming, Mother."

The very word is an accomplishment. "What have you done in this world?" they may ask in court mundane or celestial, and my instantaneous reply, assured as a duchess, will be: "Him. I made him. Whatever he is."

And I will do Anything to make him happy—even if it makes me happy too.

The day that boy beat up my Wallace, I felt no hesitation. I did not sob and fret. I went out and beat him, not Wallace, though a different mother might thrash her own son from misdirected humiliation. I beat the other boy, the neighbor boy, with a garbage can lid. It rang on his five-year-old skull like a heavenly cymbal. Then I drove him into the basement with my shoulder, frail and brassiered. His ear swelled up, and I hit him again as he cringed and pled mercy.

"Please, did you say?" I taunted him. "Wallace said 'please' and begged you not to bloody his lip. It's fat now and tender," and I hit him with objects from deep storage, things that had once served a domestic function, first a broom and then a router. I picked up a brick left over from when the patio with the built-in barbecue was constructed, and I would have hit him again if his yelps had not summoned his parents, both of them, a man with a moustache and a woman with a hat, who swore at me and dragged him away. What was she doing wearing a hat in the middle of the day anyway? I followed them to the perimeter of my property and stood with the brick, and then I heaved it through my own living room window, and left the splintered glass to remind them forever of their own son's tendencies.

The police come here frequently. They know the address, the area code. Wallace and I seem to have problems with the community. But our taxes are paid. The lawyer takes care of that as long as I promise to cease making awkward phone calls. I never see accounts. I receive checks. I pay bills, occasionally on time.

Their blue lights illuminate the crumbling driveway and barbecue, and they voice the same suspicious inquiries as always. But I say, "No warrant, no entry." I know my rights.

After they leave, I say, "Come here, Wallace."

His lip was blue and thick as an earthworm. I dabbed antiseptic cream on it, but he winced. I knew of only one more sure cure, but for a moment I hesitated. For whom?

For them? To satisfy their notion of who I should be?

I have an obligation, because no tie is tighter, no bond stronger, no glue stickier. I clamped my own lips down upon his wound to draw the poison from his flesh.

Wallace murmured and his eyes rolled up inside his head as I drank of his fluids as he had once mine. I might as well have inserted a syringe into my pulse, strung a clear plastic tube from wrist to mouth. Circulation of the blood. The taste was delicious. We were one.

I had given him my breast half a decade ago, when another man who played stupid games with tools shared the twin cones that grew from my ribcage, items of flagrant, mysterious appeal. If I saw them in the freezer at the supermarket, I would pass them by for the veal that I find more seductive. But there's no accounting for tastes; the cones served their purpose when they were not so large, but more refined

in angle and texture, when their tips pointed north, like soft mag-
netic needles.

No man has seen those breasts since Wallace's first teeth, nibs
barely protruding from his pink gums, created a cavity of blood
beneath their dimpled surfaces. In those days, I lay back against the
tasseled brown velvet couch in the living room and cried for pleasure. The hunger he felt—that slight, uncharmed child.

My shoulder was bruised where it had jammed the neighbor
child's chin. The strap of brassiere was burning my skin, as if a film
of gasoline was brushed down the blades and across my back and
over my shoulders to form twin bull's-eyes on my bosoms, and set
aflame. I quenched the flame. The air was cool. I offered Wallace
the only comfort I could. Just like I had five, or was it five hundred,
years ago. Or five million? I always thought I could have become an
archaeologist.

Wallace did not wish to return to school the next day. The guidance
counselor reported to me. Wallace was afraid, so I had to give him
strength.

So I did. The guidance counselor called again, because he thought
something was "wrong." We don't shy away from words in this age.
There is none of the between-the-lines delicacy that gave *Five
Smooth Stones* its scandalous flavor in my youth. I know how to
read, even if Wallace cannot distinguish "here" from "hear" or even
"to" from "too" from "two." We don't need two; we are one.

The counselor thinks I'm an idiot, but I have a degree. I studied
algebra. I knew what I had to do.

Every day. On the same couch, now threadbare, untasseled and
stained.

Alone we lived, and the neighbors peeked through the slats of the
dirty Venetian blinds in order to witness my nudity while I held him,
that no longer tiny, incandescent creature.

He was so hungry. I was a fertile field. There was no scarecrow to
chase him.

Neighbor men, all but the father with the moustache, offered their
tools when they saw me, dressed in Bermuda shorts and a halter top,
attempting to maintain the premises. For more than a year I mowed
the lawn, cleaned the barbecue. There I was, crawling across the
shingles, dredging gutters, tossing handfuls of rotted sycamore leaves

from the holes they had plugged, causing overflows and leaks.

I spurned their offers, but I couldn't stop the leaks. Tears of rusty brown water streaked the wallboards. Floorboards buckled, mildew spread.

Wallace and I moved into the basement, searching out the depths to escape from the encroaching damp. It has a stall shower like a vertical coffin and a miniature stove and sink, so that I felt like I was living in one of the doll houses my own father—a thin, brown goatee—once purchased for me when I was Wallace's age.

A parabolic volume of snow drifted through the living room window, but the basement was insulated right down to China, except for one air well with one window. The light at night must have been like the glow on a telephone.

Our new subterranean dwelling bothered the neighbors, but they are easily bothered by many things—more every day—like the quarter acre of grass, knee high, spread with wildflowers come the spring, which come summer began to spread creepers up the brick wall of the untended barbecue where steaks ought to be dripping fat onto hot coals. Instead, the blind plant growth probes at the mortar with tentacles with tiny puckers like octopuses. The mortar seeps out and accumulates in tiny drifts like snow, which returns come winter.

"Appalachia," they whisper disdainfully, and in the supermarket when I shop for veal—for even a mother must eat—their women—no different, no different, no different no matter what they think—shun me.

But I don't care. I enter the house, ignore the loosened and scattered strips of parquet, the befungused couch, as I skip down the stairs to the basement. It has one bed.

He had to go to school or else yet another authority, a man or a woman who wears a hat and walks like a man with a clipboard tucked under her arm, would appear unwanted in our lives. Every morning I gave him strength and every day they made fun of him, all of them except for the boy who beat up my Wallace. He fled whenever I stepped outside to examine my property.

Wallace didn't mind, but kept the same sweet, baffled expression and displayed the same intractable inability to read and to count.

Six, seven, eight—Wallace grew and struggled, and I read primers to him. "Go, dog, go."

Together we tried to memorize multiplication tables with flash cards dealt across a converted shop bench under a pegboard. "Three times three equals nine. Three times four equals twelve. Three times five equals fifteen." I tried to teach him about the world beyond the basement, because I believed that was how I was supposed to behave.

But when he'd stare at the numbers as if they were ancient hieroglyphics, I was the one who learned that none of those numbers mattered. Add, subtract, divide or multiply, whichever process you choose, all digits always reduce to one, the only truly prime number.

Wallace was sated by his daily dose of sacramental fluid, but I wasn't. The more he taught me, the more I understood my ignorance. The more I fed him, the hungrier I grew.

The man with the moustache offered to feed me during one of my less frequent fits of responsibility. I was examining my property when he shocked me by speaking from the opposite side of the shrubs he had planted between his yard and mine. His moustache through the foliage reminded me of a centipede.

Then he was gone and then he reappeared by my side—no clipboard—safe.

He had circled, and strode calmly forward to investigate the remains of the barbecue, collapsed in on itself.

"Can't fix that," he said.

"Can't fix anything," I replied.

"Can fix some things," he said and moved hands forward. He was offering me relief, though I knew it was wrong. I ought to have scorned him, but once again I felt the boiling deep inside me, like the broth of the guts of a witch at the stake.

Flat, shielded by shrubs, vines and the ruined barbecue, I obliged, in hopes of cooling the heat. Hairs bristled, a wild boar, snuffling and grunting.

I was on fire, but he was consumed; I was unconsumable—at least by his light. And unlike a witch, I was not lashed down by hemp. I was tied only by thin, insignificant strands of propriety. I watched the invisible strands fray then fly apart. My hand spidered across the ground. I took a brick.

Wallace turned ten—one plus zero.

He attended a "special" class with children who gibbered and wet their pants.

A recording informed me that the phone number I dialed had been changed, and that the new number was not listed. I knew then that the checks wouldn't come anymore and the bills come due, but I didn't care.

The house next door was for sale.

In the supermarket, I learned to slide plastic-wrapped packages of veal under my skirt. Still I was hungry. Doesn't that count?

Letters with official seals piled high. The telephone ceased to work, but the dial still glowed, until the electricity was shut off.

Only water remained, the damp from the living room coming down, puddling at the feet of our bed with no place to drain, and the shower springing on the inexorable power of its flow from the main from the reservoir from the sky from the ocean in an eternal go-round.

And what if I ate? Finally. After years of yearning. It took as long from the day Wallace's lip was bruised until the day of dominion as it had from the day that smiling, squirming beast appeared out of my belly until the day his lip was bruised.

Eleven. One plus one. The logic was impeccable.

A night when nothing out of the ordinary happened, when none of the neighbor boys made faces at our solitary window and none of the fathers next door spied upon that window with his binoculars.

I looked at the moon and became an enemy to all that's defined as sane in the world. "Wallace, come here," I said.

Although the hour was late, he thought this was merely a variation on our daily ritual, and he drank deeply. For the first time, Wallace was wrong. This was no midnight snack, no indulgence. It was time for a meal more nourishing than the raw veal we had been eating for weeks. I felt his head, hair thinning, scalp smooth. It was wonderful, as always, but . . . my fingers felt something new as they roamed over his pate, traced his ear, cupped his chin and discovered—hair. Not a bristle, but a wisp.

Invisible in the light of day. A glowing filament in the dark.

For the first time, the well did not slake our thirst.

Jeans on the floor—whose?—Colonial Jamestown by the bed—his. The traditional preliminaries weren't enough. So easy and so vital to continue. When everything is dark and there is one light, that is the direction you travel—without asking why.

"I'll show you what to do," I said.

Living with me, Wallace had not imbibed all of society's values or science's truths, but somehow he knew that what I contemplated went beyond. He hesitated. Eden grew faint.

"Come here, Wallace."

He backed off and bumped into the pegboard. Tools clattered to the floor.

"What's fair is fair, Wallace," I said.

He danced about the basement, retreated into the shower, but that was a trap. I turned on the water in order to teach him without distraction. This, Wallace could learn. Knowledge brings its own reward. Hair on the chin and a trembling from the source deep in the earth, from where all liquid flows. My reluctant scholar. Now he was brilliant.

And why is that wrong? Is there something cosmically untuned about taking the body that emerged from your own and returning it to the home it came from? On the contrary, Judge. That doesn't seem wrong to me. Together, we rectify all wrongs. Together, we straighten the curly tail. Together, we take everything that is broken and make it whole. We do it so you will have a reason to hate us. Because you have never known ecstasy.

Seven Veils
Thalia Field

COMETS

Bodies vary in importance and distance from the star. Bodies can be sand-sized or huge.
Sal was seen by early people dancing on her hands, her feet dangling by her ears.
She was painted this way with blazing eyes and glowing skin and many saw her.
The sun of the world she knows is only an average one. The moon a low-grade rock.
But they center the system and so are important and familiar and exert this power.
On an average day, people may not know exactly where Sal is and they may wonder.
She spends her time as someone's sentence: looking like, at, how.

Other bodies include satellites and moons, soldiers, stepfathers, prophets.
Sal wanders farthest past the sun at the edge of this limited imagination.
She walks the beach of the horizon so closely she does not appear to move.
Mike and Sal and Stacey have been friends since the shaded library.
Mike and Stacey know Sal better than anyone and can tell a mood from skin trouble.
Her ears are small, barely noticeable, unless she dangles her ankles around them.
Squint as she passes upside-down and she'll appear to smile.

Thalia Field

People interviewed later stress that Sal is not nearly as distant as she was made to look.
Even in broad daylight her total weight is less than most meteors.
They say that Sal is the "nearest approach to nothing that can still be anything."
You are looking at layers of ice, some small particles, some gas.
The hard part of Sal is tiny, but the coma surrounding it can be wider than earth's orbit.
Her coma consists of ammonia, frozen water, iron and nickel and sweeps the universe clean.
Unlike most, her tail is gentle, a curtain of cotton amnesia.

Left to her own devices, Sal would not shine in the night at all.
When she rounds the sun she is illuminated only by reflection.
There is nothing to her fluorescence but one energy oscillating into another.
Close to the shrill heat of her mother, there's corrosion of her flimsy materials.
Solar wind, pressure from radiation, all of these contribute to her steady wasting.
Every weekend practically there is something to celebrate, some boredom to dispel.
In this frenzy, Stacey helps choose a dress.

Mike teases Sal about her hair and her shadowy shoulders.
He calls her his "dirty little iceball" and she smiles that he loves her enough to name her.
Sal and Mike and Stacey share a secret oath: no superfluous circus.
It was believed by the Greeks that hot evaporations caused Sal's baleful loitering.
Or hot exhalations bursting into flame over kings who insisted the omens were not theirs.
Their enemies, they announced, had better take heed of the hairy torches.
Vespasian, Macrinus and other emperors perished in the years of their comets nonetheless.

284

Even with her friends beside her, Sal is mistaken for a corrupter of stars.
She has been accused of earthquakes, famines, and distrust among men.
She has been accused of aiming at earth with suicidal ambition.
End-of-the-world scares occur in all countries.
Herod procures a few hours of blasphemy for a political fund-raiser.
Sal can be mistaken for a weapon or an omen as she lingers by the hot tub.
Reason just cannot compete with the misguided faith of insecure men.

During her lifetime, Sal weaves an eccentric circle.
Most bright naked-eye comets can't be forced to the table.
No one was sure how she could be so non-parabolic.
Yet anyone with a certain demeanor twists her orbit violently.
One of these bodies could hurl Sal into deep space altogether.
For this reason, Mike gave Sal his house key and an invitation to crash there anytime.
Amateur comet hunters seek their trophies ruthlessly.

Turns out that the planets in our solar system form an almost perfect plane.
Drawing quietly on sheets of paper, circles within circles, children get it right.
But Sal comes in from other directions, ripping the paper to pieces.
So teachers, parents, governments downplay her role in the grand design.
Around the children her visit is filtered with idiomatic language.
In most cases a comet is named for its discoverer and labeled with years and letters.
Mike and Stacey know her better than anyone and can't quite find the words either.

Once Sal has been hypothesized, her angle must be found with respect to heaven.
By observing resultant actions she can be tracked by trained eyes.
Displacing the banquet hall, the library, she cuts a swath through each room.
Her face and body tangle dirty looks and muffled laughs into data arrows.
Anyone caught looking directly at her may experience nausea.
She'd displace the most massive mythology for the sake of a peaceful moment.
If only some joker hadn't painted her upside-down with ankles dangling . . .

Some historical, many mythological and most celestial beings have long worded lives.
Only Sal and her adolescent friends slip past silently.
Daylight, boredom, curiosity, clouds overcome them.
Sometimes they pass exceptionally close and once in a thousand years you feel them.
Mike and Stacey tolerate the occasional shattering of Sal into pieces.
In unlit corners of the palace they wait while she reassembles.
Never assume a comet dies; she's often safe in her bedroom by morning.

Whenever Sal breaks apart for good there will be showers of meteorites.
An investigation into Siberia found a twenty-mile circle of dead reindeer and pine.
But nothing solid, no evidence from the closet or the bank vault.
A visiting ship, a missile, would have left traces of some material.
Most likely the ice in her head simply melted on impact.
Most likely something dirty and delicate evaporated into the atmosphere.
News reporters can't find Mike and Stacey for comment.

It is said that Sal was born from a hot planet, a miniature sun ejecting a chip of itself.
Or perhaps a sun passed through a gravitational cloud which pulled Sal out like a splinter.
Perhaps all the most insubstantial material in the universe pulled together.
Then there are those who think Sal is just the leftovers of all the leftovers.
This would explain why someone's always looking at her, spotting her likeness.
This would explain why she is never liked, never likes to be so looked on, looking like.
Naked-eyed and ankles to ears, she casts curses on all astronomers.

SPECIES

The discus fish sucks instinctively but other fish must be taught to take the nipple.
A mother lioness teaches what food to eat and how and where to find it.
Even birds who fly intuitively need demonstrations on the finer points.
The secrets of the air can be taught by either parent or by a "helper" at the nest.
Baby birds of monogamous species develop an ear only for certain pitches.
And they can produce only the exact sequence of notes as the adults who raise them.

Sal called her friends from the gate house and offered them half the kingdom. Plus dinner.
Bring something to watch on television, she adds. Like a cheetah cub she knows she will be left.
The mother cheetah rushes the lessons to get in all the information.
The mother brings prey, half-dead and in a choke-hold, back to the lair. Go to it, she orders.
The cub isn't strong enough and botches the job while the mother stands by, distracted.
Ready or not, she's gone as fast as any question unasked.

Judging by what's written, the human mind is full of rats.
Status on the *scale natura* is based on what you will do at key points in a maze.
Or how quickly you'll humiliate yourself for dinner.
But rats manipulate a complex world beyond the palace walls.
And mice and salmon and monkeys notice that people aren't learning anything.
Except how best to test how well they can test what little they know how to test for.

A kangaroo is unaware of giving birth and so escapes knowledge of her cruelty.
She is able to neglect, without stress or guilt, a less than perfect baby.
If the tiny newborn falls to the ground, the mother will not reach down and help her.
Her nipple is waiting but if the girl becomes detached, *de facto* she's unfit.
A hardy infant will cling so tightly she can't be dislodged for all the tea in China.
But faced with danger the mother clears her pouch of any child found there.

The king once thought if you kill half the frog in the egg, you end up with half a frog.
No one who sees Sal can predict how she'll look in other circumstances.
Baboon daughters study protocol from their mothers: which favors for which leaders.
Is she maze dull, bright? Genetically, is she less than likely to survive?
She displays discontinuous stereotypes.
Glancing at her mother's cleavage, that first selfish gene, Sal sees an enormous shadow.

The king is a scientist of behavior and restricts evolution to his one priceless prisoner.
Populations tend to overproduce so the ugly, altruistic and zealous should die.
Eventually everyone resembles the survivors; everyone comes from a real winner.
Basic bio as the king understands it.
Only the urine, the raised lips, the bristled back, the drooling, indicate to Sal what he's on about.
As the distance between potential competitors decreases, no one can relax.

At the first sign of a problem, display your weapons.
Sharks deploy as much of their bodies as possible, maximizing surface.
Lions rub themselves on each other to create a smell of the pride.
Extend, fan out, bare teeth, build dungeons. Aggression shouldn't hurt.
Once you've scared the other guy, you should quickly decrease your appearance.
The king gets agitated, however, at this suggestion; he likes to go all the way.

Sal's dancing came out fully functioning and needed no social gestation.
Still, everyone knows the queen's fitness will be measured by Sal's survival.
The mole rat controls the sexual state of the entire community through her toiletries.
The king yawns because he isn't stimulated. The others yawn too. These are deceitful signals.
Sal observes these costly communications as the selfish herd backs into a circle.
Bleating and staring from their paranoid crescent, they scramble toward the bar.

Sal tries to conjure a signal that would scare off everyone except Mike and Stacey.
Her instincts arrive like foreign guests and are impossible to ignore. Greet or run?
Greeting the army is useless when they've got orders. Running from soldiers is stupid.
She wishes the queen might have bred with a better class of shoe-salesman.
Envy is practically impossible to notice in species which don't interact with humans.
The rarer you are, the less likely you'll be preyed upon, the less you have to lose.

Still, masquerade is the best defense; stand colored like the background, shaped like it.
Twig caterpillars who look like bird droppings avoid being picked for dinner.
Moths and fish flap erratically, appearing sick and unappetizing.
Disguise your face by painting eyes on your ass. Harlequin. Coral Snake.
Mark yourself distinctly and people will assume you are noxious. Vamp.
Fair warning comes in colors; mimic the warning and save the cost of poison.

Fireflies go home with any beetle who sends out their wives' signals.
Each has its own flash, a particular way of turning the phrase.
Signals in drunken, dark-lit cacaphonous crowds are messy and hard to discern.
The beetles easily rip their flattered hearts from their sleeves.
Turns out being "individual" is nothing more than pushing a shopping cart of cues.
The more copying goes on, the more cues are needed to identify the deadly.

Still, antlers get costly, making Sal even more conspicuous.
Soon the imitators all have them and you find yourself needing a new cue, asap.
A rat in trouble jumps to startle the snake. A sea cucumber turns inside out.
Some prey are so poisonous they kill themselves in the process of surviving.
Both die and no "learning" happens. A cricket'll tell you playing dead can backfire.
Natural selection favors anyone who can survive this pile-up of images.

MARGINS

Something's wrong with Sal: her calls come too late at night, too often.
She wants to do too many things over the course of a day.
She speaks endlessly into the answering machine. Then calls back.
Late at night, I stand back from the windows as she aims badly with stones.
Then the doorbell starts ringing as I lay deeply in the couch.

Would you like a ride tonight? It's awful weather, I don't mind waiting.
Maybe it's true that a person should always help others.
One's generosity is their humanity, their soul food; I guess you'd call Sal a glutton.
No one wants to grab the food out of someone's mouth or deprive them of a meal.
But Sal's a binge eater; one you suspect is off vomiting somewhere.

Anything you need or want she'll find for you; anything you don't know, she'll explain.
Even things you've barely dreamt she'll conjure.
Directions? She laughs and tells stories, going to the car to lend you her map.
Suggestions for a restaurant, a mechanic, a doctor, a quiet place to read?
Her every idea blooms more fully and perfectly than the last; her every privilege, yours.

Anyone she knows she'd love you to meet; anything she's won you can have.
Into fantasies you've never gone and desires you haven't felt, she'll coax you with ease.
A few drinks when you're lonely, a casual, methodical, flattering examination of your soul.
Fears you've never expressed she'll soothe and repackage into a common humanity.
And all with a feeling of contagious pleasure that in her you see what you might love.

Once I was stuck underground, a bad scene with god, prophecies of doom.
Sal called me to an intimate bar and led me into conversations about archetypes.
She sopped up my self-pity with careful teasing and rounds of compliments and beer.
I plunged into her consuming attention, while she deftly worked my faith.
Within an hour I saw the outline of a dungeon I'd never imagined.

Her voice is certain temptation: a path deep beneath a mountain.
See, I am a man of a different persuasion, never desiring any woman.
I thought: If I make it through this night, I don't have to see her mouth shining.
She rarely spoke about herself, only kept questions coming.
My edges started dulling and the colors around us drained of definition.

When finally she spoke of herself it was like a kid bringing favorite toys from the attic.
She made me feel careful and worthy as each piece was ceremoniously handed over.
Somehow she knew I needed these feelings and so even my helping her helped me.
Her gaze took root and her stories bore into my chest.
Still I remained suspicious, not of any real agenda, but of her childish way of speaking.

Yet I knew that this was the purpose, some secret reversal of healing.
And in the touching, which amounted to nothing more than listening, her words took flesh.
Here was the invitation to a fearful intimacy; that I might consider fucking her.
Her mouth, her mind, the contours of her experience—bringing all of them into warmth.
I should really stop drinking, I interrupted, calling a halt to the whole idea.

I thought if I make it out of this scene, I'll never have to see her mouth again.
It's not like she asked me for anything, I'm just a good target.
Unwillingly I took her hand, stroked her fingers and suffered a wave of desire.
She wants me to be something I'm not, suddenly washed up in kissing her.
I must be drunk. Drunk and attracted to the wrong sort of person. God forgive.

It's getting late for me, me with my obligations and activities. She offered more help.
Endless little strings; logistical details serving no purpose but to bind me to her.
Webs of times, places, reasons to see her. The present moment can't hold what she offers.
So it stretches and disfigures, its pieces graft and splice onto upcoming days, months.
In short, I blame her for everything. For making me feel like I could stay forever.

293

My brain starts to burn and she rushes over to put it out even as she sparks it again. This wasn't the emergency I planned for. I'll never see her again if I make it out of here alive. Really, I'd love to go with you, she says. I'm going to be there anyway. It's no trouble. I want to. But days pass and I was supposed to have called her back. Every hour is an hour I don't see her. A week becomes a week and a day. It's becoming obvious again that life is simple.

When I see her now I can tell any weight on this bridge will have to be mine. She won't look at me. She's laughing with someone I know at the other end of the party. Her temptations tailor to each perfect victim. We can torture her all night. She could come up and smile and I could look at her, touch her, take her home and fuck her. Or ignore her and forget about her completely. She never looks over.

TONGUES

And yet, Mike continues, she appears never to contradict anyone directly. She's so passive she doesn't say an idea until she knows it'll work, Stacey adds. The bar's getting crowded and they won't seat for dinner unless the whole party's there. They leave her a message: it's too rainy to walk around, we'll do it another time.

Sal sits and waits for food. Days go by and when it passes in front of her she eats it. She doesn't go after it. When it's there, she's suddenly hungry. She eats and has metabolism. She speeds around for a while. She'll sink her teeth in if your paralysis is covenient. Then she waits again, still as stone. Barely breathing. Body temperature cold. Thoughts slow.

Others eat and drink and laugh. Others wear jewels and make history and cry. Sal watches.
Her body temperature cools as night comes on and the torches are lit along the paths.
Fire reflects in the fish-pools and the flames dance, licking the shoes of the soldiers.
They play their flutes to charm her, but of course she can't hear them, though she sways.

Underground once, her legs became of so little use as to fall off.
Bones and skulls line the damp cisterns where sound doesn't bother coming.
In this place 145 million years pass without a clue. Friends don't call again.
Sal rejected the abundance of small land mammals in order to escape her habitat.

Some of the king's guests try to catch Sal alone during cocktail hour.
Their slithering and elongated physiques don't fool her; their hips give them away.
Unlike hers, their skulls can't protect their brains at dinner, and they are easily crushed.
Trying to kiss her they meet the misfortune of distensible jaws; her saliva of burning acid.

The similes grow as thick as vines as Sal stands farther and farther from the action.
Her jewels lack lids and widely never blink; their glassiness sloughed off in slow time.
Sal only hears things traveling through the ground, ignoring the things in the air.
With her internal ear she listens to someone praying.

On shifting sand it is impossible to get a good grip, so Sal sidewinds slowly.
Her metabolism keeps her creeping, unable to spring for long, she's careful who she knows.
The prophecy her feet feel is one man's extreme futility. His very presence someone's vanity.
Ignorant of the glitter, her tongue finds a special taste from his words rising through the ground.

Since old and new layers of skin are no longer touching, Sal secretes fluid between them. The old waits until the new disguise is complete before coming undone. Her smile grows over. Don't look at her when her eyes are milky, her blindness lasts a good week. She fumbles. She's in hiding. Storing up. Saving herself. Faithful to destiny.

Later, when all are drunk, she starts splitting at the lips, her smile peeling back from the edges. Wriggling free in the firelight, she rubs against surrounding objects: tables, candlesticks. Now she's at her best, her sharpest hues, her brightest eyes; total iridescence. Looking around at the colorless cast of herself she knows what she wants.

Sal is very shortsighted. She demands without thinking through and can't judge distances. Immobile bodies usually go unseen but his prison of prayer is exotic. She thinks she loves him. As he called to heaven she was in the way. She shows a tongue which is long and split. But he cannot see; he can judge her only by the tiny sounds it makes flickering in and out.

The ground trembles as Sal senses the infrared of his warm body and grows meaner. He hears, interrupting his prayer, the noise of chains, warfare, crowds above him. Sal's tongue, disturbed, constantly beats at the earth. She really needs his help, you see. She insists he help her, though she could, of course, help him. There's a movie in her eyes.

She can swallow someone much larger than herself. Her stomach is a damn straight line. He refuses to alternate any type of message with her so she answers him whole. Sal would like to co-star in his epic, ride away on horseback. She'd like his warm mouth. She'd like to back in his prayer or hibernate in his face, becoming his perfect likeness.

DUMMIES

Her first real dummy was witty, charming, looked like her. You'd swear he was alive.
Sal took care not to humiliate him, never doubling him over backward. No suitcases.
She did her unpacking offstage where no one could see the dismemberment.

From the first, Sal had completely custom controls made for him.
Seven years she spent designing his mouth. Four years on his real blinking eyelids.
She read *10 Steps to Building a Perfect Dummy* but decided to hire a professional.

A taxidermist collects the best hair, eyes, tear ducts and skin for amateur dolls.
There's a complex series of moving parts in their hollow bodies. Sal wanted deluxe.
His musculature and face should mimic hers; only his expression should be less ambivalent.

All day he sat for her in a child-sized chair while she danced and primped.
At first she practiced with him twenty or thirty times a day: 1. Don't move your lips.
Use the mirror to watch your mouth for any cheating: "Slay-the-ree" "Ad-then-cher."

She understood he needed to *appear* to act completely independently of her.
This system took time. She strove to string together words she had mastered.
She learned there is no such thing as *throwing* your voice, it has to be done the hard way.

As a child, Sal discovered that hearing is the most untrustworthy sense.
So she found a contrasting voice and the dummy didn't sound just like her.
And on video tape she practiced unclenching her jaw and laughing without smiling.

As the days went by, she assembled a litany of counterfeit words, a phoneme away. "Thor you I hoo-ud do anything." "I luth you there-ee nuch." His jaws flapped as she spoke. The essence of the act is that her character is real; the dummy fools everybody.

In order to keep the routine lifelike, some part of the dummy should be moving at all times. Sal's act has a simple plot and dummy movements follow it. Stare. Laugh. Stare. She keeps the audience engaged by alternately frightening and ignoring them.

Once Sal made the dummy do a headspin, causing demented laughter. It was the best house she played to, and even though it ruined the illusion, she profited. From then on the dummy got assembled and stuffed into his suitcase onstage as well.

She disposed of her first dummy after several years. Anything can be made to talk. Hands, socks, clouds, policemen, stars, governments, statues, train stations, dogs. Sal wanted the world to speak to her by itself.

From then on the dummy got emotionally out of control. Double takes. Crying. He went into her room and chewed at furniture. "I hate you" "I hate you like . . ." Technically, those are easy words to say. She covered her ears.

But increasingly Sal felt hunger for an audience and so she developed stage fright. Open with her second-best joke. Keep routines short. Been seen and not heard. But once you give it, the audience keeps the upper hand, so Sal stopped the show.

HOW-TO'S

If you pay attention, Sal can help you clean up households, schools, governments. Anything that comes in contact with people can be returned to its original luster.

But she won't argue if you insist on doing it your own way. She won't look. Millions of people can be wrong at once, turning unwanted filth into democracy.

On wood, some say use wax. Some say don't use wax. Surfaces grow dull with fingerprints. Cockroaches can sense crumbs as small as two thousand times the diameter of a hydrogen atom.

Sal knows that delay does not always cause stains to become permanent performances. Their permanence is about scrubbing. So stop it. Left alone, will the stain give up?

Adding protective shine is an incentive to free markets, a clear conscience. But even the cleanest body is home to a billion bacteria converting secretions into body odor.

As Sal points out, you must allow soiled items to soak overnight. For removal of ink: cover the area with earth and alcohol, wrap in plastic.

Before you blink, Sal's inspected your metal. Is it maintained?
Polish can often collect in the details, causing streaking, requiring scrubbing.

Moody houses harbor polluted air. If Sal tells you it stinks, don't drop it.
In a loose house, outdoor replaces indoor air at the rate of once per hour.

Irritants often do not leave traces; particles are hardest to detect or control.
You can use a tabletop air-cleaner, but these are less effective than open windows.

In your own best interest, use shaving cream or hairspray on urine; do not ignore Sal.
Newsprint is impossible to remove without bleach. Recycle as much as possible.

Every day: wash the dishes, put them away. Every day: pray. Dust and vacuum weekly.
Every month, focus on a special area for cleaning: mattresses, bookshelves, pictures, car.

Sal knows you're too busy to listen, or think that in your position this stuff doesn't matter.
Seasonally, take inventory of closets. Every year hold an unsparing garage sale.

COLORS

Wending over the orange hills, there is a path of pure blue. On it, Sal wears a crimson smock.
Her shiny black shoes are question marks on the stones. Sal doesn't tint her smile.
Through the window overlooking the meadows, Sal's hair turns a virgin, tarnished copper.
When you see her sitting upside-down on the yellow bench, don't look at her lack of gardening.
As vain as daylight she prepares the most violent similes in creation.
White peacocks wander the multi-colored meadows, Sal armadillo gray against them.
Purple soldiers exercise creamy stallions. Sal throws her darkest shadow there.
The husband drops the woman's bruised arm from his fingers. The saffron bruise smears off.
He calls for his soldiers. The wife pulls off her electron wig, shaking loose a laugh.
Sal in studded iodine stares for a moment until the air is a moony pepper mist.
Listening through her eyelids, Sal radiates the spectrum of invisible light.
Where she bought a kiss, the marble stairs wipe themselves clean of the mess.

Rome Burns
Michael Counts

NOTE

The following monologues are excerpted from GAle GAtes et al.'s *The Field of Mars*, performed last year at the theater company's Exhibition/Performance Space in Brooklyn, New York. The production took place, in four acts, throughout a 37,000 square foot warehouse; at times the audience was seated, at times they wandered, and often several performance areas could be viewed simultaneously. This text is from the second scene, second act, during which the audience was seated. While "Rome Burns" was performed, four upstage walls were removed one by one. With the removal of the last wall a forest was revealed at the back of the space (a 13,000 square foot room) where Act Three occurred with the audience traversing between two opposing proscenium stages. The English version of Tacitus's monologue was sampled from Tacitus's account of the burning of Rome in A.D. 64, from *Eyewitness to History* (Harvard University Press), edited by John Carey. Adapted and performed by Michelle Stern, this monologue was presented in super script. As a blind prophet, Stern simultaneously delivered the gibberish retranslation written by Molly Gallagher.

*

Froom Froom Gawhumpy froom el klismet frommer Rome bleep. ga whumpel yorkel nosmer fiv bet ilior fra konkel gosmer. El schneiser ligort ulija et fiyonnel trikka ma yondri holitreen. Seekl El mangiferrous et yew sheel fuind. ga whiffle porkel kosmet yoon Kloom y motzel Marcus Agrippa's rook. Et Yo tolden

Nero tried to make it appear that Rome was his favorite abode. He gave feasts in public places as if the whole city were his own home. I shall describe one as a model of its kind. The entertainment took place on a raft constructed on Marcus Agrippa's lake. It was towed about by other vessels, with gold and ivory fittings. Their

estan escavulus todel dwee
whort eyezener ssajil periff
fronsmer ree. Re whiffa whiffa
tork. qwelmer trekle dasner
snorf. ela onleeta ciudawk
gawhumpy. elkaspan da sneider
inta tungels yo speeken. Nero
Carltonian whumpire esta
uliver quand I thunka eet ways
thrine porklent furrpoict livert
een todal lous klamker. por oie
would leek toe veesat wythe
hinkel boojum eioe cayn
nayvort admeat thays afloocul
Pythagorie toe otar perkels
noy yorkels. klismer frommel
batter em mooly yommel
lorkit treen. Tome free snikter
borfel porpy boff. siyi fork leer
oye weent toe takel mees
michichinopulisses theet miu
morsheelly korsmelter smoom.
worken toe womatchula my
yaa en corfu shorkel bleeter
gommel room ort fizzel et for
hagie et por sophista por
transtinople yon. Rome oyr
hoipe theet mee brohombus
ees sauvit favus circus. cunert
yolik ka whorty bloop.

*(Beth and Ben cross
downstage.)*

hooler yoniferous el porgy
poopula quaan oopel reen
trakka toy thee fr izzle ba
winkel cormel floomer. oill
tale hout aye sceeret. quain
aiye wooz leelit aiye bigroo
pork une meenuit aye ehoi
woild lait moi een to dos

rowers were degenerates,
assorted according to age and
vice. On the quays were
brothels stocked with high-
ranking ladies. Opposite them
could be seen naked prostitutes,
indecently posturing and
gesturing. Nero was already
corrupted by every lust, natural
and unnatural. But now, he
refuted any surmises that no
further degradation was
possible for him. For a few days
later he went through a formal
wedding ceremony with one of
the perverted gang called
Pythagoras. The Emperor, in the
presence of witnesses, put on
the bridal veil. Dowry, marriage
bed, wedding torches, all were
there. Indeed everything was
public which even in a natural
union is veiled by night.
Disaster followed. Whether it
was accidental or caused by a
criminal act on the part of the
Emperor is uncertain—both
versions have supporters. Now
started the most terrible and
destructive fire which Rome had
ever experienced. It began in the
Circus. The fire then swept
violently over the level spaces.
Then it climbed the hills—but
returned to ravage the lower
ground again. Terrified,
shrieking women, helpless old
and young, people intent on
their own safety, people
unselfishly supporting invalids
or waiting for them, fugitives

304

apardimento intriputuis
eyggreen tokoodle fra romr
dreefink in thees yonil oiye
eem soo teerad bor gootnuiit
seek. ta wingle rootifer mooni
igualea roonie fortnum ir
mira riroony blatt to
Prophet/Stern:

and lingerers alike—all
heightened the confusion.
Nobody dared fight the flames.
Attempts to do so were
prevented by menacing gangs.
Torches were openly thrown in
by men crying that they acted
under orders. Nero was at

Michael Counts

(Apartment dialogue starts.)

yorkel voitlin greelly snoo. Somebordy aylse morst spreekel thoov moik porcoosa mees gabities boot in Tome de fled de Mars nort lee snievel roon kawhismet fa rooney snort mikel seekren lorking froo le churnula muut son vivida morst bree Nero fieessgarumble de konigree et desring tor Troy bykletta Rome esht la nuevra yorkel orf yorel. leesander froot zaser tergul. kllortle snoo fa whump. Strukula en loebert weetc me mooker yo seetman thort heye esht theye moost woomjf mo irronhel grool. Thymer groot yo jifron hormel sa whitty nosmer. teerad you caymz dleepmy e yekel oopen.

Antium. He returned to the city only when the fire was approaching his mansion. The flames could not be prevented from overwhelming the whole of the Palatine. Nevertheless, for the relief of the homeless, fugitive masses he threw open the Field Of Mars. Yet these measures, for all their popular character, earned no gratitude. For a rumor had spread that, while the city was burning, Nero had gone on his private stage and, comparing modern calamities with ancient, had sung of the destruction of Troy. By the sixth day the fire was finally stamped out. Of Rome's fourteen districts only four remained intact. Three were leveled to the ground. The other seven were reduced to a few scorched and mangled ruins.

306

Heldenplatz
Thomas Bernhard

—Translated from German and with
a postscript by Gitta Honegger

Characters:
ROBERT SCHUSTER, PROFESSOR, the brother of the late Professor
   Josef Schuster
ANNA and
OLGA, daughters
LUKAS, son
HEDWIG, called Frau Professor, the wife of the deceased
PROFESSOR LIEBIG, a colleague
FRAU LIEBIG
HERR LANDAUER, an admirer
FRAU ZITTEL, the housekeeper of the deceased
HERTA, his maid

March 1988

Scenes One and Three:
Apartment of Professor Schuster,
   near Heldenplatz, third floor

Scene Two:
Volksgarten ("people's garden," the park between Heldenplatz and
the Burgtheater)

After the funeral

Thomas Bernhard

SCENE ONE

Large dressing room
A high window with wooden shutters
Two high doors to the left
One high door to the right
Several wardrobes, some open, some closed, along all walls
  reaching all the way up to the ceiling
Some closed trunks and suitcases addressed to Oxford
Early midmorning
HERTA *stands at the window, dust rag in hand and looks down*
  to the street

FRAU ZITTEL. (*Enters with a suit on a hanger, hangs it up and*
  examines it.) The suit isn't even torn
A small hole in the vest
My university suit the Professor always said

> (*She smells the suit, holds it up against the light and hangs*
> *it up again.*)

Now everything is even worse
than fifty years ago he said
Actually I should have gone to see mother
I dread the nursing home

> (HERTA *starts cleaning the shoes that are scattered on the*
> *floor.*)

I either cut her nails
or I read Tolstoy to her
Only because the Professor told me fifteen years ago
read Tolstoy to your mother
it's excellent therapy
I've been reading Tolstoy to her for fifteen years

> (*She brushes the suit.*)

When I try to put her dentures in her mouth
she pushes me away
She never paid any attention to me
I want to put the dentures in her mouth
and she pushes me away
old people are pigheaded

(She smells the suit.)

Even so I lasted twenty years
he said
Who knows whether the Professor could have
settled in England once again
Frau Professor always hated Vienna
She only loved the theater
She hated Vienna
If she goes to Neuhaus now
it surely won't be for long
Frau Professor is a city person
The apartment has been sold
sold far too fast
it has to be cleared
by the nineteenth at the very latest
that's day after tomorrow

(HERTA *stands at the window polishing shoes and looking
down to the street.)*

The Professor is dead
you can look down there as long as you want
it won't bring him back to life
Suicide is always a panicked action
The shirt was torn not the suit
You of all people had to see
how he fell to his death
I have seen quite a few corpses in my life
you'll make me sick the way you keep
looking down
Frau Professor hears the screaming again
At lunch not at dinner
She barely eats a few spoonfuls
and gets pale in the face and stiffens all over
Steinhof sanitarium didn't do any good
She can no longer relax in Neuhaus either
In Oxford she won't have any more fits
you'll see Frau Zittel
the Professor said
There is no Heldenplatz in Oxford
Hitler never went to Oxford

Thomas Bernhard

There are no Viennese in Oxford
the masses don't shout in Oxford

HERTA. Frau Professor is going to take me along to Neuhaus

FRAU ZITTEL. She needs you there
I convinced her that she needs you
She spent Christmas in bed
New Year's too
In Neuhaus she also lies in bed all day
or on the terrace inactive
she also reads the same thing
over and over again

HERTA. I wanted to visit her in Steinhof

FRAU ZITTEL. She didn't let me in either
and I bought her such good pastries
Frau Professor didn't want any visitors
they said
she had that beautiful room with the terrace again
The Pavillon Friedrich is for the depressed rich
they are not really sick and yet
every time she was in Steinhof
she caught a cold
Professor Schober the head of psychiatry is a relative
of Professor Kuddlich
whom Herr Professor Schuster had met in England
through Professor Wasserbauer
an uncle of Professor Wasserbauer
got Professor Schober the top position in Steinhof

HERTA. Frau Professor has something against me

FRAU ZITTEL. She eats a few spoonfuls of soup
and gets pale in the face and stiff all over
Frau Professor is a lonely woman
The Professor never treated her well
I'll never forgive you
that your mother was an actress
the Professor often told her
even though it's not your fault
Often in Neuhaus she doesn't leave the house for weeks
Highstrung individual he kept saying to her

310

To be born in Linz is a horrible enough thought
he said

HERTA. Frau Professor doesn't like me

FRAU ZITTEL. She doesn't like me any better
she doesn't even like herself
My wife is a lost creature
utterly unhappy
she should have never been born
there are so many who should have never been born
One has to tread gently with that sort of people
but they won't let you
the Professor always said
that sort of person always ruins everyone and everything

   (*She smells the suit.*)

Every year he went to England
and bought himself a suit
English suits still are the best

HERTA. Herr Professor owns twenty-two suits

FRAU ZITTEL. Yet he always wore the same one
he could have worn it for many more years
All his life the Professor
cleaned his shoes himself
no one was allowed to clean his shoes
I made creamed soup
and a loin roast from Ziegler
that should do
Instead of Oxford
they all go to Neuhaus now
The way the Professor sold the apartment
was much too rushed
The kitchen is already cleared out

   (*Looks around.*)

This year everything would have had to be painted
A Persian rug dealer
He wants everything changed
next week he wants to start with the renovations

Thomas Bernhard

> *(She takes the shoes from one of the wardrobes and throws them in front of* HERTA.*)*

Herr Lukas will take the shoes
Herr Lukas wears the same size
A decent man wears a size eleven shoes
The Professor always said
Whenever the Professor was in Turin
he bought himself shoes
but he only wore the English ones

> *(*HERTA *cleans the shoes* FRAU ZITTEL *threw to her.)*

The Professor's death is the death of Oxford

> *(She opens all wardrobes, one after the other.)*

The shoes go into the black gunnysack

> *(She throws dirty laundry on a pile.)*

The dirty laundry goes to the laundry
I don't know whether Frau Professor will take
the dirty laundry to Neuhaus
In Neuhaus it's still really cold in March
we never went to Neuhaus in winter
but we have no choice
we have to go to Neuhaus
They were barely five years old
when they met in Neuhaus
It never works when people get married
who knew each other as children
The chauffeur always brought them
honey candy from Baden

> *(Directly to* HERTA.*)*

You can't look down at the street
all morning
it won't change anything

> *(She takes a shoe from* HERTA.*)*

That's not the way to shine shoes

> *(She shows* HERTA *how the shoe should be shined.)*

There there

(*She gives the shoe back to* HERTA.)

All you would have done in Graz
was carry his winter coat for him
you dummy
That's all I did
when I was in Graz with him
I carried his winter coat for him
the Professor hated Graz

HERTA. Herr Professor promised to take me along
to Graz

FRAU ZITTEL. All you would have done is
carry his winter coat for him
and he would have made you stay
at the Archduke Johann Hotel
in a dark closet-sized room
with a window on the air shaft
that's how he was
you would have nearly choked to death
while he had the best room in the hotel
the Professor was an egotist
through and through

HERTA. His head was

FRAU ZITTEL. You've said it a hundred times already
his head was totally smashed

(*Takes the pile of dirty laundry and throws it into another
corner.*)

The Professor wasn't sick
Professor Robert is sick he wasn't sick
Professor Robert has been sick since childhood
Professor Robert has a very bad heart
he can't breathe
when he climbs the stairs to the apartment
he has to stop at least fifteen times
Professor Robert has good reason to live in Neuhaus
he comes here so rarely
because the stairs are so difficult for him

313

> they promised to put in an elevator for thirty years
> I guess there never will be an elevator
> Professor Robert can't breathe even
> when he's standing
> but sometimes he has no problems whatsoever
> they say that's also psychological

HERTA. There are so many sunflowers in Neuhaus

FRAU ZITTEL. (*Gets an ironing board, opens it and starts to iron shirts.*) The Professor has a weak heart
> the final stage
> now we get into the season
> that's the worst for him
> spring is always bad
> If only I make it through April Frau Zittel
> I won
> then I get through another year he says
> he reads the *Neue Zürich Zeitung* every day
> Only old and stupid people live in Graz
> the Professor always said
> Dullness that's Graz
> I don't understand
> that there are people
> who love Graz
> Where should I have gone in Graz
> I was always bored in Graz

HERTA. Herr Professor promised
> to take me along to Graz

FRAU ZITTEL. No one needs to have been to Graz

HERTA. Suicides don't get a church funeral

FRAU ZITTEL. The Professor wasn't Catholic
> That's Herr Professor's suit
> I said at the cleaners
> the Professor passed away last night
> I didn't say he jumped out the window
> You need an explanation
> when you take a bloody suit
> to the cleaners

They probably thought
he was run over by a car

(*She takes a comb from her dress pocket, steps behind*
HERTA *and combs her hair.*)

You mended your stockings in the dining room
if the Professor had seen that
if the Professor had known
how you really are
I always stood up for you
Jews get buried
in a plain unfinished pine coffin

(*Looks around.*)

The Professor hated disorder
Professor Robert didn't care
not the Professor
everything had to be in its place
the Professor was one of the most disciplined people
all hell broke loose if the window handles weren't straight
It wasn't easy for Frau Professor
European diving champion at twenty-three
the Professor had a good build
He hated fitted shirts
I'll miss your crème tortes
he told Handlos the pastry chef
I am Jewish you know Herr Handlos
I have to go back to Oxford for my wife's sake
I'll miss your crème tortes Herr Handlos
In Oxford there are no crème tortes by Handlos

HERTA. People say they will kill themselves
and they do kill themselves

FRAU ZITTEL. (*Notices that* HERTA'*s collar is unbuttoned and but-*
tons it.) All week you've been standing there
looking down at the street
You should only wear black
black looks best on you
everybody dresses in such crazy colors
The Professor didn't like it

Thomas Bernhard

when I wore colors
the Professor liked me only in black
most people look best in black
you should dye all your clothes black
I also like you best in black

HERTA. Now Professor Robert
won't live much longer

FRAU ZITTEL. Professor Robert knows how to live
an existential champion as the Professor always said

> (*They move even closer to the window and look directly down on the street.*)

I wouldn't have the courage to do it
He probably remembered you too
in his will

> (*She combs* HERTA's *hair.*)

I am not a good man
he always said
One day China will rule the world Frau Zittel
the Asian Age has already begun
In Oxford you'll get the nicest room
in the attic
with a view far into the countryside
You don't know how beautiful England is

> (*Puts up* HERTA's *hair, smooths it against her head.*)

England is crucial for a man of the mind
the Professor said
people who never spent any time in England
don't count the Professor always said
It would have been good for you too

> (*Goes to the ironing board and keeps ironing.*)

You'll get my cottage in Schachhalm Frau Zittel
you can retire there
should anything happen to me

HERTA. Frau Professor won't stay long in Neuhaus
she is a city person

FRAU ZITTEL. Now she thinks
  she'll stay in Neuhaus
  spending her twilight years in Neuhaus
  she'll come back to Vienna right away you'll see
  she isn't used to country life
  country people are the death of the mind and the spirit
  the Professor always said
  a city person has nothing to do in the country
  city folk move to the country
  and are destroyed in the shortest time
  everything in the country is against the city person
  a city person deteriorates in the country
  and is destroyed in the shortest time

HERTA. Frau Professor went to the Josefstadt Theater
  twice a week

FRAU ZITTEL. She doesn't go to the Burgtheater
  she goes to the Josefstadt
  I am a born Josefstadt fan
  she always said
  It's too hard to get there from Neuhaus
  Other than the church there is no good theater out in the country
  the Professor always said
  and once you've got a taste for theater
  you can't live without it
  When the Professor went to the Concert Hall
  she went to the Josefstadt
  He really only loved his brother
  the Professor did

  (*She folds a shirt.*)

He hated everybody except his brother Robert
He would have liked to be French
he said
not English not Russian
only French
being Austrian
is my greatest misfortune

  (*Irons the shirt until it is completely flat.*)

317

Thomas Bernhard

He worked up a rage
explaining to me how shirts are to be folded
he showed me how the shirts have to be creased
when they are folded

(*Demonstrates it for* HERTA *who turned to her.*)

There you see
that's the way he folded the shirt
then he yanked it up in the air
and folded it again
and yanked it up
and folded it again

(*Looks at her watch.*)

Seven or eight times he yanked the shirt up in the air
and folded it again
and then he said now you fold it Frau Zittel
you fold it exactly
the way I did
I couldn't do it
my hands were shaking so badly
I couldn't fold the shirt
This way said the Professor this way
and he folded the shirt sleeves
this way Frau Zittel here here here
he threw the shirt in my face
and I was to fold the shirt
he was relentless
The stupidity of mankind is limitless
No no Frau Zittel I'm not crazy
I'm just a perfectionist not a madman
I'm just a perfectionist not a madman
a fanatic perfectionist that's me Frau Zittel
I am not sick I am not sick he screamed
I am just a fanatic perfectionist
I am the most famous perfectionist fanatic
Professor Schuster I can't do it I can't do it I said
Unbearable individual he screamed unbearable individual
he said this is the way you fold a shirt
I couldn't do it
I couldn't even look at the shirt

318

Thomas Bernhard

(HERTA *brushes a shoe.*)

Frau Zittel Frau Zittel he screamed and ran to the window
Do you see Heldenplatz he screamed do you see Heldenplatz
Heroes' Square
all day long she hears the screams from Heldenplatz
all day long all the time
all the time Frau Zittel all the time
it can drive you crazy
crazy Frau Zittel
It's going to drive me crazy crazy

(HERTA *has moved to the window and looks down on the street.*)

For ten years or so
Frau Professor has been hearing the screams on Heldenplatz
nobody hears it she hears it
It drives me crazy Frau Zittel it drives me crazy
Of course I see Heldenplatz I said
Right there where you are standing now
he ran right there to the window and screamed
Frau Zittel Frau Zittel Frau Zittel
leaning against the window completely exhausted he said
If you don't even know
how to iron a shirt Frau Zittel
you are in the wrong place here
the Professor was pale he moved
away from the window over here
Now you fold the shirt Frau Zittel he said
he said it very calmly
I folded the shirt very calmly
See now Frau Zittel
calm down now Frau Zittel he said
he looked at the folded shirt and said
calm down now Frau Zittel
and then he said
come now come with me to the kitchen
and make us a cup of tea
have a cup of tea with me he said

(*Puts the shirt away and irons a second one.*)

319

Thomas Bernhard

HERTA. In Steinhof in January
  in the Pavillon Friedrich Frau Professor
  had another electroshock treatment

FRAU ZITTEL. But it didn't help
  she barely gets to the dining room
  and hears the screams from Heldenplatz
  Again and again she begged him
  to give up the apartment
  but he didn't do it
  I can't give up the apartment
  just because you keep hearing the screams from Heldenplatz
  he kept saying
  that would mean that Hitler drove me from my home
  a second time
  he thought it would help
  if she plugged her ears
  but of course it didn't help
  even at night she hears the Heldenplatz screams
  she covers her ears
  that's when she has to leave the dining room
  it's been going on for ten or twelve years now
  they could have moved
  the dining room to the bedroom
  but the Professor didn't do it
  just as an experiment she thought
  he always rejected it
  then you won't sleep at all he said
  first they thought plugging her ears would do
  but of course it didn't
  There is only one option
  that is to give up the apartment
  Professor Schober told them
  as long as you don't give up the apartment
  the illness won't recede
  Professor Schober said
  You'll see you won't hear the screaming
  once we are in Oxford
  she didn't hear it for ten years
  now she's been hearing the screams
  for more than ten years

Thomas Bernhard

It won't destroy the auditory channels
Professor Schober said
but it's entirely possible
that your wife will lose her mind
one of these days
the Professor said

HERTA. In Neuhaus she doesn't hear anything

FRAU ZITTEL. She is hardly back in Vienna and she hears the
screaming
but I can't give up the apartment because of it
the Professor always said
I can't do it

> (*She puts away the shirt and irons a third one.* HERTA
> *brushes the shoe.*)

He couldn't drink any alcohol
do you like Sarasate he asked
yes of course I like Sarasate I said
that's good that you like Sarasate he said
Please make sure in the future to fold my shirts
the way I want them
it always was awful
when he came in and saw me iron his shirts
the same thing happened every time
The fact that you like Sarasate earns you
a substantial advance of my trust
he always said
I don't trust people
who don't like Sarasate
they are always horrible people
And how about Glenn Gould
do you like Glenn Gould
He kept asking me again and again
I knew I had to answer again and again
I like Glenn Gould
do you like to listen to Glenn Gould
do you like Sarasate do you like Glenn Gould
Yes I always answered I like Glenn Gould
I like to listen to Sarasate and I like Glenn Gould
People who don't like Glenn Gould

and don't like to listen to Sarasate
are horrible people Frau Zittel you know
I don't want to have anything to do with such people
they are dangerous
those people who don't like Sarasate
and don't like to listen to Glenn Gould
I also demanded from my wife
that she likes Sarasate
and likes to listen to Glenn Gould
in that regard I am a maniac Frau Zittel
I certainly could think of better things to do
than listen to Sarasate on a Saturday
or to Glenn Gould
I don't even like the piano

HERTA. Frau Professor will feel much better in Neuhaus

FRAU ZITTEL. (*Crosses to the pile of dirty laundry, grabs it and throws it in another corner.*) She wanted to go to Paris
but he didn't let her
to Paris with Professor Widrich
would you believe it
then he didn't talk to her for three weeks

(*Continues to iron.*)

Because of you I accepted the position
only because of you he told her
do you think I'd voluntarily go back to Oxford
I hate England
and especially Oxford
but I simply can't take your fits anymore
Professor Schober is all for Oxford he said
the English atmosphere will be good for you
I wouldn't have thought that Vienna
is that bad for you

HERTA. The Professor didn't want to go back to England at all

FRAU ZITTEL. He saw no other way

(*Directly to* HERTA.)

The super turned over the body

(HERTA *nods.*)

All supers in Vienna
are from Yugoslavia these days
When I tell mother I am exhausted
she doesn't even hear it
I can't read to you today I say
that doesn't move her
she demands that I read the same chapter twice
You'll see you'll calm her down with Tolstoy
the Professor said
You don't even know what Tolstoy means
Your parents didn't do anything for you
not your mother not your father
if it weren't for me
I talked the Professor into hiring you
but I only did it out of gratitude
to your grandparents
a girl from Upper Austria from the Hausruck mountain region you
    say
the Professor said
yes I said
from a peasant family

HERTA. That's not even true

FRAU ZITTEL. How often did I lie for your sake
  again and again I lied to the Professor because of you
  I did it all the time
  otherwise he would have thrown you out long ago

HERTA. That's not true

FRAU ZITTEL. You bet it is
  She doesn't steal does she
  the Professor asked
  I said no
  she does help you doesn't she Frau Zittel wherever she can
  yes I said all lies
  you steal and you don't help me wherever you can
  you are a lazy person
  like your mother
  you have to be pushed all the time

you've been in this house for four years now
and you learned nothing
but I gave up
it makes no sense

HERTA. Herr Professor invited me to Graz

FRAU ZITTEL. To Graz that Nazi nest
the absolute anti-city
as he always said
Carrying the Professor's coat
All he ever did was abuse
everybody
he abused me
he abused Frau Professor
he abused his daughters all the time
me you everybody
I am the biggest egotist he said of himself
The position in Oxford is my salvation
he said
it might mean the end of my wife
it might utterly destroy her
I can't prevent it
In Oxford you'll be cured right away
he told Frau Professor

(*Directly to* HERTA, *increasingly agitated.*)

He felt only hate for his own daughters
Frau Professor Anna hasn't bothered to see him
in two years
She didn't have to get a divorce
she drove her husband out of their marriage
now both are alone
my two academic monster daughters
as the Professor calls them
my daughters are the death of me he said
they deserted him
but he never paid much attention to them
they exploited him no end
there is nothing more depressing than single daughters
Frau Zittel
who pursue a so-called intellectual career

My daughters are my gravediggers
and my son Lukas is a loser
To have to watch for decades
how a helpless child
develops into a repulsive monster
The children we hope to have are always different
from what we finally must accept
They are together for decades playing together
studying together turning into adults together
suddenly at forty they marry with great ado
and divorce right after
and become a burden to their father
Frau Professor Anna never paid any attention to her husband
Frau Professor Olga didn't either
All Frau Professor Anna cared about was the National Library
that was always more important to her
To realize one day that your own children
are monsters he said
we think we create humans
and all we get are carnivorous idiots
overwrought megalomaniac chaotic creatures

HERTA. They don't have a washing machine in Neuhaus either

FRAU ZITTEL. The rich have a monopoly on discord
and they have always been married to discord
they all look for a way out
but they don't find one
Don't ever pity these people
the Professor said
they don't deserve any pity
But you don't understand a thing
one could keep on talking to you for decades
and still you would understand nothing

HERTA. In Lisbon he always bought shirts

FRAU ZITTEL. But the sleeves were always too short
his arms were too long for his body
My father's arms were too long too Frau Zittel he said
strangely I can't stand silk Frau Zittel
cotton yes but no silk
silk is the utmost luxury for most of mankind

325

Thomas Bernhard

I am repulsed by silk
what mankind loves
repels me all of it

> (*Folds the ironed shirt and looks at her watch.*)

All the rich people are buried
in Döbling cemetery
the Schusters have a grave in perpetuity
This is how the Professor wanted me
to fold his shirts

> (*She shakes out the folded shirt and folds it again while she continues talking.*)

like that you see like that

> (*Again she shakes out the shirt and laughs.*)

like that you see

> (*Again she folds the shirt carefully.*)

The Professor was a pedant

> (*Very calmly, putting the folded shirt next to the others.*)

You aren't going to stand at the window
and look down at the street all day
as long as we're here
The Professor is done with it
he simply didn't want to go back to Oxford
For him it's no longer tragic
he's dead
it's tragic for Frau Professor
and for Professor Robert
and for you

HERTA. (*Wiping dust off the window.*) Herr Professor promised
to take me along to Graz

FRAU ZITTEL. To Graz to Graz
The Professor was instantly dead
In Vienna it often takes two weeks
to get a funeral
In Vienna the dead often lie for weeks
in municipal refrigerators

HERTA. It was a good thing Frau Professor wasn't there
  when the Professor threw himself out the window

FRAU ZITTEL. It's tragic that you had to see the dead Professor first
  He hated ties and winter coats
  in the dead of winter he walked around without a coat
  at seven thirty in the morning his English papers
  He wouldn't let me get them for him
  the only thing mankind is really afraid of
  is the human mind the Professor said
  the Professor wasn't a popular man
  On Tuesday mother will be ninety-two
  I found the Professor a beautiful man
  I am glad we already set the table
  There'll only be two more dinners in this house
  everything is already packed

    (Looks at the suitcases.)

Everything is marked Oxford
now everything goes to Neuhaus

    (Bends over one of the big suitcases.)

Oxford Oxford
now everything goes to Neuhaus
If the apartment hadn't been sold
but the Professor couldn't sell the apartment
fast enough
Professor Lukas and Frau Professor Anna are the only ones
to go to Oxford
I hear some other professor from Oxford
came to the funeral

    (Exclaims.)

Only the immediate family
that's no good either

    (Calm again.)

The spoons were already packed

    (Gets up and irons a shirt.)

The shirts have to be ironed
even though the Professor is dead

they all go to Professor Lukas
they fit him

HERTA. The shoes also fit him

FRAU ZITTEL. When a person no longer has a way out
he has to kill himself the Professor said

(*Directly to* HERTA.)

Open the windows and shutters in the dining room
that'll get us some nice air now

(HERTA *exits.* FRAU ZITTEL *calls into the dining room.*)

The Professor's youngest brother
jumped from the window in Neuhaus
in thirty-eight
he died instantly
nineteen years old
still a student
It took the Professor years
to get over it
Suicide runs in the family
more rich people kill themselves than poor ones
We have to beat the others to it
the Professor said
You have to open the shutters all the way
so that the air can get in

(*One can hear the opening of the windows and shutters.*)

If it had been up to Frau Professor
you wouldn't even be here anymore
you can thank me
that you're still here
She doesn't like fresh air
Twice in Graz
I had to take care of the Professor
in the Archduke Johann Hotel
he had the flu
you can't imagine
how he tortured me
but I was at his mercy
everyone always was at his mercy

Herr Professor Lukas is his victim too
and he always dominated his daughters
Frau Professor Olga more than Frau Professor Anna
but neither had much to laugh about
when they were children
they couldn't even go sledding
he wouldn't let them
he wouldn't let them do anything
he was always afraid
they might hurt themselves

(HERTA *opens the shutters in the dining room so noisily that*
it can be heard clearly all the way to the dressing room.)

It was only a question of
how they would get through it
a person never meant anything to the Professor
The only one worth anything is you Frau Zittel
he once said

(*Calls into the dining room.*)

Eight settings Herta
there have to be eight will there be eight
Frau Liebig Professor Liebig Herr Landauer

HERTA. (*Calls back.*) Eight there are eight settings Frau Zittel

FRAU ZITTEL. Once I'm in Oxford
I'll be able to breathe the Professor said
Things are worse now in Vienna
than they were fifty years ago Frau Zittel
They spat at my daughter Frau Zittel
To be afraid every day Frau Zittel
I can't take it anymore
I'm too old and too weak for Austria
living in Vienna is inhuman
My wife's mental condition is reason enough
to leave Vienna
now she hears the Heldenplatz screams
even at night
I shouldn't have given up
our English citizenship
that was a mistake

Thomas Bernhard

(HERTA *returns, continues to shine shoes.*)

When we walk out the door
all hell breaks loose
In the University it's a race through hatred
when you buy yourself a roll at the corner store
seek cover the Professor said
all the boxes in the basement go to Neuhaus
the postal service could have picked them up already
Herr Lukas will get the lion's share
Frau Professor Anna took time off
Frau Professor Olga gets four weeks off
Frau Professor said she'll visit mother
but she has said it so often
One has to dress warmly
for the Döbling cemetery

(*Folds the shirt.*)

Ironing is an art
the Professor said
ironing is always underestimated
the art of ironing is one of the highest arts

(*She walks to the window and looks down on the street
with* HERTA.)

Professor Robert
won't last long in Neuhaus
with Frau Professor
he doesn't like his sister-in-law
no one could stand it
under one roof with Frau Professor
All she does in Neuhaus is
sit in her easy chair and read
twice a week she is driven to the city
to the Josefstadt Theater
yet it was she who hired me
he didn't want me
he took me in against his will

(*She takes several walking canes from the closet.*)

I didn't even want it
mother wanted me to take the job

with a famous professor
it happens once in a lifetime she said

(*With the canes she walks to the window and looks down.*)

mother never let me contradict her
it's different nowadays
now everyone does whatever they want
it was quite different then
there was nothing but orders
and all the orders were executed
Do you know how guests are to be received
the Professor asked me

(*She walks with the canes to the table.*)

I didn't say anything
You don't know of course
do you know how guests are to be sent on their way
of course you don't know
You'll learn it all from me my dear
the Professor said
my wife has got it in her head
that I must hire you
but I think you are all wrong for here

(*She puts the Professor's canes on the table and wipes them
with a dust rag.*)

The whole family
went through Steinhof
every one of us was in Steinhof
the so-called upper class Viennese
were in Steinhof at least once
even if just as outpatients
the Professor said quite often
Men always had a much deeper connection to Steinhof
than women
and accordingly a majority of us
died in Steinhof
I can say said the Professor that for most of us
Steinhof was the final stop
Our family received all higher and the highest orders
only in Steinhof

Thomas Bernhard

> (*She ties the canes together with a cord.*)

The Professor himself was in Steinhof three times
before the war
the Schusters went from Steinhof
to England
they gathered in Steinhof
and went to England overnight
Professor Strotzka
who was here in December
got the Professor the Chair at Oxford

> (*She puts the canes in a corner, walks to the window and
> looks down to the street, to* HERTA.)

They would have taken you to England
if you had learned English
but you didn't even try
in four years you could have learned to speak perfect English
but that's no longer a problem
If the Professor had known
that you don't even speak English
he wouldn't have hired you
he thought that's a given
When the trees are barren you can even see the people
who sit behind the windows of the Imperial Palace
At this time of year the lights are on
even in the morning
On Saturdays the Professor loved to have breakfast
in Volksgarten at the Meierei restaurant
once during his breakfast a sparrow
it probably had diarrhea
dropped doo on his shoulder

> (*She turns around.*)

Frau Professor hates cooking
now that the Professor is dead
we can even put caraway seeds
in the soup

> (*Looks at her watch.*)

Mother insisted to be put
in the Catholic nursing home in Kritzendorf

332

I said a municipal one
she insisted on a Catholic one

(*Walks to the wardrobes, looks inside all of them.*)

she wanted a new robe
The Professor wanted to give me the money for it
In Graz I couldn't breathe
Graz has the worst air
people always say it's Linz
but the worst air is in Graz

(*Looks under the table.*)

In Oxford they wanted to get
English furniture
You would have liked it in England
but they wouldn't have taken you along

(*She exits through the right door.* HERTA *looks after her.* FRAU ZITTEL *returns with a big vase with irises and stops in front of the table.*)

Now that the Professor is dead I thought
I could also put some flowers on the table

(*She puts the vase on the table and moves back a few steps to get a better look at the vase.*)

The Professor hated flowers
I never was allowed to put flowers anywhere
Such beautiful irises

(*She arranges the irises in the vase and steps back again.*)

Irises have a deadly smell
he used to say

(*She arranges the irises.*)

They won't look good in the dining room either

(*Takes the vase back to the dining room and calls out from there.*)

No they don't look good in the dining room

Thomas Bernhard

    (HERTA *crosses to the dining room door and looks into the dining room.*)

Tomorrow I'll just take them
to the cemetery

    (*Returns to the dressing room.*)

He didn't even want flowers
at his funeral
I want no flowers at my funeral
the Professor said
no flowers and no people
he made his brother promise
to come to his funeral all by himself
not even my wife is allowed at my funeral
he once said
the thought of having all these sub-humans at my grave
is unbearable

    (*She inspects a few pieces in the pile of dirty laundry on the floor in the corner.*)

HERTA. Professor Robert will be next

FRAU ZITTEL. Döbling cemetery is my favorite cemetery
all the famous people are buried there
When you're older you know
how to get along with death
I'll buy mother's robe
in Währing street
Not a word of thanks in fifteen years
We get through Tolstoy
she insists I start all over again
she doesn't want anything else
Blindness is the worst my child
Old people are merciless
Gogol I said
because the Professor said
I should give Gogol a try
he'll make your mother laugh Frau Zittel
she wouldn't let me
Last week he wanted to know

when I lost my virginity
You're blushing Frau Zittel he said
that was the last time he laughed out loud
Herr Lukas won't drive his sisters home
but that Niederreiter woman he will
first the Niederreiter
then his mother
Good God you have no clue
That Niederreiter woman was married twice before
first to a Turkish Bey
then to a bottler of mineral water
who left her all his money
she probably will go to Oxford with Herr Lukas
Herta sleeps the solid sleep of the stupid
the Professor always said

HERTA. That's not true

FRAU ZITTEL. It certainly is
if you know of a young woman
who could take on some of the dirty work
he said
I thought of you
in case he was thinking about someone related
I said I am related to you

(*Irons a shirt.*)

From the outside in
that's how shirts have to be ironed
then you don't get creases in the collar
Once the Professor even contemplated
sending you to nursing school
in Glanzing
But I talked him out of it
that's not for Herta I said
it only costs money and it would all be for nothing
In Graz you'd only have carried
his winter coat for him
I either cut her toe nails
or read Tolstoy to her

HERTA. Herr Lukas won't be home for dinner

Thomas Bernhard

FRAU ZITTEL. I feel as if I live in a museum
the Professor always said
The Professor was a sensitive person
Professor Robert still writes poems
He always read them to us
on Sundays during winter
Once we get through April
we're saved Professor Robert said

(*Looks at her watch.*)

All I did in Neuhaus
was scrub floors day and night
I won't do that anymore
no matter how often Frau Professor asks me to
I did everything for Herr Professor
but not for her
she only gives orders

HERTA. That's all he did

FRAU ZITTEL. But it was different

HERTA. Why

FRAU ZITTEL. You wouldn't understand
The Professor was a gentleman
He was the most cultivated person I knew
In Neuhaus I'll be carrying the folding chairs
out on the terrace and back inside again
one moment she wants to sit outside
the next inside
In Neuhaus Frau Professor is unbearable
in Vienna she has to control herself
here she can't do as she pleases
She never was allowed to come to the University
the Professor didn't let her

(*She takes the shirts which she just ironed out of the suit-case and counts them.*)

All my life
I lived in a museum the Professor said
He simply should never have come back
to Austria

they had a nice life in Oxford
you can't imagine how nice
the Professor was famous in Oxford
Professor Robert invited me to his house in Salmannsdorf
my brother is dead he said
now you can come with me
to Salmannsdorf
but I don't want to

    (*She puts the shirts she counted back into the suitcase.*)

Again and again Professor Robert wanted me
to go with him to Salmannsdorf
I'd be crazy to do it
Professor Robert needs professional care
Such an old man in such a big house
The Professor always said
his brother will die first
Professor Robert was always the sick one
the Professor always was healthy
my brother Josef will outlive us all
Professor Robert always said

    (*She leans against the table.*)

They shipped the piano ahead
by boat
I always made absolutely sure
that the socks are in order
the socks and the shirts

    (*She crosses to the window and stands next to* HERTA.)

I am not there a minute
before she insists
that I read to her

    (*Turns around and looks at the dressing room.*)

You have to watch out for cripples Frau Zittel
he said
above all blind people
The Professor looked right through people

Thomas Bernhard

(She notices some dust on the table, takes the dust rag and meticulously wipes the table, stopping now and then to examine the desktop.)

The dust is the first thing
Frau Professor notices when she comes in
All rich Viennese are buried
in Döbling cemetery
I think she still owns the vinegar factory
in Mattersburg
The Professor never bothered about money

(She inspects the tabletop, then standing up straight.)

The Professor only sold the apartment
because she always begged him
not to sell the apartment
she begged and begged
until he sold the apartment
to a Persian

(Directly to HERTA.*)*

You're probably lucky
you don't have parents anymore

(She bends down and dusts the legs of the table.)

People without parents are always pitied
the Professor said
yet they have a lifelong advantage

(She stands up and speaks directly to HERTA.*)*

You can't stand me can you
I know what you think
the sixty-year-old daughter
lets herself be tyrannized
by her ninety-two-year-old mother

(Looks at her watch, then toward the door to the hallway.)

When Professor Robert spends the night here
I don't get any sleep at all
he constantly asks for something
You take his hat

338

as soon as he comes in
I always knew
that Vienna would be my death
the Professor said
I feel as little at home in Oxford
as I do in Vienna

(*She takes the suit and holds it up.*)

The Professor must have known
what he was doing
the Professor wasn't crazy
the Professor had a sharp mind
he wasn't tired of life
The family never understood him
his son docsn't understand him
his daughters don't understand him
A man of thc mind is never understood
the Professor said
the man of the mind walks alone
through life
even if it means letting down those close to him
the Professor said

(*She smells his suit.*)

I shouldn't have taken the suit to the cleaners
it's my fault
I'll ask Professor Lukas
to let me have the suit

(*She holds up the suit.*)

The Professor has been wearing this suit
for thirty years

(*She threads a needle to mend a hole in the vest.*)

Even though we get separated from our beloved

(*She puts the vest on the table.*)

their beloved clothes stay with us
The Professor had no other choice
it probably was the weather
he said he'd pick up Frau Professor

339

at Mohr's beauty parlor
she always went to Mohr
every Thursday before the Josefstadt Theater

(*She hangs up the suit without the vest and buttons up the
jacket as she speaks.*)

The son gave him much more trouble
than the daughters
he made sure they obeyed him
Professor Lukas destroyed his father's life
He found everything repulsive in Vienna
I have to force myself to go downtown he said

(*Directly to* HERTA.)

He wouldn't have known what to do with you
in Oxford
You've been here for so long now
and you still don't understand a thing

(*She prepares the vest for mending. She looks at the suit-
case.*)

in the end
I have to do it all
no one has ever done anything
in this household
ten twelve thirteen suitcases
and the bags
it's a good thing that a few tables and chairs are still here
and the beds
Professor Robert will probably spend the night here
Mother never understood when I told her
I am overworked

(*Looks around the dressing room.*)

Forty years and barely a kind word
But I never had the strength
to leave
I would never have left the Professor to himself
he needed me

(*Directly to* HERTA.)

340

Once you get to the big city
you don't want to go back to the country
On Tuesdays I always see mother
The Professor hated nursing homes
I can't stand the smell of nursing homes
he always said
You look to it Frau Zittel
that you don't get sick
You can't afford to be sick

HERTA. (*With the dust rag in her hand, looking down on the street.*) In Graz the Professor wanted to buy me
a pair of shoes

FRAU ZITTEL. He always promised me shoes too
when we went to Graz
but he never bought me shoes in Graz
As often as I've been to Graz with him
he never bought me shoes in Graz

> (*She shuts the suitcase, then looks up to* HERTA.)

He talked me into reading Tolstoy
to mother
When I get there late mother threatens me
and insults me

> (*She crosses to* HERTA *and lightly presses her hand. Both look out the window.*)

The family will be here soon

SCENE TWO

In Volksgarten
Noon
Gloomy weather

ANNA *and* OLGA *are walking after their father's funeral;* PROFESSOR SCHUSTER, *their uncle, remains in the back, he isn't visible yet; but one can see the Burgtheater in the fog.*

ANNA. (*Stops a few steps away from a bench.*) That was the short-
   est funeral
   I ever attended
   And the most awful

OLGA. (*Has stopped, too.*) It will be hard
   to sell the house in Oxford
   half a year of looking and finally found at the last moment
   now it has to be sold again

ANNA. (*Looks back.*) Father dreaded Oxford
   everyone he knew
   had died
   he would have had no one in Oxford
   He hated Vienna
   but in Oxford he wouldn't have found anything
   that was still familiar
   everything has changed in Oxford too

OLGA. One could tell how bitter he was
   he couldn't take it anymore
   but it wouldn't have helped either
   if he had gone back to Oxford
   a few years sooner

ANNA. He wouldn't have gotten the chair then
   Professor Strotzka put everything on the line
   for him

OLGA. It was mother's idea

ANNA. Mother didn't ever want to return to Oxford
   but she resigned herself to it
   Mother wanted to move to another place in Vienna
   not to Oxford
   it didn't matter what she wanted
   father never paid any attention to it
   he never cared what she was thinking
   she never got through to him
   Oxford is a nightmare
   but every day Vienna becomes
   a much bigger nightmare for me
   I can't exist here anymore
   I wake up and I am afraid to go ahead

conditions today really are the same
as they were in thirty-eight
there are more Nazis in Vienna now
than in thirty-eight
it'll come to a bad end
you'll see
it doesn't even take an extra sharp mind
now they're coming back out
of every hole
that's been sealed for over forty years
just talk with anybody
you'll see
they're a Nazi
whether you go to the baker
or the cleaners to the pharmacy
or the market
in the National Library
I think I am among Nazis only
they're just waiting for the signal
to openly proceed against us

(*She calls out.*)

Take your time uncle Robert
we are waiting right here

(*To* OLGA.)

In Austria you must be either Catholic
or a Nationalist Socialist
nothing else is tolerated
everything else is destroyed
that is to say one hundred percent Catholic
or one hundred percent National Socialist

OLGA. Mother won't last long in Neuhaus

ANNA. On Saturday they're playing *Minna von Barnhelm*
in the Josefstadt Theater
I'm sure she'll see it
in Neuhaus she can order Zittel around

OLGA. What about Herta
is she taking her too

343

Thomas Bernhard

ANNA. One more won't matter anymore
  let her keep her
  Zittel can't do the heavy work anymore
  Zittel is already the mistress of the house
  and housekeeper second
  During the last years
  father spoke more to Zittel
  than with mother
  without Zittel nothing would have worked

OLGA. Is her mother still alive

ANNA. She is ninety-two
  in a nursing home in Kritzendorf
  father paid for it
  that won't work anymore

OLGA. Mother doesn't have to live on her pension alone

ANNA. She still has the vinegar factory
  and the fez factory
  even though she doesn't look after them these days
  she makes a fortune
  even father couldn't destroy
  those factories

    (Calls to her uncle.)

We're waiting here uncle Robert
we have time
Zittel did the cooking

    (To OLGA.*)*

He wanted to finish his book in Oxford
now nothing will come of it
Shipping the piano ahead
what nonsense
As long as I can work in the National Library
everything will be fine
but even that has become unbearable for me
you can't imagine
how stupid these people are
The director is an unbearable man
at lunch he sits down at the table

right across from me
a Salzburger or Tyrolian
every time I see his face it ruins
my appetite
good God those people
but in this country every job is determined
by party politics
people can't be stupid enough
to get the highest positions
those idiots sit everywhere
that's what drove father crazy too
the University is also filled with idiots
he suffered for twenty years
Idiots from Styria asses from Salzburg
for colleagues
intellectual life in this city
has almost choked to death
from the abominations
and idiocies of its position peddlers
Only ninety percent of my colleagues are Nazis
father said
they represent either the Catholic
or the National Socialist mindlessness
but they all are malicious and abominable
the city of Vienna is one single idiotic abomination
He was no longer able to have a conversation
in the end he only had uncle Robert

OLGA. You don't have to stay
at the National Library

ANNA. What else would I do
without the National Library
I wouldn't be able to bear it
I wouldn't know what to do with my life
you don't really believe
I could sit at home doing nothing
I never managed to do that
Waiting like mother for earnings from the factory
I always dreaded that
she wouldn't be where she is now
All that Josefstadt playgoing is just a whim

an escape into sickness
I am going to see *Minna von Barnhelm*
that's not using your mind
the theater does nothing for those people
but regulate their digestion

OLGA. If she didn't have the theater
she'd have nothing

ANNA. That's what's so pitiful
to be honest mother was ruined by father

OLGA. And father by her

ANNA. People always kill each other
Husbands and wives always kill each other
it's only a question who is killed first
who lets himself be destroyed
and annihilated first
that's what marriage is built on
there are countless stories out there
Her fits are her means of power
that's how she controlled father for two decades
at first it probably wasn't an act
and it probably isn't an act now
illnesses of that sort
are real illnesses and they are also performance

(*Calls to her uncle.*)

We don't have to rush uncle Robert

(*To* OLGA.)

That's the end of uncle Robert as well
only uncle Robert isn't the suicidal type
People like uncle Robert
don't jump out the window
they aren't hunted by Nazis either
most of the time they ignore what's going on around them
it's dangerous only for people like father
who constantly see everything and hear everything
and therefore are always afraid
Uncle Robert isn't always afraid
uncle Robert still enjoys his life

father never enjoyed his life
uncle Robert doesn't believe that
basically there are only Nazis in Vienna
he hears it but he doesn't believe it
it doesn't faze him at all
that's why he can stand it in Neuhaus
father could never stand it in Neuhaus
And when he goes to a concert it doesn't bother him
that the hall is filled with Nazis
uncle Robert can listen to Beethoven
without thinking of the Reichsparteitag in Nürnberg
father couldn't do that
We always preferred uncle Robert
to father
as children we ran to uncle Robert
whenever we could
because father was too dangerous for us
Thinking people have always been the dangerous ones
the unsuspecting who can listen to Beethoven undisturbed
are more liked
Thanks to uncle Robert
we had a nice childhood

OLGA. But father also went regularly
to concerts

ANNA. Yes but it was always a nightmare
because of the doubled effort
since he could only listen to the music
after he first forced himself not to listen
to the concert goers'
National Socialist mind-set
he had to look and listen the other way so to speak
so he could hear the music
Father was too complicated for this life
He thought in Oxford
he could start all over again
that was a mistake
it doesn't work to persevere in Vienna for twenty years
against your better judgment
and then simply go back to Oxford

347

OLGA. *(Watching uncle Robert.)* Uncle Robert never understood
father

ANNA. The two loved each other
they loved each other more than anything
but they didn't understand each other

OLGA. I told uncle Robert
he doesn't have to come to the funeral
in this cold awful weather

ANNA. It goes without saying that a brother
must attend his brother's funeral

OLGA. I didn't think
it would be over that quickly

ANNA. When nothing is said at the grave
and the weather is that bad
and there are so few people
it's over quickly
I always feel
at home in Döbling cemetery
that's because our parents took us so often
to Döbling cemetery

OLGA. *(About uncle Robert.)* Uncle Robert has gotten old
he stops every few steps
and watches the crows

ANNA. Everybody has to stop
when they're out of breath
and then people think it's out of love
for the birds
Uncle Robert was always
the professor of philosophy
but father was more philosophical
At some point your uncle Robert fell behind
father said
first they both developed at the same speed
then uncle Robert fell behind
but uncle Robert always was
a kind man unlike father
father was always unpredictable

One could say that father
was married to Zittel
mother only got on his nerves
he didn't know what to do with mother
while Zittel developed more and more
into a real companion
mother became a minor characer
and just a bother basically
she didn't count
she didn't make any effort
your mother has an empty head
father kept saying for decades
In the end Zittel
spoke only English with him
Zittel finally was the only one
with whom he could have a philosophical argument
all mother could think about was the vinegar factory
and the fez factory
Zittel read Descartes and Spinoza
Zittlel was his creature
something mother could never be
and didn't want to be
mother was an accomplished hostess
that didn't interest father
father hated everything social
he called himself a foe of society
and company
uncle Robert didn't mind going to parties
even the most awful ones

> (OLGA *walks toward uncle* ROBERT *while* ANNA *looks in the opposite direction; she guides uncle* ROBERT *who walks with two canes to the bench.*)

Zittel is cooking one last time
Tomorrow the last breakfast
in the apartment
You aren't going back to Neuhaus tonight are you

PROFESSOR ROBERT. No no the Russian crows are still here

OLGA. In any case Zittel will go with you
to Neuhaus

PROFESSOR ROBERT. (*To* ANNA *who turned around.*) When do you
  go to Oxford

ANNA. Day after tomorrow
  as planned uncle Robert

PROFESSOR ROBERT. It won't be easy
  to sell the house
  you worked so hard to find it

ANNA. A house like that
  is hard to sell in England
  first it's hard to find
  then it can't be sold

PROFESSOR ROBERT. I would think that this type of house
  can only be sold at a loss

ANNA. Maybe I'll stay for a while with Lukas
  in Oxford
  the house isn't furnished

PROFESSOR ROBERT. For that kind of money you could have gotten
  a nice big property in Neuhaus

ANNA. But father wanted to go back to Oxford
  not to Neuhaus

PROFESSOR ROBERT. But he made the mistake to believe
  he just can pick up and leave for Oxford
  in the end he saw
  it wasn't possible
  I am so used to Neuhaus

  (*Looks around.*)

  Vienna is far too exhausting
  this time of year
  in March Vienna's not the place for me
  before June Vienna's not for me

ANNA. In Neuhaus you have everything you need
  mother is happy she has you in Neuhaus
  without you mother would perish in Neuhaus

PROFESSOR ROBERT. Neuhaus is full of old people
  who can't get around in Vienna anymore

350

The old the sick and the crippled
but I loved Neuhaus since I was a child
it's more difficult for your mother
she always hated Neuhaus
there was nothing she hated more than Neuhaus
father banished her to Neuhaus
still and all she's gotten used to it
she does nothing all day
but sit in her chair either on the terrace or
in the dining room
There is a curse on the woman
if she were a fictional character
but she's real
I used to tell your father
that's the tragedy

OLGA. You want to sit

PROFESSOR ROBERT. (*Sits down on the bench with the help of his
nieces.*) In Vienna it's still winter in March
At the end of January the Viennese already say it's spring
but here it's still winter at the end of March
During my student days
I always had lunch here in the Volksgarten
not your father
he always went straight home to Herrengasse
I can't remember him ever going
to Volksgarten
except for breakfast
which he had at the Meierei restaurant

ANNA. Aren't they building a road
through the orchard in Neuhaus
have you done anything against it

PROFESSOR ROBERT. It'll take them years
I won't even live to see it
it'll take five or six years
until they start building that road

ANNA. But it will reduce the property value

PROFESSOR ROBERT. That's possible

Thomas Bernhard

ANNA. Mother wrote a letter of protest
  to the mayor

PROFESSOR ROBERT. I know
  I don't protest
  I don't protest against anything
  I no longer protest against anything
  There's no point to protests at the end of one's life

ANNA. You should also write a letter of protest
  to the mayor
  and to the ministry
  it counts when it comes from you
  it counts more than anything else

PROFESSOR ROBERT. I don't write letters of protest
  I don't care
  whether or not they build a road through the orchard

ANNA: But that makes no sense
  if for no other reason you've got to write the letter
  for our sake

PROFESSOR ROBERT. I protested all my life
  and it didn't do any good

ANNA: All you have to do is sign
  we draft the letter
  you read it
  we write it
  you sign it

PROFESSOR ROBERT. I don't care whether they build the road
  or not
  it doesn't mean a thing to me anymore

ANNA. Father would have done something against it
  that beautiful apple orchard

PROFESSOR ROBERT. But not even your father could have made me
  write that kind of protest letter
  now if they'd bulldoze my house I'd protest
  but not for the orchard
  the apple trees are old
  they'll die with me at the latest

I don't need any hostility in Neuhaus
What your mother does is none of my business
she can do what she wants
but you have to leave me alone with such trifles

(He takes ANNA's *hand.)*

You are always the same
daring and ready to battle
In Neuhaus I want to have my peace
I can't be at war with the mayor
These are the last years of my life
which will bc over soon

ANNA: Aren't you cold on the bench

PROFESSOR ROBERT. I am not cold
   Your father always staked everything on one card
   I wasn't surprised by his suicide
   It just took too long
   he should have gone to Oxford six months ago
   it was too late for him
   he always said
   all one can do in Vienna is get out
   or kill oneself
   To be honest
   I never considered suicide
   your father toyed with the thought even as a child
   When I didn't even know what suicide was
   he was already thinking about it
   The decisive factor was
   that the mayor of Vienna asked him in person
   to come back to Vienna
   it was the mayor who offered him the Chair
   But the first mistake was
   buying an apartment
   right across from Heldenplatz of all places
   even though he was offered apartments
   in Grinzing and Sievering
   I advised him against downtown from the start
   he didn't listen
   your mother was the first victim
   of this unfortunate decision

Thomas Bernhard

We understood each other best
when your father was in Oxford
and I in Cambridge
it was a really close relationship then I must say
I was prepared
to go back to Vienna
not your father
I could always go back
to my beloved Neuhaus
your father couldn't
I always felt comfortable in the country
your father hated the country
he hated nothing as much as country life
He banished your mother to Neuhaus
who hated country life as much as he did
and he ruined himself in Vienna
every year in Vienna was one big step further
toward his tragic end that's the truth
your father had the sharper mind
and he was the more sensitive character
Neuhaus he used to exclaim
I can only take it for a few hours
that's a death sentence for a man of the mind
he was right

(OLGA *sits down on the bench.*)

In a way
he suffered from persecution mania
just like your mother

ANNA. (*Vehemently.*) Persecution mania
how can you say that
You know yourself
what the situation is
it is much worse
than in thirty-eight
and it will be even more horrifying
Their hatred of Jews shows itself quite openly
their hostility is out in the open
You say you don't hear or see anything
because you don't want to hear or see

354

because with age
it became too much for you
to hear and see
that's the difference
for forty years in Vienna father never stopped
hearing and seeing
mother didn't either
you don't really think
that she is faking her fits
you can't really believe that
what a perfidious thought
Forgive me uncle Robert
but you were always hard of hearing
and you never saw anything
while our parents always heard and saw everything
You escaped into old age
your forget that father was two years older
than you
And if he had gone back to Oxford once again
you know what that meant
he would have gone to Oxford again
because he couldn't bear the atmosphere in Vienna
while you retreated to Neuhaus
into old age
In Neuhaus you see nothing and hear nothing
but in Vienna you see and hear everything
more clearly day by day
the Jews are afraid in Vienna
they always have been
and they always will be
you can't tell the Jews not to be afraid
no one will ever do that
because no one wants to be in their place
In Neuhaus you have nothing to fear
not yet
in the country they don't even know
what a Jew is

OLGA. Maybe we should walk a bit

ANNA. (*To* OLGA.) You think like uncle Robert
you think it's not that bad

while it's the worst
you always make yourself believe something isn't true
when it's not supposed to be true
you always retreated into yourself
away from the truth
like uncle Robert to Neuhaus
you both don't see
you both don't hear

PROFESSOR ROBERT. I understand you
but you shouldn't get upset about something
that can't be changed
the Viennese are Jew haters
and they always will be Jew haters
for all eternity
I know that too
but you don't really think
that I'm going to make my life miserable because of it
you can't ask me to do that
I live in Neuhaus and every week I come to town for a concert
I want to have my peace
it has always been up to the young to wrack their brains

ANNA. Father killed himself
and that leaves both of you quite cold basically

PROFESSOR ROBERT. (*Gestures to her she should sit down on the
bench with them.*) Such arguments lead nowhere
all our lives we had those arguments
I am no longer willing
to have that kind of argument

ANNA. (*Sits down.*) That's what's so horrible
that's what's so horrifying

PROFESSOR ROBERT. I know exactly what's going on
but I won't let it get to me
I don't want to let it get to me anymore
no one can ask me to do that
I am an old man that's no excuse
but I can expect some understanding can't I

ANNA. All of Neuhaus will be destroyed
if they build the road through the orchard

it will mean the end of Neuhaus

PROFESSOR ROBERT. You would have to protest all the time
    day and night
    because everywhere everything gets destroyed
    nature gets ruined everywhere
    nature and architecture everything
    Soon everything will be destroyed
    the whole world won't be recognizable anymore

ANNA. It would be enough if you just put your signature
    on the letter of protest
    just your name

PROFESSOR ROBERT. I haven't signed anything in years
    I haven't protested anything in decades

ANNA. That's what's so terrible
    they all get upset all the time
    but they don't protest
    they all get upset about everything
    but nobody does anything about it

PROFESSOR ROBERT. An utterly useless road
    I know
    a total disfigurement of Neuhaus
    but I am not signing any protest
    All of life is one single protest
    and it does no good
    they all wasted themselves protesting
    they protest against anything these days
    and it does no good

ANNA. You who have the best connections
    to the ministries
    you who know so many influential people
    who even is friends with most of them

PROFESSOR ROBERT. I no longer get involved
    my life has come to an end more or less
    I don't care what happens to Neuhaus
    just as I don't care what happens to other places
    let them do what they want
    I don't protest against anything anymore

Thomas Bernhard

that doesn't mean that I am not against it
but protesting it the way you imagine it no
I don't sign things like that anymore
At least in Neuhaus I want to have my peace and quiet

ANNA. They aren't just building a road through the apple orchard
they are building a road through the forest
by May half the forest will be cut down

PROFESSOR ROBERT. I know
I am aware
that everything will be destroyed
you act as if I didn't know
I also know that the school will be torn down
but I don't protest anymore
that's your job
the next generation
Our world is already a completely destroyed
unbearably ugly world
wherever one goes
the world today is one ugly
and thoroughly stupid world
deterioration everywhere
devastation all around
I'd rather not wake up anymore
in the last fifty years those in power
have ruined everything
and it's beyond repair
the architects ruined everything
with their stupidity
the intellectuals ruined everything
with their stupidity
the people ruined everything
with their stupidity
the parties and the Church
ruined everything with their stupidity
which has always been a pernicious stupidity
and Austrian stupidity is repulsive through and through
Big Business and the Church
are to blame for the Austrian misery
The Church and Big Business always were to blame
for Austrian misery

Governments are totally dependent
on Big Business and the Church
that's always been that way
and in Austria it's been the worst
they always courted stupidity
the mind was always trampled on
Big Business and the clergy are the puppeteers
of Austrian calamity
Actually I understand your father very well
I am only amazed the entire Austrian population
didn't commit suicide a long time ago
but nowadays the Austrians as a mass
are a stupid and brutal people
In this city a person with eyes in his head would have to
go berserk out of his mind

(*He looks in the direction of the Burgtheater.*)

All that's left for this pitiful immature people
is the theater
Austria itself is nothing but a stage
on which everything has gone to rack and ruin
a population of extras bound by mutual hate
six and a half million people left all alone
six and a half million retards and maniacs
who keep screaming for a director at the top of their voice
The director will come
and throw them into the abyss once and for all
six and a half million extras
pushed around and bullied every day
and finally thrown into the abyss
by a few criminal leading actors who sit
in the Imperial Palace's government suites
The Austrians are obsessed with misery
the Austrian is unhappy by nature
and if he is happy he's ashamed of it
and hides his happiness in despair

ANNA. Father saw things as they were
father always was consistent

PROFESSOR ROBERT. Jumping out the window
is not the solution either

even if it was consistent
as far as your father was concerned
Your father never saw a way out
I quite simply don't go out among people anymore
I don't go out among people
therefore I don't hear what they say
and I don't see their mugs
but your father couldn't bear it without people
I was strong enough to go to Neuhaus
your father couldn't do it
He probably would have failed completely in Oxford
after all the Oxford of nineteen eighty-eight
isn't the same as the Oxford of nineteen fifty-seven
in England there also is a Fascist undertow
people tend to forget that
the English also have their Fascism
in Oxford there also was and still is
hatred of Jews
no matter where a Jew goes in Europe
he is hated everywhere

ANNA. You shouldn't exert yourself uncle Robert

PROFESSOR ROBERT. I'm not exerting myself
but every now and then I permit myself to get worked up
so that you won't think
I'm already dead quite the opposite
the body is gone but the mind is reborn
every single day
that's a horrible condition
in the morning I can't imagine how
to get on my feet again
but I don't give up
I don't give in and I don't give up
of course I couldn't live in the city anymore
who would have thought we would move
to Neuhaus once again
and be happy about it
the childhood summer home
the old age refuge
I often wondered whether your father
wasn't crazy insane or crazy

but again and again he came up with a precise lecture
your father had a mathematical mind
it's an Austrian intellectual specialty
there never was
any rivalry between us
neither was there admiration
We always respected each other that was all
aside from siblings' love
Both of us quickly disassociated ourselves
from our parents
I for philosophy he for mathematics
yet your father was the philosophical mind
while I was the professor of philosophy
the legacy of the grand bourgeoisie
it always burdened us
our thinking always moved far apart
always in opposition to each other
being born in Vienna was a lifelong source of strength
And so much lack of understanding all around
it could never be anything but a doomed life
a so-called fated existence no other
England was good for us
another country is always good for people
going abroad can only benefit you
But anyone who lived abroad as long as we did
especially in England
can't go back
and certainly not to Vienna
in Vienna he'll be hit over the head
until he's destroyed
I told him he shouldn't go back to Oxford
he wouldn't listen
your mother was against it
he never listened to her
But of course all of us have come to a pitiful end

(*He wants to get up but can't manage.*)

We have time
it's not very comfortable
in the empty apartment
it would have been better to eat

at the Sacher or Ambassador

ANNA. Zittel insisted
on making filet mignon
even though the dishes were already packed

PROFESSOR ROBERT. As always Zittel is the center of attention

ANNA. Lukas is driving Niederreiter home first
he's making a detour to Hütteldorf

PROFESSOR ROBERT. That's the actress right

ANNA. She hasn't acted in years

PROFESSOR ROBERT. How long has he known her

ANNA. Two or three years

PROFESSOR ROBERT. Is she good I mean on stage

ANNA. I never saw her
supposedly she played at the Burgtheater

PROFESSOR ROBERT. Oh did she
a leading role

ANNA. That's what they say

PROFESSOR ROBERT. Then she can't be too bad

ANNA. Nowadays there's bad acting even at the Burgtheater

PROFESSOR ROBERT. That's sad
that there's bad acting even at the Burgtheater
I haven't been to the theater in years
concerts yes, the Musikverein, yes
my hearing's still pretty good

ANNA. The plays are no good
and the actors are no good either

PROFESSOR ROBERT. This Niederreiter woman
wasn't she married twice before

ANNA. Yes

OLGA. With a Turkish Bey
and with a mineral water manufacturer

PROFESSOR ROBERT. Why Lukas has to always get involved
with that sort of person
Actresses, dancers that's no good
Your mother was an actress too
I forgot all about that
but of course she never played the Burgtheater
only in Graz as far as I remember

ANNA. Did you ever see her on stage

PROFESSOR ROBERT. In a very small part
I can't remember in what play
it's been so long
We all staged plays as children
ours was real theater
either in the attic
or in the gazebo in Neuhaus
at the end of August
when we finally had memorized the text
one performance only and very private
for a select audience
it's really something that he drives Niederreiter home
together with mother

ANNA: Tasteless
but that's always been our brother
Niederreiter and mother in one car
on the day of father's funeral
only Lukas would do such a thing
He didn't even think of driving his sisters home
he could have taken you too

PROFESSOR ROBERT. I always prefer taking a cab
and never all the way to the house
I like to be dropped off in front of the Burgtheater
so I can walk through Volksgarten
I've done it for decades

(*Looks toward the Parliament building.*)

Now everything is at an all time low
not just everything politically
people culture everything
in just a few decades everything has been gambled away

it can't be undone for centuries
if one considers
what Austria once was
one can't even think about it
without considering suicide
I never was a fan of the monarchy
that's understood
none of us was
but what these people made of Austria
is unspeakable
a mindless cultureless cesspool
which spreads its penetrating odor all over Europe
and not just Europe
this megalomaniac Republicanism
and this megalomaniac Socialism
which for half a century now
had nothing to do with Socialism
the way the Socialists carry on in Austria
is criminal no less
but the Socialists are no longer Socialists
today Socialists are basically
Catholic National Socialists
Socialism was killed by Austrian Socialists
in the early fifties
since then Socialism hasn't existed in Austria
only this nauseating pseudo-Socialism
which turns your stomach first thing in the morning
it's those so-called Socialists who brought on
this new National Socialism in Austria
those so-called Socialists made National Socialism
possible today
they didn't only make it possible
they brought it on
These so-called Socialists who hadn't been Socialists
for half a century
are the true gravediggers of Austria
that's the horror of it the daily disgust with it
the Socialists are the exploiters today
the Socialists have Austria on their conscience
the Socialists are the gravediggers of this nation
the Socialists are the capitalists of today

the Socialists who aren't Socialists
are the real criminals against this nation
compared to them the Catholic rabble is insignificant
If today nearly all Austrians are National Socialists again
it's the Socialists' doing
If Austria today has such a rotten population
if it is such an unappealing utterly corrupt country
we can thank those fat greasy pseudo-Socialists for it
a pseudo-Socialist perfidiousness that's our democracy
To my ears the word Socialism has long since become
a disgusting invective
which frightens me as much as National Socialism
all those parties
but basically all Austrians the whole lot of them
are the gravediggers of their country today
everything is prey to their depravity
and chokes on their treachery their hypocrisy every single day
But I'm too old now and I don't feel like
getting involved anywhere anymore
it would make no sense anyway
where everything stinks of disintegration
and where everything screams for destruction
the single voice has become pointless
not that nothing has been said or written
against these disastrous conditions
every day something is being said against them
and written against them
but what's being said against them and written against them
is not heard and it is not read
Austrians no longer hear they no longer see
that is to say they do hear something about catastrophic conditions
but they don't do anything against it
the Austrians turned into a people of absolute indifference
toward their catastrophic conditions
that's their tragedy that's their catastrophe

(*Wants to get up but can't manage.*)

OLGA. We can sit a bit longer
we don't have far to go
Anna thinks she might stay

    in Oxford for a while
    she can take a leave from the National Library
    that's not a bad idea I think

PROFESSOR ROBERT. The Austrians have long been condemned to death
    they just don't know yet
    they haven't taken note of it
    the sentence was passed long ago
    the execution is only a question of time
    in my opinion it is imminent

ANNA. Mother will go back to Neuhaus today
    Lukas will take her there
    Zittel goes Saturday
    Does Frau Kronenberger light the stove
    in your study too

PROFESSOR ROBERT. Of course
    if I didn't have Kronenberger
    Neuhaus would be totally unmanageable for me
    I couldn't live in Vienna anymore
    A building without an elevator
    that's out of the question for me
    the reason I visit you so rarely is
    that there is no elevator
    to the third floor
    that's a catastrophe for me
    The doctor insists
    that I don't climb stairs
    that I avoid all exertion

ANNA. I hope the funeral
    wasn't too much for you

PROFESSOR ROBERT. It was short
    and I was dressed warmly
    that's still the winter coat
    from your grandfather
    your grandfather wore it in Russia
    nineteen twenty-two imagine

       (*Looks at the Burgtheater.*)

Every epoch is a horrible one
your grandfather always said
but you only notice it when you're old
How everything disgusts me here
I don't talk about it
but I think about it all the time
how everything disgusts me
the nation a cesspool stinking and deadly
the Church a worldwide perfidy
the people around thoroughly ugly and stupid
the President a cunning lying philistine
an altogether depressing figure
the chancellor a crafty peddler selling off the state
the Pope inviting some homeless people to his residence
for a so-called hot meal
and announcing the event worldwide
a cynical world
the whole world is one single cynicism
megalomaniacal actors
exploit the sub-Saharan famine
perverted heads of religious charities
fly first class to Eritrea
to have their pictures taken with the starving
for worldwide media coverage
the chancellor steps up to the podium in his pinstripe suit
and carries on about comrades
the union chiefs juggle billions
in their mountain villas
unscrupulous bank deals their top priority
Fat bellied writers
visit jails
and read their phony crap called art
to the inmates
a cynical world
a thoroughly corrupt world
with which I don't want to have anything to do anymore
In the end your father was the weaker one
he couldn't withstand this kind of pressure
it simply was too much for him
the philosophical tricks didn't do any good
When the limits are stretched too far

Thomas Bernhard

a catastrophe is bound to happen
Your father in Neuhaus is unthinkable
he couldn't even have finished his book
in Neuhaus
the quiet always bothered him
noise never bothered him only the quiet
and in Neuhaus there's almost total quiet most of the time
that wasn't your father
looking for quiet
only able to work in quiet
on the contrary the more chaos around him
the greater his inspiration
he had that in common with all those Russian writers
he admired so deeply throughout his life
Tolstoy Dostoyevsky Gogol Turgenyev
they were his world
not even philosophy
it was the Russian writers
not the French not the English
it was the Russian writers
and music
but recently not even Russian writers
nor music could satisfy him
it has no meaning anymore he said
it hasn't been like that for long he said
today I am neither interested in music nor in literature
everything has come down to one single declaration of bankruptcy
in the end I miscalculated
probably miscalculated my own megalomania
I no longer understand the signs of our time
no one understands the signs of our time
Oxford would have been
the biggest disappointment of his life
which he was spared
the way he died is also a big relief
believe me
that sort of death lacks
all horror
on the contrary
That I have lost my brother only means
I know he is in a good place

not being is the goal
It would be terrible
to come into the world again everything again
that's the most terrible thought
All over that's the goal
it is the only comforting thought

> (*Wants to get up, he can't do it at first, then he manages
> with the help of his nieces.*)

My biggest advantage in life was
that I didn't believe in God
and that I always knew
the end is the goal
You can be assured
your father thought the same
All of life is nothing but
a continuous infliction of pain
one long pain that's life
everybody exists in lifelong self-deception
The Church replaces the people's brain
she lets everyone have his one and only God
she leases the good lord so to speak
not just for ninety-nine years but in perpetuity
and she vouches for that
I mean not just the Catholic Church
all religions lease their good lord
faith is nothing but a rental agreement
billions of leaseholders pay a high annual rent
to their churches
and thereby bleed to death

ANNA. Father didn't want
printed announcements of his death

PROFESSOR ROBERT. I was very surprised
that a man like your father
made a will
and what's more with very precise stipulations
My brother and a will
was quite inconceivable to me
I wouldn't have thought it possible

ANNA. He left the house in Schalchham
   to Zittel

PROFESSOR ROBERT. I knew Zittel would get the house
   and that's only right
   she earned it
   Ultimately Zittel was the most important person
   he had
   My sister-in-law your mother
   came second
   but that's no secret
   the Schusters' wives
   never came first

ANNA. In the evening Zittel goes to Sluka

PROFESSOR ROBERT. I hope she'll bring me some venison paté

ANNA. Of course uncle Robert
   You'll stay the night in Vienna

PROFESSOR ROBERT. It means extra work for you I'm sure
   but I really can't go back to Neuhaus today
   that would be too much
   I won't need anything special
   as long as I have my own room
   Is there any furniture left in the apartment

ANNA. Of course uncle Robert

PROFESSOR ROBERT. (*To* OLGA.) You always were the silent one even
   as a child
   Being silent isn't a bad thing my girl
   I never thought that Josef
   would die before me

ANNA. I hope it all
   wasn't too much for you uncle Robert

PROFESSOR ROBERT. The Austrians' pettiness and meanness
   always enraged your father
   Maybe he should have returned to Oxford
   back in the sixties
   He always thought
   I'd die before he did

I was the one with the bad heart
he always was the healthy one

OLGA. (*To* ANNA.) Could I have your scarf

ANNA: (*Takes the scarf and gives it to* OLGA.) Poor freezing sister

PROFESSOR ROBERT. You have to study old age
young people can't start early enough
study the old folks I always say
the dying ones

OLGA. Do you think father would have found
happiness in Oxford again

(*She wraps the scarf around both hands.*)

PROFESSOR ROBERT. I don't think so
your father had been unhappy for decades
he would have remained unhappy in England
In fifty-five no one could change his resolve
to go back to Vienna
he was obsessed by the idea

OLGA. But mother was against it

PROFESSOR ROBERT. Your mother always was against it
your mother hated Vienna
she never had a good word
for Vienna or Austria
I wouldn't think
of going back to Vienna
she always said
the Viennese threw you out viciously
just think of your colleagues at the University
Jew haters all of them
He didn't listen to her
Even on the day of their departure
she said to me
Only horror waits for us in Vienna
you'll see Robert it will be the end of us
your mother foresaw everything
and your father couldn't gain a foothold in Vienna
his new Viennese colleagues hated him from the start
at best he had to put up with their idiotic hypocrisy

Thomas Bernhard

OLGA. There is so much I don't understand
  I don't even want to understand

PROFESSOR ROBERT. Oxford was also too small for him too narrow
  he always called the atmosphere in Oxford
  provincial philistine
  a man like him had to feel
  closed in locked up in Oxford
  I know how it was in Cambridge
  those English study towns are awful basically
  just as everything English gets to be a nuisance soon enough
  I could understand that he wanted to get back to Vienna
  but it was predictable
  that things wouldn't work out
  On the one hand Vienna lured him back
  on the other it betrayed him
  Nobody backed him up
  everybody was against him of course
  because he was so much better than anyone else
  they couldn't bear
  that he was placed above them more or less
  If I could only live in London
  he always said
  Oxford isn't London don't forget
  What do I live on in London
  not my wife's vinegar factory
  To be honest I went back to Vienna
  because of the music
  probably only because of the music
  but in all honesty
  after my return I didn't like any of the concerts
  Walter Klemperer Kleiber Barbirolli my God
  they're all dead
  I always came home disappointed
  but I still go to a concert now and then
  as long as I'm still mobile
  I remember your father saying
  I walk down Mariahilfer Street
  and I look for Mariahilfer Street
  and I am on Mariahilfer Street
  and I can't find it

No one was better suited than your father
if one wanted to study an unhappy person

(*Looks toward the Parliament building.*)

The tragedy is no surprise
He wanted music
he wanted his childhood
but the Viennese weren't the way
he remembered them
the Austrians weren't
nothing was
But memory is always deceptive
memory always offers a completely wrong picture
I can't just throw away
the professorship in Vienna
he couldn't do that he said
he didn't expect
that after the war the Austrians
were more venomous and much more hostile to Jews
than before the war
nobody expected that
He walked as he himself said so often
straight into the Viennese trap
He forgot
that Vienna and all of Austria for that matter
is home to falsehood and deceit

OLGA. Uncle Robert you exaggerate

PROFESSOR ROBERT. How can you say that
Every day you have to put up with the Viennese
the way they really are
how can you say that
when only last week you were spat on
for being Jewish

OLGA. I'm sure it was a mistake

PROFESSOR ROBERT. A mistake a mistake you think
that was no mistake
of course if one didn't actually live through those times
but for those who did live through it all

Thomas Bernhard

OLGA. Not really spat at

PROFESSOR ROBERT. But you told me yourself
   that you had been spat on in Schottengasse
   now you say it was a mistake
   what kind of mistake was it supposed to be
   does someone spit on somebody in the street
   when he doesn't even know the person
   just because he can see she is a Jew
   What time is it

ANNA. One-thirty

PROFESSOR ROBERT. The Viennese and the Austrians
   are much worse
   than your father could ever imagine
   just listen to what people are saying
   look at them
   they show you only
   hatred and disdain
   whether it's in the streets or in a restaurant
   a Jew of all people can't
   always sit within his four walls
   even a Jew needs to get out in the streets
   and if they notice he is a Jew
   he is punished with hatred and disdain
   Being a Jew in Austria always means
   being condemned to death
   People can write and talk however they want
   hating Jews is the purest absolutely most unadulterated essence
   of being an Austrian
   Before thirty-eight the Viennese
   had gotten used to the Jews
   now after the war they aren't used to the Jews anymore
   they'll never get used to them
   I also knew
   that by going to Vienna I went to hell
   If I had the strength
   to write a book
   about the conditions in this city today
   but I don't have the strength anymore
   The head could do it

but not the body
the body is abandoning me as you can see

ANNA. Zittel has made us hot soup
I'm sure

PROFESSOR ROBERT. What writers write
is nothing compared to reality
yes yes they do write that everything is awful
that everything is rotten and corrupt
that everything is catastrophic
and everything is hopeless
but whatever they write
is nothing compared to reality
reality is so bad
it defies description
no writer has ever described reality
as it really is
that's the horror

    (They walk a few steps and stop again.)

If they had their way
if they were honest
they'd love to do what they did fifty years ago
they'd gas us
it's in the people
I am certain
if they could
they wouldn't think twice
about killing us
My brother fled all that horror
into Kleist Goethe Kafka
but one can't keep running away all the time
into poetry and music
from a certain point it doesn't work anymore
then it is possible that suicide is all that is left
Probably it is only a question
of the most favorable moment
that's it a question of the most favorable moment

    (Directly to OLGA.*)*

You never had an affinity for music

Thomas Bernhard

that's strange
Anna does you don't
your father couldn't understand that
maybe it's because you were born
in Switzerland

(*Looks in the direction of the Burgtheater.*)

When people perform in the Burgtheater
they think
they are somebody
that Niederreiter woman isn't coming
to lunch is she
Actors and actresses at the table
never was my thing
My secretary also wanted to become an actress
nothing came of it
being a good typist also takes talent
Austrians are still a musical people
but one day
they won't even be a musical people anymore

(*They keep walking.*)

SCENE THREE

Dining room
Only one long table and seven different chairs remain
The table is set in a makeshift way
A high door to the left, a high door to the right
Three big high windows with a view of Heldenplatz
The shutters are open
Boxes and suitcases marked Oxford

PROFESSOR ROBERT, PROFESSOR LIEBIG *and his wife,* HERR LAN-
DAUER *and* ANNA *sit against the walls,* OLGA *on a box, they are*
waiting for FRAU PROFESSOR SCHUSTER *and* LUKAS

PROFESSOR ROBERT. To challenge thinking
  it was never more than that
  Listeners always have deaf ears
  one talks but isn't understood
  Incapable of self-denial
  all those faces showing nothing but arrogance
  All fields of knowledge violated
  all culture destroyed
  the mind driven out
  In the old days it was a pleasure
  to go out into
  the streets
  naturally that also was a mistake
  a mistake everything naturally

  (*He looks down at the street.*)

  Just talk to anybody
  you'll find he is an idiot
  every Viennese is a born mass murderer
  but you can't let them ruin your day
  It only makes sense you're bound to suffocate
  in the world you're born into
  Vienna is a cold gray city provincial
  all that American influence makes it so disgusting
  Americanism destroyed everything here
  I never let them ruin my mood
  Austrianness what is it
  I always ask myself
  absurdity of the first order
  it attracts us and repels us
  totally corrupt Socialism
  totally corrupt Christianity
  All it does in the end is disgust us
  that's what's so depressing

ANNA. I'll draft the letter to the mayor in any case
  you don't have to sign it right away uncle Robert
  The road cuts right through the property
  mother is helpless
  the authorities do whatever they want with mother

mother won't take any action
The church is supposed to be torn down too

OLGA. Neuhaus is wrecked already anyway

PROFESSOR LIEBIG. I remember Neuhaus very well
every summer we went to Neuhaus for two weeks

PROFESSOR ROBERT. For us it was just a summer place too
When we were in England the house pretty much fell apart

ANNA. Uncle Robert fixed it up so nicely
He planted a big garden
and now the new road will wreck everything

FRAU LIEBIG. The government does what it wants with the individual

PROFESSOR LIEBIG. That's always been that way

PROFESSOR ROBERT. The government always walks all over the
individual

PROFESSOR LIEBIG. A terrible time

PROFESSOR ROBERT. The thinking person can't help but vomit first
thing in the morning

PROFESSOR LIEBIG. Chaotic conditions are everywhere
Deceit dominates everything
and ineptness

HERR LANDAUER. They will probably form a new government next
fall

PROFESSOR LIEBIG. That's not the point
it makes no difference what government it is
one is like the other
always the same people
always the same deals
always the same interests
always the same totally corrupt people
who keep running the nation into the ground

PROFESSOR ROBERT. The language alone of those people
is so appalling
just listen to the chancellor

he can't even finish a sentence correctly
and the others can't either
what's coming out of those people is nothing but garbage
what they think is garbage
even their pronunciation is garbage

PROFESSOR LIEBIG. And the papers print garbage
the papers are written in a language
that turns one's stomach
with every page I assure you
aside from the lies that are printed there
hundreds of mistakes
editorial offices in Austria
are nothing but unscrupulous party driven pigsties

PROFESSOR ROBERT. They're all unqualified people
who don't think and therefore can't write

PROFESSOR LIEBIG. It's no wonder given their stupid readership
it's the most undemanding readers in all of Europe

PROFESSOR ROBERT. But we keep gobbling up this crap every day
because it interests us
because we are fascinated by it
You have to admit dear colleague
that in all honesty you are more interested in those idiotic tabloids
with their downright infernal stupidity
than say the *Neue Zürcher Zeitung*
So-called high standards were always boring
What we look for in those papers
is muck
I don't need a paper for daily intellectual input
it is the absolute primitiveness of these Austrian rags
I have to have every morning
admittedly I'd rather immerse myself in crap
than in the tasteless culture section of the *Frankfurter Allgemeine Zeitung*
I'd rather read Descartes right after breakfast
than the *Frankfurter Allgemeine*
My world has shrunk
to a few old books
But still I can't do without these rags
I need the filth

filth is vital
at my age

PROFESSOR LIEBIG. What's missing here is a newspaper culture

PROFESSOR ROBERT. Don't be ridiculous
What is a newspaper culture
newspaper culture newspaper culture
that's exactly what's so disgusting
But I admit that here in Austria
there is a need for a paper like the *Neue Zürcher Zeitung*
I admit that
even though I'm always bored when I read
the *Neue Zürcher Zeitung*
to which I subscribe out of habit
because for decades I've been thinking
I can't live without the *Neue Zürcher Zeitung*
it's my stupidity
no no I'd choke to death
without my Austrian rags
You can save yourself a fortune in pills
if you surrender early in the morning
to the total stupidity of the *Kronenzeitung* and the *Kurier*
it whips your circulation into a frenzy first thing in the morning
I am not talking about the *Presse*
that rotten paper for ten schillings is much too expensive
even as a sleeping pill

(*Looks at Heldenplatz.*)

This Niederreiter woman
with her proletarian roots
studies acting and turns into a slut
Lukas my nephew always messes around with such unsavory
    types
sons from good families so to speak
have always been the victims
of the theater
the slaves of actresses
The leap from the stage even the Burgtheater stage
to high aristocracy
is not an infrequent occurrence

PROFESSOR LIEBIG. Did you ever want to go back
  to Oxford again

PROFESSOR ROBERT. No not I
  I never was happy in England
  England for me was always a temporary solution
  Unlike my brother
  I never was crazy about England
  there was a time
  when my brother was crazy about England
  England saved me as it saved him
  but I would have never stayed in England
  and I never went back there
  it never would have occurred to me
  I never found everything as murderous
  as Josef did
  But I can well understand why he ended it
  For many years now I've been living in Neuhaus
  no matter where I was
  one could say I've been dead for a long time
  my brother committed suicide
  I went to Neuhaus
  it probably amounts to the same thing
  I haven't existed for the longest time
  while I observe everything
  in my death you understand

HERR LANDAUER. But you do go to concerts now and then

PROFESSOR ROBERT. Out of habit
  I can't think of anything else
  I read I walk a little around Neuhaus
  I'm not a nature lover I actually hate nature
  that's the truth
  nature does nothing for me
  and I come to town once or twice a week
  to go to a concert
  but my musical expectations are no longer very high
  I am just waiting to be completely dead once and for all
  I don't have the stomach for suicide

ANNA. (*To him.*) Mother wants to talk to you about Zittel

Thomas Bernhard

PROFESSOR ROBERT. About Zittel
  what does she want to talk to me about Zittel

ANNA. Father paid the nursing home
  for Zittel's mother

PROFESSOR ROBERT. So

ANNA. She wants to know whether you want to continue

PROFESSOR ROBERT. Zittel isn't my housekeeper
  or manager or whatever
  she goes to Neuhaus with your mother where she'll probably stay
  it's none of my business
  I have Kronenberger
  for decades now
  Kronenberger and I
  got used to each other in Neuhaus
  Your mother is drowning in money
  she should pay

      (*To everybody.*)

My sister-in-law has always been the Capitalist in the family
Besides what sort of dinner conversation is this
Herr Landauer what do you think will the Socialists win the next
    election
the Socialists have no character
and the conservatives are all stupid
and sleaze is the driving force of all parties
When you elect a politician in Austria these days
all you elect is a corrupt pig
that's how it is

      (FRAU ZITTEL *enters with a stack of plates and distributes
      them around the table.*)

My sister-in-law should be here by now
she left with Lukas
before I got into the taxi
This Niederreiter person messes up everything
What kind of person is she Frau Zittel

ANNA. It was in such bad taste
  to show up at the funeral

382

PROFESSOR ROBERT. A good looking person all in all

(*To* ANNA.)

Did Josef know her

ANNA. He brought her over twice
father wasn't thrilled

PROFESSOR ROBERT. Lukas always specialized in actresses

ANNA. Second and third rate ones

PROFESSOR ROBERT. It was utterly inexcusable
to take that person home
with mother in the car

ANNA. An outrage

PROFESSOR ROBERT. But of course we will wait Frau Zittel

(HERTA *has entered and stopped at the door.*)

Two years then she'll be a nuisance to him
it's always the same
It starts out as some great romance
a few weeks later it's a nuisance
it's normal really
Sometimes I think Lukas will never find a wife
At his age it doesn't work anymore
you get too picky
and you know you can see right through everything
nothing can come out of it but boredom and ennui

FRAU ZITTEL. Last week one day before the tragedy
Herr Professor went to Scheer to have
a new pair of shoes made for him
I just wanted to mention that

(*She distributes napkins.*)

ANNA. Lukas wears the same size

PROFESSOR ROBERT. Josef was the classic shoe fetishist
I only wore three pairs in twenty years
he owned over a hundred pairs of shoes
sixty pairs in Vienna alone
in Neuhaus there are shoes everywhere

Thomas Bernhard

    also in Salmannsdorf

FRAU ZITTEL. I put the mail in a small white bag

ANNA. I didn't write anyone
  that father is dead
  they think he's already in Oxford

     (FRAU ZITTEL *whispers into* HERTA'*s ear, they both exit.*)

FRAU LIEBIG. I always visited cemeteries
  my grandmother took me there as a child

PROFESSOR LIEBIG. Cemeteries are the perfect place to study
  the various histories
  of certain families

PROFESSOR ROBERT. Cemetery visits are most useful
  they are instructive like nothing else
  and soothing
  where else can the mind
  attacked as it is today from all sides
  achieve such concentration
  I am used to my sister-in-law's lateness
  it drove my brother to despair
  that she was always so late
  I dreaded any kind of appointment with her
  That Niederreiter person and your mother in one car
  it's inconceivable

     (HERTA *enters with a bread basket and puts it on the table.*)

It would have been best
to go to the Sacher
or just have a bite at Sluka
only Zittel would cook at a time like this

     (*To* HERTA.)

You know I have a nephew in Wolfsegg
that's right past Ottnang
the Hausruck mountain region is beautiful
mining country
as far as I remember
only the friendliest the very best people are from there
aren't you from that region

HERTA. Yes Herr Professor

PROFESSOR ROBERT. Wasn't your grandfather a miner
whom the Nazis put in a concentration camp
because he listened to a Swiss station

HERTA. Yes Herr Professor

PROFESSOR ROBERT. A neighbor reported your grandfather
and they stuck him in a concentration camp
in Holland right
my brother told me about it
The grandparents were still courageous people

(HERTA *exits.*)

ANNA: Her father was an alcoholic
and her mother sat in jail for a year
a convicted thief

PROFESSOR ROBERT. Are the parents still alive

ANNA. No one knows where they are
they aren't dead that much is known
but no one knows where they are

PROFESSOR LIEBIG. Upper Austrian
one can tell right away

PROFESSOR ROBERT. (*Looks out the window.*) People have no idea
when a catastrophe is about to happen
everything distracts them from the catastrophe
but it's only a distraction
Fräulein Niederreiter
will marry your brother
and destroy the Schusters for good
it's possible
Fräulein Niederreiter
kills everything
you'll see
A world of gawkers
who forgot how to think
the dumbing down can't be stopped
We are talking about Shakespeare he said
so what she said

we are talking about Kleist
she didn't care

ANNA. I thought a big wreath of narcissus would be appropriate
but I was wrong

PROFESSOR LIEBIG. Every dead person leaves behind bad consciences

HERR LANDAUER. But it was a successful funeral

PROFESSOR ROBERT. All funerals are failures
if they are pompous
they are repulsive if they are the simplest
they are repulsive
turning death into a show never works
Fräulein Niederreiter
will destroy Lukas
it will wreck him
Actresses have ruined
every single family
Sometimes I considered
a trip to Cambridge
but not anymore
my time in England was the best
childhood and the time in England

(*To* ANNA.)

You always were
the tough one

(*To* OLGA.)

And you the sensitive one
the pampered one
You were always cold
do you still have the muff

OLGA. Mother's muff

PROFESSOR ROBERT. Yes your mother's muff

OLGA. I don't know what happened to the muff

PROFESSOR ROBERT. In winter the ladies never
went out without a muff
the muff went out of fashion completely

after the war I never saw a muff
I last saw Robert
on Rotenturmstraße at Lugeck
I wanted to have coffee with him
but he declined
the brother with the bad heart survived him
we get ourselves all set
to die first and then we're left behind
He would've had to go back in the sixties
not nineteen eighty-eight
We shouldn't have come back to Vienna period
It was clear to me already in England
that Austria was no longer possible
Walked into the trap that's all
Mother was the only consistent one
but nobody listened to mother
I don't even want to be buried in Vienna
she always said
it didn't do any good
It's the Viennese spirit that's so destructive corrosive
she always said
The politicians squeezed this country to the bone
smashed disfigured and destroyed it
What do you think

HERR LANDAUER. Austrians have no choice
anything Austrians vote for
is corrupt

PROFESSOR LIEBIG. It is only a question of time
until the Nazis come to power again
all signs point to it
the Socialists and Conservatives play everything
into the Nazi's hands

PROFESSOR ROBERT. And that is exactly
what the majority of Austrians want
for National Socialism to rule again
just beneath the surface National Socialism
has always been in power

HERR LANDAUER. Overnight the ghost will suddenly come out as
the strong man

Thomas Bernhard

PROFESSOR ROBERT. (*Looks at Heldenplatz.*) The future in fact the
    immediate future Herr Landauer
    will prove you right
    For me personally it's no longer a problem
    not in Döbling cemetery
    my brother can consider himself lucky
    that he managed such a quick exit
    I always admired people who killed themselves
    I never thought my brother had it in him
    Oh you know life is truly a comedy

    (*Points to the scattered boxes and suitcases.*)

all those boxes and suitcases are marked Oxford
and everything goes to Neuhaus
my brother had already sold the apartment
to a Persian businessman
who lives in Istanbul
I don't know for how much
and I don't care how much the Persian paid
The Bösendorf was already shipped to Oxford
on a boat as in the old days

    (*To* ANNA.)

Now it's up to you to get the Bösendorf
back to Vienna
Your mother never played well
dilettantish banging away
even Ännchen's aria from the *Freischütz*
was beyond her
but let's not forget what she did for us
all her life

    (*To* PROFESSOR ROBERT *and* HERR LANDAUER.)

At first we thought
it was just an isolated episode
over time it developed into a chronic disease

    (*Leans forward.*)

For months now she keeps hearing
the masses scream in Heldenplatz
in a way that's truly terrifying

388

You know March fifteenth
Hitler marches into Heldenplatz

ANNA. In Neuhaus she doesn't have those episodes

PROFESSOR ROBERT. Medically easy to explain
but impossible to cure

ANNA. I am glad the apartment is sold
The apartment brought us no luck

PROFESSOR ROBERT. I always said
don't live downtown
the windows overlooking Heldenplatz
pure madness

OLGA. Mother didn't want the apartment

PROFESSOR ROBERT. Deep seated shock so to speak
she fought tooth and nail
against this apartment
but Josef was obsessed by it
I don't have far to go to the University
Right after they moved in
right on the first day she had her first episode
a passing whim they thought
since your mother was always theatrical
but her sickness is real
it wasn't just for show
She of all people who always put on a show
finally a chronic illness
What time is it

OLGA. Three o'clock

> (FRAU ZITTEL *enters, puts a glass pitcher filled with water on the table and exits.*)

PROFESSOR ROBERT. Frau Professor Liebig
you know Karlsbad very well
what do you think of a cure in Karlsbad

FRAU LIEBIG. I haven't been to Karlsbad
in fifty years

PROFESSOR ROBERT. But you know how it looks there

Thomas Bernhard

FRAU LIEBIG. I know how Karlsbad looked fifty years ago

PROFESSOR ROBERT. Fifty years ago of course
   probably Karlsbad looks quite different now
   I've never been back to the Czech region
   I hear there are some nice hotels in Karlsbad

FRAU LIEBIG. You can't go to Karlsbad
   Could be the hotels are the same
   the facades the same
   but the atmosphere today is unbearable
   wherever the Communists are

PROFESSOR ROBERT. It probably would be stupid at my age
   to go to Karlsbad
   given our present situation
   my parents took the express train
   it took five hours from Vienna to Karlsbad
   in a first class sleeping car

PROFESSOR LIEBIG. Going to a spa after sixty
   if one never went to a spa before
   is utter nonsense
   the monarchy wasn't the idea either
   Do you think there will ever be such a thing
   as the Austrian monarchy again

PROFESSOR ROBERT. No never
   There won't be anything nothing

PROFESSOR LIEBIG. Nothing

PROFESSOR ROBERT. Nothing

PROFESSOR LIEBIG. How did you manage to get a Chair
   in Cambridge back in those days

PROFESSOR ROBERT. Through Professor Strotzka
   whom I knew from Vienna
   he came to England in thirty-four
   terrific man
   after the war he also got me and my brother
   our professorships in Vienna again
   Professor Strotzka saved our lives
   now he is buried in Döbling cemetery too

so many terrific people are in Döbling cemetery
Austria's true thinkers are buried
in Döbling cemetery and in Grinzing cemetery

(*Exclaims.*)

Strotzka
Picked us up in Dover
and brought us to his house in Redding a small villa
always lived modestly but he was demanding
conditions in England were not the best at that time
the English government was feebleminded
Fled to Steinhof to Strotzka's brother
who was the head of psychiatrists in Steinhof
twelve days hidden in Steinhof
then to Switzerland
in Geneva we lived in a basement hovel
I don't have fond memories of the Swiss
the Swiss as a people have no character whatsoever
But as you know exceptions prove the rule
Read Goethe's *Tasso* in a basement hovel
and Anna and Olga being children at that time
Josef went to Oxford I to Cambridge
but it took two years
before we were allowed to lecture
and during that time we didn't make any money at all

PROFESSOR LIEBIG. For eight years my wife and I
were in hiding like you
in Caltanisetta you know

PROFESSOR ROBERT. Strotzka saved us no doubt
an outstanding scientist by the way

> (FRAU ZITTEL *enters with a second glass pitcher filled with water, puts it on the table and exits.*)

ANNA. (*To her uncle.*) If you just invited the mayor for dinner
we'd have won
You do so well with those people

PROFESSOR ROBERT. (*To* PROFESSOR LIEBIG.) We were very lucky to
get to England
I saw Professor Strotzka a few times in the Pagageno

that smoke-filled restaurant
where he and his wife always went to eat
now he's dead too
I always pass his grave
in Döbling cemetery
One half of the Schusters are in Grinzing cemetery
the other in Döbling cemetery
my wife never went to a park
only to cemeteries
and indeed nowhere is it as beautiful as
in cemeteries

    (Looks around.)

The sight of luggage
was always dreadful to me
It's always meant a journey into disaster

    (FRAU ZITTEL *enters with a vase filled with irises, puts them
on the table and exits.)*

He hated flowers
flowers and cats
This is the first time Frau Zittel
put flowers on the table
she would never have dared to do that
while my brother was alive
The first time and the last time
Out in nature yes
he always said
in the house no

HERR LANDAUER. I attended every lecture of Herr Professor
Schuster

PROFESSOR ROBERT. He always started on time
and he did precision work
that was a given
And he did have the biggest audiences
Of course he was mistrustful
he didn't trust his audiences
When they tried to approach him about his books
he bluntly turned them away
he had no tolerance in that regard

he didn't want to talk about his books
all in all he wasn't talkative
He hated debates
he hated nothing like debates
debates lead nowhere
the whole world debates and only nonsense comes of it
he always said
He never talked with me about his work
and he wasn't really interested
in what I was doing he never asked
You are just fine he always said
that was it
All our lives
we never had a real conversation
he was an inaccessible man as they say
Any effort even the most strenuous one will lead to nothing
he always said
everything that's done is senseless
because usually it is done without thinking
he was too complicated to endure the world

HERR LANDAUER. Once I met him in Schönbrunn at the palm house
and he regretted
that he hadn't lived a century earlier
We always live in the wrong time he said
we all want to live only in the past
we fixed up the past so nicely
just the way we like it
nobody wants the future
but everybody has to enter the future
where it's cold and unfriendly
I always admired the Professor

PROFESSOR ROBERT. He detested admiration
He hated nothing more than being admired
he loathed it
he hated admirers like poison

(*Directly to* HERR LANDAUER.)

But I know his relationship with you was excellent
a mutually excellent relationship
He wasn't even comfortable with affection

he perceived all of that as taking possession
the price for admiration was too high for him
he wasn't willing to pay it
Whatever he published was definitive no doubt
but he didn't want to be admired for it
Not being bothered was his ultimate happiness
if in his case one can talk about happiness at all

HERR LANDAUER. There are days when I see only happy people
around me
that's the truth Herr Landauer he said
everybody is happy you see everybody looks happy
and I am not mistaken
everything about everybody even the poorest the most miserable
is happy Landauer
and then again I only see
what an utterly unhappy bunch they are

PROFESSOR LIEBIG. He did live a very isolated life
turned inward as they say

HERR LANDAUER. Some of his students planned
to go to Oxford with him
I am sure you didn't know that

PROFESSOR ROBERT. I know he had honorable followers
but he never knew that

HERR LANDAUER. Professor Schuster had the greatest influence

PROFESSOR ROBERT. That didn't necessarily help his popularity
his colleagues didn't accept him
indeed they hated him
University professors are thoroughly provincial these days
almost without exception
what they call thinking has nothing to do with it
they lack the simplest prerequisites
They don't even come close to thinking
at our universities any more
and on top of that you have the absolutely National Socialist and
the absolutely Catholic mind-set ruling everything
Today's university professors
are unbelievably primitive
their ignorance is catastrophic

If you consider that in our universities the most important chairs
are occupied by Tyrolian and Salzburg Nazis
it only can be catastrophic
Alpine stupidity is being taught today
that's the truth collapse of Communism kitsch
an unbearable philistinism is all that gets taught
Alpine stupidity that's all there is
in the old days university professors came from the grand bourgeoisie
from the Jewish bourgeoisie
today they come from the spoiled petty bourgeois proletariat
or from the feebleminded peasantry
the situation is embarrassing
nowadays even a fat little editorial writer for the *Kurier*
is considered an intellectual genius
and a suburban dummy who still struggles with illiteracy
the caricature of a Socialist that's our chancellor
call that a statesman
these are the facts
in this small state everything is retarded
and intellectual needs are reduced to the absolute minimum
It's possible to enjoy Vienna
a few times a year
when you walk on Kohlmarkt
or across the Graben
or down Singerstraße in the spring air
but only if in utter self-denial
if you don't allow yourself to think
about the absolute ridiculousness of this country
about its irresponsibility
You constantly get taken in by Austria
but even if you eat well once in a while in a restaurant
or enjoy a good coffee in a coffee house
you must not forget
that you are in the most dangerously criminal of all European
  states
where corruption is the highest commandment
and human rights are trampled on
What an enviable person is he
who had the strength
to rescue himself from this anti-state by ending it all

395

then simply Döbling cemetery
For us the cemetery always was the only way out
my dear colleague

FRAU ZITTEL. (*Enters, whispers.*) Frau Professor is coming

(*And exits again.*)

PROFESSOR ROBERT. Well then

(*He wants to get up, but can't manage,* ANNA *helps him.
Everybody gets up.*)

Here she is my sister-in-law

(FRAU PROFESSOR SCHUSTER *is led in by her son* LUKAS *and*
FRAU ZITTEL. PROFESSOR ROBERT *walks up to her and kisses
her hand.* FRAU ZITTEL *exits again and returns with the
soup tureen, stops at the door with the tureen.*)

LUKAS. We made a detour
we took Fräulein Niederreiter home

PROFESSOR ROBERT. At my age waiting has become
a habit

FRAU PROFESSOR SCHUSTER. It is an exceptional day after all

(PROFESSOR LIEBIG *and* FRAU LIEBIG *as well as* HERR LAN-
DAUER *greet* FRAU PROFESSOR SCHUSTER.)

PROFESSOR ROBERT. One has to accept everything so we have
learned

(*Wants to sit down at the table.*)

(ANNA *and* OLGA *move the chairs to the table, also a box
because they need one more chair.* LUKAS *leads* FRAU PRO-
FESSOR SCHUSTER *to the table, she sits down.* PROFESSOR
ROBERT *sits down across from her.* PROFESSOR LIEBIG *and*
FRAU LIEBIG *sit down, as well as* OLGA *and* HERR LANDAUER.
OLGA *sits down on the box.* FRAU ZITTEL *serves the soup.*)

This is probably the last time
we eat here

ANNA. There's also dinner

PROFESSOR ROBERT. Wouldn't it be better
  to eat out
  in some restaurant

  (*Looks around.*)

ANNA. Frau Zittel has already prepared everything
  she got the venison paté from Sluka

PROFESSOR ROBERT. From Sluka
  my favorite treat even as a child

  (*To* FRAU PROFESSOR SCHUSTER.)

  I would have loved to take a taxi with you
  I didn't want to meet
  that Niederreiter woman

FRAU PROFESSOR SCHUSTER. It was arranged with Lukas
  that he would bring me home

PROFESSOR ROBERT. You and that Niederreiter
  If you don't mind
  I'll spend the night here
  I can't get back to Neuhaus today

FRAU PROFESSOR SCHUSTER. Certainly

FRAU ZITTEL. The bed for Herr Professor Robert
  is already made

  (HERTA *enters, takes the pitchers and exits.*)

LUKAS. (*Exclaims.*) *Minna von Barnhelm*
  such tasteless theater
  but it works taking the mind
  off one's problems

  (*To his mother.*)

  I'd have come with you
  to see *Nathan the Wise*
  with all its phony pathos
  but *Minna von Barnhelm*
  is just too ludicrous

  (*To everybody.*)

In fact it would be worth considering
if it is appropriate at all
in the state of mourning so to speak
to see such a grimly comical play
A requiem at the concert hall would more likely
meet with general approval
wouldn't it uncle Robert
Minna von Barnhelm on the other hand is pure operetta
A mourner should be permitted to see *Minna*
that nice little German national operetta
A mourner of all people
must not be picky
Incidentally the Josefstadt Theater
presents the most serious tragedies
as operettas
it is a trademark of the Josefstadt
that they turn everything into an operetta
Faust Miss Julie Danton's Death
it makes no difference
In the Josefstadt they've been staging operettas
for two hundred years now

PROFESSOR ROBERT. The Burgtheater suffers from having
contracted seriousness so to speak
for ninety-nine years at a time
all that laughter that makes people so mean in the Josefstadt
is wiped off their faces in the most brutal fashion
when they go to the Burgtheater
The state of theater in Vienna has always been disastrous
absolutely irreparable

LUKAS. That's typically Viennese
going to one's father's and brother's funeral in the morning
then to *Minna von Barnhelm* that night

PROFESSOR ROBERT. It is the height of tastelessness

LUKAS. Absolute tastelessness
that's exactly what's so Viennese uncle Robert
Fräulein Niederreiter by the way expresses her deepest condolences
to the family

398

FRAU PROFESSOR SCHUSTER. (*Eating the soup.*) I can imagine myself
living alone in Oxford
for a while

(*Everybody eats the soup.*)

But maybe it is silly
to go to Oxford all by myself
It will be best if Anna and Lukas go there
and sell the house as quickly as possible

(*To* ANNA.)

Did you get any mail

ANNA. From the realtors

FRAU PROFESSOR SCHUSTER. Yes

ANNA. No

FRAU PROFESSOR SCHUSTER. It won't be easy
to sell the house
I haven't even seen it

ANNA. Maybe I'll stay in Oxford for a while
I can take a leave
from the National Library
Olga can come too

FRAU PROFESSOR SCHUSTER. That's a good idea

ANNA. It will take months
to sell the house

FRAU PROFESSOR SCHUSTER. We should have turned around
and gone back to Oxford
as soon as we got to Vienna
I wanted to go back right away

ANNA. It is a very beautiful house
almost too beautiful for a professor of philosophy

FRAU PROFESSOR SCHUSTER. Josef was not going to be talked out of it
I didn't want to go
he had his mind set on it

At first he didn't want to I did
then I didn't want to
and he did
He wanted to go back to Vienna
I didn't
We should have stayed in Oxford

PROFESSOR ROBERT. He called Oxford
an intellectual dump
He always envied me Cambridge
Professor Liebig thinks
you might want to keep the house
and rent it
as your English hide-away as it were
a back-up

ANNA. Now that father's dead
it doesn't make sense

FRAU PROFESSOR SCHUSTER. The house will be sold
not to just anyone of course
And I don't need to see it
not anymore

PROFESSOR ROBERT. You can recuperate in Neuhaus
Olga will stay with you for a while
won't you Olga

OLGA. If mother wants me to

FRAU PROFESSOR SCHUSTER. I won't stay in Neuhaus
I can't take Neuhaus
What's there for me to do in Neuhaus
I always was bored in Neuhaus
I didn't spend my childhood in Neuhaus
like Josef
I could never breathe in Neuhaus
actually not even Josef liked being in Neuhaus
he just kept telling himself he did
because Robert talked him into it
No Neuhaus is out of the question
I will buy myself an apartment in the first district
ideally between Kohlmarkt and Graben
one of those penthouse apartments they are building everywhere

as central as possible
We will sell the vinegar factory

> (*Directly to* PROFESSOR ROBERT.)

I never understood how you could stand it
in Neuhaus

PROFESSOR ROBERT. Herr Landauer will take care of the sale
of the Oxford house
he will go there with Anna and Lukas

> (HERTA *enters with freshly filled pitchers of water and puts*
> *them on the table.*)

So there will be no formal death announcements

FRAU PROFESSOR SCHUSTER. No

ANNA. Father didn't want announcements
He hated death announcements
more than anything

OLGA. His will is very specific

ANNA. Down to the smallest detail

PROFESSOR ROBERT. It wasn't at all like him
I'm very surprised that Josef
even made a will
it really surprised me

> (*To the* LIEBIGS *and* HERR LANDAUER.)

Aren't you surprised

LUKAS. I am not at all surprised
father was a precision fanatic
He had everything under control
the idea of chance didn't exist for him
By the way he hated plays like *Minna von Barnhelm*
Lessing is a typically German pedant passing for a poet
pathetic sentimental humorless he said
All the Germans who are fed up with Goethe
cling to Lessing
as the lifesaver of their hypocrisy

PROFESSOR ROBERT. The theater has always been obnoxious grand-
standing
but of course it's always been useful
as a breeding ground for romance

FRAU PROFESSOR SCHUSTER. (*To the* LIEBIGS *and* HERR LANDAUER.)
Everything is packed
the furniture is already in England
we wanted to leave the dining room table in Vienna
The silverware was also packed

PROFESSOR ROBERT. It's lucky the luggage
hadn't gone off to England already
That would have been a perfect comedy

(*Everybody looks up.*)

Tomorrow morning Professor Liebig
will notify the faculty
there will be no mention of suicide
a sudden death at his age
is perfectly normal
every day thousands die a natural death in this city
Many will sigh with relief
when they hear that Professor Schuster is dead

FRAU PROFESSOR SCHUSTER. My husband stipulated
that his death is not to be announced until
one week after the funeral

PROFESSOR ROBERT. We can announce it tomorrow
no one will care
after all it really is all over now

(HERTA, *who had been standing behind* PROFESSOR ROBERT,
*exits. Slowly increasing screaming of the masses at Hitler's
arrival in Heldenplatz nineteen thirty-eight, which only*
FRAU PROFESSOR SCHUSTER *can hear.*)

Death is the most natural thing
in the world
don't you agree Professor Liebig

(*To* FRAU PROFESSOR SCHUSTER *who suddenly stiffened in
her chair and stopped eating her soup.*)

402

In Neuhaus Frau Zittel will make you
her famous compresses
I am sure Neuhaus will be good for you Hedwig
You can leave everything in Neuhaus
until you find a new apartment
there is plenty of room
Kronenberger gets along well
with Frau Zittel
And maybe you will stay a bit longer
in Neuhaus
Once you are in Neuhaus
everything will fall into place

(*All except* FRAU PROFESSOR SCHUSTER *calmly continue eating their soup.*)

Funerals always are
a horror
As long as they don't take place in Central cemetery
I always thought
Even I would be horrified to be buried
at Central cemetery
but Döbling cemetery

FRAU PROFESSOR SCHUSTER. Neuhaus always made me nervous
I always dreaded Neuhaus
the quiet there always made me nervous
Josef never understood that
the quiet in Neuhaus always made me sick

PROFESSOR ROBERT. Everything always had an entirely different
effect on you
always the opposite

OLGA. I always enjoyed being in Neuhaus

LUKAS. I would have sold Neuhaus long ago
Retreating to those stupid rural dumps
is the same as
ending it all
I always hated Neuhaus
and I never liked it in Baden

PROFESSOR ROBERT. (*To everybody.*) My brother Josef hated spas

Thomas Bernhard

LUKAS. People age twice as fast in the country
  as they do in the city

ANNA. Ideally you have both
  a bit of Neuhaus
  then Vienna
  then Neuhaus

PROFESSOR ROBERT. (*To* PROFESSOR LIEBIG.) You should come to
  Neuhaus
  some time
  for twenty years now you promised
  to come to Neuhaus
  and to this day you haven't been to Neuhaus
  Neuhaus is much more beautiful than Baden
  Our father bought the house in Neuhaus
  in nineteen seventeen
  back then forty acres of meadows went with it

> (FRAU ZITTEL *enters, but stops at the door. The screaming of
> the masses grows increasingly louder.*)

The climate in Oxford was totally different
from Cambridge
In Oxford it was pretty unpleasant

> (FRAU ZITTEL *crosses to the windows and closes the
> shutters.*)

The tragedy is not
that my brother is dead
the horror is that we are left behind

> (HERTA *also crosses to the windows and stays close to* FRAU
> ZITTEL.)

Lifelong exertion
and everything geared toward the highest achievement
then absolute pointlessness at the end
He planned three volumes
You know *The Signs of the Times*
it remains unfinished
piles and piles of notes that's it

*(The screaming from Heldenplatz gets louder and louder
even through the closed shutters.)*

To be honest I
only returned to Vienna because I love music
It wasn't for the University
It wasn't for anything other than music
Vienna is no longer an intellectual city
before the war yes
but after the war not at all
everything artificially inflated and vulgar
don't you think so Professor Liebig

PROFESSOR LIEBIG. Certainly my dear colleague

LUKAS. I still find Vienna
quite amusing
amusing interesting amusing

PROFESSOR ROBERT. We should have turned around the moment we
arrived
at Western Station
We walked right into the Viennese trap
we walked into the Austria trap
We all thought we had a fatherland
but we don't

LUKAS. Maybe I will go with mother
to *Minna*
A stupid play like that
has worked miracles for me before

PROFESSOR ROBERT. Josef was fooled
all of us were fooled
But Oxford surely wouldn't have been the solution
The problem was that for my brother
there was no solution

> (FRAU PROFESSOR SCHUSTER *sits up even straighter in her
> chair and remains that way, seated stiffly in her chair.)*

In this most horrible of countries
the only choice you have is
between Conservative and Socialist pigs
an unbearable stench keeps spreading

Thomas Bernhard

from the Imperial Palace to Ballhausplatz
and from the Parliament
across the whole corrupt and wasted country

(*Exclaims.*)

This tiny state is one gigantic dung heap

PROFESSOR LIEBIG. People with a vision
should see a doctor
our chancellor said

PROFESSOR ROBERT. Yes an abomination
passing for stupidity
Our unhappy brother
couldn't put up with it any longer
But since all Austrians are unhappy
it can't be said
that he was the only unhappy man

> (FRAU ZITTEL *crosses with* HERTA *to the table and serves
> more soup to* PROFESSOR ROBERT, PROFESSOR LIEBIG, *his wife
> and* HERR LANDAUER. PROFESSOR ROBERT *loudly as the
> screaming of the masses on Heldenplatz reaches the limits
> of what's bearable.*)

Coming back to Vienna
was such an absurd idea

(*Even louder.*)

But the world only consists of absurd ideas

> (FRAU PROFESSOR SCHUSTER *falls forward, face first, onto
> the table. Everyone is startled.*)

Translator's Postscript

Thomas Bernhard wrote *Heldenplatz* for the fiftieth anniversary commemoration of Austria's annexation to Hitler's Reich. Heldenplatz (Hero's Square) is the monumental square in front of the Hapsburg Palace where Hitler and his troops were greeted by throngs of enthusiastic Austrians when they arrived in Vienna on March 15, 1938. The play was commissioned by Claus Peymann, the Burgtheater's controversial artistic director. After rehearsals in June 1988 prior to its scheduled fall opening at the Burgtheater, passages of Bernhard's script were leaked to the press. Quoted out of context again and again, in various commentaries and interviews, they provoked mass hysteria which ironically seemed to validate the play's attacks on then-President Waldheim's Austria even before it premiered.

On opening night, November 5, Right Wing activists dumped horse manure in front of the theater. The daily *Der Standard* printed a scathing pre-opening review of the text by Peter Sichrovsky with the incendiary headline "Storm Heldenplatz." Sichrovsky, himself the son of returning refugees and known in Austria as the author of *Born Guilty*, a compilation of interviews with the children of Nazi criminals, attacked Peymann, a Northern German and former "theater director from Bochum who, with the help of an Austrian writer, makes a Viennese Jew bark like a German shepherd."

Kronenzeitung featured a front-page photo-montage depicting the Burgtheater engulfed in flames, with the caption "Uns ist nichts zu heiß" ("Nothing is too hot for us"). The headline on the same page ominously announced "Heldenplatz Premiere: Burgtheater under Police Protection." And, in fact, two hundred policemen in plainclothes and uniform were positioned around all entrances prior to curtain time.

Boohs and bravos accompanied the performance that ended with a forty minute standing ovation. What caught the audience by surprise was best described by critic Benjamin Henrichs in the influential weekly, *Die Zeit:* "The people of Heldenplatz, who wrangle with Austria, attack Austria and want to destroy it with their hate arias (which would also destroy their contradictory love for it), are Austrian Jews. As Jews they claim the right of the victim. As Austrians they speak the language of the perpetrators. . . . In Bernhard's courageous and certainly diabolical construction he doesn't show the Jews in roles that would move even the hardcore anti-Semite to tears. Not as decent, cultured, attractive victims of barbarity, but—oh my God— as Austrians. And what Austrians hate, whoever they are, is always also who they are and will be, to the end of their days."

Despite the opening night controversy, *Heldenplatz* continued through the Burgtheater's 1988/89 repertory season. Distanced from its immediate political purpose, the play managed to subvert the tradition from which it came. Here is the world, or rather the vanishing worlds, of Chekhov and Hugo von Hofmannsthal. The Schusters—as in Chekhov's *Three Sisters* and Hofmannsthal's *Der Schwierige* (*The Difficult One*) or, for that matter, Musil's *The Man Without Qualities*—cling to an older order of class, culture and status, a milieu Bernhard himself, an illegitimate child from an impoverished rural family, aspired to (which didn't prevent him from attacking its pretenses). Professor Robert's language is distilled from the casual lilt that separated Hofmannsthal's old-time grand bourgeoisie from wannabes. It is as if in his last work, his final legacy, so to speak, Bernhard wanted to make himself legitimate—the bona fide heir to Vienna's intellectual, social elite.

As in the case of Hofmannsthal's exquisite comedies *Der Schwierige* and *Der Unbestechliche,* the cultural nuances of *Heldenplatz* with their unspoken innuendoes cue a multi-layered subtext that is lost in translation. The geography of Vienna, as inhabited by the Schusters, resonates with history, and maps the family's quasi-aristocratic status. In Vienna's fin-de-siecle tradition, the latter is synonymous with Bildung and culture. Their apartment with a view of Heldenplatz is located in the historic compound of the Hapsburg Palace. Professor Robert's father acquired their family's sprawling summer estate in Neuhaus, a village south of Vienna, not far from Mayerling where Crown Prince Rudolph killed himself. Bernhard makes a passing reference that he purchased the property in 1917, a period of desperate hunger and poverty all across Europe. Baden is a historic spa, not far from Neuhaus, which became overpopulated due to Vienna's post-war urban growth. Fräulein Neidermeier, the actress-lover of Professor Robert's nephew, lives in Hütteldorf, a predominantly working-class suburb of Vienna, far below the Schusters' station. Their liaison, gossiped about during the Schusters' "last supper" in Vienna, suggests all the trappings of a comedy of manners.

The cemeteries in the play tell yet another story of status consciousness. Döbling and Grinzing are exclusive suburbs of Vienna. Bernhard himself is buried in Grinzing, as are Paul Wittgenstein, Gustav and Alma Mahler among other famous artists and dignitaries. By contrast, Zentralfriedhof, which makes Professor Robert shudder, is located in a bleak area on the industrial outskirts of Vienna. Steinhof, Vienna's famous mental institution is a favorite Bernhard setting, best known from his memoir *Wittgenstein's Nephew.* Robert's reference to the chancellor as "a crafty peddler selling off the state" is an allusion to the privatization of state-owned industries under chancellor Vranitzky during the eighties. In the process, jobs were created for (Socialist) party members and friends in these newly created (Capitalist) enterprises.

Finally, the chancellor is quoted as saying: "People with a vision/should see a doctor." This is a reference to a statement that has been variously attributed to German Chancellor Konrad Adenauer as well as Austrian Chancellor Franz Vranitzky. Bernhard uses it as a thinly disguised allusion to another imbroglio triggered by Austria's Minister of Culture and Education who declared Bernhard "a case for science, albeit not in the field of literature." Austria's artists demanded an apology (which they didn't get) for the insinuation that artists are pathological cases. By its placement in the play the quote sets the stage for the traumatic finale of Frau Professor Schuster's collapse. With this in-joke Bernhard underhandedly suggests that the voices Frau Professor hears on Heldenplatz are real, that the mentality of those who screamed persists.

Special thanks to Bradford Morrow for his insightful suggestions during the course of my translation of the play.

—Gitta Honegger

NOTES ON CONTRIBUTORS

JOHN ASHBERY's latest book is *Girls on the Run: A Poem* (Farrar, Straus & Giroux). He teaches at Bard College.

Irish writer CAROL AZADEH's first book, *Marriage in Antibes*, is forthcoming from Carroll & Graf Publishers in February 2000. "The Country Road" marks her first appearance in print in America.

THOMAS BERNHARD (1931-1989) was a novelist, playwright and poet whose works include *Gargoyles, Correction, Woodcutters, The Lime Works, Wittgenstein's Nephew, The Loser* and, most recently, a collection of plays, *Histrionics*, and of stories, *The Voice Imitator*. Bernhard, who lived in Austria, is widely considered to be one of the most important writers of his generation.

SUSAN BERNOFSKY teaches in the German Studies program at Bard College and has published translations of Robert Walser, Gregor von Rezzori, Durs Grünbein and others. Her translation of Walser's novel, *The Robber*, is forthcoming from University of Nebraska Press.

MEI-MEI BERSSENBRUGGE's recent works include *Endocrinology* and *The Four Year Old Girl*, both published by Kelsey Street Press. She lives in New Mexico with the artist Richard Tuttle and their daughter.

MELVIN JULES BUKIET's most recent novels are *After* and *Signs and Wonders*. His next novel, *Strange Fire*, is forthcoming from W. W. Norton. He teaches at Sarah Lawrence College and lives in New York City.

MICHAEL COUNTS is Artistic Director of GAle GAtes et. al., a performance and visual arts company co-founded with Michelle Stern in 1995. Recent productions include *Tilly Losch, The Field of Mars* and *1839*. The next GAle GAtes et. al. production, *So Long Ago I Can't Remember*, will have a workshop production during a residency at the California Institute of the Arts in early 2000.

THALIA FIELD's first collection, *Point and Line*, is forthcoming in spring 2000 from New Directions. She teaches in the Writing and Poetics department at Naropa University.

JONATHAN SAFRAN FOER is completing work on a novel, *The Beginning of the World Often Comes*. He edited an anthology of writing inspired by Joseph Cornell's bird boxes.

MARK FRIED has translated four books by Eduardo Galeano, as well as other works of Latin American literature. He lives in Ottawa, Canada.

SARAH GADDIS is the author of *Swallow Hard*. She is currently working on her second novel, tentatively entitled *Man at the End of His Rope.*

EDUARDO GALEANO is the author of the trilogy *Memory of Fire* and the classic work, *Open Veins of Latin America*, among others. He lives in Uruguay and was a 1999 recipient of the Lannan Award for Cultural Freedom. "The Impunity of the Sacred Car" is excerpted from *Upside-Down: A Primer for the Looking-Glass World*, to be published next year by Holt/Metropolitan.

WILLIAM H. GASS is the director of the International Writers Center at Washington University. His most recent book is *Reading Rilke*, published by Knopf.

FRANK O. GEHRY established the architecture firm of Frank O. Gehry & Associates in 1962. Since that time, Mr. Gehry has built an architectural career that has spanned four decades and produced public and private buildings in America, Europe and Asia.

NOY HOLLAND's first book, *The Spectacle of the Body*, was published by Knopf. She teaches in the MFA program at the University of Massachusetts.

GITTA HONEGGER is chair of the Department of Drama at the Catholic University of America, and is the American representative of the Thomas Bernhard International Foundation. She is completing a book on Bernhard, *Whereof One Cannot Speak . . . The Making of an Austrian*, to be published by Yale University Press.

NORMAN MANEA's most recent publication in English is the novel *The Black Envelope*. "The New Calendar" is an excerpt from *A Return of the Hooligan*, to be published by Farrar Straus & Giroux in 2000.

MALINDA MARKHAM has poems published or forthcoming in *The Paris Review, Volt, American Letters & Commentary, Colorado Review* and elsewhere.

CAROLE MASO is the author of six books, most recently *Defiance* (Dutton/Plume). A book of essays, *Break Every Rule*, a journal of pregnancy, *Music of the Spheres* and a volume of poems in prose, *Beauty is Convulsive*, are all forthcoming from Counterpoint.

ANTHONY McCALL, designer and film maker, directs Anthony McCall Associates, the prominent art world graphic design studio, and recently founded the web design company Narrative Rooms. He lives in New York.

MARK McMORRIS is the author of *Moth-Wings* (Burning Deck) and *The Black Reeds* (University of Georgia). He teaches in the English Department at Georgetown University.

SANDRA NEWMAN writes fiction and plays. Her first play, *The Lenin's Head*, is being produced at the Hackney Empire Studio this autumn. She lives in London. "Medium" is her first appearance in print.

JOYCE CAROL OATES is the author most recently of the novel *Broke Heart Blues* and the essay collection *Where I've Been, and Where I'm Going*. "The Sharpshooter" is the first published excerpt from her monumental forthcoming novel *Blonde*.

D. A. PENNEBAKER is a documentary filmmaker, best known for his film on Bob Dylan in the 1960's, *Don't Look Back*, and, more recently, *The War Room*, an obbligato to the Clinton presidential campaign which he made with his partner and wife, Chris Hegedus, and for which they received an Academy Award nomination.

JOSÉ GUADALUPE POSADA (1852–1913) was a Mexican artist and engraver whose work was a primary source of inspiration for Diego Rivera, José Clemente Orozco and David Alfaro Siqueiros, among others.

RICHARD POWERS is the author of *Three Farmers on Their Way to a Dance, The Gold Bug Variations, Galatea 2.2*, and *Gain*, among other novels. His new novel, *Plowing the Dark*, is forthcoming from Farrar, Straus & Giroux in the spring of 2000.

PETER SACKS is the author of *Natal Command* (University of Chicago Press) and the forthcoming *O Wheel*.

JULIAN SCHNABEL has had over 100 solo exhibitions internationally. His work is in the permanent collections of numerous institutions including the Metropolitan Museum of Art, New York, and the Guggenheim Museums in New York and Bilbao, Spain. In 1996, he wrote and directed the feature film, *Basquiat*.

PETER DALE SCOTT is a writer, former Canadian diplomat, and emeritus English professor at the University of California, Berkeley. Two volumes of his poetic trilogy *Seculum* have so far appeared: *Listening to the Candle* (1992) and *Coming to Jakarta* (1988). The final volume, *Minding the Darkness*, will appear from New Directions in the fall of 2000.

RICHARD SERRA is a sculptor who lives and works in New York City and Cape Breton, Nova Scotia.

REGINALD SHEPHERD is the author of two books, *Some Are Drowning* and *Angel, Interrupted*. His third collection, *Wrong*, is forthcoming from the University of Pittsburgh Press.

ISAAC BASHEVIS SINGER (1904-1991) was the author of many novels, stories, children's books and a memoir. He won the Nobel Prize in Literature in 1978.

GILBERT SORRENTINO's new novel, *Gold Fools*, and his *New and Selected Poems, 1958–1998*, will be published by Sun & Moon Press in 2000.

ARTHUR SZE is a participant in the College of Santa Fe's National Millennium Survey, and is a recipient of a Lila Wallace-Reader's Digest Writers' Award. His latest book, *The Redshifting Web: Poems 1970–1998*, from Copper Canyon Press, was selected for the 1999 Balcones Poetry Prize.

YOKO TAWADA, a native of Tokyo, has lived in Hamburg, Germany, since 1982 and writes in both Japanese and German. She has received numerous prizes, including Japan's prestigious Akutagawa Prize for *The Bridgegroom Was a Dog* and the Adalbert von Chamisson Prize awarded in Germany to foreign writers who have made significant contributions to German culture. "Where Europe Begins" was Tawada's first story written in German, now published here for the first time in English.

ROSMARIE WALDROP's most recent books of poems are *Reluctant Gravities* (New Directions), *Split Infinites* (Singing Horse Press) and *Another Language: Selected Poems* (Talisman House). She lives in Providence, Rhode Island, where she co-edits Burning Deck books with Keith Waldrop.

Forthcoming work from PAUL WEST includes *O.K.*, a novel about Doc Holliday (Scribner); *The Secret Lives of Words: A Fan's Album* (Harcourt Brace); and *The Dry Danube: A Hitler Forgery* (New Directions). Excerpts from all three books have been published in *Conjunctions* and on *Web Conjunctions*.

JOY WILLIAMS is the author of numerous books, including *The Changling, Escapes: Stories* and *The Florida Keys, 1996: A History & Guide*.

LOIS-ANN YAMANAKA is the author of a book of poetry, *Saturday Night at the Pahala Theatre* (Bamboo Ridge Press), and the novels *Wild Meat and the Bully Burgers, Blu's Hanging* and *Heads by Harry*, all published by Farrar, Straus & Giroux. She is at work on her fourth novel, *Father of the Four Passages*.

Back issues of
CONJUNCTIONS

"A must read"—*The Village Voice*

A limited number of back issues are available to those who would like to discover for themselves the range of innovative writing published in CONJUNCTIONS over the course of nearly two decades.

Conjunctions:1, A Festschrift in Honor of James Laughlin. Paul Bowles, Gary Snyder, John Hawkes, Robert Creeley, Thom Gunn, Denise Levertov, Tennessee Williams, James Purdy, William Everson, Jerome Rothenberg, George Oppen, Joel Oppenheimer, Eva Hesse, Michael McClure, Octavio Paz, Hayden Carruth, over 50 others. Kenneth Rexroth interview. 304 pages.

Conjunctions:2. Nathaniel Tarn, William H. Gass, Mei-mei Berssenbrugge, Walter Abish, Gustaf Sobin, Edward Dorn, Kay Boyle, Kenneth Irby, Thomas Meyer, Gilbert Sorrentino, Carl Rakosi, and others. H.D.'s letters to Sylvia Dobson. Czeslaw Milosz interview. 232 pages.

Conjunctions:3. Guy Davenport, Michael Palmer, Don Van Vliet, Michel Deguy, Toby Olson, René Char, Coleman Dowell, Cid Corman, Ann Lauterbach, Robert Fitzgerald, Jackson Mac Low, Cecile Abish, Anne Waldman, and others. James Purdy interview. 232 pages.*

Conjunctions:4. Luis Buñuel, Aimé Césaire, Armand Schwerner, Rae Armantrout, Harold Schimmel, Gerrit Lansing, Jonathan Williams, Ron Silliman, Theodore Enslin, and others. Excerpts from Kenneth Rexroth's unpublished autobiography. Robert Duncan and William H. Gass interviews. 232 pages.

Conjunctions:5. Coleman Dowell, Nathaniel Mackey, Kenneth Gangemi, Paul Bowles, Hayden Carruth, John Taggart, Guy Mendes, John Ashbery, Francesco Clemente, and others. Lorine Niedecker's letters to Cid Corman. Barry Hannah and Basil Bunting interviews. 248 pages.

Conjunctions:6. Joseph McElroy, Ron Loewinsohn, Susan Howe, William Wegman, Barbara Tedlock, Edmond Jabès, Jerome Rothenberg, Keith Waldrop, James Clifford, Janet Rodney, and others. The *Symposium of the Whole* papers. Irving Layton interview. 320 pages.*

Conjunctions:7, Writers Interview Writers. John Hawkes, Mary Caponegro, Leslie Scalapino, Marjorie Welish, Gerrit Lansing, Douglas Messerli, Gilbert Sorrentino, and others. *Writers Interview Writers:* Robert Duncan/Michael McClure, Jonathan Williams/Ronald Johnson, Edmund White/Edouard Roditi. 284 pages.*

Conjunctions:8. Robert Duncan, Coleman Dowell, Barbara Einzig, R.B. Kitaj, Paul Metcalf, Barbara Guest, Robert Kelly, Claude Royet-Journoud, Guy Davenport, Karin Lessing, Hilda Morley, and others. *Basil Bunting Tribute,* guest-edited by Jonathan Williams, nearly 50 contributors. 272 pages.*

Conjunctions:9. William S. Burroughs, Dennis Silk, Michel Deguy, Peter Cole, Paul West, Laura Moriarty, Michael Palmer, Hayden Carruth, Mei-mei Berssenbrugge, Thomas Meyer, Aaron Shurin, Barbara Tedlock, and others. Edmond Jabés interview. 296 pages.*

Conjunctions:10, Fifth Anniversary Issue. Walter Abish, Bruce Duffy, Keith Waldrop, Harry Mathews, Kenward Elmslie, Beverley Dahlen, Jan Groover, Ronald Johnson, David Rattray, Leslie Scalapino, George Oppen, Elizabeth Murray, and others. Joseph McElroy interview. 320 pages.*

Conjunctions:11. Lydia Davis, John Taggart, Marjorie Welish, Dennis Silk, Susan Howe, Robert Creeley, Charles Stein, Charles Bernstein, Kenneth Irby, Nathaniel Tarn, Robert Kelly, Ann Lauterbach, Joel Shapiro, Richard Tuttle, and others. Carl Rakosi interview. 296 pages.

Conjunctions:12. David Foster Wallace, Robert Coover, Georges Perec, Norma Cole, Laura Moriarty, Joseph McElroy, Yannick Murphy, Diane Williams, Harry Mathews, Trevor Winkfield, Ron Silliman, Armand Schwerner, and others. John Hawkes and Paul West interviews. 320 pages.

Conjunctions:13. Maxine Hong Kingston, Ben Okri, Jim Crace, William S. Burroughs, Guy Davenport, Barbara Tedlock, Rachel Blau DuPlessis, Walter Abish, Jackson Mac Low, Lydia Davis, Fielding Dawson, Toby Olson, Eric Fischl, and others. Robert Kelly interview. 288 pages.*

Conjunctions:14, The New Gothic. Guest-edited by Patrick McGrath. Kathy Acker, John Edgar Wideman, Jamaica Kincaid, Peter Straub, Clegg & Guttmann, Robert Coover, Lynne Tillman, Bradford Morrow, William T. Vollmann, Gary Indiana, Mary Caponegro, Brice Marden, and others. Salman Rushdie interview. 296 pages.*

Conjunctions:15, The Poetry Issue. 33 poets, including Susan Howe, John Ashbery, Rachel Blau DuPlessis, Barbara Einzig, Norma Cole, John Ash, Ronald Johnson, Forrest Gander, Michael Palmer, Diane Ward, and others. Fiction by John Barth, Jay Cantor, Diane Williams, and others. Michael Ondaatje interview. 424 pages.

Conjunctions:16, The Music Issue. Nathaniel Mackey, Leon Botstein, Albert Goldman, Paul West, Amiri Baraka, Quincy Troupe, Lukas Foss, Walter Mosley, David Shields, Seth Morgan, Gerald Early, Clark Coolidge, Hilton Als, and others. John Abercrombie and David Starobin interview. 360 pages.

Conjunctions:17, Tenth Anniversary Issue. Kathy Acker, Janice Galloway, David Foster Wallace, Robert Coover, Diana Michener, Juan Goytisolo, Rae Armantrout, John Hawkes, William T. Vollmann, Charlie Smith, Lynn Davis, Mary Caponegro, Keith Waldrop, Carla Lemos, C.D. Wright, and others. Chinua Achebe interview. 424 pages. Out of print.

Conjunctions:18, Fables, Yarns, Fairy Tales. Scott Bradfield, Sally Pont, John Ash, Theodore Enslin, Patricia Eakins, Joanna Scott, Lynne Tillman, Can Xue, Gary Indiana, Russell Edson, David Rattray, James Purdy, Wendy Walker, Norman Manea, Paola Capriolo, O.V. de Milosz, Rosario Ferré, Jacques Roubaud, and others. 376 pages.

Conjunctions:19, Other Worlds. Guest-edited by Peter Cole. David Antin, John Barth, Pat Califia, Thom Gunn, Barbara Einzig, Ewa Kuryluk, Carl Rakosi, Eliot Weinberger, John Adams, Peter Reading, John Cage, Marjorie Welish, Barbara Guest, Cid Corman, Elaine Equi, John Weiners, and others. 336 pages.

Conjunctions:20, Unfinished Business. Robert Antoni, Janice Galloway, Martine Bellen, Paul Gervais, Ann Lauterbach, Jessica Hagedorn, Jim Lewis, Carole Maso, Leslie Scalapino, Gilbert Sorrentino, David Foster Wallace, Robert Creeley, Ben Marcus, Paul West, Mei-mei Berssenbrugge, Susan Rothenberg, Yannick Murphy, and others. 352 pages.

Conjunctions:21, The Credos Issue. Coedited with Quincy Troupe. Robert Olen Butler, Ishmael Reed, Kathy Acker, Walter Mosley, Robert Coover, Joanna Scott, Victor Hernandez Cruz, Frank Chin, Simon Ortiz, Martine Bellen, Melanie Neilson, Kenward Elmslie, David Mura, Jonathan Williams, Cole Swensen, John Ashbery, Forrest Gander, Myung Mi Kim, and others. 352 pages.

Conjunctions:22, The Novellas Issue. Allan Gurganus, Barbara Guest, John Hawkes, Wendy Walker, Stacy Doris, Harry Mathews, Robert Olen Butler, Nathaniel Tarn, Stephen Ratcliffe, Melanie Neilson, John Barth, Ann Lauterbach, Donald Revell, Robert Antoni, Lynne Tillman, Arno Schmidt, Paul West, and others. 384 pages.

Conjunctions:23, New World Writing. Bei Dao, Eduardo Galeano, Olga Sedakova, Abd al-Hakim Qasim, Yang Lian, Claudio Magris, Coral Bracho, Faiz Ahmed Faiz, Nuruddin Farah, Carlos German Belli, Jean Echenoz, Nina Iskrenko, Juan Goytisolo, Paola Capriolo, Peter Cole, Botho Strauss, Semezdin Mehmedinovic, Pascalle Monnier, and others. 344 pages.

Conjunctions:24, Critical Mass. Yoel Hoffmann, Githa Hariharan, Kathleen Fraser, John Taggart, Thalia Field, Lydia Davis, Guy Davenport, Myung Mi Kim, Marjorie Welish, Leslie Scalapino, Peter Gizzi, Cole Swensen, D.E. Steward, Mary Caponegro, Robert Creeley, Martine Bellen, William T. Vollmann, Louis-Ferdinand Céline, and others. 360 pages.

Conjunctions:25, The New American Theater. Guest-edited by John Guare. Tony Kushner, Suzan-Lori Parks, Jon Robin Baitz, Han Ong, Mac Wellman, Paula Vogel, Eric Overmyer, Wendy Wasserstein, Christopher Durang, Donald Margulies, Ellen McLaughlin, Nicky Silver, Jonathan Marc Sherman, Joyce Carol Oates, Arthur Kopit, Doug Wright, Robert O'Hara, Erik Ehn, John Guare, Harry Kondoleon, and others. 360 pages.

Conjunctions:26, Sticks and Stones. With a Special Fiction Portfolio guest-edited by Ben Marcus. Angela Carter, Ann Lauterbach, Rikki Ducornet, Paul Auster, Arthur Sze, David Mamet, Robert Coover, Rick Moody, Gary Lutz, Lois-Ann Yamanaka, Terese Svoboda, Brian Evenson, Dawn Raffel, David Ohle, Liz Tucillo, Martine Bellen, Robert Kelly, Michael Palmer, and others. 360 pages.

Conjunctions:27, The Archipelago. Coedited with Robert Antoni. Gabriel García Márquez, Derek Walcott, Cristina García, Wilson Harris, Olive Senior, Senel Paz, Kamau Brathwaite, Julia Alvarez, Manno Charlemagne, Rosario Ferré, Severo Sarduy, Edwidge Danticat, Madison Smartt Bell, Fred D'Aguiar, Glenville Lovell, Mayra Montero, Lorna Goodison, Bob Shacochis, and others. 360 ages.

Conjunctions:28, Secular Psalms. With a special Music Theater portfolio guest-edited by Thalia Field. Maureen Howard, Julio Cortázar, Joanna Scott, David Foster Wallace, Stephen Dixon, Susan Gevirtz, Gilbert Sorrentino, Anselm Hollo, Can Xue, Harry Partch, Robert Ashley, Meredith Monk, John Moran, Alice Farley, Ann T. Greene, Ruth E. Margraff, Jeffrey Eugenides, Jackson Mac Low, and others. 380 pages.

Conjunctions:29, Tributes. American Writers on American Writers. Coedited with Martine Bellen and Lee Smith. Ntozake Shange, John Sayles, Nathaniel Mackey, Joanna Scott, Rick Moody, Dale Peck, Carole Maso, Peter Straub, Robert Creeley, Paul West, Quincy Troupe, Ana Castillo, Amiri Baraka, Eli Gottlieb, Joyce Carol Oates, Sven Birkerts, Siri Hustvedt, Lydia Davis, and others. 416 pages.

Conjunctions:30, Paper Airplane. Franz Kafka, Günter Grass, Jorie Graham, Susan Sontag, John Ashbery, Rosmarie Waldrop, Joy Williams, Shelley Jackson, William T. Vollmann, Rae Armantrout, Fred D'Aguiar, Robert Kelly, and others. 400 pages.

Conjunctions:31, Radical Shadows. Previously Untranslated and Unpublished Works by 19th and 20th Century Masters. Coedited with Peter Constantine. Anna Akhmatova, George Seferis, Djuna Barnes, Elizabeth Bishop, Truman Capote, Anton Chekhov, Fyodor Dostoevsky, Yasunari Kawabata, Vaslav Nijinsky, Marcel Proust, E.M. Cioran, Robert Musil, and others. 400 pages.

Conjunctions:32, Eye to Eye. Writers and Artists. William H. Gass and Mary Gass, C. D. Wright and Deborah Luster, Camille Guthrie and Louise Bourgeois, Rikki Ducornet, John Yau and Trevor Winkfield, Diane Michener, Robert Creeley and Archie Rand, Lynne Tillman and Haim Steinbach, Thomas Bernhard, Suzan-Lori Parks, and others. 400 pages.

Send your order to:
CONJUNCTIONS, Bard College, Annandale-on-Hudson, NY 12504.
Issues 1–15 are $15.00 each, plus $3.00 shipping.
Issues 16–32 are $12.00 each, plus $3.00 shipping.

Issues with asterisks are available in very limited quantities.
Please inquire.

What did Jean-Paul Sartre say to his mother when he gave her his book?

What did **Elias Canetti, Michel Leiris,** and **Raymond Carver** say to their mothers? What did **Walt Whitman** say to **Peter Doyle** when he gave him his book? What did **Delmore Schwartz** say to **W.H. Auden?** Or for that matter, to **John Crowe Ransom?** What did **Tristan Tzara** say to **Richard Huelsenbeck? Alan Watts** to **Mircea Eliade? Wilhelm Reich** or **Otto Rank** to their wives? **Henry Miller** to **Kenneth Patchen? Frank O'Hara** to **Barbara Guest? Michel Foucault** to **René Magritte? Søren Kierkegaard** to **Johannes Heiberg? William James** to **Charles W. Eliot? Theodor Herzl** to **Max Nordau? Edmond Goncourt** to **J.-K. Huysmans? William Faulkner** to **Ben Wasson? Marcel Duchamp** to **Jean Paulhan? Hart Crane** to **Paul Rosenfeld? Constantin Cavafy** to **Christopher Nomikos? Georges Bataille** to **Jacques Lacan?**

Find out at **LAME DUCK BOOKS** in Boston, where we offer these and other unique presentation copies and exquisitely rare first editions of many of the greatest books of the 20th Century.

You may also visit us at the following upcoming antiquarian book fairs:

Eastside Trinity Antiquarian Book Fair (New York)
at the 26th Street Street Armory, October 23 & 24

Hamburg Antiquarian Book Fair (Quod Libet)
at the Hamburg Bourse, November 12-14

Boston Antiquarian Book Fair
at the Hynes Convention Center, November 19-21

Madrid International Book Fair
December 16-19

MLA
at the Hyatt Regency, Chicago, IL, December 27-30

California Antiquarian Book Fair
at the Los Angeles Airport Marriott, February 11-13

NOON

EDITED BY DIANE WILLIAMS

NEW

PLEASE SEND FICTION

1369 MADISON AVENUE   PMB 298   NEW YORK   NEW YORK   10128-0711

HEREWITH PAYMENT FOR MY ISSUE OF NOON

NAME

ADDRESS

CITY   STATE   ZIP

ENCLOSED IS MY CHECK FOR $9.00 DOMESTIC AND $14.00 FOREIGN TO

NOON, INC.
1369 MADISON AVENUE   PMB 298
NEW YORK   NEW YORK   10128-0711

Allison Amend
J. T. Barbarese
T. Coraghessan Boyle
Oliver Broudy
John Callaway
Michael Czyzniejewski
Laurence Davies
Stephen Dixon
Anthony Doerr
Andre Dubus
Amy Schildhouse Greenberg
David Halberstam
Jana Harris
Lois Hauselman
Hoag Holmgren
Betsy Isbell
Thomas E. Kennedy
Kerry Langan
Paul Maliszewski
Michael McGregor
James McManus
Kirk Nesset
Lisa Sandlin
Norman Waksler   Barry Silesky
Sarah Williams
Karen Wolf
Nancy Zafris

35

STORYQUARTERLY

P.O.B Box 1416 Northbrook, IL 60065
Co-Editors: Anne Brashler & M. M. M. Hayes

SINGLE ISSUE: $5   LIFE MEMBERSHIP:
SUBSCRIPTION: 5 issues $20 $75 (3 priority critiques/yr)